A CLASS ACT

JULIE HOUSTON

Boldwood

First published in Great Britain in 2024 by Boldwood Books Ltd.

Copyright © Julie Houston, 2024

Cover Design by Alice Moore Design

Cover Photography: Shutterstock and iStock

Every effort has been made to obtain the necessary permissions with reference to copyright material, both illustrative and quoted. We apologise for any omissions in this respect and will be pleased to make the appropriate acknowledgements in any future edition.

A CIP catalogue record for this book is available from the British Library.

Paperback ISBN 978-1-83561-006-0

Large Print ISBN 978-1-83561-007-7

Hardback ISBN 978-1-83561-005-3

Ebook ISBN 978-1-83561-008-4

Kindle ISBN 978-1-83561-009-1

Audio CD ISBN 978-1-83561-000-8

MP3 CD ISBN 978-1-83561-001-5

Digital audio download ISBN 978-1-83561-004-6

Boldwood Books Ltd
23 Bowerdean Street
London SW6 3TN
www.boldwoodbooks.com

For my wonderful women friends who've been there for me with their love, support and friendship.

PART I

LONDON, MAY 2023

1

I'd first encountered Carrington when chasing the part of a female barrister. Wanting to gen up on how my character might act in real life (and now, knowing the man – in *every* sense of the word – I'm more convinced than ever that those called to the bar are actors worthy of any Sunday evening TV series) I'd taken myself off one morning and joined the burgeoning queue outside the Central Criminal Court on Newgate Street.

Together with those nervously waiting to support family and friends – as well as others nosily, or downright ghoulishly, hoping to catch some unfolding excitement – once instructed, I followed the uniformed court official and trooped in after him. We all self-consciously kept our eyes and thoughts to ourselves as we were ushered up and into the public gallery, which reminded me of balcony seats in a small provincial theatre.

Having hoped to make notes on, and emulate, a *woman* barrister, I was disappointed to see the only female in the legal profession present was the judge and immediately wondered how I could extract myself from my seat to try my luck in another court. It was like being at the theatre when you're suddenly desperate for a pee but don't dare disturb the whole row, knowing each and every one will have to rise like a Mexican wave, dropping jackets and coats, tutting crossly while doing so.

Making the decision to count to ten before attempting to make my exit, I'd got to nine when I saw him.

'Fabian Mansfield Carrington KC,' my neighbour informed me knowingly as I started to rise, before sitting back down, transfixed. 'One of the youngest – if not *the* youngest – to become a King's Counsel.'

'How on earth do you know that?' I whispered back, unable to take my eyes from the man in question.

'Oh, I know everything about my boys,' she said importantly, exhaling a cloud of minty breath in my direction.

'Your *boys*?'

'Yes, been coming here for years. Know 'em all,' she boasted. 'I'll often manage to have a chat with them at some point.'

'Really?' I stared.

'Absolutely,' she whispered again. 'Fabian down there is set on becoming a top judge one day. Bit of all right, isn't he?' she added, surreptitiously offering me a Polo mint as though it were an illegal class A drug. 'He's my favourite at the moment; never miss one of his performances if I can help it. So, how do you know the defendant, then? Is he a loved one? Your brother? Boyfriend?'

'No. No, nothing like that.' I laughed, to her obvious disappointment: I could see she'd have loved to have been offering a hanky or a sympathetic hand if my 'loved one' was about to be sent down for ten years. 'I don't know him at all. I'm an actor. Out of work at the moment. Well, no, I do work – at Graphite. On Conduit Street in Mayfair?' I might not particularly enjoy the shifts I put in there three times a week, but I wasn't averse to a bit of showing off about the restaurant – it was, after all, listed in *Time Out* and *Esquire* as one of London's top ten restaurants.

'Fancy.' Minty Breath sniffed, somewhat disdainfully. I'd bet any money, three hundred years ago she'd have bagged a good seat, knitting in hand, at every public hanging at Tyburn Gallows.

'Right.' I dithered, probing with the tip of my tongue the hole in the mint, knowing I really should move to another court to observe a female barrister, but completely entranced by the man now standing in the well of the court. He paused, shuffling papers in front of him, and then bent to speak to a colleague who, catching his arm, was obviously determined to have his full attention. After a few seconds, Carrington turned slightly, his attention moving from those involved in the legal business of the day to those of us in the public gallery, idly surveying the audience to the drama that was about to unfold. As his eyes met mine, I felt myself utter an involuntary gasp: this man was quite devastating, but, after first giving me what could only be described as an incredibly intense stare, he looked away taking no further interest in what he'd seen.

'Hard luck,' Minty Breath cackled, nudging me in the ribs. 'He almost makes love with those incredible eyes of his to hopeful girls who've come specially to watch him in action – I've seen it. You're obviously not his type.'

Although what I really needed was to know what footwear a female barrister would have on, what hairdo she could get away with under her judicial wig, I reckoned I could learn at least *something* from the man now holding court with the twelve good men and women of the jury. I soon began to realise it wasn't simply a matter of assembling a better narrative than the other side. Presentation was just as, if not more, important and this Fabian Carrington had obviously prepared his role with the same zeal as any method actor.

Carrington stood erect – no slouching shoulders, which might portray indecision or lack of confidence – keeping perfectly still and limiting hand movements to open, relaxed gestures. Everything about him communicated composure, authority and honesty. But it was his tone, his easy delivery and the repetition of phrases to emphasise a particular point that really marked out his professional skill. He moved from gentle solicitude, offering empathy with, and compassion for, his client, to suddenly changing tack and holding forth, with a scornful ennui as to the preposterous, even risible, allegations his client was having to answer to. Just five minutes into his opening speech, Fabian Carrington was already stirring the jury's emotional responses.

As well as stirring lustful longing in every single little bit of me.

And very probably I'd have left it at that, leaving the Old Bailey not just with ideas and actions to accompany the lines I was learning for the forthcoming audition at the Queen Mary theatre in Paddington, but also with a sense of unfinished business. No doubt Carrington would have remained the object of my fantasies for a couple of days, a few weeks even. Then, with nothing to revive the memory of that dark hair escaping from beneath his wig, that easy melodic voice and those searching brown eyes – as well as having been turned down flat for the role of the female barrister in the TV drama – the image would gradually have faded from my mind.

After leaving school, I'd spent three years at Manchester Met, crossing the Pennines from my native Yorkshire village of Beddingfield where I'd grown up, to work for and gain a somewhat desultory degree in English and drama. I should have quit once I realised that three years in Manchester were going to do absolutely nothing to help me achieve my ambition of performing musical theatre in London, but my father, who only rarely deigned to visit Mum and his three daughters, had told me to hang on in there and graduate to the Manchester School of Theatre, which was, basically, just another department in the same university. When I'd demurred, told Jayden (we'd never called him Dad) that would mean adding to my already eye-watering student debt, he'd simply laughed, peeled off an equally eye-watering roll of fifties and told me to follow my dream. Weren't Julie Walters and Richard Griffiths both past alumni of Manchester? he'd ventured. And look how they'd turned out. As *Mamma Mia!*, starring the irrepressible Julie Walters, was one of my absolute favourites, I did as Jayden suggested and remained in Manchester.

I adored every single minute of my latter years there, eking out my student loan and erratic handouts from Jayden by working in numerous bars and restaurants in the city centre. But I knew I never wanted to do anything else with my life but musical theatre. And I also knew that once I'd graduated I'd be fighting off every theatre producer – Andrew Lloyd Webber on my doorstep was a favourite fantasy – in the West End. They'd all be banging on my door, demanding I play the lead in their brand-new productions.

Some of it I got right. Heading to London in my mid-twenties, I found myself not only an agent (of somewhat dubious credentials, I'll admit, but an agent nonetheless) but also the much-revered Equity card, as well, a particularly damp and noisome flatshare above a Turkish barber (with equally dubious credentials) and doner kebab joint in a badly lit back street of Hammersmith.

Despite my doing everything advised by Leonard, my agent, interviews and actual work were sporadic, if not downright non-existent, and I was more practised in pulling pints and waiting on tables in central London than applying greasepaint and being put through my paces in a chorus line. During my second year in the big city, however, things did finally start to happen and I spent two wonderful months in the chorus of *Big*, the musical, at the Dominion. I was on my way, loving every minute of being on stage and able, at last, to give up both my part-time waitress and barmaid jobs in Covent Garden. I had enough money – almost – to pay the rent and eat, and I knew this was just the start. And it was. As a consequence of my two-month run in *Big*, I auditioned and was given the part of Ernestina Money in a revival of Jerry Herman's *Hello, Dolly!*. I was ecstatic, ringing Jayden, who was touring in Germany at the time, as well as Mum and my older sister Jess, both at home in Beddingfield. I was going places, moving up in the world: on the verge of global domination.

Unfortunately, so was Covid.

The show was put on hold before it ever got going and the restaurants and bars – my previous means of survival in London – closed, and in desperation I did what most unemployed twenty-some-year-olds had to do and retreated back home to the small terraced cottage of my childhood: to Mum and to Yorkshire. I'd not lived at home since the age of eighteen, but now found myself sharing my old bedroom with a twelve-year-old sister, the result of yet another of Jayden's habitual returns to Lisa – my mum – and his family up north.

This reinstatement of a father figure in our lives, when I was thirteen and Jess fifteen s had lasted a couple of months before Jayden was off again – leaving Mum pregnant with Sorrel – touring with yet another band (think UB40 and you'll get the picture) and, presumably, shacking up with one or more of his other women along the way. Mum had long since stopped questioning Jayden Allen, despite Jess and I having a go at her once we were in our teens and able to judge for ourselves this ridiculous relationship she'd put up with since she was just seventeen.

So, Covid-bound along with the rest of the nation, and having no idea when, or even if, I would ever be able to return to my first love, musical theatre, I made what was probably my first ever grown-up decision and enrolled on a Postgraduate Certificate in Education. It was all done online, and not validated until eighteen months later when I spent twenty-four weeks in various West Yorkshire comprehensives on school placements teaching English, dance and drama. The result of these terrifying placements was the authority to teach in any school in the UK, but also had me vowing *never ever* to set foot in a classroom again. Ever.

So, here I was, back in London post-Covid, my uncurbed enthusiasm for musical theatre and a life treading the boards brimming over once again. I was now in my late twenties, still broke and sharing a somewhat dubious flat above yet another Turkish doner kebab joint near Berwick Street Market, on the edge of Soho, this time along with two other actors.

Leonard, my agent, had gone into some sort of decline during Covid, retiring to St Anne's on the chilly Lancashire coast with his long-term boyfriend, but had come up trumps by passing me on to a new, upcoming agent called Dorcas O'Hara. When she'd learned I'd previously had a part in *Big,* but, more importantly, my father was Jayden Allen, she had immediately taken me on and was forging ahead with trying to get me the theatre work I craved.

I divided my daytime hours between being put through my paces at auditions for the big shows in the West End (I was confidently aiming high), reading for smaller parts in plays in the more provincial theatres (hence the visit to the Old Bailey and my first sight of Fabian Carrington), and earning enough to pay the rent and for own-brand basics from Aldi by waitressing at an upmarket and very on-trend French haute cuisine restaurant called Graphite on Conduit Street.

My tiny room – big enough to fit just a single bed and chest of drawers – horrified even Jayden who, gigging and touring since the age of seventeen with his many reggae bands, was used to dossing down in less than salubrious places. But it was perfectly placed between theatre-land and Graphite at the junction with New Bond Street in Mayfair.

I'd never been afraid of hard work – just terrified of the bolshy adolescents to whom I'd naively attempted an introduction to Shakespeare and Wordsworth as instructed on teaching placements back home in Yorkshire.

Now, those horrible, interminable classroom hours left behind back in the north, I was fighting fit and raring to go, ready to showcase once more just what I was capable of. The long hours on my feet at the restaurant didn't deter me from spending time, whenever I could, practising routines over and over again in a nearby gym and dance studio owned by an ex-boyfriend, in exchange for teaching a couple of his weekly Zumba classes. I just couldn't afford the exorbitant London gym memberships I'd have had to take out in order to keep up my fitness. I had to be ready, at the drop of a hat, for any potential auditions with sometimes sanguine, often short-tempered, theatrical directors and this did mean I had to keep on the right side of Xander, the owner of the gym.

* * *

Three weeks after the heart-stopping morning spent at the Old Bailey, I walked through the closing of another unusually hot and beautiful May day in central London. Nature seemed intent on unfurling and unfolding before me, the acidic green leaves of the street's plane trees a sharp contrast to the candyfloss pink cherry blossoms' playful bobbing on the evening breeze. I breathed in the scents and sounds at the end of Friday's rush hour: diesel and frustrated hooting of black cabs; warm pavements already dominated by tables, chairs and throngs of newly released office workers, jackets discarded, holding bottles of Sauvignon Blanc aloft while air-kissing new arrivals.

And I didn't want to be anywhere else but in the centre of this seething, gorgeous throng of humanity.

Well, other than joining the queues snaking patiently along the pavements of each theatre I now walked past on my way to my six-hour shift at Graphite, but a girl has to pay her rent and eat. Knowing I was going to be late yet again, I picked up speed as I weaved haphazardly towards Mayfair.

'You're early,' Bess Bridger, yet another out-of-work actor, managed to say through a mouthful of cake as I headed to the row of lockers in the staff rest room. That was a misnomer for a start – the waiting staff were rarely given any breaks, let alone an actual rest, even less so on Friday and Saturday evenings when the work was hectic. I kept meaning to google how much rest we were legally entitled to, but Miss Muffler, the German-born harridan masquerading as line manager, had little truck with either comfort breaks or anyone having the temerity to demand workers' rights.

Bess pushed what remained of the Colin the Caterpillar cake in my direction. 'Stefan's birthday cake,' she volunteered, pointing a sponge-, cream- and chocolate-smeared knife towards one of the sous chefs, who responded with a friendly wave of his own, extremely dangerous-looking, cook's knife. 'I can't believe we work in one of the poshest restaurants in London and yet all we get is a sodding kid's cake to eat.'

'Hell,' I said, suddenly ravenously hungry and wishing I'd finished the remains of the sliced loaf and peanut butter I'd left in the kitchen back at the flat. 'Is that all you lot have left me? Colin's arse?'

'If you'd been as late as you usually are, you wouldn't even have got that. I'd be quick if I were you – Godzilla's on the warpath.'

Shoving Colin's last white-chocolate leg into my mouth, I quickly changed into the blue and cream long-sleeved matelot-style T-shirt and cream waistcoat, before tying around my waist, in authentic French bistro fashion, the long cream apron. Damn. In my hurry to be ready when Walburga Muffler arrived for her pre-shift pep talk and inspection I'd got a huge dollop of melted chocolate on my waistcoat.

'Bugger.'

'Act your way out of that.' Bess grinned as our boss appeared and I folded my arms against the offending brown stain.

'Ah, Robyn, you decided to join us?' she barked, eyeing me through slightly closed eyes. 'You have stomach ache?'

'Stomach ache?' I stood my ground.

'You are hanging onto your middle as though you need the appendix whipped out?'

'Already out, years ago,' I lied.

'Well, do stand up straight,' she ordered, as though I were a recalcitrant nine-year-old. 'The restaurant is full to capacity this evening. Go. Stand by your station. Head up, shoulders back. Smile.'

2

In order to eat out in the most expensive square of the Monopoly board, I've always reckoned, those being seated by Claude, the restaurant's front of house, must have either a) saved up for years, or b) just won a shedload on the lottery. Or c), as was more often the case at Graphite, the diners simply had more dosh than they knew what to do with and didn't give a second thought to spending obscene amounts of it there, where a starter of oysters with just a squeeze of lemon would set them back the same as feeding a whole family living on the brown square of the Old Kent Road.

Whether it was my own working-class roots, or a steadily increasing leaning to the political left, the more I saw of this blatant squandering of wealth, the more I questioned my own part in pandering to the wealthy while helping to further this inequality. When I'd raised this with Jess, my big sister, who worked long hours as a carer in a home for the elderly on the outskirts of our pretty Yorkshire village of Beddingfield, she'd just given me one of her looks. It was just the way of the world, it always had been, and, as far as she could see, always would be.

Giving a surreptitious glance down at the offending stain on my waistcoat, I realised I could just about hide it by hitching up my apron and retying it over the chocolate. While this did nothing to ensure sartorial elegance, at least it gave me cover until I could beg Claude – who was my mate and disliked Miss Muffler as much as the rest of us did – to look out another in the pile back from the laundry.

I was making my way over to Claude when the front door opened, bringing in the remains of the heavenly late-spring evening and a party of nine. I quickly and perhaps prejudicially surmised they fell into my category c) guests. The women, all slim, tanned, manicured and coiffed with swishy locks, wearing tiny designer dresses the price of which would have kept me in hummus for a decade, stepped through the door with the confidence and elan found only in women who've been born into wealth and privilege. While the five women wore the colours of exotically plumaged birds, the men were soberly suited in conventional city blacks and greys and still to loosen, let alone remove, their neckwear.

Claude greeted and immediately escorted the nine to the far table in my assigned station and I followed at a distance, conscious of my apron hovering somewhere below my breasts instead of on my hips, turning to check my cart of linen, silver, glasses, and china had been adequately restocked by the outgoing waiter. Although a large group like this would mean a lot of extra work depending on how much alcohol they put away – and Friday usually meant more than average – tips were often in direct proportion to booze drunk. I sent up a tiny prayer of thanks to the Front of House in that Great Restaurant in the Sky: if all went well I might have enough by the end of the evening to treat myself to a good seat at the musical *Mrs. Doubtfire* at the Shaftesbury Theatre.

'Good evening and welcome,' I trilled, conscious that

Walburga Muffler was hovering, watching my every move while probably desperate to readjust my pinny now anchored snugly beneath my armpit. Graphite was getting a name for its fabulous selection of cocktails and that old 1970's favourite, The Harvey Wallbanger – a heady mix of vodka, Galliano, and orange juice – was making a comeback. Because of this, Bess, Claude and I had rechristened Walburga 'Wallbanger' and every order for it had me wanting to titter.

'Wallbangers all round, I think,' the diminutive, slightly rotund and balding chap who'd taken charge demanded of me without deigning to look my way. I stood smiling benignly while biting the inside of my lip at the thought of asking Marcel, tonight's bar steward, for nine *Walburgas*.

'Lovely, you've made a good choice there.' I beamed, not one person at the table apparently interested in my opinion. 'I'll fetch menus for you,' I went on, 'but we have a specials board just to your right...' I interrupted their conversation, indicating in the manner of an air stewardess pointing out emergency exits. The response was that doubtless expected by any airline attendant: total lack of interest, bordering on irritation.

'Any allergies?' I asked, poised to take note on my iPad.

That piqued a flurry of interest.

'Sesame, gluten intolerant,' one beautiful brunette said, without looking up.

'Any crustacean,' the girl at the end of the table offered with a wintry smile. At least she'd made eye contact.

'Any tree nut,' a third said. I pulled a face, mystified. Weren't all nuts grown on trees? 'Oh, and tinned fish,' she added.

'Don't worry, we don't have *tinned* fish here at Graphite.' I smiled, with slight condescension, my chance to get one back at this snooty lot.

'Well, that's good.' She visibly shuddered. 'But I actually said, if you'd been listening, *any finned fish*.'

There were fish *without* fins? Fish with physical disabilities, then? 'But you're OK with crustaceans?' I asked, now slightly pink and feverishly making notes, wanting to laugh but conscious that my apron was descending asymmetrically to reveal the chocolate stain. 'Is that it? Lovely.'

'We are waiting for one more of us,' Ms Fish Face, a stunning blonde who really was the most strikingly attractive girl I'd ever seen, now chirruped. 'Don't take our food orders until he arrives,' she commanded.

'Make that *ten* Wallbangers, then,' the little chap shouted in my direction.

Did his nanny not teach him to say please and thank you? 'Of course.' I smiled. 'I'll get that sorted straight away and take your food orders once your colleague arrives.'

'Ten *Walburgas*,' I said with a laugh in my best pronounced German accent, 'for the city slickers in the corner.' I grinned at Marcel, who didn't respond as he usually did to our little joke, but instead lowered his eyes from mine and got on with the order.

'Ms Allen,' Walburga Muffler, snapping at my heels like the terrifying Rottweiler she was, had me up against the bar, pulling unceremoniously at my apron to reveal the smeared chocolate stain, which now resembled, somewhat uncannily, a map of Italy. 'I will take this order for Harvey Wallbangers while you go and change that waistcoat. There are clean ones in the rest room. I have my eye on you, tonight, Ms Allen. Now go.'

I went.

Oh, Lordy, I sent up a silent prayer as I grabbed a newly laundered and ironed waistcoat, please give me a job. A *proper* job on stage. I'll act my tush off and dance until I drop like the girl in the red shoes. Well, maybe not: didn't she end up cutting off her feet to stop dancing? Mind you, anything to get out of having to serve pillocks like the table for ten upstairs.

I plastered on a smile – as well as more lipstick – before heading for the restaurant floor, glancing towards the main door as another couple of guests arrived. And I swear my heart actually stopped and then did a quite spectacular lurch because there, in front of me, was the missing tenth guest.

Fabian Mansfield Carrington. Three weeks on from my research outing to the Central Criminal Court, his name was still emblazoned in my memory. The only thing different about him this evening was the lack of judicial wig, which now allowed a full reveal of fairly long dark, curling hair.

'Fabian!' Ms Fish Face jumped out of her seat, flinging beautifully toned and bronzed arms around him, before leading him to the vacant chair at her side. 'You are naughty being so late, when it's *such* a special occasion.'

I hesitated, trying to work out from the others' greetings what this occasion might be. The four men were now standing, shaking Carrington's hand, patting his back, while the little bloke had him in an ill-thought-out bear hug that didn't quite come off, his bald head bumping unceremoniously and somewhat embarrassingly into Carrington's armpit.

Lucky bloke to be in such near contact, I mused as Miss Muffler shoved ten menus in my direction.

'Good evening,' I addressed the back of Carrington's head. 'I believe you're all here now? Are you ready to order?' Nervous excitement at having Carrington within touching distance was making me forget the right way to go about things.

'No, of course not,' Fish Face snapped crossly. 'Would you mind just giving us some time, waitress?'

Waitress? I looked slightly askance at the woman but, remembering I needed this job to pay the rent, which was now two weeks

overdue, I nodded demurely and went to help Miss Muffler with
the drinks order.

'Excuse me?' I moved towards Carrington with my tray,
placing the sliced-orange-and-cherry-adorned frosted glass in
front of him.

'Thank you so much.' He glanced up at me, his brown eyes
meeting mine, appraising. He was even more beautiful close up.
Often, seeing and being near someone at close range when only
previously viewing from afar can be a bitter let down: eyes cold
and with no soul, teeth that need work, a shoulder full of
dandruff; blackheads in a pitted nose; halitosis even.

Fabian Mansfield Carrington did not disappoint. Tall, with
olive skin and brown eyes, he was as utterly devastating as I
remembered. He picked up his glass, taking a long, obviously
much-needed drink, but then turned back to me, holding my gaze
until I had to look away.

'Don't I know you from somewhere?' He smiled. 'You look very
familiar.'

'She's just the waitress, Fabian,' Fish Face said slightly irritably, taking his arm in an obvious attempt to regain his attention.
'Come on, it's your birthday – let's celebrate.'

Ah, his birthday? Suddenly, not caring, I smiled down at him
as he turned once more in my direction. 'I'm sure I know *you* from
somewhere too. TV perhaps?' I pretended to hesitate. 'Aren't you
the presenter on that kids' programme? *Shaboom*, is it?' I held his
eye for a good few seconds, enjoying the excuse to have his
attention.

'Kids' programme?' Fish Face snorted disparagingly. 'Fabian
here happens to be one of the top defence barristers in London. If
you recognise him from *anywhere*, maybe you've found yourself at
the Old Bailey at some point? Hmm? For some reason?'

'Ah.' I nodded slowly, giving Carrington the benefit of what I

hoped was a mysterious and engaging smile, one I'd often practised for a part. 'Of *course*. That explains it.'

And with that, I moved round the table, taking orders, offering
recommendations, and suggesting dishes, aware that not only
Miss Muffler, but now Fabian Mansfield Carrington as well, were
keeping a close eye on my performance.

The evening passed in the usual flurry of greeting guests,
being at my most charming, listening and always putting the
interests of the customer before my own. Even though I was
desperate for, in no particular order: a glass of iced water, a pee, a
foot massage, a sodding great G and T and, if I'd smoked, a quick
fag outside the back door of the kitchen.

But this evening was different. My smile was genuine, my feet
almost skipping round my station, while Carrington was
constantly glancing my way, trying to work out if he really did
know me.

His table became clamorous, rowdy, one step from raucous, as
the evening went on and glasses were refilled, raised and downed
in celebration of Carrington's birthday. And yet Fabian Carrington
himself appeared to be drinking very little. His hand, I noticed,
was often held over his glass as one of his companions endeavoured to share with him yet another bottle of expensive champagne and, when I took the bottle from the ice bucket and offered
to fill his glass, he placed a warm hand over my own, holding it
there for longer than necessary while smiling and shaking his
head. It was a wonderful, exciting game the two of us were playing, cleverly carried out secretly – by me because it was the restaurant's policy for staff not to fraternise with guests, and, I assumed,
by him because Miss Fish Face kept a steely eye on his every
movement that didn't involve her.

As midnight approached, Carrington's table was the only one
left and Bess, Claude, Marcel and Miss Muffler were, despite Miss

Muffler's usually unbreakable rule of not to start the clearing-up process while any guests were still in situ, doing just that. I went to join them, helping to restock each station's cart ready for the following day's lunch session.

'Tell 'em to eff off now,' Bess whispered in my direction, yawning discreetly as she did so. 'I've had enough. Mind you, there is one hell of a gorgeous man on that table.'

'Oh?' I said, folding the starched Graphite-logoed napkins. 'Is there? I hadn't noticed.'

'Hmm,' Bess went on. 'Apparently it's his birthday and yet he's drinking *water*.'

'Maybe he's a recovering alcoholic?' I ventured.

'I don't think alcoholics ever recover, do they?' She frowned, considering. 'My Uncle Trevor who was—' She broke off, dropping the knife she was polishing in her excitement. 'Shhh, shhh, he's coming over...'

Carrington walked towards us and, ignoring Bess – who was now openly gawping – and me, addressed Miss Muffler. In perfect German to boot, my boss melting like snow in spring as the pair conversed in her native tongue. Carrington finally turned to the rest of us and said, 'I'm so sorry to keep you from your beds. It really is incredibly rude of us, and I apologise. We're on our way now.'

'Do come on, Fabian, we're heading off to Kadies. We need you to get us in.' The little bald bloke was obviously the worse for wear, tottering slightly on his stacked heels, his pink pate and forehead sweating as he tried to manoeuvre Carrington towards the door.

'Not me.' Fabian Carrington shook his head. 'It's been a long, long hard day.'

'Oh, come on, Fabian,' Fish Face wheedled. 'You've so much to celebrate, darling.'

'Sorry, all of you. Taxi for me and home.'

This was promising, then, if Fish Face didn't appear to have an open invitation to join him in his taxi and, presumably, his bed. The nine of them drunkenly tumbled out of the restaurant and Carrington turned to follow, offering a final wave and 'sorry' in our direction.

I made my way back over to their abandoned table, knowing just another ten minutes and I'd be heading off myself, but feeling the same sense of unfinished business I'd experienced on leaving Carrington at the criminal courts a few weeks earlier.

Finally I joined Bess in the rest room, quickly chucking my uniform into the laundry basket and pulling on the jeans and T-shirt I'd changed out of hours earlier.

'Blimey, *he* was a bit of all right, wasn't he?' Bess sighed. 'And way out of *your* league, Claude,' she called over her shoulder. 'Don't you go having fantasies about *him, mon petit chou.*' She planted a kiss on Claude's cheek. 'Come on, let's find some entertainment. The night is but young.'

Claude turned, tutting. '*Merde*, I suppose I *have* to do this?' He raised an eye crossly.

'What, come out on the town with me?' Bess grinned. 'It's all right, we can head for Ku Bar,' she added, naming one of Soho's favourite gay bars and clubs.

'*Non.*' Claude tutted again. 'This here.' He handed me a piece of paper.

Please ring me.

Followed by a phone number.

Oh! Glory be! He'd left his number. Fabian Mansfield Carrington had *left his number* for me! I felt as though I'd won the lottery, my pulse racing, my feet ready to dance all the way back home to Soho.

'Robyn, she wins again.' Claude sniffed crossly. 'Ah, to be born so *jolie*,' he added, somewhat cattily, as if every evening spent working at Graphite culminated in some sort of contest. 'Come on,' he conceded, linking my arm with his. 'I'm still not talking to you. But, we'll walk your way, anyway,' he added. 'And we're not in danger any more.'

'Danger?'

'That *bâtard* who abducts women and does horrible things to them before, you know' – Claude pulled his arm from my own, taking a dramatic hand across his throat – 'has been caught. You've not heard?'

'Oh, really?' I felt total relief that the man dubbed the Soho Slasher, who'd abducted, raped and murdered six young women in the past couple of years, had been caught. One of his victims had been found only a couple of streets down from my own in Soho.

Could this evening get any better?

3

That summer was one I'll never forget.

Walking back towards Soho, the streets, despite the late hour, still alive with Friday night revellers enjoying the warm evening after what had been a fairly miserable spring, Bess and Claude advised me to play it cool with Carrington.

'Play it cool?' I scoffed. 'I'm not in the sixth form, playing hard to get with the school's star football jock, for heaven's sake. I'm pushing thirty. I really can't be doing with playing games at my age.'

'I bet 'e was,' Claude replied dreamily, sidestepping a couple on the pavement.

'Was what?' Bess and I both turned to Claude.

'You know, captain of *le rugby quinze* and *le football* team.'

'Can you play *both*?' I frowned. '*We* had to make a choice between hockey and netball when I was at school. We weren't allowed to play both at Beddingfield Comp.'

'Well, tennis squad, then,' Claude replied. '*Mon Dieu*, I can see 'im in leetle white shorts on the centre court.'

'He's a *barrister*,' Bess jeered. 'In the *criminal* court. If he plays anything, it'll be golf. You know, like they all do once they're in the city and clawing their way to the top. They all end up joining Daddy's golf club and turning into their fathers.'

'Stop it.' I laughed. 'I'm rapidly going off him.'

'Oh, you did fancy him, then?' Bess glanced at me sideways as we came to Lisle Street just off Leicester Square. She stopped. 'Did you know him? Had you met him before?'

'Of course, she fancy him,' Claude put in, before I could reply. 'Who wouldn't? Right, we 'ere now, Robyn. Do not phone 'im 'til at least tomorrow. 'Ang on until Sunday if eet at all possible. I am *un 'omme* and I know these things.' Claude kissed me on both cheeks before disappearing up the steps and through the entrance of Ku, his attention now on other pleasures.

'You OK the rest of the way by yourself?' Bess asked, turning to follow Claude. 'You don't need to get an Uber now that the Soho Slasher has apparently been caught?'

'Of course,' I replied.

And I was.

* * *

I left it until Saturday evening before ringing Carrington. This wasn't a conscious attempt at 'playing hard to get', which, now I was twenty-eight I was more than ready to denounce as juvenile and overrated – as well as full of nuance and subtlety, which, without practice, is not always easy to pull off. Not only was I utterly beyond playing such games at my age, I was genuinely busy the next day. As I went about my Saturday tasks of laun-derette, food shopping and going over some lines for a forth-coming voice-over job (a tin of famous baked beans being hoovered up in a kitchen up north), I knew that, in reality, Fabian Carrington in the flesh wouldn't be able to live up to the fantasy I was enjoying of the man. I didn't want my bubble to burst in a soggy mess of disappointment.

It didn't.

I'd actually managed to persuade myself that no one could be so attractive as the man I'd been fantasising about for three weeks. That, in reality, he would be boring, right wing, lack a sense of humour, be disparaging about the acting profession: the list of his demeanours was endless. At 9 p.m. on the Saturday, with a glass of wine on the tiny kitchen table in front of me, I finally made myself sit down with my phone and rang the number. I assumed he'd be out wining and dining, entertaining any number of women to whom he'd passed his phone number, and I'd just be able to leave a message.

'Hello?' He answered on the second ring and, expecting voice-mail, I felt the power of speech desert me.

'Hello?' he repeated. 'Fabian Carrington.'

'Hello, Fabian. This is Robyn.'

'Robyn?' I heard puzzlement in his voice.

'Robyn, the waitress at Graphite? Last night?' Oh, hell, he'd no idea who I was.

'Ah, Robyn. I'm so sorry, I didn't actually know your name. How lovely that you've rung.'

'And did you want me to ring you so you could work out where you think you've seen me before?'

He laughed. 'No, not at all – although that would be good. I was hoping you'd come out for lunch with me.' His voice was teasing.

'Lunch?' I didn't really do lunch. A coffee and slice of toast with Marmite and peanut butter late morning usually took me, via a packet of digestives and an apple, through to whatever was left in the shared kitchen fridge in the evening. I was a whizz with a pot of cottage cheese and a bag of rocket leaves.

'You know, that meal one sometimes manages to fit in between breakfast and dinner?' His voice, educated, warm, held humour.

'Right, OK, lovely, thank you. That would be very pleasant.' For heaven's sake, woman, I chided my stuttering self, my Yorkshire accent sounding conspicuously broad in comparison to his southern articulation.

'Are you free tomorrow?'

'Tomorrow?'

'The day after this one, I believe, is the definition.' He said the words without an ounce of pomposity and I found myself smiling at his rhetoric.

I *had* promised myself a day at the studio, really getting to grips with the routine I was working on in readiness for a possible audition the following week. 'What time were you thinking?'

'Lunchtime?' He laughed again and I just loved the sound of his amused response.

'OK, thank you. I'd like that.'

'I can pick you up. Where are you?'

'Soho.'

'No, I mean where do you actually *live*?'

'Soho.' Top London barristers obviously didn't realise people actually *lived* in the area.

'Really? I thought Soho was just home to Chinatown, rather sleazy bars and, you know...?'

'The sex industry?' Heavens, I hope he didn't think I was a sex worker and that by taking me out for lunch, he'd end up with a freebie. 'I can see I'm going to have to educate you,' I replied, somewhat huffily. Oh, hell, now that sounded as though I were going to educate him with a whip, standing over him in a mask, basque and high heels. 'This whole area,' I said quickly, now sounding as if I were narrating a BBC documentary on the area, 'is the centre of the UK's film production and post-production industries, so many locals are top professionals working in the film industry.'

'Right. Sorry. I was actually going to say the hunting ground of the man they've dubbed the Soho Slasher. You can't be too careful there at the moment...' He paused. 'Ah, so you're an actress...?'

'*Actor*, please.'

'An *actor* when you're not waiting on tables?'

'Trying to be.' I nodded into the phone and then, remembering he couldn't actually see me, added, 'Covid has a lot to answer for.'

'So, would that be where I've seen you before, then? On TV?'

Doubtful, seeing as I'd only ever managed the tiniest of one-line speaking parts in a couple of TV soaps and dramas. 'Possibly,' I said. 'Although musical theatre is my first love and where I really want to be—' I broke off as I realised he was talking to someone who'd obviously just come into the room. Oh, God, don't say he was married.

'I'm sorry, Robyn, something's just cropped up. Text me your address and I'll pick you up at one. That OK with you?'

'Lovely,' I said faintly, realising he'd already rung off.

* * *

I spent Sunday morning at the studio, putting myself through a gruelling routine over and over again, encouraged by Xander, the owner and ex-boyfriend who allowed me free use of the space in return for teaching Zumba classes.

'Not bad.' He applauded. 'Not quite Jennifer Beals yet, but...'

'Who?' I panted, sweat dripping as I downed a full bottle of water.

Xander tutted. 'She who executed one of the greatest dance routines ever? *Flashdance*?'

'Bit before my time.' I wiped my face. 'You OK with me tarting myself up here? The shower at my place is prone to a sulk at the best of times and any hot water there will have been used up by Tanya and Jacques by the time I get home.'

'As long as you'll come out with me afterwards. We could do lunch?' Xander looked hopeful.

'Sorry, already spoken for.'

'Oh?'

'Just a friend. Probably a pie and a pint somewhere.' I smiled, trying to let Xander down gently. I didn't want to fall out with him – I needed the studio space at my disposal.

* * *

I went through the usual shampooing, conditioning, leg-shaving routine that was always a prequel to a first date and wondered, idly, if men put themselves through the same regime. I bet they didn't. I bet it was a quick shower, an equally quick glance at the previous day's boxers to see if they'd pass muster for another outing, a clean shirt and that was it.

I walked back to the flat, where Tanya was eating rice pudding straight from the tin while perusing the latest edition of *Spotlight*.

'You off out?' She deigned to look up in my direction.

'Got a lunch date,' I said, making for my room.

'Lunch? Get you.' She held up the tin of Ambrosia. 'What's wrong with a snack in a tin?' I didn't find Tanya the easiest of flat-mates, especially as she appeared to be constantly in work and didn't mind letting me know of her success. 'Anyone I know? What's he in?'

'The Old Bailey.' I grinned.

'Oh,' she said, sucking on her spoon thoughtfully. 'Daniel—'

her agent '—wanted me to go for a part in that, but I said, "no way".'

With twenty minutes to spare, I now had the momentous decision which of my few clothes were going to be suitable for a date with Fabian Mansfield Carrington. There wasn't a huge choice: being permanently broke meant my wardrobe consisted mainly of charity-shop finds. But Jayden had had a recent financially worthwhile tour of Sweden, Norway and Denmark and had rolled up a month ago with his usual wad of tenners and with the strict instruction to buy myself something lovely. 'Never mind the council tax,' he'd dictated, 'you need to look good when you go for auditions. Every time I see you, you're in the same leggings or sweatpants.'

So I'd gone along to Beyond Retro on Great Marlborough Street and there, amongst the fabulous vintage forties and fifties frocks, was an utterly beautiful pink, pure cotton, 1960s Ossie Clark sundress.

I reached for it now, pulling it off the clothes rail, and fell in love with the beautiful dress all over again. Hell, shoes? Oh, sod it, everyone wore trainers now in London wherever they were going and, luckily, the spotless white trainers Miss Muffler insisted we wear at Graphite were at my disposal.

Lipstick, blusher and a hand through my – always unruly – mass of black curls and I was off. With five minutes to spare, I made my way down the downright dangerous threadbare-carpeted stairs, stepping over the holes but unable to avoid the nausea-inducing stink from the meats on the vertical rotisserie, and out through the flat's entrance adjacent to the Turkish kebab joint below. Hasad, who owned the place and was our landlord, whistled. 'Hey, Robyn, you looking good,' he called. 'That doesn't let you off paying the rent you owe me,' he added, grinning.

'Next week, I promise,' I soothed. 'I always pay up, you know that.'

'You come out with me instead. I show you good time.' He leered wolfishly as I sat down on the pavement, unsure from which direction Fabian would be coming. I closed my eyes against the cloudless cerulean sky, breathing in the warm Sunday lunchtime air. In doing so I also blotted out the throng of humanity, the garishly coloured street signs advertising every sybaritic enticement known to man as well as the piled-up rubbish and abandoned food waste. Nervous that Fabian wouldn't be able to find me, but just as terrified that he would, I glanced longingly at my front door. I needed a pee. How much easier on my whole nervous system to go back upstairs to the flat, take off my posh frock and make-up and lie on my bed, going over the words for the baked-bean ad.

'He-e-ey-y,' Hasad called from his vantage point at the kebab counter, 'nice car.'

A silver Porsche was making its way at a snail's pace down the street towards us, its driver obviously uncertain of his bearings, and I jumped up from the pavement as Hasad whistled once more. '*Tanrinin anessi* – that is some car, Robyn – you take care... *Eğlence...* Enjoy!'

I peered in through the car window as it cruised past me, feeling for all the world as if I were on the set of *Pretty Woman*, one of my all-time favourite films. Similar gorgeous car, similar gorgeous man. I just prayed he didn't think I was a similar sort of hooker. I pulled frantically at the hem of my short dress that had ridden up as I sat on the pavement waiting.

The silver car came to a standstill and the offside window slid slowly down.

'Robyn?' The door unlocked with a click. 'Do get in.'

Once seated, I turned towards the man, knowing my face was

flushed with the warmth of the afternoon, the exertion of lowering myself into the black leather interior as well as nervous tension. He was wearing an expensive-looking dark blue short-sleeved shirt, jeans and trainers, his olive-skinned face bearing a subtle but very becoming stubble.

'You OK? Really lovely to see you again.' He grinned across at me, taking in every bit of me, from my pink dress, equally pink face and obviously nervous disposition. This wasn't the confident, sassy waitress who'd made constant eye contact with him just two days earlier.

'OK,' I breathed.

'Are you up for a drive?'

'Well, we're in a car, so I guess that's the best way forward,' I said, wanting to immediately take back and swallow the banal words. Oh, for slick, easy conversation to slip effortlessly from my lips. 'Where are we heading?'

The car shot forward and a group of Japanese tourists, following their guide with a fluorescent flag held aloft, scrambled for safety. 'Marlow.' He smiled.

'Wasn't he a poet?'

Fabian laughed. '"Who ever loved, that loved not at first sight?"'

I was impressed. Not many men knew lines of poetry, and even fewer had ever quoted them at me.

'I'm actually at my parents' house for the weekend – they're away and I'm dog-sitting their new puppy. I'm sorry to drag you all the way over there, but my sister, who was supposed to be doing a shift with the dog, has had to fly off to a meeting in Copenhagen.'

'Oh?'

He didn't expand further, but simply raised an eyebrow in my direction as if sisters *flying off* to Copenhagen for meetings at the drop of a hat on a Sunday morning was the norm. I thought about my own sister, who would be taking my ten-year-old niece, Lola, round to Mum's place in order that she could *fly off* to Hudson House, the care home on the outskirts of Beddingfield where Jess put in long and gruelling shifts to pay the rent now that Dean, Lola's father, had gone AWOL once more.

'So, Marlow?' I asked.

'I grew up there.'

'But you don't live there any more?'

'No, no, it would take me far too long to commute every day into London.'

'And it's no place for young hipsters on their way up?'

He laughed at that. 'You're right. Once I'm ready to settle down, I might make my way back there.' He gave me such an intense look, I was almost on the point of saying: '*I do. I'll* settle down with you; have the 2.5 kids, the dog, the pony and the orangery off the kitchen.' 'Today, it won't take an hour.' He was speaking again but, submerged as I was in a lovely dream of hosting fabulous suppers for his barrister colleagues in our beautiful five-bedroomed (all en suite) house in Bucks, I didn't quite catch all he was saying. All a bit daft anyway, as I can't cook unless it's cottage cheese and a bag of the old rocket. Would that suffice for kitchen sups for eight? Jess, a superb cook, keeps telling me that producing a fabulous meal's not exactly rocket salad, but I would disagree with that sentiment.

'Sorry, you were saying?'

'Once we get onto the M40 it'll be less than an hour's drive. I thought we could have a picnic on the river?' He looked a little unsure. 'Unless you'd rather a restaurant? There's Heston's place over at Bray. I did wonder about that...'

'What? *The Fat Duck*?' I stared at Fabian. Even I, connoisseur of baked beans and cheese on toast, and utterly uninformed about posh restaurants – apart from Graphite – had heard of Heston Blumenthal. 'It must be booked up years ahead.'

'Dad's mate,' he said, slightly embarrassed. 'He'd probably fit us in somewhere. Having said that, there's Boris...'

'Boris?' Oh, for heaven's sake, please don't say his dad was mates with the ex-prime minister.

'The dog.'

'You've called a new puppy Boris?' I stared across at Fabian again.

'After Boris Becker. My mother spends a lot of her time, when she's not working, playing tennis. Becker was her idol when she was a teen.'

'Even though he's totally fallen from grace? Tax evasion? Prison?' I wasn't impressed.

'Mum was a top London judge at one point. She came out of retirement to help the team defending him at his trial last year.'

'Right.'

I sat back in my seat as the Porsche hit the fast lane on the M40 and Fabian concentrated on the road ahead. I turned slightly, taking in the dark features of this man who was whisking me off into a world so alien to my own. What the hell was I getting into?

4

'I'll have to pick up Boris,' Fabian said smiling, once we'd driven through miles of incredibly gorgeous countryside on the way out to Marlow. I've always considered the beautiful village of Beddingfield, where I'd grown up in West Yorkshire, stunning, and the scenery and sheer majesty of North Yorkshire, particularly around the Dales, and even round the bleak Pennines, unsurpassable, but as we passed through picture-box villages and expensive-looking towns with upmarket bars and restaurants, I could see why commuters would yearn to break out of London to live here. 'You OK with dogs?' Fabian asked, when I didn't reply.

'Depends what it is,' I said. 'If it's a great big pit bull or a horrible yappy little lapdog, then probably not. I didn't grow up with dogs. Mum's house is surrounded by fields and amazing countryside but she's never been keen on having one. Particularly as we have Roger.'

'Roger? A cat?'

'A rabbit,' I said. 'He's a house rabbit. He'd probably see off any dog that dared to venture onto his territory. He's particularly territorial about the sofa – we have to wrestle with him to get the best view of the TV.'

'I'm sure Boris will pass muster.' He grinned, slowing down as, a mile or so out of the riverside town of Marlow itself, we approached a long country drive. After passing through an electric gate, we drove along a tree-lined avenue planted richly on either side with herbaceous borders, mature trees and topiary. Fabian slowed with a crunch onto a gravel driveway in front of probably the most heavenly house I'd ever seen.

'Is this all yours?' I asked faintly as Fabian cut the engine.

'Well, my parents'.' Fabian smiled. 'And my grandparents' before that. Been in the family donkey's years. I grew up here. Right, come on, I'll just get Boris and his lead and the picnic.' I followed Fabian as he bounded up a flight of honey-coloured stone steps, pressed a few buttons on the alarm and walked through a magnificent reception hall, a pillared archway leading to the main, cream-carpeted staircase. While the house must have been designed and built with grandeur in mind, the rooms weren't stuffy, but instead portrayed generations of family life. I walked behind Fabian into a spacious kitchen, which my sister Jess, with her love of cooking, would have sold her soul to get her hands on. A huge six-door navy Aga obviously hadn't been thought sufficient because to one side of it was a bank of stainless-steel ovens, steam oven, microwaves and coffee maker that wouldn't have looked out of place in Costa. Hundreds of cookery books, as well as myriad gardening tomes, overflowed from a bank of bookshelves on one wall. As I gazed round in wonder, Fabian moved across the kitchen, opening what I assumed to be a utility room.

'Oh!' I jumped back in surprise as a blond bundle of energy flung itself upon me, knocking me backwards onto a kitchen chair.

'Meet Boris.' Fabian grinned.

'Hell, he's big.' I laughed, both the dog and I enjoying the attention. 'I thought you said he was a puppy.' Big lion's feet, out of all proportion to his slender legs, paddled furiously across the floor back to Fabian. 'What the hell is he?'

'Goldendoodle,' Fabian replied, wrestling the dog to the floor where he lay supine as Fabian cleverly avoided puppy teeth while rubbing at the dog's pink speckled tummy.

'Right, OK,' he said, standing up before moving to the sink to wash his hands. (I do like a man who washes his hands before touching food and, believe me, a hell of a lot of men don't.) 'Just give me a moment to sort the picnic. Red or white?'

'Oh, erm, white, please.' I wandered over to the huge window, taking in the acres of kitchen garden, greenhouses, a summer house and, the *pièce de résistance*, a large outdoor swimming pool, ornamented by expensive-looking, artistically arranged sunbeds, tables and chairs. This certainly beat my mum's two splintered deckchairs she'd bought years ago at B&Q.

'Right, would you mind awfully taking Boris while I bring the picnic? It's a fifteen-minute walk down to the river, if that's OK with you?'

'Of course.'

Concentrating all my efforts on reining in the exuberant puppy, who was intent on making a bid for freedom, I didn't speak much as we walked along country lanes awash with the new season's gifts of nature. Frothy cow parsley dominated as far as the eye could see, its delicate creamy lace umbellifers creating a sea of doylies through which we walked, Boris having me hanging onto his lead like a cartoon character. The last of the spring bluebells coordinated a veritable Union Jack with the addition of red campion, while acres of meadowland on either side of us were ablaze with glossy buttercups the colour of workmen's high-vis jackets.

'That looks terribly heavy,' I ventured, glancing across at Fabian's right hand gripping the basket handles. 'What on earth have you got in there?' A picnic, to me, was a cheese sandwich, a bag of crisps and a bottle of pop with, if you were lucky, a roll of Jaffa Cakes or Jammy Dodgers to finish.

'Nearly there.' Fabian smiled, cutting through a copse of trees and taking us down onto the banks of the Thames. 'Best place on the riverbank,' he said, taking Boris from me. 'Is this OK for you?'

'OK?' I glanced across at him. Surely someone as certain, so self-assured as the man I'd seen in action at the Central Criminal Court couldn't be feeling unsure about the place to have a picnic?

'Bit of a family secret, this spot.' Fabian smiled, retrieving a blanket from the basket. 'It's a tradition that we meet here on Boxing Day.'

'Boxing Day?' I stared. 'Isn't it cold, wet and miserable?'

'Well, yes, it can be, but lovely if it's been snowing. We bring pies and bacon sandwiches as well as warm glühwein and meet up with my horde of cousins and their offspring. A bit of a rite of passage to be allowed the glühwein instead of warm Ribena when you're sixteen. Irrelevant that you've probably been knocking vodka back at school in the dorm since you were twelve...'

'Right.' Fabian, I could see, inhabited a society – a world – vastly different from my own.

'You OK?' Fabian asked.

'You keep asking me that,' I said, trying to smile through my unease. 'I'm fine, really.'

'Well, why don't we have a drink first and you can spill the beans?' Fabian brought out a bottle of expensive-looking white wine, poured us both a glass – actual glass not plastic – and handed me one.

'The beans?' I took a sip of the deliciously cold and crisp wine and realised Fabian was gazing at me intently.

'OK.' He smiled. 'You are an incredibly beautiful girl. Where are you from?'

'Beddingfield, a large and pretty village on the outskirts of what was the industrial textile area of West Yorkshire.'

'Well, yes, it's fairly obvious you're from the north.'

'Is it? And does that bother you?'

'Why on earth should it bother me? But I'm curious. You're obviously not a rosy-cheeked Yorkshire lass with Anglo-Saxon roots.'

'Is that how you southerners see anyone hailing from north of Watford Gap?'

'Not at all.' Fabian drank deeply from his own glass, but he wasn't in the least embarrassed at probing. Years of experience in court, I supposed. 'So?'

'So?' I repeated.

'What's your heritage?'

Nicely put, Fabian.

I took another sip from my glass, relenting slightly. 'So, both my parents are dual heritage: my father's mother was English, but his father was originally from Jamaica.'

'Was?' Fabian asked.

'I never knew my paternal grandmother: she died when my dad was just a baby. Or my grandfather...' I trailed off, not wanting to explain further.

Fabian nodded, but said nothing.

'My mother's...' I paused '...lineage is more complex. She was adopted at birth, and her adopted parents never wanted her to find out her heritage so she really has no idea who her natural parents were. She knows her birth mother was English and her father from India. But apart from that, nothing.'

'Wow, that's an incredibly exotic background.'

'Exotic?' I frowned.

'Yes. Here am I, able to trace my own family tree almost right back to the Normans – pure English, the lot of them.'

'Weren't the Normans French?'

'You know what I mean.' He laughed. 'Whereas you are…'

'Half English, a quarter Jamaican and a quarter Indian,' I parroted. 'I learned to do fractions at junior school while working that lot out.'

'And your mum's adopted parents?'

I put down my glass and looked across at Fabian, feeling as though I were some strange creature under a magnifying glass he couldn't quite work out. 'Why the third degree?'

'I'm sorry.' He laughed easily. 'It's my job to find out everything about a person. And, Robyn…'

'Yes?'

'For some reason, I want to find out all about you. The minute I saw you in the restaurant…'

'Yes?'

'Oh, I don't know.' Fabian pulled a hand through his dark hair. 'I suppose you're so different from the crowd I was with on Friday. You know, all the women with their blonde, streaked, straightened hair; identical clothes from some designer of the moment; ridiculously expensive handbags that are too big for gym-toned arms.'

I laughed. 'Well, I like to think *every bit* of me is toned – I do enough dancing to tone the lot – but, my bag, I'm afraid, is M&S. And second-hand to boot.'

'And your grandparents?'

'Back to them?' I shook my head. 'According to my mum, she was brought up by a very upright – and uptight – teacher and his neurotic wife. She's always refused to speak about them, despite Jess and I wanting to know more.'

'Jess?'

'My big sister. There's just twenty-one months between us. She lives next door to Mum, back in Yorkshire, with my niece, Lola.'

'So, they were your grandparents, then?'

'Well, yes, although no blood relation obviously. I've never met them – my mum refused to have anything to do with them once she met my dad, and they've never tried to get in touch with us or have any relationship with me and my sisters.' I shrugged. 'I don't suppose they approved of their daughter running off with a dreadlocked mixed-race musician.'

'Famous?'

I laughed at that. 'Depends what you mean by famous. Probably more infamous when I hear what he's been up to next. Jayden Allen? Heard of him?'

'Erm no, can't say I have.' Fabian put his head on one side. 'Look, I don't think I've ever met anyone more...'

I raised an eye. 'More?'

'I'm sorry. I'm being utterly nosy. Downright rude almost. Shall we eat?'

I was already so full of this heavenly man in front of me I didn't think I'd be able to eat a single thing, but I smiled. 'I can always eat a cheese and pickle sandwich.'

'Oh.' For a split second Fabian looked worried. 'I should have asked what you'd prefer. Are you vegetarian?'

'No, why? What have you rustled up?'

'So,' he said, delving into the basket and bringing out what appeared to be half a deli counter, 'we've a blue Stilton and broccoli quiche, coronation chicken, a sourdough loaf and the rest, I'm afraid, is straight from Waitrose.'

'And the quiche isn't? Did you get your mum to make it?'

'Not at all.' Fabian affected mock offence. 'As soon as you

agreed to meet me for lunch last night, I looked in the fridge and freezer, and got my pinny on.'

'Really?' I stared and then laughed. 'No, you *didn't*! Your sister, then? Or the cook. I bet you've a cook.'

Fabian smiled. 'I can assure you, M'Lud, the defendant in front of you this afternoon is speaking nothing but the truth. I actually find cooking relaxing; in fact, I love being in the kitchen.'

'Oh, sorry to disappoint you: I'm utterly hopeless with anything culinary.'

'Right, what would you like? A slice of quiche? Some coleslaw? That's mine too.'

'Thank you.' I was suddenly ridiculously nervous again, my mouth dry, no appetite at all. Sitting within a foot of this exceptionally gorgeous man, who had been at the heart of my lustful fantasies for the past weeks, wasn't conducive to tucking in with zestful abandon. Hell, what if I couldn't swallow? I took another slug of wine – what on earth was I even doing here, a fish out of water, gasping for air?

I nibbled at the quiche Fabian handed to me on a plate. It was truly delicious and if I'd been at home, by myself, I'd have devoured the lot in three greedy mouthfuls. Fabian was buttering bread lavishly, piling on a garlicky pâté and tucking in, but turned when he saw I was struggling.

'You don't like it?' He pulled an anxious face.

'I do, I do. It's absolutely divine. I'm eating slowly, cherishing every morsel,' I lied, offering up a face of appreciation. 'You didn't make the bread as well?' I added, trying to get his attention from my dry mouth and seemingly closed throat.

'Certainly did. I got into bread making during lockdown.'

'Like lots of people.' I smiled. 'You should meet my sister Jess, she's a superb cook: can produce a fabulous meal out of just a few ingredients... I keep telling her I'm going to get her onto *Master-*

Chef...' I trailed off, realising I was gabbling when I should have been eating. 'So,' I said, 'you appear to have got my life story out of me. What about you?'

'The usual,' he said easily. 'I'm one of three: I've an older brother – half-brother actually – and younger sister, born to white, very English, very, you know, conservative parents. Both in the legal profession.'

'Oh? Solicitors? Lawyers?'

'Something like that.'

'Something like that?'

'Yes... So, try some of the coronation chicken. I add apricots – my own recipe.'

'What?' I laughed, sensing a reluctance on Fabian's part to continue as he spooned out creamy cold chicken and poured more wine. 'Thank you.' I hesitated. 'So, your dad's a top judge or something, is he? And your mum was on Boris Becker's defence team...?' I trailed off: something was beginning to turn cogs in my brain. 'Roland Carrington?' I finally said, staring across at Fabian for confirmation.

He nodded, a mixture of pride and embarrassment on his beautiful face.

'Your dad is the Lord Chief Justice of England?'

'And Wales.' He smiled, nodding again. 'I'm amazed you know that. Most people don't even know who the foreign secretary is.'

'I do,' I said, immediately giving the correct name.

'Or even the home secretary...'

'Easy,' I said scornfully. 'I'm in a pub quiz team,' I explained. 'When it doesn't clash with my shift at Graphite. "Who is the Lord Chief Justice of England and Wales?" was a question a month or so ago. No one knew.'

'Even you?'

'No, not at the time. I do now though.'

'Well, there we go,' Fabian said lightly. 'So, your dad's a musician?'

'Yes, been with various reggae bands ever since he was expelled from school. He does have quite a following in the Netherlands and Scandinavia.'

'Something to be proud of.' It was a statement rather than a question.

'Is it?' I looked directly at Fabian before relenting. 'I suppose it is.'

'Ice cream?'

'Home-made?' I smiled.

'Is there any better?'

'Well, I'm not averse to a Magnum if pushed.'

Fabian laughed, cleared away the remains of the picnic before opening some sort of thermos cool box. 'Hmm.' He frowned, looking down. 'Not quite as hard as I'd have liked.'

For some childish reason, that made me want to titter and I had to look away, folding the starched linen napkin Fabian had passed me earlier. Grow up, Robyn, I silently chastised myself. This man is a sophisticated adult: a barrister, the son of England and Wales's Lord Chief Justice.

I turned, the actor in me coming to the rescue as I offered a totally straight face in Fabian's direction, only to find him laughing himself. 'Sorry,' he apologised, unable to stop. 'So sorry.' He turned to the box, scooping out a soft spoonful of vanilla ice cream before standing and moving right over to where I was sitting. 'Now,' he ordered, 'try this. Hang on, close your eyes…'

'My eyes?'

'Yes. You can't savour the exquisite vanilla taste if your other senses are still on full alert.'

'I can *smell* the vanilla,' I argued. I could also feel my pulse racing, my heart going nineteen to the dozen.

'Close your eyes,' he insisted again.

I did as I was told, parting my lips slightly, anticipating sweet, vanilla-flavoured coldness.

Instead, there was a soft touch of cotton as his shirt brushed my bare arm, followed by warm, equally soft, lips on my own. My eyes fluttered open in surprise, but Fabian smiled. 'Just an experiment,' he explained, seriously. 'I read ice cream tastes so much better and colder if alternating with something warm.' He offered the spoon and, laughing, I licked the ice cream this time, but he leaned forwards, kissing my mouth once again until I wasn't sure which was the kiss and which was ice cream, both so utterly delicious I truly wondered if I'd died and gone to heaven.

5

We stayed on the riverbank that wonderful warm and sunny afternoon for hours, chasing after Boris, who was intent on pinching the remains of the picnic, nibbling on a selection of French cheese and fruit – grapes, fresh lychees, lusciously dark crimson cherries – and chatting, but Fabian didn't kiss me again. It was as if he'd given me a taste of something sweet and delicious and was now withdrawing the treat. Whether this was a deliberate tactic – remember, I'd seen him in action in court – or whether the two kisses were enough to make him realise he didn't relish more, I was quite unable to work out.

As if to reinforce the second option, Fabian glanced at his watch and suddenly jumped up. 'Goodness, I didn't realise the time. Are you working at the restaurant this evening? I need to get you back.'

'No, I rarely work Sundays – Sunday's my day for sorting myself out for the coming week, going over routines at the gym – I'm lucky: my friend owns Xander's gym on Prestbury Street and lets me in free of charge. Anyway, you know, Sundays are for the usual stuff.'

Fabian nodded. 'Me too, I'm afraid.'

'Going over routines at the gym?' I quipped, using humour to keep a smile on my face when I had the awful feeling that my Sunday spent with Fabian Carrington was about to fizzle and I should log it as a one-off. A Sunday with a beautiful, smart and interesting man – who, in reality, was way out of my league.

He laughed. 'I have a potentially very heavy case I'm going to be working on over the next few weeks. I really need to get back to London and get stuck in.'

I jumped up, hoping he might take my hand and pull me back down beside him on the picnic blanket, but he stood, packed away the remains of the cheese and prodded Boris, who was sleeping soundly in the shade of a great oak, gently with his foot.

'All ready?'

We strolled back with Boris walking sedately on the lead, any conversation that of polite strangers.

The ice-cream kisses might never have happened.

'Oh.' Fabian stopped as we approached the house to find a large red flashy car pulled up at the side of Fabian's silver Porsche. 'My brother appears to be home.'

'Weren't you expecting him?'

'Not really. Come on, I'll sort the remains of the picnic stuff and grab my keys.'

I wasn't quite sure if that was an invitation to follow Fabian back into the house or remain where I was in the garden, but Boris, whining and pulling on the lead, made the decision for me and I followed in Fabian's wake through the open front door.

A sandy-haired man, without Fabian's devastating good looks but obviously his brother, was sitting at the kitchen table, feet up on the chair opposite, glued to the football match on the small TV on the wall, a huge doorstep of a chicken sandwich in one hand and a bottled beer in the other.

'Didn't know you were home?' Fabian was saying as he emptied the picnic basket, wrapping cheese and quiche neatly before replacing them back in the huge stainless-steel American fridge.

'Was in the area, so thought I'd grab a beer and see what was on the agenda. Mum and Dad not back, then, I see?'

'No, not until this evening. I've been here all weekend to dog-sit.'

'And other things as well, by the look of it.' The man glanced in my direction and then, taking a bite of his sandwich, nodded at me.

'Robyn, this is Julius, my brother. Julius, Robyn.'

There came another nod, followed by a full-frontal appraising examination as Julius looked me up and down and then proceeded to undress me with his eyes, while continuing to make his way stolidly through the sandwich. 'Where's Jemima?' he finally asked, turning back to Fabian as he swallowed and wiped his mouth on a paper napkin. 'Thought *she* was the one looking after the damned dog.'

'Had to fly off to Copenhagen. Some trouble brewing there – in-house politics of some sort.'

'Well, that's what happens when you abandon the family profession and go off in a different direction. Always said there'd be trouble there.'

'Right,' Fabian said, ignoring Julius and picking up a large black bulging briefcase, a navy sweater and his car keys. 'We're off. If you leave before Mum and Dad are back, make sure you put Boris back in his crate in the utility, with plenty of water.'

'I'll just nip to the loo, if I may?' I smiled across at Fabian. Not having wanted to squat down behind a tree on the riverbank, I was at the crossing-my-legs stage of wanting to pee.

'First door on the left.' Fabian smiled back at me, but he appeared tense.

I left the two of them to it and headed out of the door. I could have stayed in that downstairs cloakroom for ever. A loo and huge white basin dominated a room bigger than my entire bedroom in Soho, the walls filled with family photographs, surfaces sporting Jo Malone candles and diffusers, as well as towering piles of folded and rolled white and navy soft fluffy towels. Behind me, an open Fortnum & Mason wicker basket held croquet paraphernalia, while a plethora of expensive-looking tennis racquets stood idly against the wall by the door.

I smiled at my reflection in the huge mirror, fancying myself ensconced in a copy of *Ideal Home* magazine. As I washed my hands, I perused the myriad wooden-framed photographs of Eton where hundreds of boys, frozen in time behind the glass protection, grinned down at me. Where was Fabian? I wondered. I spotted him almost instantly, a boy of thirteen or so, sitting cross-legged in front of a row of unsmiling staff, his dark hair flopping onto his starched stiff white collar, his large eyes as captivatingly magnetic and enticing then as now, twenty years or so on.

I spent a long time taking in the tall, dark-haired, dark-eyed image of a much younger Roland Carrington, the current Lord Chief Justice, and another of him with a tall, raw-boned, reddish-haired woman who must be both Fabian's as well as Julius's mother – and from whom Julius Carrington had obviously inherited his looks.

I made my way back, but stopped when I realised Fabian and Julius were in the middle of a discussion and, from its heated tone, apparently at odds with one another.

'You have to drop the Warrender case,' Julius was saying, his tone bullying. 'There's so much—'

'I don't *have to* do anything, Julius,' Fabian interrupted crisply.

'I'm more than able to make my own decisions on clients I do or don't take on.'

'Some pretty *strange* decisions you appear to be making lately...' Julius paused, a snort of ribald mirth following. 'So, where'd you pick *that one* up?' I could almost see Julius Carrington's head nodding in the direction of the downstairs loo. 'Don't think Ma would be overly impressed... you know what I'm saying? Oops, sorry, not very woke of me, that, was it? Mind you, she's a looker, I'll give you that. You can pass her on to me once you've finished with her.'

'You're utterly disgusting,' Fabian snapped and, hearing him taking his leave, I quickly moved back to the open front door, desperate for him not to realise I'd overheard the words that were making my heart thump with fury and embarrassment. Not to mention disappointment. So much disappointment.

Fabian led the way to his car without a word, the actor in me conjuring up an expression of beatific normality on my features while, in reality, my insides were churning and I just wanted to get the car ride over and tell someone what I'd overheard.

Jess. I needed to talk to Jess, my sister.

'I've a confession to make, Robyn,' Fabian eventually said, when, five minutes after we'd set off, neither of us had said a word.

'Oh?' He'd slipped the note to Claude in Graphite the other night as a bet laid down by the other men on the table? He couldn't cook any more than I could – he'd ordered all that delicious food online from Waitrose and decanted the lot into his own dishes? He was allergic to out-of-work actors? *Any* kind of actors?

'Oh?' I said again when he didn't speak, now not only furious and humiliated but also irritable.

Eventually he started to laugh, a little amused moue of embar-

rassment on his face as I turned to look at him while he concentrated on the road ahead. 'I *knew* you worked at Graphite, Robyn.'

Well, I wasn't expecting that.

'Oh?' I said for the third time. 'Did you? How?'

'Robyn, I saw you in the public gallery the morning you came
to court.'

'Right?' This was news to me. From what I remembered, it was
me doing all the gawping – I didn't recall Fabian looking back
again towards me after that first initial meeting of eyes, when he'd
appeared to look away without interest.

'And from that one chilly, superior glance into the audience...'

'The audience?'

'...you were able to ascertain I was a waitress? At a particular
restaurant in Mayfair?' Anger at what I'd just overhead Julius
Carrington say was rendering me sarcastic, the smile I'd plastered
on my face to get us through the drive home slipping in direct
proportion to the Porsche eating up the miles on the motorway.

Fabian looked sheepish. 'No, of course not... I...'

'What?'

'Robyn, I'm sorry. I've upset you. I shouldn't have said anything.'

'You've still not told me. Did you follow me? Stalk me?'

'No, of course not!' Fabian was laughing at the very idea. 'I
asked Shirley who you were.'

'Shirley?'

'Who you were sitting with in the public gallery.'

'Oh, Shirl, the famous Old Bailey groupie?'

Fabian smiled at that. 'Shirley's been sitting in the public
gallery as long as I've been defending. I made sure I was on the
concourse at lunchtime, hoping to bump into you, but you'd
already left. Shirley, as always, was there, ready to say hello, and I
simply asked who she'd been sitting with. She didn't know your

name, but did know where you worked, which was obviously handy.'

When I didn't say anything, Fabian apologised once more. 'I'm sorry, I wasn't stalking you.'

'Well, I think you probably were. And you were lucky I was working on the Friday shift – I don't work every evening.' I paused. 'And lucky that you managed to get a table.' I still couldn't smile and show Fabian how ridiculously happy I was to be at the centre of his detective work. Not now, not after hearing Julius Carrington's unpleasant words.

'It did take three weeks for a table to be free.'

'Which coincided with your birthday? That was fortunate.'

'I thought so.'

We drove in silence until we hit the centre of London, and I realised I'd no idea where Fabian actually lived in the city. 'So,' I finally asked, 'does Shirl often score women for you?'

'Goodness, that's harsh.' Fabian appeared genuinely shocked. 'Robyn? What is it? I've really enjoyed this afternoon, really enjoyed talking to you, and I'm so sorry if my method of finding out who you were, my wanting to get to know you, seems underhand. Sleazy even? But I wanted to be upfront with you. I can't think of any other way I could have had of making contact with you.'

We were heading for Marylebone and I saw my chance at a red light: 'You can let me out here, Fabian, please. Really. You've a lot to do and I can get the bus from here.'

'Don't be silly.' Fabian put out a hand. 'I don't understand.'

'Fabian, I've had such a lovely afternoon. Thank you so much...' I hesitated. 'The thing is, you see, I heard what your brother said...'

Fabian closed his eyes briefly. 'He's my half-brother and a

pillock into the bargain. Always has been. I'm so sorry you had to hear that... I didn't realise...'

'It's OK, really.' It wasn't. 'Thank you again... Look, there's a 453 bus... that's mine...'

'Robyn...'

I opened the car door and, with as much dignity as I could muster, ran towards the town hall where my bus was just about to leave.

6

And that, I decided, was that.

Never mind falling in love at first sight with a man who was not only way out of my league but had a horrible racist brother to boot. I had other things to concentrate on, namely getting back into the West End. While I'd loved every single second I'd spent with Fabian Mansfield Carrington on the riverbank, and couldn't stop reliving the ice-cream kiss, it was a fairy tale. I intended putting him and his repugnant brother where they belonged – in Marlow – and out of my head and dreams.

'You OK?' Jess answered my call on its first ring. 'How's the big city?'

'Big. You?'

'Oh, you know.'

'Tell me.' I took my mug of liquorice tea and settled back on the bed. Our chats could go on for hours.

'The usual.' I heard Jess sigh. 'I'm having to spend a lot of time trying to sort Sorrel. Mum just can't handle her.'

'Has Mum been called into school again?'

'Worse. Sorrel's been excluded once more.'

'How long for this time?'

'A week. And after that it's half-term, so she's going to be driving Mum to distraction not knowing where she is, what she's up to. Apparently, she totally disrupts every class – apart from dance and drama, which she loves – and the new head at the comp is on a mission: zero tolerance. You know the sort of thing – the kids having to ask if they want to take off their school jumper; no trainers, no phones...'

'I should think not. In class? Take her phone off her. That'll stop her.'

'I doubt it. Knowing Sorrel, she might go and nick one. I don't suppose you could have her down to stay with you for a few days? Give Mum a break?'

'Not really, Jess. I've a single bed in a tiny room and I'm out working all the time. I can't leave a fifteen-year-old girl to her own devices in the middle of Soho.'

'No, I get that.' Silence for a while. 'Mind you, I bet you're relieved the Soho Slasher's been caught. It's in all the papers.'

'Look, I'll try and get up for a few days... How is Mum?'

'Not wonderful. Jayden's not been in touch for a while now. She tries to get on with her life, but she's low.'

'Is she taking her medication? Seeing the doctor?'

'Robyn, you know what it's like. Someone like Mum, living with long-term physical health problems, doesn't always get the proper help or treatment they need. I just have to do what I can for her on a daily basis.'

'I'm so sorry, Jess. I know you're having to shoulder it all. How's Dean?'

'Oh, you know,' she said once more, obviously not wanting to go into details.

'Jess, *tell* me.'

'He's got another woman.'

'Again?' Jess's husband and father of Lola, my gorgeous ten-year-old niece, was a waste of space. In my eyes, anyway. 'Get rid of him, Jess. You're a strong, independent woman with a career.'

Jess laughed out loud at that. 'You call working shifts in a care home a career?'

'What about the outside catering job you had? Working for Home Dining? You loved that, cooking all day.'

'Robyn,' she said crossly, 'the place folded during lockdown.'

'Yes, I know, I *do* know that, but what's happened to your dream of running your own catering company? Weddings and christenings and such? You've got all your health and food hygiene certificates.'

'D'you know how much it is to even *rent* a place to do that? And all the catering equipment I'd need? It's just a dream, Robyn.'

'Get yourself on *MasterChef*. You'd win, hands down, and then everyone would pay you lots to cook their dinner for them.'

A snort of derision came down the phone.

'Or you could at least get a job with another outside caterer. They must be crying out for people like you who love and are brilliant at cooking.' My heart gave a little lurch as I recalled Fabian's expertise with his quiche and ice cream, not to mention his kissing.

'I know, I know, and I will, but at the moment I need the job I have to pay the rent and feed and clothe Lola. And I've enough on, keeping an eye on Mum – and now Sorrel – without taking on catering jobs when I might not actually get there to cook and serve the stuff.' She laughed. 'The bloody van's got something wrong with it again.'

'Dean's a mechanic, for heaven's sake. Get *him* to fix it.'

'He's too busy fixing himself up with the new barmaid at The Green Dragon.'

'Jess, throw him out. You don't need him. He's a bunion.'

'A bunion?' She actually chortled at that.

'A useless lump of flesh,' I snapped. 'Cut him out.'

'I will, I will. One of these days. Right, enough about me,' she finally said, and I could almost hear her smiling. Jess just got on with what life threw at her, as did Mum on the whole. My mother had been utterly stunning in her time, apparently catching the eye of every red-blooded male in the area. Now she was in her early fifties, a rare and possibly inherited complaint called acute porphyria – as well as Jayden – appeared to have got the better of her. I really should ring her more, visit her more. 'What are *you* up to?' Jess was saying. 'How did the audition for the female barrister go?'

'It didn't.' (At the mention of *barrister* my heart did a little lurch.) 'And, to be honest, I just want to sing and dance and have a steady job in musicals. I'm hoping Dorcas, my agent, will be in touch this week with something.'

'How on earth are you living? Paying the rent? In the middle of London?'

'Oh,' I said, more cheerfully than I felt, 'the shifts at Graphite keep my head above water. Just. And Jayden, when he's in the money, always hands over a wad. I'm assuming he does the same with you and Mum?'

'Very erratic, very sporadic, but yes, every now and again – when he remembers he has three daughters and a wife in Yorkshire.'

'Jess, Jayden never married Mum.'

'She likes to think he did: wears a wedding ring and calls herself Mrs Allen. Sorrel won't have anything to do with him at the moment.'

'Can't say I blame her... Oh, Jess... Jess...' I just had to talk to her about Fabian.

'What? What is it? Robyn?' There was concern in Jess's voice and I felt immediately sorry I'd said anything.

'I've fallen in love.'

'Oh, thank God for that. I thought you'd murdered someone.'

I closed my eyes, wincing at her choice of words, and knew, on the other end of the phone, sitting at the kitchen table in her little terraced cottage in Beddingfield, Jess would be doing the same.

'And?' she probed. 'Is that a bad thing? He's not married, is he?'

'No.'

'Gay and unavailable?'

'No.'

'*Famous* and unavailable? Is it James Norton?'

'What?'

'He was brilliant in *Happy Valley*. You know they filmed it just down the road from here?'

'I do know. He's in *A Little Life* at the Harold Pinter Theatre,' I said vaguely, not overly interested in any production that didn't involve singing and dancing. 'He's a barrister.'

'No, no, he plays the part of a New York lawyer, I think, not a barrister.'

I tutted, dying to get back to Fabian Mansfield Carrington. 'No, Jess, I've fallen in love – in lust, if you like – with a barrister at the Old Bailey.'

'Well,' she finally said, after a long silence, 'there's a novelty.'

'Yep.'

'And with our family history?'

'Yep.'

'And has he, you know, fallen in love with you as well? Or is he someone you've just seen from afar?'

'He came looking for me.'

'What do you mean?'

'He knew I worked at Graphite.'

'Right?'

'And he fed me little ice-cream kisses on the riverbank in some place called Marlow.'

'Have you been drinking, Robyn?'

I smiled, even though remembering those kisses made me want to cry, knowing I'd never have them again.

'Ice-cream kisses?' she asked. 'Are they like those little Iced Gems biscuits? Those little midget things? They've got BOGOF on them at the Co-op at the moment. Lola loves them, although,' she added, 'I do have to think about her teeth. Pure sugar.'

'Don't think you can say *midget* any more.' I laughed.

'We do up here in Yorkshire,' she said dryly. 'Remember your roots, Robyn.'

'He's a top London barrister, his brother is in the legal profession, his mother *was* a top London judge. Oh, and, er, his father is the Lord Chief Justice of England and Wales.'

'Fuck!' Followed by silence. 'Hang on...' I could sense her googling Roland Carrington as the expletive hung, accusingly, in the two hundred miles of air separating us. 'And yet,' she eventually said, 'all he feeds you is cheap little biscuits?'

'Oh, and his brother is unpleasant. Misogynist from what I saw... and heard... of him.' I hesitated. 'And racist.'

'Ditch him,' Jess snapped. 'A barrister is bad enough. A racist barrister is just not on.'

'I didn't say Fabian was racist,' I protested.

'A barrister? Called Fabian? And from Buckinghamshire, for heaven's sake? I bet he went to Eton, or one of those other top-knob public schools for the privileged rich. Don't go there, Robyn.'

'Do you not think you're being slightly prejudiced, Jess? You know...'

'Robyn,' she said, but more gently now, 'don't talk to me about prejudice. I've lived with prejudice of different kinds all my life. Only last week a new inmate... guest,' she corrected herself '...at Hudson House said she didn't want "a darkie" serving her food.' I could almost see Jess air-quoting the words.

'Oh, for heaven's sake. Surely not? I thought we'd moved on from all that?'

'You're setting yourself up for heartache, Robyn,' Jess warned.

'No, I'm not,' I said sadly. 'Because I won't be seeing him again.'

* * *

'Ah, Robyn, caught you.'

I was very tempted to reply to my agent, Dorcas, that I wasn't actually running away from her, but I swallowed the words wholesale and, instead, said, 'Hello, Dorcas, how are you?'

'Well, very well, as will you be when I tell you.'

My pulse raced and I put down the kettle I was just about to fill at the kitchen sink. 'Tell me what? You have something for me?'

'Sounds promising, Robyn, but, as always, don't get your hopes up too high.'

'OK. What?'

'Now, as you know, the casting process is different for every show...'

Just cut to the quick without the homilies, I urged her silently. 'What is it, Dorcas?'

'A speaking chorus part.'

'Right.' I held my breath. Don't get too excited, Robyn.

'You're up for the part of Arabella Plumpton-Jones.'

'In *Dance On*? At The Mercury?' I closed my eyes, my fingernails stabbing into the closed fist of my hand not holding my phone. 'I only went to see a performance of it a couple of weeks ago. I absolutely adored it.'

'That's right. Anyway, auditions at the end of the week.'

'Can you be more specific?' It wasn't easy trying to remain calm when, if Dorcas had actually been in front of me, I feared I'd have her up against the wall by the scruff of her neck to get the information from her more speedily.

'Right, OK, today's Monday – erm, Friday, 9.30 a.m. at The Mercury on East Street. It's a dance group audition with both the director and choreographer. The girl who's had the part of Arabella P-J is pregnant apparently. Didn't tell anyone she was up the duff and is now throwing up at every turn and they need someone PDQ. Lots of girls up for it, of course, so...'

'Don't get my hopes up. I know, I know.' If there'd been a chandelier in the kitchen of the Soho flat, I'd have been swinging from it.

'But do give it your best, Robyn. Dance audition, so turn up in your gear ready to go on. Oh, and they want two songs.'

'From the show?'

'Not necessarily. Two songs of your choice, so choose two that you know well and which showcase your voice to its best advantage. Text me later when you've decided and I'll see if I agree with you and then let them know.'

I already knew the songs I'd be singing: 'Don't Rain on My Parade' from *Funny Girl*, a notoriously difficult number to carry off, and 'He's My Boy' from *Everybody's Talking About Jamie*, which was enough to have me in genuine floods of tears, no acting required.

I looked at my watch. I was working the eleven-to-five lunchtime shift at Graphite but, scanning the studio timetable at Xander's gym, saw I could squeeze in three quarters of an hour between Bums and Tums with Tony and a hatha yoga class, with the gym's rather good sound system. I needed the acoustics of the large studio to belt out my audition pieces, taping and playing back the singing until I'd got it just right.

Monday, Tuesday and Wednesday passed in a flurry of practising, and performing dance routines, teaching two Zumba classes, as well as the repeated recording and playing back of my audition songs, interspersed with a couple more shifts at Graphite. All this meant I had no time whatsoever (I think the lady doth protest too much, Your Honour) to let my mind wander anywhere near the enticing but dangerous subject of Fabian Mansfield Carrington. I tried hard not to glance hopefully at the restaurant door every time it swung open, and left my phone safely in my locker. Apart from Tuesday evening, when I was working the late shift at Graphite once more, I managed a couple of early nights, despite suffering the hyperbolic cries of ecstasy (if she was putting it on then she was a better actor than I'd ever given her credit for) coming through the thin walls of Tanya's room as she gave some new man a good seeing-to.

By 9 p.m. on the Thursday, I felt I couldn't do one more thing to ensure the best possible performance the following morning and, after a shower and light meal, decided on another early night. Then I remembered: I'd left my music at Xander's. How could I have been so stupid? I quickly dressed in the gym gear I'd just pulled off, grabbed my trainers and ran through the still light and busy Soho streets to Xander's. The last session of the evening – a Pilates class – was coming to an end and once the participants had been taken through their final cool downs, I made my way in.

'Yours?' the instructor, a middle-aged woman with a long greying plait and sporting a pair of garish lemon tights, held up my USB stick.

'Gosh, yes, thank you,' I breathed, utterly relieved.

'Xander said you'd an important audition in the morning.' She picked up her things and went to follow the last people out of the studio. 'Good luck.'

'Thank you.' I suddenly knew I just *had* to go through the dance routine once more and, plugging the stick back in, gestured to Xander – who was at the studio door indicating with his watch – that I'd lock up once I'd finished. He was obviously off on some hot date because, showered and dressed to kill, he didn't demur as he normally would at my offer.

The routine had just one tricky *tour jeté* – a jump in which one foot steps out to the side, and the other foot kicks around in a leap to meet the other, the dancer then landing on the kicking foot. I shucked off my trainers, steadied myself, took a deep breath and took off, arms outstretched over my head during the leap, before bringing them down once more. Perfect. Pleased, I went for it again and then again and again. Jennifer Beals, eat your heart out.

Heart racing with the effort, it suddenly went into overdrive as I realised I was no longer alone in the studio. Oh God, that was all I needed – some weirdo who'd come in off the street and was now standing in the doorway, arms folded, watching my every move. (If he hadn't been caught, it could have been the Soho Slasher, for heaven's sake.)

'You're good,' Fabian said.

'Jesus, do you make a habit of creeping up on women when they're practising?' My heart didn't calm down once I'd realised just who that man was.

'I wasn't *creeping up* on you. The guy – the owner? – was on his way out and let me in when I asked if you were here.'

'You were lucky – he doesn't usually let anyone in who's not a member. And he's very protective of me...' I broke off, staring. 'How on earth did you know I'd be here? Are you stalking me again?'

'You told me you were always here when you weren't at the restaurant.'

'No, I didn't.' I frowned. 'I'm not *always here*. Very often on a Sunday, yes, but apart from that I have to grab the time when I possibly can, usually early mornings or late in the evening.'

'You said.'

'Right.'

'You're good,' Fabian said again. 'Very good.'

'Thank you.' I didn't know what else to say. I picked up my trainers and unplugged the precious USB stick from the sound system. 'I need to go,' I said, walking towards the door where Fabian still stood. Dressed in a beautifully cut black suit, crisp white shirt and maroon silk tie, he'd obviously come straight from chambers. He pulled a hand through his hair, looking across at me with those deep brown eyes of his until I had to look away.

'I'm sorry.'

'Sorry?' I was standing in front of him now, but, unless I bobbed round him, or physically pushed him to one side, unable to exit the studio.

'For startling you.'

'You did.'

'Don't go.' His voice was still low as he put out a hand to my arm, but then moved it to my face where he took an escaped tendril of hair, twisting it almost thoughtfully around his finger before replacing it neatly behind my ear. 'I needed to see you again.'

'Needed to? Or wanted to?'

'Is there a difference? Yes, I suppose there is,' he added, almost to himself. 'Needed to,' he went on. 'I needed to apologise for my brother's behaviour.'

'You already did. It's fine. I've heard worse.'

'And, if I'm to focus on my work, and get defendants off who're paying me a hell of a lot of money to do just that, then I need to concentrate on the job in hand.'

'Oh?'

'But, Robyn, the thing is, knowing until I saw you again, I've not been able to do just that. Concentrate on my work, I mean.'

'So, are you saying that I'm the cause of some poor bloke looking at twenty years' hard labour because you can't defend him properly?'

'Something like that.' He nodded, his voice softly caressing, his beautiful face impassive, but his eyes full of humour. 'You see, all I can think of, when I'm putting questions to a witness, is not their answer, but the need to kiss you again.' His hand came up once more and this time I found myself leaning into it as he moved his thumb slowly across my bottom lip. He bent his face down to mine, a faint citrus aftershave flooding my senses as he did so, kissing my mouth, which had slightly, and almost involuntarily, opened in response. And I was lost. Utterly lost.

7

For the hugely coveted chorus role in *Dance On* I was up against twenty-five other girls, all determined to make the gift on offer that morning theirs.

'You're as good as the rest, better than most, Robyn,' Jayden had scolded me over the phone as we'd chatted while I made my way through an already busy Leicester Square and into East Street. 'Just give it all you've got. And don't forget to drop into the conversation that you're Jayden Allen's daughter.'

'As if.' I'd snorted, ringing off before entering the theatre through the back door.

I'd handed in the two hard copies of my CV and the required headshot – needed so the casting and musical directors could put a name to a face – and we then proceeded to warm up, most of us sipping compulsively from bottles of water, too nervous to chat; I could see there was stiff competition and my confidence wavered. I noticed a tall, lithe redhead who'd been with me the two months I'd spent in the line-up in *Big* but, as I waved tentatively in her direction, pleased to see at least one friendly face, we were called forward.

Once we'd assembled on the stage, we were given the low-down by Carl Farmer, the musical director, of what was expected of us, and then the choreographer, a tiny girl with a swishy blonde ponytail, took us through a short dance routine. She then left us to join the director in the front seats, and they both watched, making notes as we performed what she'd instructed. This was good, I could do this, and my confidence grew as a couple of the girls missed steps, leaping in the wrong direction as nerves got the better of them.

We then came back on singly, had a thirty-second chat as to our career so far before being instructed to perform our own practised routine, the one big chance to showcase one's skill and talent as a dancer.

I let myself go, not thinking of anything but the music I'd chosen and my routine, giving it all I'd got and dancing to the very best of my ability.

My two-minute dance routine came to an end, I thanked the judges and retreated offstage to await my next instructions. It was unusual at this stage in the proceedings for cuts to be made but after we'd all done our auditions just fifteen out of the original twenty-five were called back on stage, while the others were released.

We were taken through another, much more taxing dance routine and then split into three groups, so that just five at any one time were performing on stage.

I couldn't believe we'd got through all this in under ninety minutes – the producer was clearly determined to whittle the options down quickly. At 11 a.m., we were told we could leave but were requested to remain nearby, our phones switched on, as some of us would be called back that very afternoon to sing.

I went for a coffee in Pret on Coventry Street, sitting at a table by the window while phoning Jess, Mum and finally Jayden, biting my nails when not one of them answered. Knowing Mum, she'd have seen a bit of sunshine and be out weeding and planting and doing far too much, with little regard for her condition. I drank my coffee, playing down any hope that I might have a recall later that day by planning what to do with the rest of my life once I was given the big 'thanks, but no thanks'.

As I sat at the window, looking out over the street, my thoughts came back again and again to Fabian.

After leaving Xander's the previous evening, Fabian had walked me back to the flat, wished me luck for the audition before bending to kiss my cheek. He'd turned, as if to walk away, but then retraced his steps. 'Will you come out with me?'

'Out with you?' I smiled at that – it reminded me of being back at Beddingfield Comp when one of the red-faced, cheese-and-onion-breathing Year 9 lads finally got up the courage to ask you to meet him outside the Co-op, where, with safety in numbers and bottles of cheap cider, we kids used to hang out.

'Thank you,' I said. 'I'd like that.'

'I'll be in touch,' he replied and, this time, turned and actually walked away.

Now, unable to sit a minute longer, I left my window seat in Pret, my Fitbit clocking up the steps as I walked the length and breadth of the West End, from Shaftesbury Avenue and down James Street to Covent Garden before heading down The Strand to Charing Cross. I was passing in front of the National Gallery, considering taking myself in there to kill some time, when my phone rang.

'Ms Allen? Could you make your way back to The Mercury? We'd like you to come back in, if you're happy to do that?'

* * *

'Oh, Robyn, you got it?' Jess was almost as ecstatic as I was, and I loved her all the more for it. Some sisters, some mates (I was thinking here of Tanya back at the flat) are not averse to finding little ways to burst one's bubble of success in order to bolster their own sense of importance: *Is that all they're paying you? That producer is the absolute devil to work for. My cousin's best friend's sister couldn't stand the other members of the cast – totally bullied, she was – left with a nervous breakdown...* But not Jess. Her excitement down the phone was palpable, and I knew she was already mentally scanning her kitchen calendar, as well as her credit-card statement, to see when she could bring Lola down to see her Aunty Robyn on stage.

Jayden, characteristically, sent an over-the-top bouquet of flowers and a bottle of champagne: it was all or nothing with my father – boom or bust – but apparently my successful audition coincided with a new record release, which, for once, was not only selling well but was even being played on the radio.

A couple of hours after Dorcas, my agent, rang with the wonderful news that I was successful, a text came through from Fabian:

> Come and celebrate.

> How on earth do you know whether I'm celebrating or not?

> Aren't you?

> Yes.

> There you go, then. I'll pick you up at 7.30, if you're free.

Was I really going to waste time and energy playing games by replying that I already had plans or by not responding for an hour or so? Of course not: I was far too old for such juvenile nonsense, and I couldn't think of anyone I'd rather be celebrating with.

> Thank you, I'd like that.

I'll cook dinner. Don't go eating sweets and spoiling your appetite

That made me laugh.

> Don't pick me up. I'll get the bus. Where are you?

Westminster

Bloody hell, posh or what?

> 88 bus. No problem. Text me your address. I'll find you.

* * *

It was another beautiful evening and, after showering, I found my trusty trainers and set off, eschewing any transport except my own two feet. The great thing about living in central London was that, by walking everywhere in order to save money, it had become something of a challenge – like doing The Knowledge, so loved by the city's black cab drivers. London had become a village for me and not a huge metropolis. Now that the alleged Soho Slasher – Rupert Henderson-Smith, I saw from the free newspaper reports – was in police custody, I was even up for walking the streets after dark.

I walked a route taking me along Wardour Street, Shaftesbury Avenue and Drury Lane relishing as I always did, the buzz of London's theatreland and, although I sometimes longed for the green fields and unspoiled woods surrounding Mum's place, I'd lived so long away from the countryside that I was beginning to consider myself a city girl. I knew, as I made my way past myriad theatres and then on towards Fabian's apartment, I was right where I wanted to be.

It took me twenty minutes of brisk walking, using my phone to navigate to Fabian's place. I'd assumed it would be a bit more upmarket than the dive I was renting in Soho, but even this assumption didn't prepare me for the actual reality of his apartment in St James's Place between Mayfair and Westminster.

'You found me?' Fabian said as he let me in.

'You were hiding?' I quipped, immediately wishing I didn't turn every question into another. An old boyfriend had once said this habit of mine used to infuriate him. Why couldn't I just float in serenely and say 'hi' before arranging myself seductively on the leather sofa to await being served a cocktail?

'Oh, you shouldn't have.' Fabian smiled, taking the bottle of champagne from me.

'I didn't really. My father was exceptionally quick off the mark and sent over the bottle, together with some flowers. Don't know if it's any good... Not sure how he managed it within a couple of hours of me knowing I'd got the part...' I was gabbling now.

'Sounds an interesting bloke. I'd like to meet him.'

'I don't think you would... Oh, wow—' I broke off, moving over to the huge picture window through which, from four floors up, a huge expanse of Green Park was on view.

'Forty acres of greenery down there apparently.' Fabian smiled, coming to stand behind me and handing me a glass of champagne, which, being deliciously ice cold, couldn't have come from the bottle I'd carted in my hot sweaty mitts all the way from Soho. 'It's one of eight Royal Parks in London, the royal being Charles II who decided to build a wall around an area of the Poultenay estate, a former lepers' ground on the city outskirts, before renaming it Upper St James's Park.'

'So originally a leper colony?' I gazed down at the park, now awash with evening joggers, dog walkers and those late leaving work from the many surrounding offices.

'Congratulations, Robyn,' Fabian said, clinking my glass with his own. 'You must be very happy?'

'Ecstatic.' I smiled. 'I really, really am.'

'Does that mean you can give up your job at Graphite?'

I nodded. 'Thank goodness. Don't really think I'm cut out to serve the public – the posh public at that...' I trailed off, looking round at the beautiful apartment, taking in the understated décor, the obviously expensive fabric at the window and the white baby grand piano in the corner, before bringing my gaze back to Fabian himself.

He was wearing jeans and an immaculate white T-shirt: apart from a narrow tan leather belt that accentuated not only his slim waist but also his broad chest, that was it. Nothing on his feet and the plain gold watch on his left wrist. I took a long gulp from my glass, suddenly feeling shy, vulnerable even. Here I was, in the ultra-chic fourth-floor apartment of a man I knew very little about, drinking champagne while wondering what was going to happen next. What I was supposed to *say* next.

'How long have you lived here?' I asked, sounding like a hairdresser. 'It must be well placed, central for your work?'

'It is.'

'Right.'

Fabian smiled, relenting a little. 'The apartment was originally my great-grandfather's. My grandfather, my mother and then, until recently, my brother Julius have all lived here for a while before moving out to the sticks.'

'You're very lucky.'

'Lucky?'

'To have things handed to you on a plate.'

Fabian pulled a face. 'Bit unfair, that. I've worked many years and long hours to get where I am with my work. I don't just swan in at 10 a.m. and say a few words to persuade the judge and jury of my client's innocence, you know.'

'But you have somewhere very lovely to come back to, once you've done that.'

'You disapprove?'

'I approve very much of the apartment – although, to be honest, I think I'd miss a front door and a garden. And some countryside.'

'Which is why my family moved out and I moved in. I guess Julius's and Jemima's kids will have the apartment next...'

'And your own?' I had a sudden thought. 'Hang on, are you married? Your wife and 2.4 children farmed out in deepest darkest Bucks while you continue to frolic and live the sybaritic single life during the week, before heading back to them at the weekend?'

Fabian laughed at that. 'Sybaritic?' He held up his own glass of champagne. 'I can assure you, Robyn, this is as self-indulgent as it gets on a Friday evening. And you were with me at the weekend. Did you see any evidence of a wife and children?'

'What about Fish Face?'

'I beg your pardon?'

'The girl you were with at Graphite who has an allergy to all finned fish.'

Fabian pulled a face. 'Does she? Don't all fish have fins?' He considered for a few seconds. 'Well, not prawns and oysters *et al*, but are they fish?'

'She's very beautiful.'

'She is.'

There was polite reservation in Fabian Carrington that I'd

never come across in the men I usually hung out with, and I wasn't quite sure how to handle it. I drank more of my champagne, but saw that Fabian took only a few sips of his own.

It was clear he wasn't about to divulge any possible relationships he was in. And why should he? Dating rules, especially in big cities like London, had evolved into something quite different from those extravagant little scenarios I'd acted out with my Barbie and Ken as a kid. *One* Barbie – and definitely *one* Ken – living happily ever after as Barbie donned her wedding finery and walked up the aisle. Maybe I'd overindulged myself in such idealistic yet unrealistic scenes to compensate for the reality of Mum and Jayden's relationship. And why I loved the romance of musical theatre so much. A psychoanalyst would have a field day with me, I reckoned.

'You live here alone?' I finally asked.

'I do. I like the solitude.'

'And your brother? Julius?' I thought I'd better wave hello to the elephant in the room. After all, it was his fault I'd jumped out of Fabian's car the other night.

'He got married last year and moved out to Surrey.'

'Goodness, he actually found someone to marry him?' Instantly I could have bitten my tongue. Slating a man's relatives when you hardly know the man himself is not exactly conducive to a harmonious evening ahead. 'I'm so sorry,' I said. 'That was very rude of me.'

'But understandable.' Fabian smiled. 'I can only apologise again for his words and that you overheard them. OK, are you hungry?'

I realised I was famished. Apart from the bowl of porridge and banana I'd forced down before the audition – knowing I needed the energy to leap around on stage – and the coffee in Pret, I'd been far too nervous and excited to think about food. 'Thank you,' I said. 'I am.'

Fabian moved to the open-plan kitchen area, bending to retrieve dishes from the fridge. 'Is it usual for you to be told that you've got the part on the same day of audition?' he asked, removing cling film from a bowl and adding a salad dressing to its contents, tossing the whole thing as he spoke.

'It hardly ever happens.' I shook my head. 'Usually takes a good week before they let your agent know. But this one was a bit different – the girl was pregnant and throwing up everywhere. For her own sake, as well as the rest of the cast, she had to give up the part. Lucky for me, of course.'

'Come and sit down,' Fabian directed, moving to the far end of the room where a table was set meticulously with silver and linen for two.

'You are very precise.' I smiled, sitting down and loving the fact that Fabian had pulled out the chair for me.

'Is that a bad thing?' he asked, looking slightly worried.

'Just not what I'm used to. Having dinner with someone usually means a takeaway curry or a spag bol on my knee in front of the TV... Oh, goodness, this looks wonderful.'

Fabian set down two plates of something I couldn't quite identify.

'*Palourdes au gratin.*' He smiled. 'Baked clams with garlic butter.'

They were utterly delicious and as the alcohol went down and I dipped focaccia (apparently home-made, although when Fabian had had time to bash the dough and stud with rosemary, salt and tiny little tomato halves was anyone's guess) into the garlicky butter, I found myself beginning to relax.

'Where did you learn to cook?' I asked. His eyes lingered on me longer than they should and I felt myself grow pink.

'I studied languages at Oxford,' he replied. 'Had a year out in Germany and then France...'

'Ah, that's why you were able to converse with Wallbanger so well the other night.'

'Wallbanger?' Fabian raised an eyebrow. God, did he realise just how effortlessly sexy he was when he did that?

'Miss Muffler, my boss at Graphite. You were chatting to her before you left on Friday evening.'

'Oh, right, yes. And she's actually called *Wallbanger*?' Fabian started to laugh.

'Long story.' I smiled. 'So, what were you saying to her?'

'I was simply telling her that the evening had been totally enhanced by the beautiful, quite intoxicating waitress at our table who had not only captured my every sense, but who I simply had to get to know because—'

'You didn't!'

'No, you're right, I didn't. I simply asked her to compliment the chef on his *confit de canard*... I've never quite managed to get the right balance of thyme and bay leaf when I've attempted to make it myself.'

I put down my fork and stared. 'And I guess that's what you do all day? Spin a story of what *could* have happened, rather than what, in reality, you know to be the truth?'

'You'll never know, unless you ask Miss Muffler herself, just *which* is the true version.' He smiled as he removed plates. 'So, where did I learn to cook? I spent almost eight months at the University of Burgundy in Dijon.'

'Where the mustard comes from?'

'And the most sublime food. There's a great mix of fine dining and relaxed restaurants in the region. My favourite – and an absolutely incredible one – is Au Fil du Zinc, but there's also a cookery school called The Cook's Atelier in the heart of Beaune where they only use ingredients from local artisan producers. I was supposed to be helping students converse in English at the university, but no one seemed bothered if I went AWOL.'

'You miss it?'

'It's a long time ago now.' Fabian's brown eyes were sad. 'I *longed* to stay there. I *would* have stayed there if I could.'

'And why couldn't you?'

'What, not finish Oxford? And not go into law as the Carringtons have done since time immemorial? Not quite the done thing, Your Honour.' He stroked my arm fleetingly as he took the plates into the kitchen area. As he stood at the worktop, his back to me, I sat and marvelled at his physique. He must have been six foot two and everything was in proportion, from the muscles working beneath the white T-shirt as he squeezed lime, tapering to the slim waist and taut buttocks clad in denim.

'You fell in love?'

'Sorry?'

'In France, when you were there in your early twenties, you met someone...?'

Fabian smiled, but there was the same sadness, regret almost, on his face as he placed Caesar salad in front of me. 'Parmesan?' he asked. 'Black pepper?'

8

I knew I'd fallen irrevocably in love with this beautiful, intelligent and seemingly sensitive man. I'd had two previous long-term relationships back in Manchester – one particularly we both thought would end in commitment, but were simultaneously relieved when we realised we were going nowhere, neither of us wanting the same things in life.

But this thing with Fabian was like nothing I'd ever experienced before: I felt I was drowning in those eyes of his, wanting to touch him constantly when I was in his presence, desperate to see him again the minute I wasn't.

That first evening, after we'd eaten the clams and the Caesar salad, we stayed at the table, drinking coffee and just talking, getting to know everything about each other: he was Taurus to my Capricorn; favourite colour navy blue to my mauve; couldn't be without French cheese, whereas I had withdrawal symptoms if there was no Marmite and peanut butter on my one shelf of the shared kitchen cupboard.

And all the time, our fingers would accidentally touch as he poured coffee, passed the milk jug, opened the exceptionally expensive box of chocolates from Harrods his grandmother had sent over for his birthday. I was waiting for a repeat of the ice-cream kisses but none was forthcoming and I was both relieved and disappointed. I didn't want the evening to end in sex on his cream carpet – that would have been too obvious. If this was going to be worth anything, have any future, then sex on the second date was not happening.

At midnight, Fabian called an Uber, took my hand and walked me down to the street where, while we waited for the cab, he threaded his hands through my hair, pulling his face down to mine and kissing me so thoroughly I was a quivering mess and debating whether it wouldn't be a good idea to walk him all the way back up again and ravish him on that cream carpet after all.

Just a few days later – it was a Wednesday evening; I remember it so well – Fabian asked if I'd like to meet him after he'd finished work for the day. We could walk along Regent's Canal from Little Venice as it was such a beautiful evening, and stop for a drink at one of the cafes and pubs along its length. I'd spent all day at The Mercury theatre, signing contracts, and insurance documents, being fitted for outfits and completing a hundred and one other tasks. I met the cast as they trooped in and along to the dressing rooms, some with only half an hour or so to spare before curtain-up for the mid-week matinee, and I marvelled, wondering would I ever appear as sanguine as these performers. I knew on my first night's performance the following week I'd be impatiently ready to go, poised with my make-up on, as soon as the stage door was unlocked.

I watched the whole performance, singing along and acting out the steps in my head as well as with my restless tapping feet, from the safety of the side stage. My excitement and delight were only slightly marred when the girl whose part I was about to take shoved past me, deliberately knocking into my shoulder as she came off stage.

One of the leading men had seen her actions and, still smiling at me, said, 'She assumed she'd have maternity leave rather than being thrown off the production. You can't really blame her for taking it out on you.'

I wanted to retort tartly, 'I think I can,' but I was the new girl, I didn't need to be ruffling any feathers, and instead nodded with, 'I get that,' and a smile.

After that little altercation, the thought of a walk in the evening sunshine and a drink with Fabian was music to my ears. After all, how many other evenings would I have free once I was committed to seven performances – possibly eight, including two matinees – every week?

'You look tired,' I said, noting the dark shadows around his eyes.

'Been working on a very difficult case.' He nodded, taking my hand. 'Not left chambers before 10 p.m. since I last saw you.'

'Even at the weekend?'

'Saturday, I had a family commitment I was expected to be at but, yes, Sunday was spent going through indictments.' Fabian sighed, pulling a hand through his hair in a gesture I'd come to recognise very much as his own. 'You can't imagine how much I'd rather have spent the time with you, Robyn.' He stroked the area between my thumb and finger as he led the way to his parked car at Marylebone, and just that simple touch sent a spark through my whole body.

Fabian drove quickly to Little Venice, the affluent residential district in West London that sits on the junction of the Paddington arm of the Grand Union Canal, the Regent's Canal, and the entrance to Paddington Basin, before parking up. We walked and we talked, stopping for a drink at two waterside pubs – Coke for

Fabian, white wine spritzer for me – and when he bent his head to kiss me, and the kiss went on and on and two kids on bikes doing wheelies shouted, 'Oy, mate, get a room,' Fabian pulled away and groaned.

'Christ, Robyn, if I don't make love to you soon, I won't be held responsible for anything else...'

'I don't want you feeling responsible for *anything*,' I managed to get out once we both came up again for air.

'Shall we go?' he asked almost brusquely, before grabbing the attention of the waiter to pay for drinks we'd hardly touched. We set off back to the car and had only been gone thirty seconds when his phone rang.

'Sorry,' he eventually said after a short conversation to whoever was on the other end of the phone. 'I'll have to make a detour and call in for a file I need.'

'Call in?'

'At chambers.'

'I've always wanted to see where barristers hang out backstage.'

'Backstage?' He smiled and we carried on to the car, which, in the time we'd been away, had accrued a parking ticket. 'Shit, that's London for you,' he said, peeling it off the windscreen and throwing it into the car before driving us off – in a manner guaranteed to end up with another motoring offence – towards the Royal Courts of Justice.

'Handy,' I said, once he'd parked the car in its allotted spot. 'You know, your apartment, chambers and the courts all within walking distance of each other.' But Fabian didn't reply, intent on retrieving the file as quickly as possible. He pushed myriad security buttons to enter a large domed building. Several flights of marbled stairs, as well as an imposing amount of framed-photograph-covered cream painted walls, stretched ahead of us.

'Through here,' was all Fabian said as we walked the length of classically decorated corridors.

'Wow,' I finally said. 'Is this all yours?'

'The Carringtons', anyway.' He smiled over his shoulder. 'Been here for over a century. We have forty barristers.'

'Forty?' I gasped. 'Forty offices?'

'Twenty,' he corrected, somewhat vaguely. 'The more junior barristers share.'

'I bet you don't.'

Fabian smiled and gestured as we walked. 'Julius's office... my mother's... Reception... You still here, Milly? You need to get off.'

'I wanted to finish this for you, Mr Carrington,' she said, looking me up and down, obviously intent on trying to work out who I was.

'Oh, Mr Carrington,' an acne-faced young man called nervously from around an open door to my right. 'Could I have a word?'

'Go home, Hugh,' Fabian called. 'It can wait until the morning.'

'But...'

'Really, go home.'

I followed Fabian up the flight of stairs where he unlocked a door on the left and we went in. The room was immaculately – obsessively – tidy and I took in the rows and rows of leather-bound legal tomes and the huge desk under the tiniest of windows. I glanced around, recalling the notoriety of Dr Crippen and the Kray twins as well as Ruth Ellis, the last woman in the UK to be hanged for murder and, of course, the Yorkshire Ripper. All had faced judgement at the Old Bailey. Maybe, I thought, their defence could have been planned in this very building?

I shivered at the thought, finding a modicum of normality in a pair of battered sofas at one end of the room, and the drinks cabinet strategically placed between them.

'Help yourself to a drink,' Fabian said, his eyes still on the papers in front of him. 'And now we're back, I'll have one myself. There should be some mixers in the fridge – I could really do with a whiskey and ginger ale. And the lavatory is through that door if you need it,' he added.

I poured us both drinks and, after handing one to Fabian, wandered the room, taking in the many photographs of past Carringtons, slowing down at one of a younger and presumably newly called to the bar Fabian.

'I'll try not to be too long.' He smiled in my direction, before loosening his tie and unbuttoning his shirt collar with obvious relief.

Fabian was on home territory here, and for thirty minutes he appeared as though in a different world, moving from desk to computer to the large tomes and then to files on a shelf, intent on something or other before shifting back to his laptop.

Eventually he turned to me, draining his whiskey as he did so. 'I thought you'd done bar work?' He smiled. 'There must have been at least a triple shot in that.'

'Sorry.' I pulled a face. 'More used to pulling pints in pubs in Manchester than sorting spirits in a barrister's bar.' I sipped at my own drink, unable to tear my glance away from Fabian as he moved towards me, taking my glass and placing it on his desk. He was so close I could see the smattering of freckles on the bridge of his nose, was able to take in the sweep of his long eyelashes as he briefly closed his beautiful brown eyes, and then I closed my own as he kissed me again and the air between us appeared to still.

'Ah, Robyn,' was all he said as he began unbuttoning my shirt to reveal what was beneath, and my own hands went automatically to his white shirt, finishing the job of unbuttoning its front that Fabian had started when he'd loosened his tie.

'Just a moment...' He broke off as I stood back to admire his quite spectacular tanned and toned torso, before leaning in once more to pull the shirt from its mooring in the black leather belt. He moved to the door, turned the key and then, with a smile, pressed me gently back against the desk. I can never take in the tantalising scent of leather and furniture polish without remembering that first time Fabian made love to me, and it was like nothing I'd ever experienced before.

* * *

Afterwards, his arms wrapped tightly round me, he whispered, 'Stay with me tonight, Robyn.'

'I thought you liked your own company.'

'I do, but tonight I need you to come back and stay with me. We can't make love like that and then go our separate ways.'

'I've no toothbrush.'

'I've a stack.'

'Well, then, what can I say?'

9

And so, for that glorious, heavenly summer, I was doing the best job in the world, the only one I'd ever wanted to do, while utterly suffused with love for this sublime man who appeared to want to be with me as much as I with him. I threw all caution to the wind, ignoring the fact that our backgrounds and heritage were so vastly different, that I'd already encountered what his family's reaction might be to their son having a relationship with me. And that Fabian was unaware of my own family history, which I was unwilling to share with him at this early stage in our relationship. What was the point when Fabian might tire of me within a few months and move on? Would it have made any difference if I'd come clean from the start? I honestly don't know.

How we managed a relationship when he was working from 6 a.m. until late, while I was fully engrossed in being Arabella Plumpton-Jones in *Dance On*, I'll never know. Maybe it was because we *were* both so full on with our respective careers that, when we did meet up, often tired out and irritable or, more often, wired after consuming surfeits of caffeine to keep us going, the relaxing, the love making, the late-night strolls through the London streets and along the banks of the Thames were heady.

Of course, it wasn't all sweetness and light. What relationship is? My general messiness drove Fabian mad, while his pernickety attention to detail (did we really need linen napkins when a piece torn off a kitchen roll was more than sufficient as I hoovered up the delicious meals he created?) had me rolling my eyes in frustration.

I couldn't comprehend his defence of murderers and rapists when he must often have known they were guilty, and it was this that led to our first argument. We were both shattered after a particularly long day, but Fabian had messaged to say he was back at the apartment and had made food. To be honest, much as I was longing to be with him, I'd twisted my knee slightly as I'd leapt across the stage and into the arms of my stage lover and needed to get back to my flat to ice it. But I couldn't resist Fabian's persuasive words so I hobbled into an Uber (oh, the bliss of earning enough to have an Uber account) and made my way to his apartment in St James's place.

He was standing at his precious navy Rangemaster stove, fully engrossed, moving from a recipe on his iPad to the ingredients, and didn't realise I was there until I was standing right behind him.

'Jesus, you made me jump.' He actually started like a nervous deer and I laughed as the intent scowl on his beautiful face softened and he reached out the one arm not stirring the pan, drawing me into him.

'You were away with the fairies.' I smiled.

'Would that they were.'

'Who?' I asked, puzzled. 'And were what?' I accepted the glass of wine he poured and pushed towards me. 'You're not making sense, Fabian.'

'Fairies: you know, good guys.'

'Ah,' I said, understanding his mind was still on work. 'Comes with the territory, I guess? You know, dealing daily with the bad boys.'

'And girls. Don't think, just because they're female, they're less lethal than men.'

'Are you defending a woman at the moment, then?' Fabian rarely told me what he was working on.

He sighed. 'No. Just one very – allegedly – brutal and sadistic killer.'

I stood back, put down my glass and stared. '*How can you?* How can you be on the side of someone like that? How can you defend him, knowing he's guilty?'

'Who said I know he's guilty?'

'You must know. I don't *get* it.'

'Robyn, there's a huge difference between actually knowing someone is guilty and suspecting they are. We work within the law and strict guidelines: if someone who wants me to defend them *tells* me he's guilty, then I can't get him to give evidence to the contrary. Doing that, I'd be a party to his perjury. I can't stand there, in court, in front of a judge and jury, and knowingly mislead them.'

'Oh, come off it, Fabian.' I was cross. 'Your job *must* surely be to mislead the judge or the jury? To get them onto your side.'

'That's a very simplistic view you have of the judicial system, Robyn.' Fabian spoke as calmly as when I'd watched him addressing the court.

'Don't patronise me,' I snapped. My sore knee was throbbing, I was tired and I didn't like what Fabian was saying one little bit. 'How can you defend a… a murderer… a child abuser… yes, how can you defend someone who's hurt a child, taken a child? Killed a child?'

'My job before going into that courtroom is to advise a client...'

'A *client*?' I tutted. 'They're murderers, rapists...'

'...is to advise a client,' Fabian repeated calmly, turning back to the stove, 'on the strengths of the case against him, take instructions and then give honest advice as to whether they're likely to be believed. It's not up to me to make a judgement on guilt or innocence. That's why we have juries chosen from all walks of life.'

I heard myself snort disparagingly. 'Oh, yes? All walks of life? My dad's never once been called for jury service, my sister Jess has never been called and I certainly have never been.'

'Hey, hey, Robyn.' Fabian put up both hands in supplication. 'Don't take your argument with society out on me.' Unfortunately, he still had the wooden spoon he'd been using for stirring the pan in one of them and tomato and herbs – oregano, I think – dripped onto his white T-shirt, which broke the tension.

'That'll have to come off,' I said, as though addressing a naughty child who'd been playing in the mud. 'Come on, arms up, off with it.' I reached for his leather belt, unbuckling it slowly while Fabian immediately and gratifyingly hardened at my touch.

We finally ate at one in the morning.

* * *

One morning at the beginning of September, as we were both about to leave his apartment, Fabian said, 'Robyn, my parents are holding their annual charity do in the garden on Saturday. Come with me?'

'I don't think so.' I laughed. Actually, jeered is probably, to my shame, nearer the truth.

'Please come. I'm a patron of one of the charities and Mum's wanting me to make a speech. I'd really like it if you were there with me.'

'Sorry, Fabian. It's just not my thing. You know that.'

'I don't know anything of the sort. It's a charity do in aid of...' He broke off.

'In aid of?' I raised an eyebrow. 'You've no idea, have you? So, which particular aspect of society are they feeling guilty about this week? Disaffected youth? A bit of nimbyism: no bypass anywhere near the Home Counties? Fallen gentlewomen? Or are they being totally radical and going for Gay Pride? Rainbow banners across the tennis courts of Bucks?'

'Stop it, Robyn.' Fabian wasn't amused. 'Sneery sarcasm doesn't become you.'

'I'm sorry.' I was. I didn't know why I was being so petulant. Fabian's parents, as far as I knew, could be lovely, hospitable people who wanted to share what they had with others. 'Do they know you've been seeing me?'

Fabian grinned wolfishly. 'A bit more than *seeing*, I would advise, Your Honour.' He reached forwards, unbuttoning the top two buttons of my shirt I'd just fastened, and I batted away his hand. 'Yes, I've mentioned you.'

'And do they know of my... my *heritage*?'

'Robyn, *stop it*. This is London, for fuck's sake—' he added in exasperation '—50 per cent of people living in London are non-white. In Newham it's 70 per cent, if you want some statistics. In my chambers we have barristers, clerks, pupils who are many different heritages.'

'Employees, yes, and welcomed to show you've filled your quota of diversity—'

'Stop it, Robyn.'

But I went on, repeating myself like an out-of-control runaway train. 'Taking me along to a charity do in Marlow would be introducing someone quite different into your family.'

'And? And how?' Fabian was really angry now. 'Different? Why are you so *different*? You've two arms, two legs, a good brain...'

'You know exactly what I'm saying.'

'No, I don't, actually. I can't believe that a strong, independent, intelligent and beautiful girl like you in today's society could have such hang-ups... Look at Meghan Markle.'

'Exactly,' I snapped. 'Look at her. What *she* went through.'

'My parents are not the bloody royal family,' he snapped back, throwing up his hands in despair. 'For all your right-on thinking, Robyn, you might be the most prejudiced person I've ever met. I really have had enough of this. Grow up, will you? I'm going to work; I'm late as it is.' And with that he walked calmly but determinedly away from me, not looking back once as he did so.

* * *

Hell, I missed him.

For the next two days I threw myself into my work as much as I could but, with my knee still not 100 per cent, and what now appeared to be a small bursitis on the outer joint, I was advised by my doctor to take a couple of days off. Carl Farmer, the director, wasn't at all happy and was actually quite off hand with me, promoting one of the other chorus members – a rather shy girl called Yo Ming – to my part. Desperate for my knee to be back to normal, I did as the doctor told me, sitting on the tiny fire escape overlooking the bustling Soho street below, a bag of frozen peas on my elevated leg.

I'd been set on rereading some Hardy novels but in the warm sunshine my concentration soon wavered and I found myself nodding off, coming to with a dribbling but dry mouth and my whole body aching from having my leg raised at a strange angle.

When I wasn't reading, sleeping or worrying that Yo Ming's interpretation of Arabella Plumpton-Jones might be superior to my own, I was kicking myself (with my one good leg) for the way I'd behaved with Fabian. What on earth was the matter with me? I'd been given an invitation to the family home of this wonderful man and I was making cheap jibes at their expense. Fabian was right: I was pigeonholing his parents, family and friends and so was guilty as charged of holding prejudiced, working-class-hero views.

I checked my phone constantly, but there was nothing. God, I missed him. I longed for him to draw up in his fancy car outside the apartment and (still in *Pretty Woman* mode) climb up the fire escape to rescue me before bearing me off to Buckinghamshire into the bosom of its posh people.

Having soon realised that Fabian was as proud as he was gorgeous, I knew I was going to have to eat a bit of humble pie and, on the day before the Saturday charity do, I picked up my phone with sweaty hands and texted:

> I'm so sorry for my utter pig-headedness, Fabian.
> If the invitation still stands, and you forgive me,
> I'd love to come with you tomorrow. xx

His response was immediate and to the point:

> Sorry, taking someone else. You had your
> chance…

I gasped in horror as I read the text, knocking over my half-full cup of coffee with my good leg as I stood. Another text followed on a moment later:

But, on second thoughts, I'd much rather take you. It's a lunchtime do. Pick you up at eleven tomorrow...

* * *

He looked sublime. Wearing faded Levi's and the ubiquitous white T-shirt, but this time topped with a beautifully cut navy Luca Faloni jacket. I was very tempted to pull him from the car and manhandle him back upstairs to my room. Sod Marlow, my need for his hands on me, and mine on him, was almost overwhelming.

But I was on my best well-mannered behaviour, so I slid demurely into the car seat beside him.

'You look stunning,' was all he said and then he hesitated, hands on the wheel but not driving off. 'I think I'm going to have to take you right back upstairs where you came from.' He reached a hand to my bare arm, stroking it with intent.

'I think not, young sir,' I said primly. 'Unhand me at once and take me to Marlow.' I glanced across at him. 'I *am* sorry,' I said. 'I behaved like a moron.'

'You did.' He still didn't drive off, but instead, leaned across once more, kissing my cheek slowly. 'I missed you, Robyn.' He sat back, appraising me. 'I love the dress.'

'Thank you.' I'd spent the remaining hours of the previous afternoon testing out my knee by walking over to Cheval Place in Knightsbridge, blowing money I couldn't afford in Pandora, the upmarket dress agency there. I'd come out with the perfect little Roland Mouret cream shift and known I had to buy the Jimmy Choo sandals to go with it. What was the point of a bloody expensive dress without the accompanying footwear?

We chatted easily all the way there, or rather I talked and

Fabian listened. He'd rarely discussed his caseload, but there was a new hesitancy now, which I put down to my previous questioning about how he could bring himself to defend criminals. Once we hit Marlow, and I knew there was only another few minutes' drive until we turned along the private road, I felt nerves begin to kick in. Fabian took my hand, squeezing it lightly as he pulled up in front of the beautiful house.

'Come on,' Fabian said, smiling in my direction. 'Let's get this over and done with.'

10

'Fabian, glad you were able to make it.' A man I guessed to be in his late sixties, and instantly recognisable from the photos I'd googled of the Lord Chief Justice, was at the top of the steps leading to the front door. He was attempting to tie a blue striped apron round his rather rotund middle while keeping one hand on Boris, who was desperate to be off into the crowd of people gathered in the sunlit garden beyond. Sir Roland Carrington shot out his free hand in my direction, the apron draped loosely from around his neck.

'Dad, this is Robyn.'

'Good to meet you, m'dear. Do make yourself at home, have a drink, plenty to eat...' He gave up the unequal struggle with Boris, who shot forward towards Fabian who caught him, instantly calming him down with a firm but reassuring hand. 'Needs some training, does that dog.' Roland smiled. 'Right, apparently I'm on BBQ duty again. What is it about we men that women think we like nothing better than flipping a sausage over hot charcoal every time the sun comes out?'

'You love it, Dad.' Fabian smiled.

'Which charity is today in aid of?' I asked.

'Oh, several, I believe. You'll have to ask Gillian, my wife; she's in charge.' He waved a hand vaguely in the direction of a shaded copse of trees.

'Hello, darling.' A dark-haired whippet-thin woman – I'd seen more flesh on a toothpick – dressed in white cut-offs and a pink floaty top was air-kissing Fabian with some enthusiasm and yet never actually making contact with any part of him. She turned to me, scrutinising every inch of my face and dress from behind ridiculously over-the-top Victoria Beckham-type shades. Hang on, it wasn't VB herself, was it?

'Robyn, this is my sister-in-law, Claudia.'

Ah, not Victoria, then.

'She's married to Julius.'

'For my sins, darling, and not sure for how much longer: I should have realised, once we were married, his work would take precedence over me.' She turned to me. 'Don't ever marry a Carrington...' She trailed off, looking me up and down once more as if to reassure herself that that was never likely to be on the cards. 'Right, must go and help Gillian. Julius wants a word, Fabian, at some point. Told me to grab you when I found you.'

'I can do without getting into work talk with Julius,' Fabian said, shaking his head as Claudia disappeared into the gathered guests. 'Don't let him take me off to one side, will you?'

He took my hand (which I was pleased about – he might have brought me into the cradle of his family, but could have played down any relationship we were having) and we wandered through the groups of beautifully dressed women and confident, laughing men, Fabian stopping occasionally to chat to one or the other and to introduce me. Most were friendly, but several of them widened their eyes slightly – I was, as far as I could make out, the only woman of colour there – and, as we walked away, I heard one tell her neighbour in a too loud aside: 'According to Julius, she's some random reggae singer's daughter. Reggae? Can you imagine? I bet Gillian's had something to say about that...'

How did Julius know that? Had Fabian told him about Jayden?

I turned to ask him, curious rather than resentful – I was proud of being Jayden Allen's daughter – but we were being approached by a couple I knew I'd seen before.

'Fabian.' The man drew him into a bear hug and I immediately recognised him as the little chap from Graphite the night Fabian had come in for his birthday celebration.

'He-llo. I know you from somewhere?' Fish Face actually closed one eye as she tried to work out where she'd come across me before. 'Harrods,' she eventually said. 'You served me when I bought Mummy's birthday present last week? The quite darling little pink cashmere Max Mara cardigan? Mummy loved it... No?'

'Nope, try again.' I smiled as Fabian struggled to extricate himself from the other man's embrace.

'Oh, you've got me,' Fish Face trilled.

'Graphite?' I smiled.

'Oh, you were in Graphite? Were you on a table near us?'

'I was serving you: I was your waitress that evening.'

'You're a *waitress*? *The* waitress?'

'Hello, Araminta, how are you?' Fabian, having made a final bid for freedom, bent to kiss the girl's cheek.

'Well, I'd have been a lot better had you got round to answering my calls, Fabian.' She was obviously cross. 'I did tell you you'd been invited to Mummy's birthday bash. She was most put out when you didn't turn up.'

'I'm so sorry, Araminta. I'm absolutely mowed down with work at the moment.'

'Really?' Araminta glared in my direction. 'You didn't tell us you were friendly with the... the *waiting staff* at Graphite.'

'Only one of them.' Fabian smiled, reaching for my hand. 'This is Robyn.' He was saved from any further comment by Boris bowling up, shooting his head lovingly into Araminta's crotch before, having obviously fallen in love, attempting to mount her bare tanned leg.

'Come here, you damned dog.' In his wake came a tall dark-haired girl in torn jeans and white vest who, after apologising to Araminta for the dog's bad manners, flung herself into Fabian's arms.

Not another one? Were they all in love with Fabian Mansfield Carrington?

'Thank God you're here, Fabian,' I heard her whisper. 'I'm just about to turn to drink with this lot.'

'This is my little sister, Jemima.' Fabian grinned, turning to me while hugging her. 'Come on, let's get a drink...' and then, realising the little chap, and certainly Araminta, appeared to think the invitation included them too, said, 'I've not seen Jemima for weeks and the *three* of us are going to head off for a drink and a catch-up. Lovely to see you both,' he added somewhat dismissively, taking my hand and pulling Jemima's arm through his own before we all set off at pace across the lawn.

'Right, Jemima,' Fabian said when we had put some distance between ourselves and the other two, 'this is Robyn.'

'Robyn, golly, we meet at last. I feel I know everything about you.' She gave me a hug. 'Never known this big brother of mine to talk so much about any woman.'

'I'll take that as a compliment.' I grinned, instantly liking this sister of Fabian's.

'Oh, you must, you must. Let's get a bottle of wine and sit under the willow and get rat-arsed.'

'Well, one drink would be lovely,' I conceded.

'There's Pimm's actually,' Jemima said. 'Let's have Pimm's, shall we?'

'I've been off work for four days with a dicky knee,' I explained ruefully. I felt I could down a whole pitcher of Pimms. 'I've been let off this afternoon's matinee, but I have to be back at the theatre for the evening's performance. I shouldn't drink at all really, but I don't suppose one Pimm's will hurt: it's just a fruit cocktail, right?'

'One it is, then.' Jemima smiled. 'And I suppose you're driving Robyn back to London in a couple of hours, Fabes?' She sighed. 'Looks like it's just me, then... Oh, hell, hang on, Mum's on her way over.'

'Fabian? You made it?' The approaching woman glanced at Jemima. 'When did *you* arrive, dear? Any chance you could have dressed for the occasion?' Jemima raised an eyebrow and shrugged before heading off in the direction of the Pimm's, and Gillian Carrington turned to me, extending her hand. 'Hello. Thank you for attending this afternoon—'

'Mum,' Fabian interrupted, 'you're being a bit formal. This is Robyn.'

'Robyn.' She nodded almost dismissively. 'I believe you work in the theatre? You're an actress?' She said the word with as much disdain as though she'd been saying 'sex worker' or 'layabout'.

'I think we're probably all called *actors* these days, but yes, I'm currently at The Mercury in the production of *Dance On*.'

'Right, right...' She trailed off, seemingly unable to think of anything else to say on the matter of my work, and instead turned back to Fabian. 'Fabian, Lucinda is here with her parents. She's just been called to the bar and I know she'd love to have a word with you.'

I realised, despite what I'd just been telling Jemima, I could do with being called to a bar myself, but I stood stoutly in front of this red-haired, raw-boned woman, a fixed smile on my face.

'If I bump into her, Mum, of course, but, to be honest, we've only just dropped in for an hour or so. I'm taking Robyn for afternoon tea at *The Fat Duck*.'

'Oh?' Gillian Carrington frowned. 'Are you? A special occasion, is it?' She gave me a hard stare before demanding of Fabian, 'You've managed to get a table? That was very clever of you.' She turned once more to me. 'So...?'

'Robyn,' I prompted.

'So, Robyn, where are you from?'

'Well, I'm living in Soho at the moment, but I grew up in Beddingfield – it's a village in West Yorkshire.'

'West Yorkshire? Really? The industrial part of the county as opposed to Harrogate in the north?' She sniffed slightly. 'No, I meant, where are you *really* from?'

Oh, dear God, not this again. Surely, *surely*, people didn't still ask this of people who didn't look just like themselves? 'Where am I *really* from? Well, I'm reallio, trulio, from Yorkshire, although,' I said, putting on a slight West Indian patois, 'ma big man's half Jamaican and my mum is half Indian – but actually that could be half Pakistani: she was adopted at birth and has no real inkling as to her true *background*. I believe the *rest* of me is pure Yorkshire but, as you say, urban West Yorkshire as opposed to the more leafy-avenued North Yorkshire...'

If Gillian Carrington had actually put up her two hands to stop my monologue, I wouldn't have been surprised but, well-brought-up woman that she allegedly was, she simply cut me off by pointedly and meaningfully turning her back on me.

'Mum,' Fabian warned, obviously embarrassed at his mother's rudeness, 'we're going to get a drink and catch up with Jemima.'

'Well, it's of the utmost importance you speak to Julius before you go, Fabian,' Gillian Carrington said, almost crossly. 'You *know* what about. He's looking for you.'

'I'd really quite like to have some time off work...'

'You know as well as I do that the Carringtons pride themselves on always being available for their clients.'

'Not today they don't,' Fabian said firmly. 'I've shown my face here, Mum, and I'll mingle and be polite, but I'm not extending that politeness to any work business—'

'As you wish, Fabian,' Gillian interrupted icily. 'Your mind is obviously on other things this afternoon, but I *would* appreciate your having a word with Lucinda, and you absolutely *have* to speak with Julius. Now, I need to get back to overseeing the food – people will be becoming hungry. And, do *not* forget, Fabian, you've the speech to make re the charity for which you're the patron.' She glanced at her watch. 'Shall we say in an hour? Over by the pergola?' And without another word, or eye contact, she walked quickly away from us.

Fabian was angry. 'Come on, let's get out of here,' he snapped. 'I'm sorry to put you through that. She's insufferable – always has been.'

I shrugged. 'You can't go anywhere. You've your speech to make. Look, I don't mind *anyone* asking about my heritage – it's something I'm very proud of and more than happy to explain – but, unfortunately, it's the way that some people – including your mother – use the question to belittle as well as to reveal their ignorance and prejudice. And,' I went on as Fabian put out a hand to me, 'I'm sorry if on first meeting your mother I've ended up calling her ignorant...' I trailed off. 'It wasn't my intention.'

Fabian put both arms around me, kissing the top of my head, obviously upset at his mother's behaviour.

'Fabian, it's fine,' I said, 'really, but you need to know that your continuing in a relationship with me is not going to be easy. Already, I've encountered quite unpleasant disapproval from your brother, and now your mother as well. All I'm saying is that you're probably better off with a private-school-and-Oxford-educated southerner whose father's something in the City.'

'Oh, for heaven's sake, stop it, Robyn, you're doing it again: *Pride and Prejudice* could have been written about you – you've got both in spades. Ignore my brother and my mother. They'll adore you once they get to know you, and if they don't...' He broke off as Julius Carrington appeared in front of us.

'Hello, Robyn, how lovely to see you again.' He slurred the words. 'And, goodness, don't you look stunning?' Julius's hand was immediately on my backside, alcohol-laden breath on my cheek. 'I can certainly see what my brother sees in you,' he whispered wetly into my ear, 'although I bet you've not got round to telling him—'

'Get your hands off her,' Fabian snapped, pushing Julius roughly away so that some guests standing nearby turned and stared.

Julius stumbled slightly but stood his ground, both hands held upwards in apparent supplication. He moved further towards Fabian, one finger now pointing and almost touching his half-brother's collar, determination emanating from every aspect of his stance and voice. 'Fabian,' he growled, lowering his voice to exclude me from the conversation, 'you appear not to be answering my phone calls. I need to know – we, the family, need to know – what your intentions are regarding Henderson-Smith...'

Henderson-Smith? My head shot up instantly at the name that had been splashed across every newspaper. Rupert Henderson-Smith, who had finally been tracked down and arrested after the savage rape and murder of six women in London.

'*Henderson-Smith?*' I stared at Fabian. 'The Soho Slasher? You're not going to be defending Rupert Henderson-Smith?'

'Not now, Robyn.' Fabian took my shoulder to steer me away from Julius.

'How interesting, Fabian, that *she* of all people appears quite horrified at the thought of you—'

'"She of all people"?' I hissed furiously, all the pent-up nervousness from the afternoon now morphed into the anger I was feeling, not only at the treatment of myself by both Gillian and Julius Carrington, but also the utter dismay that Fabian was even considering taking on the defence of this high-society alleged murderer. 'What the hell do you mean, "she of all people"?'

'You need to ask that?' Julius sneered. 'With *your* family history?' He shook his head in apparent mock despair.

'What family history? What are you talking about?' Fabian turned to me. 'Robyn?'

I closed my eyes for a second before taking Fabian's hand in my own.

And waited for the sky to fall in on me.

11

'What, you mean you've not told him, Robyn?' Julius tutted dramatically, his eyes gleaming, not only with the excess alcohol he'd obviously put away, but the sheer malicious delight at being the one about to spill the beans.

'Robyn?' Fabian said once more. 'What? What *is it*?' He let go of the hand I'd placed in his.

Julius actually laughed out loud now. 'I suppose telling your barrister boyfriend that you come from murdering stock isn't the best way to cement a relationship. Oh no! And not great for his career and the Carrington family name. Hmm?' Julius returned his hand to my backside, patting it lasciviously. 'And I can see you've got your claws well into Fabian... seen where he comes from.' Julius now moved his hand in the direction of the beautiful house, gardens and swimming pool. 'Bet you didn't want to give up on all of this, or the chance it might come your way one day? Yep,' he added as Fabian started to propel me away, 'ask her about her murdering grandfather – not one, but two—'

'Fuck off, Julius.' Fabian grabbed my hand, ushering me down to the car, oblivious to friends and guests who put out hands of greeting, wanting him to stop and chat.

'Get in,' he snapped.

'Don't order me about,' I retaliated.

'Why is everything such a fight with you, Robyn?' Fabian was pale apart from two spots of colour in his cheeks. He turned the ignition and reversed quickly, ignoring a well-dressed middle-aged couple with a beautiful redhead – the newly called to the bar Lucinda? – who were on the point of knocking on the car window to get his attention, scattering them to one side instead. Fabian turned out of the gate and set off at speed before indicating and parking up in a lay-by as soon as he saw the opportunity. He killed the engine.

'Right,' he said. 'Out with it.'

'I think your brother put it very succinctly.'

'Your grandfather murdered two people?' Fabian stared. 'How the hell does Julius know about *your* grandfather?'

'He's obviously done his homework.'

'So, go on, then, tell me.'

'Long story, but if you're hoping I'm going to tell you he was innocent, that it was all a mistake, then sorry, I'm not.' I suddenly felt utterly bone weary. 'Look, Fabian, drop me off at the station in Marlow and I'll get the train back to London.'

'Don't be ridiculous, Robyn – I've a table booked for afternoon tea.'

'I don't think so, Fabian.'

'Why didn't you tell me?'

'Why didn't *you* tell *me*?'

Fabian stared. 'Tell you what?'

'That you're going to be defending the Soho Slasher.'

'You seem to know a lot about it. About *him*.'

'Of course I do,' I snapped crossly. 'It's the only thing anyone's been talking about: you and I have talked about him loads of times – we even had a discussion about how on earth he would ever get anyone to defend him in court—'

'No, we didn't, Robyn,' Fabian interrupted calmly. 'You spouted long and hard and I didn't respond. That's not a discussion.'

'No, you didn't dare, did you? Didn't dare tell me you're going to be on the side of the man who, despite his exceptionally privileged upbringing and his education at top public schools, chose as his sport raping and murdering women. You knew I couldn't stay with you if I learned you'd been engineering a way to get him off.'

'There's a long way to go yet. The case is at the early stages.'

'Fabian, women like me have been terrified to walk the streets at night. The Ritzy Ripper, the papers are now calling him, now they know his background and about the suite his parents kept at The Ritz hotel. Likened him to the Yorkshire Ripper, who preyed on women on my home patch back north.'

'I didn't tell you because I knew this would be your reaction; I didn't want to lose you. And presumably that's why you chose not to mention to *me* that your grandfather killed two people?'

'Let's not sweeten this with words – he *murdered* two people. And no, it's not something I bring up over a cup of tea and a custard cream.'

'When would you have told me?'

'I'm sure, if you'd done a bit of googling, you'd soon have come across an article about Jayden Allen and learned that my grandfather murdered my grandmother and her lover when Jayden was just a baby. A double murder in the early seventies by a black man – a reggae singer himself who'd come over from Jamaica on *The Windrush* – of his white wife and her white lover was the stuff of headlines in the same way that your Rupert Henderson-Smith is now.'

'He's not *my* Rupert Henderson-Smith.'

'No, but it sounds like he soon will be. How can you, Fabian? How *can* you do it? Is it for the money? The kudos?'

'Even when all of the evidence points to the guilt of a client—'

'A client?' I gave a little laugh.

'When all of the evidence points to the guilt of a client,' Fabian went on calmly, 'they are still entitled to a fair trial and representation.'

'And Julius and your mother are obviously delighted you've taken on the case?' I shook my head. 'I don't get it. Why?' Then I saw the light. 'Oh, I bet it would be a bit different if he was plain old Roy Smith from Tower Hamlets who'd gone to the local comp? Or my grandfather – yes, why not, now that that little can of worms has been opened? – my grandfather, a black man from Jamaica who'd murdered his white English-born wife? But Rupert Henderson-Smith, Eton educated, whose parents probably mix in the same social circles as your own, well, that's totally different, isn't it?'

'You're talking about something you know nothing about, Robyn,' Fabian said stiffly.

'And you're telling me that your mother and your brother would welcome the granddaughter of a convicted Jamaican double murderer into your family? Tainting those Anglo-Saxon genes you're all, oh, so proud of? Can you just picture me, eating cucumber sandwiches on the lawn with Claudia, discussing where, oh, where is the best place to send little Henry and Amelia to nursery school?' I adopted the Jamaican patois once again: 'We must enrol them where the little ones can learn Mandarin and Caribbean...'

'You're unbelievable, Robyn: you're prejudiced, proud and full of stereotypes.' Fabian shook his head.

'So I've been told.' I turned to Fabian, knowing I should have trusted my gut instinct from the very start, which had told me he was way out of my reach. 'Look, at the risk of making a habit of jumping out of your car to run for public transport, I'm going back to London. I have to be at the theatre and I need plenty of time warming up, not having danced for almost a week. Just drop me off at the station, Fabian.'

'Don't be ridiculous. I'm driving you back. You need to change.'

'You can't – you've a speech to make back there. And—' I held up my bag '—not only do I not want to be held responsible for your not turning up, everything I need's in here.' I found myself unable to meet his eyes, didn't want to see what he must really be thinking: that I was just too much trouble. That his family were right.

'Robyn...' Fabian trailed off and I knew I'd lost him. He wasn't prepared to fight for me and all the fight seemed to have gone out of me as well. He turned the ignition and we drove the five minutes to Marlow station.

'Your work and your family will always come first: we probably just met at the wrong time.' I leaned over to kiss him before opening the car door and, although Fabian moved towards me briefly, he didn't try to stop me.

* * *

'Oh, you're back? How's the knee?' Carl Farmer, the director, crouched on stage with two of the lighting technicians, looked up only briefly to acknowledge my presence.

'Fighting fit,' I lied, knowing my knee still wasn't 100 per cent. 'I've come in early to have a good warm-up.'

'Good, good, that's good,' he said vaguely, obviously more interested in the problem he was having with the lights. 'Curtain-up's not for a couple of hours.'

I changed into sweatpants and top and spent the next hour or so stretching, warming up and taking myself through various routines. It was so good to be back doing what I loved and I tried to put Fabian out of my mind.

But every step, every turn, every leap and every *jeté* was accompanied by his face, his touch, his kiss. What the hell had I been doing not fighting for him? For us? This damned pride of mine that had always stuck its neck out and tripped me up – it had well and truly done its work this time.

Leap and plié.

How could I continue with Fabian when he was on the point of defending that arrogant murdering misogynist, Rupert Henderson-Smith?

Stretch and élancer.

And how could there ever be any future for me with him and the Carringtons now that Julius bloody Carrington would be having a field day telling the world and his wife about Winston Allen, my paternal grandfather, who'd died in HMP Belmarsh while serving a life sentence?

Glissé, step, glissé.

I should have told Fabian myself. Of course I bloody well should have.

Step and tour jeté.

I landed and instantly knew my knee wasn't quite as good as I'd thought.

'Everything OK?' Carl called from down in the footlights. 'You've got one hell of a face on you, Robyn.'

'Never better,' I called in his direction. 'Just off for a five-minute break.'

'Yo Ming's more than able to carry on as Arabella Plumpton-Jones, you know!' he shouted after my departing back.

'No way!' I retorted over my shoulder. 'I'm tip top. Absolutely raring to go.'

I grabbed my towel and phone, desperate for there to be some word from Fabian. Instead, there were six missed calls from Jess. I exited the stage door with my water bottle, needing fresh air and a phone signal. Jess answered immediately.

'What's up?'

'It's Mum. She's been rushed into hospital again. Had one of her seizures but she actually stopped breathing this time.'

I closed my eyes.

'She's very poorly, Robyn. You need to come home.'

'I'll get the train tomorrow – I'll sort it. How's Sorrel?'

'I don't know where she is.'

'What d'you mean?'

'Exactly that. She and Mum had another set-to, apparently. Mum came over to my place in tears, saying she just couldn't cope with her any more. I went back with her to see what was happening. There was no sign of Sorrel – just a mass of broken crockery – and so I did my best to settle Mum while I tried to ring round and find her.'

'Why on earth didn't you stay with her, Jess?' I snapped crossly.

'Why on earth don't *you* come up and stay with her, Robyn? I can't do *everything* here.' There was panic in my sister's voice. 'Dean's buggered off with the barmaid. Haven't seen *him* for weeks, and I was already late picking Lola up from a birthday party at the other side of town.'

'I'm so sorry.' I realised I'd not been back to Yorkshire since

April when I'd gone home for the weekend to help celebrate Jess's thirtieth birthday. Almost five months ago.

'Yeah, well, so am I.'

There was silence as we both mulled over the situation.

'Look, Jess,' I said eventually, 'I've got the performance tonight, and after that I'll tell Carl—'

'Carl? Is that your posh barrister?'

'No, Jess, *he's* history.' I breathed deeply, trying to accept what I'd just vocalised to my sister, as well as to compartmentalise my life. 'Carl's the director. I'll tell him Mum's poorly, and I'll be up by tomorrow afternoon. Try everyone you know who might have some idea where Sorrel could be holed up. She'll come back when she's hungry—'

'Robyn, she's a bolshy fifteen-year-old, not a dog who'll come back wagging its tail wanting his Chappie.' I could hear the frustration in Jess's voice.

'I know, I know, I'm sorry, I'll be with you tomorrow afternoon.'

Phillipe, The Mercury's deputy stage manager and responsible for the pre-show calls, started the first of his rear-of-house orders: 'Ladies and Gentlemen of *Dance On* Company, this is your half-hour call. Thirty minutes, please.'

'Got to go, Jess, I'm not dressed or made up yet.'

I made my way up to the dressing room where I'd already checked my four changes of costume were good to go. I stopped as I went through the door, seeing my usual spot at the mirror was taken by Yo Ming, while three others from the company were standing round her, chatting, their costumed-backs to me. I caught Yo Ming's eyes through the mirror and she stood, saying something to the other three, who turned in unison my way.

'Oh, you're back?' One of the girls, a small feisty blonde,

sniffed as Yo Ming made to stand, starting to unzip the back of her Arabella Plumpton-Jones costume.

'Didn't Carl tell you?' I asked pleasantly.

'Must have slipped his mind,' the blonde replied. 'Yo has been brilliant in the role.'

'I bet she has.' I smiled. 'Thanks, Yo. I'm really grateful for your stepping in at such short notice.'

The four of them drifted away towards their own places, but not before the blonde – who I knew to be the original pregnant Arabella P-J's best mate – muttered, but loud enough for me to hear: 'She must have sucked Carl's dick to get that part.'

Scarlet-faced, my pulse racing, I slid into my seat and started on my make-up, sweeping pan stick across my cheeks with a shaking hand.

'She's a bully.' Antonio, one of the men in the chorus, laid a hand briefly on my shoulder. 'Just let her bully you until she's *done* bullying you,' he advised. 'I know that's not what you want to hear, but you know...' He patted my arm and moved towards the back of the room where he started to limber up, moving his neck and head in a smoothly hypnotic rotation.

Could this day get any worse? I took a deep breath – there was no way I was going to let any spiteful little upstart upset my equilibrium – but my head was pounding and my knee felt stiff and unwieldy. Once I was dressed, I swallowed a couple of painkillers before moving over to join Antonio and some others ready to go on stage.

Apparently, the day *could* get worse.

And did so.

Quite spectacularly.

I made my entrance ten minutes after the start of the performance, dancing suggestively around the strategically placed three men in the chorus line-up with whom I was allegedly having flirtatious affairs. I had to smile coquettishly while they turned imploring faces, gesturing their love for me. In response, I turned my own face, instead, to the audience to demonstrate my intention to flee and, taking several quick steps, I launched into the high *jeté* that would take me off stage.

At the same moment as a whole raft of stage lights in front of me flickered epileptically and, confused, I landed badly, swerving and falling and crashing onto the stage and my already dicky knee with a quite startling ferocity and speed.

And there and then, on the day I had already lost Fabian Mansfield Carrington, I lost my career in musical theatre too.

PART II

BEDDINGFIELD, WEST YORKSHIRE

12

'Oh? Oh?' Jess, opening the front door of her cottage in Beddingfield the following evening, appeared able to utter only the monosyllabic word, her head moving comically from myself to Jayden as we stood on the doorstep. Finally she opened the door fully against the early September evening chill and we trooped past her in silence, walking along the narrow carpeted hallway and into the kitchen where Jayden put down my hastily packed suitcase. It might have been packed hastily with the help of Jayden once I'd been released from A & E, but it contained my life.

Or what was left of it.

'How come *you're* here?' Jess turned to Jayden. 'We certainly didn't expect *you*.'

'He was in the audience last night.' I shrugged tiredly, not wanting the third degree. 'I didn't know he was there, Jess, and yes, yes, I know, Jess, when has he ever taken an interest before? Good job he was there: he saw me fall, saw me knacker my knee good and proper this time.'

'Oh, you're joking, Robyn?' Jess pulled a face. 'But you'll be able to go back? Surely?'

'I'm a dancer, Jess. An ACL injury—'

'ACL? Speak English, Robyn.'

'Damaged Anterior Cruciate Ligament,' I said bleakly, lifting the unwieldy brace on my left leg as proof. 'Twelve months of rest and recuperation, apparently. And can you see any director taking me on after that?' I sat down at the kitchen table because I didn't know what else to do, where to put myself.

'I got her straight to A & E.' Jayden, always mindful of Jess's sharp tongue where he was concerned, endeavoured to earn a few brownie points. 'Stayed with her until the early hours while they X-rayed and did what they had to do and then, knowing what's happening up here with your mum...' He trailed off under Jess's hard stare.

'About time you did your bit with Sorrel, Jayden,' Jess went on. 'When was the last time you saw your youngest daughter? Or Mum?'

'He's been in touch with me, Jess,' I said wearily. 'Give him a break. I'm not sure how I'd have managed without him.'

'Well, of course he has,' she snapped. 'Show business, singing; you doing well, it's right up his street. When there's his wife – sorry, his woman, you never did get round to marrying Mum, did you? – and his fifteen-year-old daughter needing his support, it's a different story.' She turned to look me in the eye. 'And where was your barrister in all this, Robyn? Why didn't he come galloping to the rescue on his white charger?'

'You know I'm away, touring most of the time,' Jayden started to protest, but quailed under Jess's continued hard stare. 'I called in last month, Jess. Has Sorrel come back? We don't have to worry about her any more?'

'Not *worry* about her? Jayden, Mum's in hospital again and just a week after starting back at school for the autumn term, Sorrel's actually been excluded again.'

'Where is she now?' I asked. 'Next door?'

'Out somewhere again.'

'Can't you keep her in?' I snapped, looking at my phone. 'It's going up to nine, Jess. Sunday night and school tomorrow.'

'Have you ever tried keeping a bolshy fifteen-year-old in when she's just as determined to stay out?' Jess snapped back. 'And *I* should be at work doing the night shift I do a couple of times a month – no choice. I've had to ring in to say I've got Covid – the one thing guaranteed to let me off the hook.'

'You haven't, have you?' Jayden stepped away from the table in alarm. 'Got Covid, I mean. Plays havoc with the vocal cords, I believe.'

'No, of course I haven't,' Jess said, sitting down as all the fight seemed to go out of her. 'Look, I need some help here.'

'Where's Lola?' I asked.

'In bed, of course.'

'No, she's not.' Jayden grinned. 'Hello, darling. Come to see your grandpa?' He scooped my pyjama-clad niece up into his arms and, delighted at seeing him, Lola snuggled into his embrace before glancing shyly in my direction. I realised I might be calling out Jayden for his lack of interest in his family, but I'd not been doing much better. I hadn't been back home since Easter – since meeting Fabian, in fact.

My heart lurched.

I wanted him so badly.

'So, you're back for a while, then, Robyn?' Jess's voice softened as she turned Lola from Jayden's embrace, directing her back towards the stairs and bed. 'I'm so sorry about your knee; what rotten luck. But I'm really not sorry you're here: I'm getting to the stage where I just can't cope with work, with...' she put two hands over Lola's ears '...with Dean buggering off again, with finding childcare for this one while I do my night shifts now Mum's back in hospital.' She sighed. 'And trying to look after Mum and Sorrel as well.'

'Look, you get yourself off to bed, Jess.' Jayden smiled winningly in her direction. 'Get a good night's sleep. Robyn and I will go next door, wait for Sorrel to come back and I'll stay the night...' He trailed off. 'But I've a gig up in Aberdeen tomorrow evening...'

'The Scots are into reggae?' I pulled a face.

Ignoring me, Jayden went on, 'We'll make sure Sorrel gets to school in the morning and then go and see Lisa at the hospital. Where is she? The usual?'

The three of us knew 'the usual' was the Green Lea wing of the town's main hospital, a dismal Victorian building a twenty-minute drive or so away from the village.

'Come on,' he said, leaning in to chuck Lola under the chin before picking up my case. 'You got the key for next door, Jess?'

* * *

Nothing from Fabian. I'd be lying if I said I hadn't hoped he'd get in touch.

But there was nothing.

I knew, for my peace of mind, I should remove all means of contact, but I was hoping against hope he'd find out about my accident and whisk me back down to London and his apartment to recuperate now that I'd told Hasad, my landlord in Soho, I wouldn't be back. Part of me, clutching at straws, had been about to pay Hasad two months' rent – the net total of my savings from my work at the theatre – to keep my room at the flat, but then my sensible head had locked on. How was I going to live? I could just see Wallbanger Muffler offering me my old job back at Graphite: she'd never liked me much when I was fit, healthy and could do her bidding. No chance now with the black functional knee brace A & E had fitted on show beneath my white apron, while trying desperately not to limp through a seven-hour shift at the restaurant.

While waiting for Sorrel to appear, Jayden and I put together a makeshift supper of the bread and cheese we'd found in Mum's fridge before settling ourselves somewhat uneasily into our respective rooms. Jayden had disappeared into the room he shared with Mum whenever he deigned to come home so I made my way to the tiny boxroom, relieved that the lumpy bed settee was still there – and actually made up – rather than a whole load of boxes and assorted stuff thrown there just for somewhere to put things. At nine forty-five I texted Sorrel.

> Sorrel, Jayden and I are at home waiting for you. You don't have to stay with Jess again tonight. But, if you're not back in the next hour, am going to get the police out. And don't think I won't.

I lay on the bed, which was just as uncomfortable as I remembered, downed more painkillers than was probably wise to overcome the steady metronome throbbing in my knee, and closed my eyes as picture after picture of the last forty-eight hours played on a never-ending loop behind them.

Should I – could I – have reacted any differently to Gillian and Julius Carrington's downright unpleasant and totally unacceptable attitude towards me? Taken on board that Fabian was about to defend what I considered to be the indefensible? Ignored the bitchiness of Yo Ming's coterie of mates at the theatre? Informed Carl, the director, I needed to have another week off to ensure my knee wouldn't let me down? As it had so spectacularly.

Was it only yesterday morning I was showering, slipping into the beautiful cream Roland Mouret dress and matching sandals? Doing my make-up and hair, desperate to impress, not only Fabian, but his family as well?

I wanted to wind the hours back, start again, go along with whatever Fabian was working on; accept his family were an unpleasant shower but that it was Fabian I wanted, not his bloody relatives. And I should have been up front from the very start with Fabian about my grandfather.

Anything, anything at all, to not be where I was now, back in Beddingfield, my life in tatters...

I broke off my *if only* thoughts as I heard the front door open and bang. I struggled off the narrow bed, limping painfully down the steep cottage staircase.

'Ah, you got my text, then?'

'What are *you* doing here?' Sorrel looked me up and down as only a disgruntled fifteen-year-old can. 'I was looking forward to having the place to myself.'

'There's no way you can stay here by yourself,' I snapped. 'You're fifteen, for God's sake.' I relented slightly. 'Now Jayden and I are here, you obviously don't need to go round to stay with Jess.'

'Don't tell me Jayden's staying for more than one night. He never has before.'

'I know, I know, he's always been the same, Sorrel. But he does care. *I* care.'

She snorted derisively, making her way to the fridge, leaving the scent of cheap hair product, fags and booze in her wake. Or was it dope?

'I'm starving.' She hacked at the loaf I'd just put back in the breadbin, cutting a huge doorstep, which she slathered generously with Philadelphia before shoving it unceremoniously into her mouth.

What *would* Gillian Carrington think of that?

Sorrel stopped chewing for a second as she noticed the brace on my knee. 'What've you done?' Not overly interested in my response, she continued to make her way through the huge slice of bread and cream cheese.

'Well, I won't be doing any dancing for twelve months.' I tried to smile, realising I was playing the sympathy card. I didn't know much about fifteen-year-olds apart from obviously having been one myself once. And, latterly, having taught – without a great deal of success – whole bunches of the species. I shuddered, remembering.

'Oh, dearie me.' Sorrel almost sneered. 'And you were going to be such a big West End star as well. Mum and Jess said you were, anyhow. Oh, God. You're not back for good, are you? Thought you were just here to see Mum.' She tutted, though the realisation obviously wasn't putting her off her food.

'So, we'll get Mum sorted, get her back home as soon as we can. But, more importantly, get you back on track. School, for instance.'

'What about it?' Sorrel chewed up to the crusts, leaving them on the kitchen worktop before wiping her T-shirt sleeve across her mouth.

'You have to go, Sorrel.'

'I *don't think so*. I can leave when I'm sixteen.'

'No, you can't. And anyway, you're fifteen. You have to be in some sort of work or education until you're eighteen.' I'd learnt *that*, if nothing else, from my PGCE course. 'Jayden and I are going to come with you in the morning; speak to your...? Head? Head of year?'

'They're all tossers,' she said calmly. 'And there's no way you're taking me into school like a five-year-old.'

'Absolutely we are. So, get that into your head right now. And

—' I looked at my phone '—it's well after ten. Go up and get a shower, get that make-up off and sort your school uniform for tomorrow. Have you got clean stuff?'

'I doubt it. Mum wasn't overly interested in making sure my shoes were polished and my shirt ironed.'

'Don't blame Mum,' I snapped. 'Mum's not well, you know that. You're big enough to sort yourself.' I relented. 'Right, I'll come up with you. Put a wash on, if necessary. Jess tells me you've a new head who's a bit of a stickler.'

'A stickler?' Sorrel laughed shortly. 'You might have *sticklers* down in London schools; up here they're pillocks and tossers, not interested in anything but league tables and the correct footwear.'

She set off up the stairs and I limped up after her. 'Jesus, Sorrel, you *have* to be joking?' I stood in the door of her bedroom, my eyes acclimatising to the gloom of the room, which, lit only from the one red bare bulb hanging from the ceiling, not only gave the impression of entering a Soho brothel, but emphasised the utter chaos in there. How on earth could one girl create such a mess? Mugs, some half full, some sporting the beginnings of a green mould, littered any surfaces not bearing the weight of crumb-filled plates, hardened-cereal-coated bowls and discarded takeaway containers. Dirty thongs, cheap plunging and padded bras, scarves and school uniform came together in a kaleidoscopic nightmare of colour and texture.

I took several deep breaths. 'OK, first job, get every bit of uniform you're going to need in the morning. Every bit, Sorrel, including clean knickers and tights. I'll wash and iron them. Then, you get your school bag ready.'

'School bag?' She gazed around the room as if I'd asked her to find her last will and testament. Which, if she was intent on carrying on in this manner, she might need sooner than later.

'Mould is lethal,' I snapped, picking up the worst of the dirty dishes and mugs and uneaten food. 'School bag?' I repeated. 'Any homework done.'

'What world do you live in?' she asked tartly.

'One a lot different from yours, obviously. Sorrel, you've got GCSEs at the end of this year.'

'Oh, I don't need those,' she said airily before yawning widely and loudly. 'I'm going to be a dancer like you.'

'You don't think I did all my exams first? Did years at uni?'

'You did it the hard way,' she scoffed. 'I'll just turn up at auditions and show them how good I am—'

She broke off as Jayden stuck his head round the door.

'Jesus.' He whistled.

'My sentiment exactly,' I said, shaking my head.

'Hello... *Dad.*' Sorrel threw him a look of disdain. 'Seems Mum has to be ill for you to get in touch with me. See that I'm OK. It was my birthday last week, you know.'

'Was it?' Panic appeared on Jayden's face and he automatically reached for his wallet.

'Your birthday is in February, Sorrel.' I tutted.

'Yes, well, *he* obviously has no idea.' She tutted in return. I wanted to move across the room and take her in my arms, gain some comfort for myself as well as for my little sister, but knew her response from old. What an utter waste of space Jayden had turned out to be, particularly over the past few years and particularly as Mum's health had deteriorated. Mum herself had always tried her very best, bringing us up as a single parent most of the time.

'Uniform?' I said again. 'Come on, Sorrel, Jayden and I are here for you now. School tomorrow.'

It was nearly one in the morning before I was able to go to bed myself. Sorrel's full uniform was washed, ironed and neatly folded on a chair outside her bedroom door, the polished black brogues the school insisted on underneath. The uniform for Beddingfield High – Beddingfield Comprehensive when Jess and I had been pupils there – had changed dramatically since the two of us were kids. Then it had been a disgusting light green polo shirt, darker green sweatshirt and the ubiquitous black polyester trousers or skirt. Trainers on our feet – the laces threaded rather than tied – were de rigueur, and those not conforming to the required fashion of the month were laughed off the school bus. Jayden, having fought his own demons the only way he knew how, with his fists, had always insisted Jess and I have the best possible trainers and, looking now at Sorrel's footwear, idly tossed into one corner of her room, I assumed he'd continued in the same vein with her.

Sorting, at least for the moment, this one tiny aspect of Sorrel's dysfunctional life, as well as giving the kitchen a jolly good clean before I went back upstairs for the final time that evening, went some way to shelving my own bomb-shelled previous two days. But once under the thin polyester duvet and accompanying floral cover, I lay, eyes wide open in the dark, and knew my life was over.

13

'Robyn? Robyn, are you up?'

Fabian was on the other end of the phone, telling me everything was going to be fine. That not only did he know some clever consultant with whom he'd been at Oxford who had the wherewithal to have me up and dancing again within the week, but he'd also been in touch with Carl Farmer, who was desperate to have me back. Fabian went on that I'd been absolutely right, no two ways about it, to object to his defending that monster Henderson-Smith in court. He should have realised he was in the wrong to even *consider* taking on the case... He was on Mum's doorstep and when was I going to come down and let him in? His mother and his brother, Julius, were with him to apologise for their lack of warmth in welcoming me into the Carrington family when in fact they totally *loved* the idea of taking a woman of colour, a double murderer's granddaughter, into their midst. They were all there to help me... to get Mum well again... to get Sorrel through her GCSEs and to make her Beddingfield High's head girl... I just needed to come down and let them all in...

'Robyn? Robyn?' Jayden was shaking me while the knocking on the front door continued.

'Who's down there? On the doorstep?' I asked, my eyes still closed as I desperately tried to cling onto the dream rather than face the reality of an overslept wet Monday morning at 8 a.m. in West Yorkshire.

'Robyn?' Jess was now yelling up at my bedroom window from down below in the garden. 'Do you know what bloody time it is? I can't get *in*. You've left the key in the door.'

'Can't you let her in?' I snapped furiously in Jayden's direction. 'Why've you let us sleep in? We have to get to school with Sorrel.'

I scrambled out of bed, shook Sorrel, who was absolutely dead to the world, and headed for the one bathroom in the cottage. I needed to sort myself before sorting my sister; Jayden was big enough and daft enough to sort himself. By the time I was dressed in the decent jeans and sweater I'd salvaged from my still unpacked suitcase, Jess had taken over, chivvying Sorrel into the shower, standing over her while she dressed before propelling her down the stairs and into the kitchen to pour the cereal and milk she'd brought round from her own kitchen and make a pot of tea in Mum's best teapot. I craved coffee, but poured myself a large mug of the weak tea.

'Lola's already at school in Early Morning Club.' Jess indicated with a nod of her head the village school we'd ourselves all attended, just two minutes down the lane. 'I'm going to have to get off to work now.'

'Your Covid?'

'Miraculously cured.' She raised an eyebrow. 'Come on,' she went on, looking at the kitchen clock, 'get off down to the school and throw yourself on the mercy of this new head teacher. Just tell them the pair of us are both alumnae of Beddingfield Comprehensive and that...'

'Alumnae?' I stared across at Jess as Sorrel pulled a face of disbelief. Either my little sister had a smattering of Latin or, much more likely the case, didn't know what the hell Jess was talking about.

'Past pupils, yes, and, as such, we're not prepared to stand for this behaviour.'

'Whose behaviour?' I was getting confused.

'The school's.'

'I thought it was Sorrel's behaviour that was in question?'

'And tell her you're a trained teacher yourself,' Jess went on. 'That should impress the woman. Mind you, from what I've heard in the village, Godzilla was a pussycat compared to this new head teacher.'

'A woman? Right! More likely to be sympathetic and on our side, then?'

'Why?' Jess looked up. 'You'd be better off using all your feminine charms on some man.'

'Feminine charms?' Sorrel smirked, looking directly at me. 'Has she got any?'

'Your sister, Sorrel, has a top London barrister for a boyfriend.' Jess, despite telling me I was only heading for heartache throwing my lot in with the Bucks Barrister Brigade, was always quick to come to my defence.

'Not any more, she hasn't,' I said bleakly, standing up and pulling on my jacket while putting up both hands to indicate I didn't want to talk about it. 'Right, come on, where's Jayden? Let's go and make peace with the school and then I have to go and see Mum. Sorrel, get that lipstick off, get those trainers off...' My knee was hurting like hell and I was in no mood for comeback from a truculent fifteen-year-old. I threw her the black shoes I'd cleaned and polished the previous evening. 'And get these on your feet.

Fasten that top button on your shirt and pull your tie up properly.'

I closed my eyes briefly before heading for the door and Jayden's car.

How on earth had it all come to this?

* * *

'Do you have an appointment with Ms Liversedge?' The woman on Reception's eyes narrowed in our direction before she turned to her diary. 'I can't see anything here... Ah, you're with Sorrel Allen?' The woman sniffed and threw a look of disdain in Sorrel's direction. Sorrel, after months of practice, caught it deftly, throwing it straight back at the woman, but with the added contempt of a confrontational teen.

'Fuck's sake,' Sorrel muttered into her chin, head swivelling to the outer door and freedom. 'Let's go.'

'And you are?' The receptionist turned to Jayden.

'Listen, sweetheart, I'm Sorrel's dad.' Jayden, who'd been gazing intently at blown-up photographs of the school musicians, spoke for the first time to the Rottweiler of a receptionist. I was fascinated by her hair – a sort of backcombed beehive held back in a tortoiseshell band – obviously fashioned to give her some height and standing amongst the staff and recalcitrant youth with whom she spent her days.

Jayden had passed his own formative years in care, as well as being excluded, expelled and moved on from myriad places of learning, and any time now spent in educational establishments – and in the presence of those who ran them – made him exception-ally nervous. As well as defensive. 'Her mum's not well – she's in hospital – and we need all the help we can get from you people. Sending Sorrel out onto the streets without an education is the worst possible thing you can do at the moment. This is her big sister here.' Jayden was warming to his theme, despite a line of mulish-looking adolescents and brand-new Year 7 kids – their too big blazers and creaking leather shoes and satchels giving them away – forming a queue behind him. He pointed a beringed finger at me. 'And Robyn here is not only a trained teacher, so knows *exactly* what she's talking about...' he paused as I glared in his direction '...but she's given up her career in London to move back up here to take care of Sorrel while their mother's in hospital. She won't stand any nonsense from her, you know, love; she'll make sure she's here on time and does her homework...'

I glared even harder in Jayden's direction. Hearing what I had to do back up here in Yorkshire was having me on the verge of panic. I knew I couldn't leave it all to Jess any longer, but I didn't want to *be* here. I didn't want this. I couldn't do it.

I was stopped in my tracks by a pleasant voice behind me. 'Ah, but will she ensure Sorrel no longer disrupts every single class she's being taught in? Can she be responsible for the safety of my staff? For the other students' personal belongings?'

We all turned in the direction of an exceptionally attractive blonde-haired woman – perhaps in her mid-thirties and obviously a go-getter to be head of a large comprehensive at her age. The woman offered an on-off smile that didn't quite reach her eyes. 'You don't have an appointment this morning, Mr Allen? No, I thought not. As far as I'm concerned, an outcome about Sorrel's future here was reached before the weekend. But I can see you appear to be in the dark about this.'

She glanced across at the wall clock above the receptionist's head. 'School started fifteen minutes ago, but I can give you half an hour now. Mrs Jackson...' she turned to the immovable receptionist, who was in the process of impatiently clicking her fingers at the queue behind us, '...please ask Mr Walters and Mrs

Saxton...' she turned back to Jayden and me, '...they're my deputies... to join us. And then postpone my 9 a.m. mentoring session with Miss Hanson, if you would. We need to get this sorted.' She took a step backwards into her office. 'Mr Allen, Ms...? Sorrel, do please come in.'

The three of us trooped in, two of us terrified, while Sorrel had the air of not giving a damn about any of it. I don't think for one minute it was bravado – she genuinely wanted to be out of there as soon as she could and get on with the rest of her life. We sat in silence for thirty seconds as the head teacher had indicated we should with the simple raising of a manicured hand, until her two deputies joined us, standing, tablets to hand, at the back of her office.

'Sorrel,' Ms Liversedge said, now the other two members of staff were in situ and she'd moved to her place of advantage behind the huge oak desk underneath the window, 'your father and sister here appear not to know about what happened last week.'

'Which bit?' Sorrel said rudely, holding the head's gaze in surly defiance.

'Which bit, Sorrel?' I hissed. 'How many *bits* are there?'

'Ms...?'

'Allen,' I offered with a smile. 'We're all Allen.'

'Ms Allen,' she started again. 'I had *Mrs* Allen sitting here at the beginning of last week, which, I'm sure you'll be aware, was only the first week of the new academic year. When I took up my headship at Beddingfield last Easter I inherited a litany of Sorrel's misdemeanours. And, I'm sure you're *also* aware,' she went on, and here she raised an eyebrow in Jayden's and my direction, 'but, I'm getting the impression you're *not*... that Sorrel was already on probation?' She ran a hand through her long blonde hair. 'My predecessor, Mr King, had excluded her several times for short periods of time but always allowed her back into school. I accepted the post here with the proviso that, together with the governors, I would be operating a zero-tolerance policy on poor student behaviour. As such, to protect the good name of the school, the other students, and particularly the parents who have constantly been to see me with complaints about Sorrel, Mrs Allen was told, as was Sorrel, that any more taking of other people's property—'

'Property?' I stared.

'A mobile phone last Tuesday. Sorrel was given a final written warning on Wednesday. On Thursday she disrupted the PE session – Sorrel has opted to take GCSE PE, as you know.'

I didn't.

'And disrupted the dance session.'

'Call that dance?' Sorrel sneered. 'It was a stupid sailors' hornpipe...'

'Sorrel,' I snapped. 'Enough.'

'Sorrel took Mrs Pemberton's phone from her hand...'

'I was just trying to get some decent music on the deck.'

'...actually snatched the phone from the teacher's hand, leaving her with a quite unpleasant scratch to her wrist...'

'It was a tiny little mark, for heaven's sake.' Sorrel sat back in her chair, arms folded, a closed-down expression on her very pretty face.

'...and then walked out of school with it.' Ms Liversedge raised an eyebrow and then a hand as Sorrel attempted to speak. 'That teacher's phone is still to be recovered, and the matter is now in the hands of the police.'

I closed my eyes briefly, then glanced across at Jayden, whose face was impassive.

'I didn't nick it.' Sorrel said, shaking her head. 'If she'd had the sense to use Find My Phone, she'd know I left it on the windowsill outside the gym.'

Ignoring Sorrel, Ms Liversedge continued. 'I asked Sorrel's mother to come into school on Friday, and that's when I told her there was no longer a place for Sorrel here at Beddingfield High.'

'Which was more than enough to make her ill again,' Jayden interrupted. 'Brought on one of the seizures which are part of her condition. She's back in hospital, you know.' Jayden, usually pretty laid-back, sat up in his chair crossly. 'Surely your ESW should have been working with Sorrel?'

'ESW?' I asked.

'Educational social worker,' Jayden snapped. 'I'm assuming the school has one, Ms Liversedge?'

'Of course,' she said smoothly. She really was an incredibly cool customer, very attractive with a quite amazing bosom on full display beneath a plunging white silk top.

'What's their role?' I asked hopefully, leaning forward. Was this someone we could turn to for help?

'An educational social worker will coordinate with parents, teachers and students to assess and resolve the student's behavioural and social problems. One of their main responsibilities is to create a plan to help students function in a school environment, participating in the special educational needs process as necessary.'

'I'm not SEN,' Sorrel hissed in fury. 'That's for the thickos who can't do the work. She was rubbish anyway.'

'Surely she should be in this meeting with us now?' I asked, pinning all my hopes – and desperation – onto this elusive demigoddess of off-the-rail fifteen-year-olds.

'Unfortunately, she's been dealing with a higher than usual number of cases and erm... erm... has gone off with... erm...

stress. We have been told a replacement for Ms Greenhough is forthcoming, but...'

'But probably not forthcoming this week or next?'

'As you say.' Ms Liversedge steepled her fingers and looked across at us over her hands. 'It's not the best of situations but... but I'm afraid the governors and myself are not prepared to back down on this. To be honest, I'm very surprised to see you all here this morning. Mr Bray – our chair of governors – and I were *quite adamant* about our decision when we spoke to Sorrel's mother on Friday afternoon.'

'As my father has already told you, she's in hospital,' I hissed. 'Possibly – in fact quite probably – *because* of all this.'

Ms Liversedge's carefully made-up face flushed a not too flattering turkey-neck red. 'I do hope, Ms Allen, you're not suggesting my governing body or I are responsible for your mother's... illness?'

'Of course we're suggesting that,' Jayden snapped.

'I can assure you...' Ms Liversedge broke off, glancing in her deputies' direction, obviously ensuring notes of the meeting were being taken. 'I can assure you all procedures were followed: a written letter outlining the governors' decision was sent first class on Friday afternoon. It included our suggested next steps: either a PRU in the town centre...'

'A PRU?' I glanced at Jayden, knowing he'd understand.

'Pupil referral unit,' he confirmed, shaking his head.

'...or, I took the liberty of speaking to Mr Donoghue, the head over at St Mede's—'

'St Mede's?' My head shot up. 'I thought that place had closed down years ago?'

'Several reprieves, I believe, especially as they're prepared to take on some quite difficult cases. And believe me, Ms Allen, Sorrel here is no angel.' She held up her hand once more as I started to speak and then she rose, flicking her long blonde hair with a nod of her head while indicating that her deputies should get back to doing what they were paid for. 'I'm so sorry if this is not what you wanted to hear. I will reiterate: we have gone down every avenue, followed all legal procedures to remove a child from our school register...'

'I'm not a sodding child,' Sorrel snapped, knowing we were dismissed.

'...and I strongly advise you make an appointment to see Mason Donoghue at St Mede's asap.'

'It doesn't work just like that, surely...?' I started as the head moved to the door. 'She gets kicked out of one school one day, and the next, the one down the road's welcoming her with open arms? And Mum's just splashed out on all this new uniform for Sorrel – the monogrammed blazer, the black shoes...'

'I never wanted this rubbish uniform,' Sorrel scoffed. She pulled off the blazer, throwing it in the direction of Ms Liversedge who, to her credit, caught it deftly with one hand, folded it neatly and handed it back to me.

'As I say, Mr Allen... Ms Allen, you're in the hands of the authority's educational social workers from now on. I repeat, your best option is to speak with the head of St Mede's directly. He's under no obligation to take Sorrel and, if he doesn't, you'll have to work with the authority and go where directed.'

'Right, let's do that, then,' I said furiously. 'Come on, Sorrel, let's go.'

'You can't just go to St Mede's without an appointment, Ms Allen. You need to be contacting the local authority for advice.'

'Watch me,' I countered, pushing Sorrel ahead of me, out of Ms Liversedge's office.

'I have to get off to Aberdeen,' Jayden protested, looking at his watch.

'Yes, and *I* have to go and see Mum,' I replied. 'But we're not doing *anything* until we've sorted Sorrel. We're not having her enrolled at the PRU, or wandering the streets or staying in bed all day, so you and I, Jayden, are going to make sure, not only that she has a place at another school, but that she goes there every day.'

'And how are you going to make me?' Sorrel asked, but some of the bravado was already leaving her. 'You'll go back to London soon; Jayden's off all over Europe and we probably won't see him again for months.' She glared in his direction. 'And we don't know how long Mum's going to be in hospital.'

'I know, I know,' I said, feeling stress in every bit of my body, but also a huge wave of sympathy for this little sister of mine who, when her guard was down, appeared terribly vulnerable. I took her arm and guided her into the back seat of Jayden's car. 'Look, Sorrel...' I fastened my seat belt and pointed Jayden in the direction of St Mede's, but then faltered as I turned and took in Sorrel's bent head and hunched shoulders. 'Sorrel?'

'I don't know what to do,' she cried, suddenly crumpling into herself.

'Pull over, Jayden,' I ordered almost immediately we'd set off, and he indicated, pulling into the Starbucks on our left.

'What is it, Sorrel?' I reached behind me for her hand.

'No one listens,' she sobbed, mascara, tears and snot amalgamating in a soggy mess, which she made no attempt to mop up, even with her chewed-to-the-quick fingers. '*He's* never around.' She pointed towards Jayden in the driving seat. 'He never has been. Jess is too busy working and has Lola to think about and you... you, well, you're going to be famous and marry some posh bloke and be rich and live in Bucks... wherever that is... Mum said so... and, and... I get nervy... I feel funny in my tummy...'

'What are you anxious about?' I asked, stroking her fingers. 'Is someone being mean to you?'

'I can't tell you. But I get anxious... what if I end up like Mum?'

'Try to tell me, Sorrel. Please?' When she didn't deign to answer, I tried to reassure her. 'But why on earth would you end up like Mum? Poor old Mum's been landed with a very rare condition. You know that. It's not hereditary.' I turned to Jayden, indicating with one look that he should lie if necessary. 'Is it, Jayden?'

'I googled it.' Sorrel sniffed. 'It can sometimes be passed on. And Mum got really depressed when she had me, didn't she? She didn't want me, and I bet he didn't either.' Sorrel glared at Jayden through her tears.

'Of course Mum and Jayden wanted you,' I soothed and, turning to my dad, added, 'Tell her, Jayden, tell her!'

While we did our utmost to convince Sorrel that she had been very much wanted, my mind went back to the time, listening over the banister and at the closed kitchen door on one of Jayden's arrivals back home. Mum was crying while Jayden was talking in a low voice and it hadn't taken long for me to realise that it was true, my parents *hadn't* wanted another child. Especially as Jess and I were both well into our teens by then.

'That was post-natal depression, Sorrel. It's horrible at the time, but a lot of women get it when they've had babies.' I was desperate to reassure her. 'Mum *wasn't* so good when you were born, and I know we were only thirteen and almost fifteen, but we – Jess in particular – helped her through it as much as we could. We used to look after you when Mum was tired and fed up with everything.' I glared at Jayden, remembering, but he shrugged and looked away, not knowing what else to do. 'It was hormones,' I went on. 'Mum got over it and absolutely *adored* having a new baby. Jess and I loved having a new baby in the house too,' I lied, remembering thinking would the baby ever shut up crying? Would Mum ever stop crying?

'The thing is, I just can't sleep sometimes, and Mum said she was like that when she was my age...'

'Well, she shouldn't have said that,' I soothed, glancing at Jayden. 'Right, Sorrel, this is what we're going to do: Jayden is going to go and get us coffee, we're going to have a bit of a chat and then... no argument... he's going to drive us to St Mede's and we're going to be on our best behaviour and plead with the head there to take you on.' I took a deep breath. 'Sorrel, you're my sister: Mum, Jayden, Jess and I love you. We're here for you. We're going to sort this all out.'

'And then you'll leave me again. Go back to London.'

I closed my eyes, rubbing at my knee, which was throbbing now. 'I'm going nowhere. I'm staying right here with you and Mum.'

14

'I really did think this place closed down when Jess and I were at Beddingfield Comp,' I said as Jayden drove into the car park. 'We were always ready to do battle with the kids who came here – bloody rough lot, they were. Jess and I used to be terrified of them.'

'I wouldn't know.' Jayden sighed, looking surreptitiously at his watch before pulling into the one vacant space, a veritable oasis amid a sea of hatchbacks.

'No, I don't suppose you would.' I shook my head slightly in his direction. When had Jayden ever been around or interested, when we were at school?

'Are we allowed to park here, d'you think?' he asked, glancing round almost guiltily, apprehension at being forced into yet another official establishment plainly manifesting itself once more.

'Come on, Sorrel, best behaviour now,' I said. 'If this school won't take you, then it's the... the other place in town...'

Sorrel rubbed at her eyes. 'I can't go in there. They'll know I've been crying.'

'Well, maybe not a bad thing. It'll show them you're sorry and ready to start again.'

* * *

'Do you have an appointment?' The woman behind the open office window, who, although not quite as much a Rottweiler as the one at the high school, clearly wasn't prepared to let us through without, if not a fight, at least a tussle.

'I wondered if Ms Liversedge at Beddingfield High had phoned?' I asked, smiling.

'Not that I know of.' She turned to the other two women in the office, who both shook their heads.

'Sorrel here,' I continued in as friendly a manner as I could muster, when all I was feeling was despair, 'has just moved into Year II at Beddingfield High, but there appear to be some clashes of personality... Could we see Mr Donoghue, please?'

'Well, not without an appointment. And it *is* Monday morning, one of the busiest days of the week as you can imagine. We always have any weekend problems to sort out—'

'We don't mind waiting,' I jumped in. 'Sorrel's father' – I pointed in the direction of Jayden, who was now standing by the main entrance making a phone call – 'has to be in Aberdeen this evening and needs to be on his way.'

'I'm sorry, really...' To be fair, the receptionist did appear to be just that. She glanced down at what I assumed to be a diary as Jayden finished his call and joined us once more. 'I can make an appointment for you to see Mr Donoghue on, erm, erm...' more turning of pages '...Thursday?'

'Oh! I know you! Jayden Allen?' The receptionist was interrupted in her perusal of the diary by a tall, well-built man in a maroon tracksuit appearing round the open door at the back of the secretary's office. 'It *is* Jayden Allen, isn't it? Or, if not, you sure as hell are his double.'

The office staff, Sorrel and I immediately shifted our attention from the man in the doorway to Jayden, and then back to the man.

'I love your stuff. Been a fan since I saw you play in Leeds when I was fifteen.'

'Oh, really?' Jayden ran a hand over his braided hair, obviously delighted at the recognition. 'That's great to hear – my music does have quite a following in Scandinavia, but not as much in this country.'

'You're wrong there. Who told you that? I heard you on Radio 1 last week. The new album you have out?' The man beamed in Jayden's direction, the smile lighting up his whole face. He was probably of the same heritage as Jayden, but while Jayden had always insisted on wearing his hair in the style he felt best accompanied his music, this other man's was short, and he was clean-shaven. He stepped fully into the doorway, almost filling it with his height and width – this was one big man – before crossing through the office and out into the reception area where we stood waiting.

'Nearly time for assembly, Mason,' the receptionist reminded him as though speaking to a recalcitrant child rather than the head teacher it was now clear he was. 'You were late last week as well, and you know you always insist on taking Monday's assembly yourself.'

Smiling beguilingly back at the receptionist, he held out his hand to Jayden before glancing across at Sorrel and me.

'Look,' he said, 'I have to get out of this tracksuit – need to set a good example to the kids – and take assembly. You're wanting a meeting with regards to...?' He raised an eyebrow in Sorrel's direction, holding her own defiant stare until, seemingly on the back foot, she rubbed at her eyes, twirled a finger through her long dark hair and eventually looked away.

'This is Sorrel, Jayden's daughter – and my sister.' I spoke quickly, not holding back: I could see there was no point. 'Sorrel has... she's... she's lost her place at Beddingfield High. We'd really like you to find her a place here if you can. The alternative is the—'

'The PRU? Pupil referral unit?' Mason Donoghue's voice was firm as he finished my sentence. 'Come to that, has it, Sorrel? And what makes you think we'd be prepared to take you here?'

'I don't want to be *taken* anywhere,' she muttered. 'I just want to go home.' She began to make for the door, but I put a warning hand on her arm.

'I have to take assembly,' the head said again, moving back towards his office, pulling at his tracksuit top as he did so. 'But I can speak with you straight after that. I'm sure Sally here will make you a coffee.'

'I think we're a bit coffee'd out actually.' I managed to smile as Sorrel scowled but made no further attempt to remove herself. 'But thank you, I'm very grateful.'

'Robyn, I really have to get off,' Jayden said, looking at his watch once the head's door closed on us. 'It's a good seven-hour drive up to Aberdeen and I promised Jess I'd call in at the hospital to see your mum.'

'How are we supposed to get home?' I snapped. 'I can't walk anywhere with this knee!'

Jayden reached into the leather bag slung across his jacket, peeling off a wad of notes. 'Get an Uber,' he said. 'Once you're back at your mum's place, her car is there.'

'It won't be insured for me.'

'It's both taxed *and* insured,' Jayden said patiently. 'I told Jess to insure it for anyone to drive – that van of hers she insists on going around in is knackered – and sent her the money to do it. It's there for you to get yourself and Sorrel about in.'

'I can't walk – I can't drive – with this knee, Jayden. I need some help here.'

'Robyn, if I'm to keep on sending money for your mum and for Sorrel, I need to work. You know that. Look, I know all this has blown up in your face and the last thing you were expecting was to have to quit your job, but I can't afford to quit mine into the bargain.'

'OK. OK!' I snapped crossly, holding up both hands, wanting him gone. Jess and I would sort things – we always had.

'Sorry, love, I have to go. I'll tell your mum you're back home and looking after Sorrel, and not to worry...' He trailed off and then appeared to cheer up somewhat. 'He seems a decent bloke.' Jayden nodded towards the closed door through which the head had gone.

'Because he recognised you?' I scoffed. 'Because he likes reggae?'

'Because he was wearing a tracksuit.' Jayden grinned. 'In all my years in all the damned places they put me, I never once saw a head teacher out of a suit and not sitting behind a great desk, peering across at me as if I was some specimen they wanted to stamp on.'

'You do exaggerate...' I began, but he was already out of the main door and gone. I knew it would be some weeks, months even, before he deigned to grace us with his presence once more. We were on our own – again.

* * *

'Do come in, both of you.' Forty minutes later, Mason Donoghue's face reappeared round his office door. While waiting for the head teacher to see us, despite my trying to engage Sorrel in conversation to find out just what was going on in her life, she'd clammed up and spent the whole time on her phone. In the end I'd joined her in the silent but addictive scrolling on my own phone, desperate for something from Fabian, but also from Carl Farmer at The Mercury to tell me he was waiting for me to return as soon as my knee was up and running once more. Up and dancing even! Fat chance. I could hardly walk without it hurting.

There was nothing from either of them.

'So, what was up with Beddingfield High?' Mr Donoghue asked as soon as Sorrel sat in front of him. 'It's a great school, from what I hear. Got more facilities than we have here at St Mede's.'

Sorrel shrugged, refusing to look at him.

'Sorrel, I won't be able to judge if St Mede's is the right place for you – if we're the right match – if you won't talk to me.'

'Sorrel,' I started irritably, but Mason Donoghue held up a hand in my direction and, censured, I sat back.

'What do you like about school?' he went on.

'Nowt.' She sniffed. 'I've *never* liked school.'

'That's not true, Sorrel,' I interrupted once more. 'You loved school when you were in the juniors. You did really well in your SATS and you were in all the school plays.'

'Sorrel, I can't offer you a place here unless you're willing to work with us.'

'Up to you.' She sat back with folded arms.

'OK, let's go,' I snapped, all the tension of the past couple of days rising to the surface and finding release in an explosion of anger. 'I've really had enough of this. If you want to ruin your life by not going to school, then that's totally up to you.'

'The thing is, Ms... Allen, is it? The thing is that if you're acting in loco parentis—'

'Acting in *Loco Parentis*?' Sorrel scoffed. 'She's acting in *Dance*

On at The Mercury Theatre in London's West End, not in something called *Loco Parentis*.'

Well, this was a turn-up for the books: my truculent little sister not only knowing what and where I was performing, but obviously prepared to blow my trumpet for me into the bargain.

The man turned fully in my direction. 'As I was about to say, if you're acting in loco parentis, Ms Allen, *you* are responsible for making sure Sorrel is in education.' Without waiting for my response, he continued: 'So, you're an actor?'

I nodded. 'Musical theatre.'

'Well, she *was*.' Sorrel sniffed again. 'Can't do much dancing at the moment with that knee.'

'I noticed you were limping,' the head said, holding my gaze.

'Look, we're here to discuss Sorrel and her schooling, not me and my career.' I could hear myself sounding like Sorrel and closed my eyes for a second before adding, 'I'm so sorry, that came out wrong.'

Mason Donoghue turned back to my sister. 'And do you like dancing, Sorrel?'

'Yes. Of course.' She gave this nice – and really rather gorgeous – head teacher such a withering look that if she'd added 'duh, Dude', I wouldn't have been a bit surprised.

'But as far as I know Beddingfield High has an excellent dance and drama department?'

'You're joking,' Sorrel scoffed. 'Excellent? It's rubbish.'

'Oh? Well, one of my teachers left to move over there during the six-week break.' He turned in my direction. 'Left me in a bit of a hole, actually. I'm having to cover some of the dance and drama lessons myself. I'm not bad with the drama side but... you know...' He trailed off, his eyes not once leaving mine.

'I'm sorry,' I said, giving him what I hoped was a sympathetic smile, but not overly interested in the man's staffing problems.

'That can't be easy. So, Mr Donoghue, I really need to know if St Mede's is able to take Sorrel. If not, I'm going to have to go back to the education authority and hand over the problem to them. Which, I believe, means a PRU?'

'Why don't we have a look round?' the head said, standing. 'You might decide we're not the school you want to come to.'

'It's not,' Sorrel mumbled.

'It is,' I hissed back, smiling beatifically at Mason Donoghue while nudging my sister in the ribs.

'Come on.' He smiled. 'Let's see if we can change your mind, Sorrel.'

We spent the next half-hour on a tour of the school, Mason greeting each student we came across by name, enquiring, congratulating or censuring each one in turn while suggesting they might like to tone down the make-up, make sure they were on time for their next class, be ready for football practice at lunchtime.

We'd rounded a corridor and were approaching the science laboratories at the far end of several dismal-looking, grey concrete tower blocks when a door banged open and two boys spilled out onto the floor in front of us, arms and legs wheeling in fury as they attempted to knock seven bells out of each other. A cheering, delighted gaggle of Year 8 kids filled the now gaping science-classroom entrance, the door having been flung back against the sludge-green corridor wall by the two wrestling adolescents. A plaintive voice was reasoning and then imploring, and eventually shouting for some semblance of order but, as more of the class poured out into the corridor, it was obvious he was being ignored wholesale by the kids in his care.

'Kyan, AJ!' (Was no one called good old John, David or Peter any more?) Mason Donoghue leapt into action, grabbing both boys by the scruff of their necks and hauling them off each other.

'Go back to your classroom and your seats,' Mr Donoghue ordered calmly to the rubbernecking gaggle of kids, one hand still attached firmly to each of the previously tussling duo.

And, to be fair, they did, without another word. 'I shall be with you in just two minutes and any one of you not in your own seat, not doing exactly as you've been asked by Mr Prentis, will have me to deal with. Understood?'

'Ger off me.' The smaller but more pugnacious of the two in the head's grasp was intent on wriggling free. 'Get the fuck off me... You're assaulting me... GBH... me dad an' all 'is mates'll be down to sort you out.'

'Bring it on, son,' Mr Donoghue said calmly. 'If he's not down to see me after school this afternoon, I'll be up to your house before your tea's on the table.' He released the pair from his grip. 'OK,' he went on, texting something into his phone, 'Mrs O'Sullivan will collect you and take you to Removal. You're there until lunchtime when I want to see both of you with a written apology for disrupting Mr Prentis's science lesson.'

Throughout this little contretemps, Sorrel had stood idly by, unimpressed by the disruption, reaching into her pocket and scrolling through her phone again.

'Put it away,' I muttered, once the head had popped his head round the science room door. He spent a good five minutes talking to the class and their teacher before making his way back in our direction.

'And that's why I'll *never* again go back into a classroom,' I vowed, shaking my head at the very idea.

'Bit different from your own schooldays?' Mr Donoghue asked with a grin.

'No, I was actually referring to the year I spent as a teacher just after lockdown.'

Mr Donoghue paused, actually stopped walking back in the

direction of his office, Sorrel trailing on behind. 'You're a qualified teacher?'

'I *was* a teacher.' I shuddered slightly. 'Never again. *Never.*'

'And your chosen subject?' he asked, sounding like the presenter of *Mastermind*. 'Your area?'

'My subject?' I glanced with some suspicion towards the man. 'English, dance and drama.'

'Great stuff. Just what I need.'

'Don't look at me.' I gave a laugh, holding up two hands.

'But you're qualified?'

'Qualified to know I'll never go back within spitting distance of any classroom.' I attempted levity. 'Being forced into just one school this morning has been enough to bring me out in hives. But now, coming here and seeing that little performance' – I nodded back down the corridor – 'puts me on the verge of a panic attack. I take my hat off to anyone who works in schools, but it is not for me...' I trailed off, realising this somewhat charismatic head teacher had stopped walking and was standing, arms folded, smiling in my direction.

'OK,' he said finally. 'Bog off, then.'

'I *beg* your pardon?' Even Sorrel's head had come up, if not in shock then in some semblance of surprise that a head teacher should speak such words to the family of a prospective new student.

'Buy one get one free.' Mason Donoghue grinned. '*You* want something *I* have, Ms Allen, i.e., a place at my school for Sorrel here—'

'I don't want a place here—' she started once more.

'And I want something *you* have, Ms Allen.'

The full-of-innuendo smirk and raised eyebrow on Sorrel's face morphed back into its habitual scowl as Donoghue continued. 'I'm offering Sorrel a place here at St Mede's, with immediate effect, with the proviso that you, Ms Allen, not only accompany her every day, but remain at school, taking up the position of temporary dance and drama teacher.'

'What?' I stared at the man. Was he mad? 'Are you *mad*?' I finally managed to get out.

'Obviously.' Sorrel shook her head sagely, for once apparently on my side.

'With some English lessons thrown in – oh, and possibly some RE and PSHE as well... How does that sound?'

'Like blackmail, Mr Donoghue,' I finally spat. 'That sounds just like *blackmail* to me.'

'He's blackmailing you, Robyn,' Sorrel agreed, in delight. 'Don't stand for that.'

'I'm not,' I said crossly. 'Come on, Sorrel.' I stood, marching as much as one can march on a dicky knee, towards the main entrance. 'We're finished here. Looks like it's the PRU for you.'

'I'm getting out here.' Sorrel was already unbuckling her seat belt in the back seat of the taxi taking us through the town centre and out towards Beddingfield and Mum's place.

'Oh, no, you don't,' I ordered, leaning over to prevent her from opening the door. 'You're coming back with me: I need to know where you are and what you're up to. Then I'm going to drive Mum's car to the hospital and you'll have to come with me.'

'No way am I going there,' Sorrel said coldly. 'I don't want to see Mum poorly again with tubes everywhere. And don't you dare say she's there because of me.'

'I wasn't going to say that,' I protested.

'I'm off,' Sorrel said, opening the door while the Uber had stopped at a red light. 'Don't worry about me.'

'Sorrel? Don't worry about...?' But she was off, crossing the dual carriageway and heading into the town centre.

'You letting her go?' The driver – he'd introduced himself as Davit from Armenia – looked askance at me through his rear-view mirror. 'You need to keep eye on young girl like that. Why she not in school?'

'Without actually keeping her under lock and key, I'm not sure how I can do that,' I said coldly, stung by his criticism. My head was aching, my knee was aching and I felt physically sick with longing for Fabian. I was going to have to message him, tell him I needed him, ask him to drive up to Yorkshire and help me. He'd do that: he loved me; he was an adult in a way Jayden, my own father, never had been; he'd help me sort things out. Talking to myself like this, reassuring myself with a plan of action, was helping to keep panic at bay.

The house, when I let myself in, was feeling cold and unloved, our unwashed breakfast dishes still on the kitchen table where we'd left them. I moved them to the sink – Mum had never wanted a dishwasher – ran hot water and added the last squirt of Fairy liquid from its bottle before chucking it into the overflowing pedal bin and reaching for the kettle. There didn't appear to be anything resembling proper coffee, but there was a tin of instant and Jess had put a couple of pints of milk in the fridge. Apart from the milk, there was little to celebrate my homecoming, and I knew I needed to do a massive shop.

I attempted a tentative feel at my knee, wincing as pain beat a steady metronomic tempo up and down my leg. The A & E department at St Thomas's hospital in London, where Jayden had driven me after my fall, had told me not to drive and said I needed to see my GP to arrange physio. Knowing I was fit, healthy and very rarely ill, I'd never got round to finding a GP during my short time back in London. And I didn't know if I was still on the books at the doctor's practice just down the lane from Mum's. That was something else I was going to have to sort.

I sat down with the – quite disgusting – coffee, desperate for the caffeine hit I hoped would clear the fog that appeared to have settled where my brain had once been. All I wanted to do was shut out the past couple of days as well as the picture of my future without the work I loved, without Fabian. It was very tempting to take more painkillers, expel Roger Rabbit from the sofa where he was guarding his territory and wrap the bright red throw – a constant and comforting feature of my childhood – around myself before finding some relief from this waking nightmare in sleep.

My eyes flew open and, draining the remainder of the coffee, I sat up, Roger gazing at me with some suspicion. I needed to be mobile, knew that if I wasn't going to be able to walk long distances with this knee, I *had* to drive. Heaving myself up off the sofa with discomfort, I went hunting for the little battered Fiesta's car keys, immediately finding them in the kitchen drawer where Mum'd always kept them.

Jayden might have insured me to drive Mum's car, but I didn't think for one minute the insurance company would pay out if they knew I was driving with a knee injury when I'd expressly been told not to. But I had to see Mum, had to do some shopping. I went outside to where the car was sitting on the drive, remembering with a little prayer of thanks that, because it had taken Mum five attempts at passing her driving test, Jess and I had persuaded her to switch to an automatic car. She'd passed her test on the next attempt and the three of us – Sorrel at that point being just a twinkle in Jayden's roving eye – had gone down to McDonald's in town to celebrate our new freedom. Surely, I could drive an automatic, my injured left leg notwithstanding?

Puffing and panting with the exertion of it all, I found myself heading into Beddingfield village and the road leading to the hospital where Mum had been blue-lighted once more. I'd worry about Sorrel – where she might be and what she might be up to – once I'd seen Mum and assessed what was happening there. As I got the feel of both the car and my knee, I realised I was driving too slowly and, fed up with the ensuing cacophony of car horns and accompanying hand gestures from impatient drivers, I made

myself catch up with the general flow of traffic, completing the
journey in just twenty minutes.

* * *

'Oh, Robyn, I'm really sorry you're here again. Although it is
lovely to see you.' Samantha, one of the wonderful nurses on
Ward 6 of Green Lea wing, looked up from her computer and
stood up to give me a hug. 'We really hoped after last time we
wouldn't see any of you back again.' She paused. 'What's with the
leg?' She nodded towards my knee. 'I heard you'd made it big
dancing in the West End?'

'Hardly.' I grimaced, lifting the offending knee in her direction. 'ACL.'

'Well, I hope you're not driving?' She frowned, noticing the
keys in my hand.

'Me? Would I?'

'Very probably.' She tutted.

'Can I see Mum?'

Samantha nodded.

'Why are you keeping her in? Is she in danger again?'

'She's had another attack of her acute porphyria. You don't
need me to tell you that can be life-threatening if it isn't promptly
treated. This was a particularly bad attack, Robyn, and Lisa was
experiencing dehydration from loss of fluids, as well as the usual
breathing problems. Her blood pressure is far too high and she's
still in danger of another seizure. Repeat acute attacks can lead to
chronic kidney failure, liver damage... even liver cancer. We have
to keep her here under observation—' She broke off. 'Hang on...'

I hung on, trying to take in that this recurrence of mum's
condition, which had repeatedly raised its ugly head throughout
my childhood and teens, appeared to be the worst yet. Symptoms

of acute porphyria can include severe pain in the chest, legs or back; digestive problems, such as constipation, nausea and vomiting; muscle pain, tingling, numbness, weakness or paralysis. And, most frightening, mental changes, such as anxiety, hallucinations or confusion as well as seizures. Mum had not had an attack like this since I was about twelve, although she'd suffered badly during her pregnancy with Sorrel. Jess had never forgiven Jayden for putting Mum's health at risk by getting Mum pregnant a third time.

'Hang on... Mr Spencer...?' Samantha stood and beckoned over a youngish man who, obviously harassed at the detour he was having to make back in our direction, walked towards us, a frown on his clean-shaven, baby-like features. Was the cliché about young policemen just the same when it came to medical consultants? 'Mr Spencer's new here,' she said in a whispered aside to me. 'He is *so* good, Robyn. Really. Lisa couldn't be in any better hands.'

'Just on my way for a quick break.' He tutted. 'What is it?'

'This is Lisa Allen's daughter, Robyn,' Samantha started. 'Can you give her a few minutes?'

'Come on.' He threw a hand in the direction of an office behind him. 'I've five minutes before I need to be somewhere else.'

'Down the pub?' I quipped, attempting levity.

'No, Ms Allen, to see a young man of eighteen who, because of his chronic illness, failed to gain the necessary A-level grades to take him off to Cambridge this autumn and who thought death a better alternative than taking up the place offered elsewhere.'

'Right. I'm so sorry.' Suitably chastened, I followed the man into his office.

'Mum's not very well, is she?' I asked, sinking gratefully, if not gracefully, into the proffered seat to one side of his desk.

'We're going to do the very best for her, but, yes, she is poorly.' The man was quickly perusing a file of notes. 'We're stabilising her and then, once we've done that, we'll run the battery of tests needed to assess her. Look, go in and see her. How much time do you have? I believe you live in London?'

'Oh, you know?'

'Jess put me in the picture. To be honest, I can see your sister needs some help, some coping strategies…'

'Sorrel?'

'Who's Sorrel?'

'My *little* sister. She's fifteen.'

'Ah yes, the catalyst for Lisa's not feeling she can manage any more.'

'Oh, please don't let Sorrel know you feel she's to blame.'

'I've never met your little sister, Ms Allen, and apportioning blame isn't helpful to anyone at the moment. I was actually talking about Jess: she's just about at her wits' end, you know.'

'I'm sorry. I didn't realise.'

'As I say, no one's pointing a finger at anyone. When do you go back?'

'Back?'

'I thought Jess said you lived in London?'

'Not any more.' I felt my heart plummet down to my injured knee. 'I'm here now. Here until I'm not needed any more. Right, I'll go in and see her. Thank you so much for all your help. It really is appreciated.'

* * *

'Mum?'

Every time I saw my mum, when I'd not seen her for a while, I marvelled anew at what an incredibly beautiful woman she was and, for a good few seconds, I simply gazed down at her. This was my mum, the woman who'd single-handedly brought up me and Jess – and then Sorrel – trying her very best to be the mum she knew we should have, though not always achieving that goal. Her slim wrists and long tapering fingers lay along the white sheet and coverlet, the wavy dark hair framing her coffee-coloured, heart-shaped face curled onto the starched white hospital pillow. Her full mouth was slightly open but, as she came round, appearing to fight the reality of the hospital room, her eyelids fluttered, she frowned and muttered something incomprehensible.

'Mum,' I said again, moving over to sit on the chair at her bedside, taking her hand in my own.

'Jayden?' For a split second, when she thought it was my dad at her side, her face lit up in a smile.

'It's me, Mum. Robyn.'

'Robyn? Oh? How lovely to see you.' She turned her face fully towards mine. 'You're looking *so* well.'

I felt immediate guilt that I'd not been home, nor really been in touch for ages, so in love had I been with my new life. With Fabian.

'Not really, Mum. I've damaged my knee; can't dance any more. But never mind about me.' I stroked her hand.

She didn't speak, but a single tear rolled down her cheek.

'Mum.' I knew, if I wasn't careful, I was going to cry myself and that was the last thing she needed. I had to try to be strong for her, get her well, get her home. 'Mum? Jess, Sorrel and I, we all love you. We're here for you, you know that.'

'I know, I know. It's just... it's just... I'm so tired. So tired of having this bloody condition. Fed up of wanting to have your dad with me all the time and now Sorrel... she really hates me.'

'Mum, Sorrel is *fifteen*. Fifteen-year-olds hate *everyone*...' I broke off, attempting levity. 'Bolshy teens don't love anyone but themselves.' I frowned, afraid that Sorrel didn't even love herself at the moment. 'And Dad? Well, Jayden is Jayden. You can't change *him*, Mum. You should know that by now...' I trailed off, realising that telling Mum off, telling her what she should be doing – and what she shouldn't – wasn't going to help at the moment. She was an intelligent woman – she *knew* she'd spent too much of her life obsessed with one man. One who most certainly did not merit all the emotion she'd poured into him.

'But...'

'I'm back up here in Yorkshire now, Mum,' I said, smiling, trying hard to take away some of the despair I knew she was feeling at finding herself back in hospital once more. 'I'm going to be looking after Sorrel, making sure she goes to school.'

'Well, good luck with that. I've tried, Robyn. She takes no notice of me. And I just don't want her to have to put up with me when I'm like this. It means she has to do a lot of things for herself, and for me – things *I* should be doing. It's not fair on a fifteen-year-old.'

'She *is* fifteen, that's the whole point, Mum. She *should* be doing things for herself at her age. Jess and I both had to, if you remember? You've spoilt her, and she needs to grow up a bit, so stop right there! I'm here now and I'm going to help you get better.'

'Thank you, Robyn.' She smiled, but one hand continued to clutch compulsively at the bed covers. Her voice wavered and another tear fell, unheeded, and then, apropos of nothing, she suddenly added, 'Never fall in love with someone so deeply that they take over your life, that you can't be without them.'

I knew this wasn't the time for me to be telling Mum I didn't believe that what she felt for Jayden was anything but obsession: a compulsive infatuation fuelled by learned behaviour reaching back, probably, to the childhood she spoke so little about. I wasn't versed in psychology. Should I advise Mum to forget Jayden, that he was never going to change, that she had to break this cycle? Or tell her what she wanted to hear to give this darling mum of mine some small shred of hope?

I chose the latter. 'Jayden's been with us for the last couple of days, Mum. He came to see me at the theatre and then, when I hurt my leg, he drove me home.'

'Jayden did?' Her eyes lit up. 'Oh, *did* he?' Her eyes moved towards the door. 'And is he here now?'

'He had to drive up to Aberdeen. He has several gigs up in Scotland...'

'Right.' Mum's face immediately began to crumple and close down once more.

'But he came to Sorrel's school with me.' I smiled.

'Did he?' Mum smiled once more. 'Oh, good. That's good. That head teacher at the high school just wouldn't listen to me. I tried, Robyn, honestly... Oh, Robyn, but she was so intimidating. She was quite terrifying... She reminded me of...'

'Of?' I leaned forward, hoping Mum was going to open up about her past, something she'd never done before.

Mum didn't speak for a few seconds. 'Liz Truss,' she eventually said.

'Liz Truss?' I stared at Mum.

'Hmm. Liz Truss with a spectacular chest.' Mum actually began to laugh at that. 'So, you managed to persuade that head-mistress to keep Sorrel?' Mum's beautiful almond-shaped brown eyes began to close and I could see she was drifting off once more.

'All will be well, Mum. Really. You just rest and get yourself better. Jess and I will sort everything.'

'Don't make my mistake,' she murmured. 'Don't ruin your life by falling in love with someone who doesn't love you back, like I did. And Jess did. That dreadful Dean...' Mum's eyes closed under the sedation, but she smiled, her facing lighting up with pleasure. 'This lovely new man of yours, though, Robyn, sounds perfect... I'm so pleased for you...'

I dropped a kiss on Mum's cheek, standing as Samantha popped her head around the door. 'Let her rest, Robyn,' she advised as I followed her out of the room. 'Anyway, I hear you've a wonderful new chap in your life?' She nudged me somewhat suggestively in the ribs. 'Jess was telling me all about him. Some posh barrister in London?'

'Yes.' I smiled, suddenly knowing I *had* to speak to Fabian. Had to tell him what was happening. 'Just off to ring him now.'

'You do right.' She laughed. 'Ooh, to be in your twenties, living in London and in love.' She patted my arm. 'Don't you worry about Lisa. She's in the best place here. You go and talk to your man. Get him to come up to Yorkshire to be with you.'

I limped my way back to the car, settling myself and breathing deeply to steady my nerves. Then, realising it wasn't yet midday and Fabian would more than likely be in court, I took the coward's way out and messaged him rather than ringing.

> Fabian, I am so very very sorry that we appear to have fallen out again. Probably all my fault! As you say, me and my pride! I'm back in Yorkshire – afraid I had a bit of an accident and damaged my knee good and proper this time. My mum's not well and I'm trying to sort out my little sister. I can't tell you how much I love and miss you. Please, give me a ring as soon as you are able.
>
> Robyn.

Knowing Fabian would more than likely be either with clients in his office or in court, I didn't anticipate an immediate response from him. I sat back in the driving seat, closed my eyes and endeavoured to get my racing pulse back to normal before turning the key in the ignition ready to make my way back to Beddingfield.

My heart did a somersault as my phone sprang to life with a message.

> I think everything that needed to be said has been said, Robyn. I also think it best for both our sakes that we formally terminate our relationship and have no further contact with each other.

> Fabian

16

"Formally terminate our relationship!" Is that barrister wanker-speak for *bugger off, I'm throwing you out of my bed and my life*?' Jess was absolutely livid. 'Give me your phone, Robyn, I'll message him back. How dare he?' She reached for my mobile, which I'd left on the kitchen table, unable to bear the thought of its pernicious presence carrying that ghastly text in my pocket or my bag. I didn't want it anywhere near me.

'Leave it, Jess,' I snapped. 'Don't you dare.'

'Well, let me at least delete that last message. Otherwise, you'll read it again and again. And *again*, in the middle of the night and then—'

'OK, OK, delete *the lot*.' I started to cry. '*Except* that last message. It'll remind me if I'm tempted to message him again. Yes, go on, all his messages except this one. All his contact details...' I put my head down on the table and sobbed.

'Probably the best way,' Jess agreed, picking up the offending object. 'You know, a bit like ripping off an Elastoplast in one swift final act. Hurts like hell to begin with, but then it's over and done with and no going back, no picking at it...'

'OK. OK, spare me the analogy.'

'Bastard,' she hissed as she reread Fabian's final text once more. 'Blimey, there's a hell of a lot of them here... oh, some really lovely things... oh... listen to this one... oh, Robyn...'

'Don't *read them*,' I pleaded. 'They're personal. Just *do it*, Jess. Get him out of my life, as I appear to be out of his.'

'Done!' Jess gave a final flick of her wrist and Fabian Mansfield Carrington was out of my life.

As though he'd not been in it for the past four months. And, apart from that last message to remind me there was no hope, he was gone. Utterly gone.

'Right,' she said, throwing the phone back down onto the table, well out of my reach, before making a great show of metaphorically washing her hands of the man I'd adored. 'I'm going to head off to the Co-op before I have to pick up Lola from school. I'm so stressed, Robyn, I need to cook and to bake. I'll make something wonderful for tea, we'll open a bottle of wine and then when – if – Sorrel gets back, we'll sit her down and tell her we mean business...' She broke off as a loud knocking came at Mum's front door and both our heads shot up in unison.

'The police?' Jess whispered, biting her lip. 'Mum said Sorrel was in trouble with them.'

'Fabian?' I whispered in turn, my heart racing as I ran down the tiny narrow passageway to open the door, conveniently forgetting he'd neatly and expertly *terminated* our relationship only an hour earlier.

'Oh.' I stared at the man standing on Mum's doorstep, for a split second trying to work out who he was, so out of context was his appearance there. 'How did you know where we lived?'

'Easy. I spoke to the head at Beddingfield High.'

'I didn't think our personal details were supposed to be bandied around like this. Data protection and all that?' Utter disappointment that the man standing there wasn't Fabian come to rescue me made me caustic in my response. 'Sorrel's not home,' I added.

'I've not come to see Sorrel.' Mason Donoghue smiled. 'May I come in?' He took a step inside.

'You appear to be doing so,' I replied somewhat tartly and then, remembering I needed to keep on the right side of this man if he was to relent and offer Sorrel a place at St Mede's, I added, 'Please. Come on in.'

'Jess, this is Mr Donoghue.' I ushered the man into Mum's kitchen. 'He's the head teacher of St Mede's.'

'Mason?' Jess looked up and stared. 'You never said.'

'You never asked.'

'You two know each other?' I looked in surprise from Jess to the man who was now easing his great height and well-toned body onto a kitchen chair, apparently making himself at home.

'Mason's granny is a guest at Hudson House.'

'A guest?' I gave a little chortle. 'Is that what you're called when you end up in an old folks' home?'

'As opposed to what?' Mason Donoghue raised an eye in my direction. 'A client? An inmate?'

'Hadn't really thought about it, to be honest.' I shrugged. 'So, at what point did you realise Sorrel was Jess's sister?'

'Not until you'd left my office and then I sort of put two and two together.' Mason smiled across at Jess.

'Oh, so does that mean you're willing to take Sorrel as a pupil without blackmailing me, then? Now that your granny's in Jess's care? We could end up blackmailing *you* in return: you know, give Sorrel a place at your school or Jess won't let your granny stroke the pet therapy dog…'

'We don't *have* a pet therapy dog…' Jess started.

'Or bar her from bridge sessions,' I said, warming to my theme.

'Tiddlywinks, ludo and, occasionally, draughts,' Jess corrected.

'Those as well.' I nodded in agreement. 'Take Sorrel, Mr Donoghue, or your granny will be blacklisted.'

'Hang on. Blackmailing you?' Jess frowned. 'What *are* you talking about, Robyn? Mason's blackmailing you? What have you *done*?'

'He says he'll take Sorrel, as long as I go and teach there as well.'

'Really? Well, how wonderful is that!' Jess beamed at both of us. 'You loved being a teacher, Robyn. Tea, Mason?'

'No need for fabrication, Jess.' I shook my head in her direction as she went to fill the kettle. 'I've already told Mr Donoghue here that I hated teaching. That I was a rubbish teacher.'

'You passed, did your NQT year,' Jess protested. 'You're qualified.'

'Qualified to know that, after a year at the chalkface, I never want to be back there again. Ever.'

'No chalk these days.' Mason smiled. 'All whiteboards and SMART boards.' He sighed. 'When they work, anyway. Look, Robyn, I'm desperate for someone to take over the drama department.'

'Take it over?' I stared. 'You didn't say I was going to be in charge of it.'

'Would that make a difference?'

'More pay, Robyn!' Jess was jubilant. 'We're going to need more funds to keep both houses warm and running now that Dean's gone and isn't sending me any money. The cost of living is horrendous. I haven't put the central heating on yet and *never* have a bath.'

'Not sure we should be a party to your personal hygiene habits, Jess.' I tutted. 'Or lack of them.'

'You know exactly what I mean.' She tutted in response. 'Look, Robyn, as your elder sister, I'm ordering you to take this lovely teaching job. It'll be right up your street.'

'*Ordering* me? Who do you think you are?'

'Your big sister. We need the money, Robyn—' She broke off as the front door banged and all three of us glanced towards the open kitchen door.

'Oh, God.' Sorrel stared at Mason Donoghue sitting comfortably, and without a trace of embarrassment, at the kitchen table.

'Almost, but not quite, Sorrel.' Mason smiled.

'I'm off.' Sorrel made for the door she'd just come through, but Jess barred her way.

'Oh, no, you don't. Listen, Sorrel, Mr Donoghue is here to offer you a place at St Mede's. Robyn and I are not prepared for any backchat.'

'You're not my mum.'

'Loco parentis,' Jess snapped.

'That again?' Sorrel raised an eyebrow as did Jess, the pair of them squaring up to each other like a couple of bantam hens. 'Look.' Sorrel glared in my direction. 'I'm definitely not going to your school if *she's* going to be there every day. How embarrassing to have your big sister there teaching, watching everything you do, knowing what you're up to and reporting back to Sturmführer Jess every night.'

'I'm impressed, Sorrel.' Mason raised an eyebrow. 'You've obviously been listening during your GCSE World War II history module.'

'I like history.' Sorrel shrugged. ''Bout the only thing I do like, apart from dance.'

'So, rather a bonus to have lessons with a professional West End dancer, then?' Mason, in turn, looked in my direction.

'Hang on,' I said, rubbing at my knee. 'For a start—'

'Perfect,' Jess began, hands on hips. 'You take the pair of them, Mason, and I'll make sure your granny is right at the front of the queue when the hairdresser comes. *And* gets a second helping of afters when it's chocolate pudding with chocolate sauce.'

'OK, OK!' Sorrel put up both hands in a show of apparent acquiescence. 'I don't want to have to go to the PRU,' she said sulkily. 'What do I do about uniform? Do I have to wear one?'

'Of course. Where uniform's concerned, I'm as strict as Beddingfield High,' Mason said seriously. 'We have second-hand stuff.'

'I'm not wearing second-hand,' Sorrel protested.

'Well, it's either that or you shelling out yourself for a new blazer, sweater and tie,' Jess said firmly. 'Mum only bought you a brand-new uniform three weeks ago. You always seem to have money on the go.' All three of us looked towards Sorrel, who, under adult scrutiny, glared back and turned away from us. But not before I'd seen her face flush slightly. Oh, hell, if it was true that she had funds, we needed to know where they were coming from.

'So,' Mason said, turning back to me, 'it's a yes from me and Sorrel, then, is it?'

'And from Robyn as well.' Jess smiled sweetly in my direction, but there was a steely determination I recognised from old behind it.

'How about, Robyn, you start with us at St Mede's on a supply basis rather than on any contract, temporary or otherwise?' Mason suggested. 'I'll be there to help and support you, as will both the PE and the English department, who've been covering the dance and drama curriculums with me. Why don't you come back in tomorrow and I'll show you round again and give you all the planning documents we have? I'll need to see all your certificates and get references from the school in which you did your NQT year, and I'm assuming your DBS is up to date? If not, we can soon sort that out.'

'Of course it is.' Jess nodded enthusiastically. 'It was only a year ago she was teaching in schools. It'll be like riding a bike,' she added. 'It'll all come flooding back, Robyn.'

'D'you think I can speak for myself, Jess?' I glared in her direction. 'Are you both not forgetting one thing?'

'What's that?' Mason and Jess, as well as Sorrel, all turned back to me.

'I'm disabled!' I lifted my leg with its black brace towards them. 'I need physio and rest on this leg, not starting a new job where I'll be on my feet all day. And how the hell do you suggest I'm going to teach dance with a knackered knee?'

Mason frowned. 'All right, OK, most of the dance lessons will continue to be covered by the PE staff and, I guess, by myself. You'd be mainly teaching drama, Robyn, which, I believe, you're qualified to do? Obviously, it would be better if you could be hands-on... knees-on... but I'm sure you'll be able to teach and guide the kids from the sideline, as it were. As I mentioned earlier, I'll also need you to cover some PSHE and English lessons.'

'Sex education and all that!' Sorrel grinned loftily in my direction as if I weren't aware of the meaning of the first acronym. 'After the mad passionate affair I hear you were having with that new man of yours, Robyn, you'll know how to teach *that*...'

'*Excuse me,*' I snapped, utterly embarrassed as Mason held my eye, his own full of humour. I glared at Sorrel who, despite her being my little sister, I was now beginning to dislike intensely.

'That's good, then.' Mason grinned. 'Looks like we're making progress. OK, it's Monday now.' He paused, obviously thinking on his feet. 'Not got my diary and, I'd forgotten, I'm actually out of school tomorrow, but I'll expect you both in on Wednesday for a bit of an induction and then, on Thursday, we'll crack on.' He turned to Sorrel, speaking softly. 'And, Sorrel, don't you go thinking St Mede's is a soft touch. My school is turning a corner: I'm determined to make it a place parents want to send their children to and I won't have *anyone* in it who disregards my rules. You play fair with me, Sorrel, and we'll be there for you and do everything in our power to help you get where you want to be. I'm telling you now, my teachers and I won't stand for any of the behaviour you've been involved in at Beddingfield High. You work with us, and we'll work with you. If not, you're out...' He raised an eye in Sorrel's direction and, while she tried to stare him out, eventually she lowered her gaze and looked away.

Mason held out a hand to me. 'Welcome to St Mede's, Ms Allen. I hope your time with us, until you're able to resume your career in London, is a happy and profitable one.'

* * *

Totally exhausted by the events of the last two days – surely it must be more than two days since my entire world had come, literally, crashing down around my ears? – I tried hard to eat the utterly wonderful food Jess had put in front of me, Sorrel and Lola. While my big sister and niece both tucked in with relish to the fragrant-smelling chicken and tarragon dish, neither Sorrel nor I were able to do justice to her cooking. I knew what had taken *my* appetite but, glancing across at my little sister's set face and demeanour, knew I was a long way from understanding what was troubling Sorrel. The bottle of cheap red wine Jess had spent her last few pounds on at the village Co-op and opened in celebration of both Sorrel's and my own new beginning at St Mede's

High School did go some way to releasing the anxiety-provoked constriction in my throat, and I was able to force down a few mouthfuls with some accompanying oohs and aahs of appreciation and approval.

'You should go on *MasterChef*,' I said, as I always did whenever I ate Jess's delicious meals.

'Really?' Sorrel sneered before replacing her fork on her half-eaten food and making to leave the table.

'We've not finished eating, Sorrel,' I said as calmly as possible. Constantly berating her would get us nowhere.

'Well, *I* have,' she said, standing. 'I'm off out.'

'No, you're not.' Both Jess and I spoke as one while Lola's head, moving in turn from her mother to her scowling fifteen-year-old aunt, followed the action like a crowd at Wimbledon.

'I'm really not sure how you're going to stop me,' Sorrel replied, her face flushed. And, screwing up the piece of kitchen roll I'd laid at each place in lieu of napkins, she stood and left the kitchen.

* * *

Later that evening, much later, I woke from an exhausted sleep full of dreams of the whole of the cast of *Dance On* laughing uproariously as I fell again and again off the stage while Mason Donoghue stood, arms folded in incredulous contempt, at the back of some windowless classroom watching as I attempted to teach a sex education lesson, using a video of Fabian making love to Fish Face as a visual aid.

I shot up in bed, covered in perspiration, my knee throbbing and stiff and, reaching for my phone, saw it was only 11 p.m. I'd been asleep for just an hour. From down below came the sound of a car door slamming and the murmur of voices. Manoeuvring myself and my knee out of bed, I moved over to the bedroom window. Sorrel, laughing at something that had obviously been said by whoever was in the back seat of the black BMW, made her way up the garden path. A few seconds later the front door banged and I heard her move to the kitchen before opening and closing the fridge door.

Well, at least she was home. I turned over in the box room's uncomfortable single bed, resolving that in the morning I'd move my things into Mum's room, and tried to sleep once more. But I was now wide awake, panic and pain threatening to engulf me in equal measure as I went over the events of the last few days.

Pulse racing, I made another decision: no way was I taking this teaching job I'd been bulldozed into accepting at Mason Donoghue's bloody awful school. No way, Pedro. I'd rather get a job down at Aldi or delivering parcels for Amazon.

No way on this planet was I *ever* going back into a classroom.

Not now. Not on Wednesday. Not ever.

17

'Look, Robyn, I don't know what to suggest,' Jess said in some exasperation the following morning when, after walking Lola down to the village school, she was back in her kitchen, emptying the dishwasher and tidying up before setting off for yet another session at Hudson House, the care home she'd worked in for years. I'd left Sorrel asleep in bed and gone round wanting advice and company. If I was expecting sympathy, Jess was obviously not about to give it. 'If you now say you're not prepared to take up this teaching job, then you'll have to go and sign on or something. Sickness benefits? Unemployment benefits? Universal Credit? *I* don't know, *I've* always worked.'

'As have I,' I retorted, stung at her sharp words. 'There's never been a time when I've not earned a living.'

'Well, if you're really not prepared to take up Mason's offer – although, you know, you did agree you would, and now you appear to be going back on your word – there's always work on offer at Hudson House. No one ever wants to be a carer.'

'I'm not surprised,' I said. 'I can't think of anything worse.'

'Not even teaching?' she shot back. 'You want jam on it, Robyn.

I suggest you come with me and see if you'd prefer wiping old ladies' bottoms and holding their hands when they're frightened, and upset that none of their family is visiting them...'

'OK.'

'OK what?'

'I'll come with you now.'

'You just want to be out of the way when Sorrel surfaces,' Jess said, pulling a face of exasperation. 'I thought the idea of your being next door was to keep an eye on her.'

'I can't be her minder. She's nearly sixteen.'

'Oh, I think you can.' Jess wasn't letting it go. 'Mum and I have been trying to do just that while you were in London.'

Ignoring this, I offered, 'No, really, I'll come with you. Is there a vacancy?'

'There are *always* vacancies in *every* care home.' Jess rinsed and wrung out the yellow dishcloth she'd used to wipe down the kitchen worktops before hanging it on the taps. 'Come on, then; I'll show you what hard work is. You'll soon be running scared and begging Mason for that teaching job.'

* * *

'Can I have a word, love?'

'Of course.' Jess put down the loaded tray she was carrying and moved to talk to the woman who I guessed to be in her late sixties, and who was now standing nervously in the reception hall of Hudson House. 'It's Mavis's daughter, isn't it?' Jess asked, smiling. 'Mrs Hattersley? How are you? I did go along to Mavis's funeral, sat at the back in the church, but didn't manage to catch you afterwards. I'm sorry – I had to get back here to help with the lunches. Come on in and sit down. Oh, this is my sister Robyn.' Jess indicated with a wave of her hand as I followed in her wake, limping behind her like some unwanted shadow. 'She's making up her mind whether she's going to come and work with us or not.'

'Rather you than me, love.' The woman raised an eyebrow in my direction. 'Absolute saints, these carers; I don't know how they do it. Jess and the others here are marvellous – absolute saints,' she said again.

Three hours into my sister's shift, and amazed at just how much Jess was fitting in, I was beginning to see what Mrs Hattersley meant.

'I won't keep you, love.' Mrs Hattersley addressed Jess once more. 'I just wanted to ask you a favour.' The woman, now running a nervous hand through her short greying hair, had obviously rehearsed her opening gambit.

'Well, I will, if I can.' Jess smiled encouragingly.

'So, my dad died.'

'Oh?' Jess stared at the woman, apparently in some surprise, and I moved forward to listen. 'I always thought your mum was a widow,' Jess said. 'And had been for many years. I'm really sorry,' she went on, patting the woman's arm in sympathy. 'You've lost your dad so soon after losing your mum? I didn't realise.' Jess frowned. 'I don't recall your dad ever coming here to visit. So, he died recently, did he?'

'Forty-one years ago, love. I was only in my late twenties when he went. Heart, it was.'

'Forty-one years ago?' Jess turned in my direction, pulling a scary face, and I wanted to laugh.

'And my mum had kept him in her wardrobe ever since. When she came here last year, when she was unable to care for herself any longer, I took him back home with me.'

'For forty-one years?' Jess stared and that was when I did start a nervous titter. 'Mavis had kept his ashes in her wardrobe for forty-one years?'

Mrs Hattersley nodded. 'Apart from the last twelve months or so – I've had him with me since we packed up Mum's things and brought her here.' I didn't like to ask if we could bring Dad with her and, to be honest, by that time she'd forgotten his name, never mind she'd been married to him for umpteen years.' She gave a little laugh herself. 'You might well stare, Jess. I'd had words with her ever since, but she'd promised him, in the hospital, she'd always keep him nearby. I reckon it was so's he could keep an eye on *her*, rather than t'other way round. If you get my meaning. Anyway, it obviously worked because she never looked at another man. And she were a right good-looking woman was my mum.'

'She was,' Jess agreed, nodding her head in my direction. 'She really was, Robyn. Always insisted on having her hair done and her lipstick on.'

'Liked a port and lemon – or two – on a night down at The Green Dragon. And bingo. She loved her bingo.' Mrs Hattersley wiped a tear. 'Anyhow, as you know, when Mum died, we had a service up at St Luke's church. They *all* seem to go through St Luke's when they leave the care homes round here,' she went on, almost accusingly, lowering her voice. 'Rick, that's my husband, reckons these homes must have got some sort of deal with St Luke's: you know, two for the price of one or something? I only say that because the parson up there isn't very *accommodating*, like. All a bit rushed, we thought. She'd have been so pleased that you managed to get to the service – even if it was a bit shorter than we'd anticipated. She thought a lot of you, Jess. We knew she was in good hands with you around.'

'Well, thank you, that's very kind...'

'So, I'm here to ask you a favour.'

'Oh? What can I do for you?' I saw Jess cock her head to one side in what I guessed she hoped was a gesture of empathy.

'My mum kept my dad for so long because she'd promised him they'd be scattered together.'

'Right, that's nice.' Jess patted the woman's arm once more.

'The thing is, I think Mum would have gone happy if she'd known someone from here at Hudson House – well, you really, Jess: you were always her favourite – could be there at the... at the... you know... the scattering.'

We plough the fields and scatter the good seed on the land came immediately to mind and I had to suppress, not only a bubbling-up giggle, but also the impulse to sing the words out loud.

'That really isn't a problem, if I can get the time off.' Jess, knowing I was on the verge of laughing, tittered slightly herself and Mrs Hattersley looked at her somewhat askance. 'So, what were your mum's wishes, Kath?' she finally managed to ask, rearranging her features in her best 'care home assistant' face. 'Where would she like to end up? Do you know?'

'Yes, I know exactly.'

'Oh?'

'The Cow and Calf.'

'Right. I don't think I know that one.' Jess frowned, turning to me where, my knee having started to give me some jip, I'd gone to sit next to one of the residents. 'Do you know it, Robyn? Is that the pub over the other side of Beddingfield?'

'A *pub*?' Kath looked slightly put out. 'I know I said she was partial to a port and lemon, but I don't want you getting any ideas she was a drinker.'

'Of course not.' Jess rearranged her features. 'So, the Cow and Calf?'

'And you a Yorkshire lass?' Kath Hattersley looked even more put out. 'Ilkley Moor, love. You know, *baht 'at*? The Cow and Calf are big stones on the moor that are supposed to look like a... well, like a cow and a calf.'

'Right. Quite a way out, then? Ilkley Moor? All the way past Bradford and through Ilkley itself. Must be a good hour from Beddingfield, Jess,' I estimated, while Jess herself appeared to be juggling all her commitments in her mental diary.

'I was conceived up there,' Kath said proudly. 'Mum never told me that until just before she died. My dad had asked her to marry him up there, they got a bit carried away, as it were, and next thing they knew the wedding was being brought forward.' Kath smiled. 'I promised her I'd leave her and my dad up there.'

'Romantic, isn't it?' I said, enjoying the story. 'A bit like Cathy and Heathcliff up on Wuthering Heights?'

Kath shook her head. 'Sorry, love, don't know them. Were they in here at Hudson House as well?' She broke into a smile. 'So, that's good: you've done this sort of thing before, then, Jess? With this Cathy Heathcliff? Part of the job spec, I suppose?'

18

———

I knew, following my visit to Hudson House care home, I was going to have to bite the bullet and take up Mason Donoghue's teaching job offer.

Having spent most of the day with Jess at the home, I was now utterly in awe of care workers, of their commitment, professionalism and hard work. And it *was* hard work for Jess: back-breaking stuff, always on call, helping, soothing, advising, sorting medication, while constantly accompanying the elderly, often incontinent, men and women both to the loo and the shower, at the same time as keeping an eye on her team of new-to-the-job care assistants. I'd shadowed Jess as she did all the usual hands-on stuff such as providing personal care, including showering, bathing and shaving the whiskery old men while persuading them to clean their teeth. Apart from the shaving, the ritual reminded me of dealing with kids. Was it any wonder that Jess was so good, not only with ten-year-old Lola, but with Sorrel as well? Although, when I was chatting to Jess as she went about these tasks, she admitted she'd come to a standstill with our little sister, intimating that Mum had ended up back in hospital because of Sorrel and she, herself, was almost at her wits' end with her.

While carefully, almost lovingly, combing and tying back with a pink ribbon the thin hair of ninety-five-year-old Sara, Jess had turned to me, looking me determinedly in the eye, and said, 'I need help, Robyn. Not sure I can cope with Sorrel any more. Please stay up here with us and take up Mason's offer.'

And then she was off once more, with me trailing after her, helping Desmond with his mobility issues and Basil with his lost spectacles before setting off down to the kitchen to check on the preparation of lunches. Then, once she'd found Annie, who'd gone AWOL, she had commenced the twice-daily monitoring of the blood pressure and heart rate before making sure she was on hand to support with feeding and hydration.

Even while taking her half-hour lunch break, Jess continued working, jumping up with a smile on her face to chat to a worried family to update them on their relative's progress. I was exhausted and all I'd done was trail after Jess, sitting, chatting and patting (as Jess called it) lonely men and women, some simply counting the days and hours until relatives were free – and willing – to visit them once more.

If they ever did.

I messaged Mason Donoghue but when after an hour there was no reply, rang him on the number he'd given me. Still no response, so I found and rang the St Mede's reception number, which was answered immediately.

'Could I speak to Mr Donoghue?'

'I'm sorry, he's not actually in today. Can I take a message?'

'It's Robyn Allen. Could you tell Mr Donoghue I'd like to take up both his offers?'

'His offers?'

I hesitated. 'Both myself and my sister, Sorrel Allen, will be in school in the morning.'

'Oh, that's in the diary. Mason has already confirmed you'll both be joining us. No problem at all. See you in the morning.'

And with that she rang off, leaving me looking at my phone like the second-rate actor I now apparently was.

'Oh, Mr Mason Donoghue! Pretty sure of yourself, aren't you, you full-of-yourself bloody headmaster?'

Ninety-eight-year-old Beryl, who'd stuck to my side most of the afternoon, cackled in delight, patting my arm in encouragement with a papery-skinned hand. 'You tell the bastard,' she whooped. 'Never liked teachers or headmasters: I was slippered more times than I can remember when I were a lass...'

* * *

Wednesday morning and Sorrel and I duly presented ourselves at St Mede's Reception, waiting a good twenty minutes until Mason Donoghue was free to see us. He immediately requested – ordered – that Sorrel accompany one of his members of staff to Lost Property where she'd be temporarily kitted out with the school blazer and tie, saying, when Sorrel started to demur: 'My school, my rules, Sorrel. You'll need to wear our stuff until you are able to buy the uniform yourself.'

'I'm not a bloody charity case,' she began.

'And rule number one at St Mede's is no swearing. Oh, and rule number two is no phones in class. You'll be given a key to a locker where you can leave your personal things as well as your phone.'

'Good luck with that.' I smiled chummily towards this new boss of mine, but he didn't respond.

'Robyn, once Sorrel is settled can we have a meeting at some point?' He looked at his watch. 'Where I'll get Petra to go through all the policies with you.'

'Petra? Policies?'

'Behaviour; Health and Safety; Safeguarding; Anti-bullying; First Aid...' He narrowed his eyes slightly. 'You know, the usual stuff?'

'Of course,' I said. 'And you'll want to see all my certification?' I could be just as professional as Mason Donoghue if I needed to be. Although to be honest, once I'd left my last school, determined never again to darken the door of any educational establishment, I'd been about to make a bonfire of all my curriculum documents, teaching plans, files and everything else that goes hand in hand with being a teacher. But Mum, proud of my achievements, had rescued the lot from the bin, placing it neatly – reverentially – in the top two drawers of the chest in the box room. Thank goodness she had: I'd spent the previous evening going through it all, my pulse racing with anxiety at the thought of standing once again in front of a class of kids, but also reminding myself of some of the lessons that, not only had been successful, but I'd actually sometimes quite enjoyed teaching.

'Ah, Petra?' Mason was making his way back to his office, but turned and called over his shoulder to a pretty blonde sporting a tracksuit who'd just made her way into Reception. 'Have you time now? This is Robyn who I was telling you about yesterday. She's joining us on supply, covering English, dance and drama and some PSHE.'

'Got everything you'll need, Robyn.' She waved a pile of stuff in my direction. 'Do you want to come down to my office and we can crack on like a pit pony?'

'Sorry?' I stared at her.

'There's a lot to get through,' she amended, obviously realising I had a deficient sense of humour as well as, when she caught sight of the brace on my knee, a knackered left leg.

'I'm not sure I can do this,' I said as I limped after this little firecracker of a woman, who was probably not much older than me, panic threatening to engulf me as I sped up in her wake. My pulse was racing and I actually felt physically sick. Sick with longing for my old life and for Fabian.

'Tie,' Petra barked at some little dot of a lad who obviously hadn't yet learned how to manoeuvre the stiff fabric hanging round his neck. She bent, flinging the material deftly round itself before adjusting the knot and sending him on his way. 'Monday's homework?' she demanded of a tall, neatly dressed girl with a headful of braids, but Petra accelerated, without waiting for any response or excuse on said homework. 'Sorry, Robyn, you were saying?' She turned to speak as we moved along corridor after gloomy corridor. 'Your leg bothering you? ACL?' she asked knowingly.

'Well spotted.' I panted after her as we went through empty classrooms, making detours and short cuts before finally arriving at a door marked:

MS P WATERS
Deputy Head Teacher

'Had one myself after skiing,' she announced, nodding in the direction of my knee. 'Mine was torn. Had to have three months off work. If you're able to walk on it like that, you've only got minor damage. I'll try and make sure you're able to sit down some of the time in the classes you'll be taking. Mind you' – she frowned – 'I know Mason's hoping you'll be able to lead us in dance and drama.'

'*Lead you?*' I stared. 'I'm here on a supply basis. I'm hoping, seeing I've not been in a classroom for over a year, someone will be *leading me.*'

'Well, of course, we'll do everything to help. Mason insists we all muck in together. I'm trained Phys Ed, so I still do a lot of the games and PE as well as mopping up lessons where we've not been able to afford a day's cover. But dance? Wow? You were in the West End? I guess they had to replace you? Temporarily? Are you able to go back?'

'I doubt it,' I said, remembering the cavalier fashion with which Carl Farmer had replaced the pregnant former dancer with me. I determined, however, I'd be ringing both Carl at the theatre and Dorcas, my agent, later on today. As well as getting a professional opinion on my knee from the local GP. If this Petra knew as much about ACLs as she appeared to, there might be some hope for me yet.

Petra waved a hand towards the chair in front of her desk, seating herself behind it before reaching for the pile of papers, sifting through each one and asking me questions as we went along.

'Cuckooing? FGM?'

'I'm sorry,' I said, 'I've forgotten what they are. I don't suppose I had any reason to be concerned about these things in London.'

'I think we have to be aware of drugs and female genital mutilation in all walks of life, not just in schools,' she admonished. 'But obviously, especially in schools when we're working daily with kids.'

'And here in a village like Beddingfield?'

'Little Micklethwaite,' she amended. 'And absolutely. The danger is in assuming that because we're *not* London, *not* in Manchester, these things don't happen out here in the sticks. You need to be aware of behaviour – of clues – that a child in your class is being manipulated either by other kids or by adults and could be involved in something they shouldn't. Not necessarily by outside influences, of course,' Petra went on. 'Kids can be in fear of their own families.'

'Right.'

Petra held my eye for a fraction longer than necessary before handing over the wad of documents. 'OK, behaviour policy. We have strict written guidelines on which you need to proceed when a student's kicking off.'

'And is that often?'

'This is St Mede's, not Eton,' Petra retorted before relenting somewhat. 'Much, much less so since Mason took over two years ago. He is an absolutely superb head. The school is on the up and up. I think he's asked you to come here because he's obviously seen something in you – believes you'll be an asset to the school.'

Or, I thought, cynically, he can't get anyone else to venture over the doorstep.

* * *

Two hours later and with my head spinning and the bell for break only adding to the pain that was starting to build over my eyes, Petra handed me the remains of enough paper to have decimated a forest and stood up. 'Come on, caffeine.' She grinned.

'Gin?' I asked.

'Safeguarding rules, remember,' she replied, laughing.

We made our way back along corridors packed with a veritable army of kids, little Year 7s in new, too big uniforms mingling awkwardly with man-sized giants sporting downy bumfluff on their top lip, but all intent on their fifteen minutes of freedom outside in the September sunshine. As we neared the main exits, streams of youths met and joined like a confluence of rivers and a couple of scuffles broke out. Petra was immediately in there, barking orders, holding back one stream while allowing another to move forward. 'Main exit's been damaged and is unsafe to open,' she explained over her shoulder. 'Hence the pushing and shoving to get out.'

The pervasive odour, peculiar only to high schools, of rubber-soled trainers, leather satchels, school dinners, sweat, cheap floor polish and disinfectant assailed my nostrils and I closed my eyes slightly, remembering how I'd sworn never again. Teaching and me just weren't a fit.

'Coffee?' Petra asked, seeing the panic in my eyes. 'Honestly, it'll all come back.' She grinned. 'Like riding a bike.'

'Never very good at bike riding,' I muttered. 'Fell off and broke my thumb when I was ten,' I added but, nevertheless, carried on through the escapees in Petra's wake, in search of coffee.

* * *

'New girl in Year 11's pretty bolshy,' a sandy-haired bloke, probably in his late fifties, was saying to no one in particular, the rest of the staff too busy grabbing sustaining coffee, tea and KitKats in their fifteen minutes' break to be interested in what he was saying. 'Been kicked out of Beddingfield High apparently. Should have been on her way to the PRU but, for whatever reason, our lord and master's decided to give her a place here.'

'Not daft though.' A tall black woman around my age turned towards the sandy-haired bloke. 'She knew almost as much as me about the Weimar democracy, its political change and unrest, and the Munich Putsch as well.'

'Well, she needs keeping an eye on.' The other sniffed,

slurping at his coffee while still masticating his biscuit. 'It won't be long before she starts showing her true colours.' Noticing me for the first time, he turned in my direction. 'Hello,' he said contemplatively, his small eyes taking in every bit of me in much the same way as Julius Carrington had mentally undressed me on the first occasion I'd met him.

'Hi.' I smiled, determined to be friendly: I needed the natives on my side if I was to be working here. 'What do you teach?'

'Wankers mainly,' he replied, the start of a smirk on his face.

'This is Robyn, everyone,' Petra said hurriedly, shooting a look of utter disdain at the man. 'She's joining us tomorrow, covering some English and drama and PSHE, but, fantastically, because she's been working in the West End, no less, will be able to give us direction in dance and theatre studies.'

'I don't think...' I started, a rictus of a smile on my face, but she'd turned to the man lavishly buttering toast in the kitchen area of the staffroom. 'Dave? Going to leave Robyn with you now. If you can go over the English stuff she'll be doing?' Petra turned back to me. 'Dave's Head of English,' she explained and then, looking at her watch, added, 'Sorry, going to have to scoot. Got a meeting with Mason and then I'm teaching Year 7 games. Half these kids can't catch a ball. And the other half are convinced they're the next Messi and it's only a matter of time before they're signed up by Man U.'

I spent the next ninety minutes sorting out more admin and being given the low-down on the English curriculum by Dave Mallinson, Head of English at St Mede's, who I found helpful if a little distant. He and Sandy Head were old retainers, he told me, been at the school for years and would probably be carried out, covered in chalk dust, breathing their last gasp.

'You still enjoy it, then?' I asked. 'The teaching, I mean?'

'Must do or I'd have taken early retirement years ago. When

we really were at rock bottom, in special measures and the authority was intent on closing us down, I was about to go then. But Mason came along and started turning the place round.' He looked steadily at me. 'It's a good place to be if you can get a handle on the pupils. Kids are not born disruptive, badly behaved you know? Most want to learn, to fit in, to please. Unfortunately, the crap they've had to put up with at home, how they've been brought up, the challenges they've had to face before they even started primary school, let alone high school, have had them at a disadvantage from the get-go.'

'I know, I know.' I smiled, slightly irritated. 'I do understand that. I've obviously done the child development, the psychology, the behaviour modules...'

'Ah, but you don't start really understanding what it's all about until you're hands-on. You'll be fine, Robyn. Just take it a day at a time. Oh, and if you need some work on that knee – ACL, is it? – my wife's a physio. I'll give you her details.'

I was starting to feel a little calmer. A little more, you know, I can do this. Maybe until Christmas? Just a term; sort my knee; sort Mum and Sorrel and then get myself back to London. Go and find Fabian and tell him I knew my bloody pride *and prejudice* had been to blame... It was all my fault...

By lunchtime I felt as though I'd never been away from the chalkface. Petra came back to the staffroom as the lunch bell sounded, inviting me along to the canteen where I'd be expected to not only do a couple of dinner duties, but actually – on Mason's insistence – sit with the kids and eat as well.

While not overly impressed with the fare on offer – the ubiquitous pizza and chips with a lettuce leaf and half a tomato masquerading as salad – I was more so with the orderly queues and level of noise. Then I understood: Mason Donoghue was not only tucking in at a table with the younger kids, but apparently keeping a friendly, if steely eye on the older ones as well. (I'd not thought it possible for an eye to be both friendly and steely until I'd seen Mason in action.)

'Mason insists he's in situ here every lunchtime,' Petra explained. 'And if he can't be, then at least one of us from the senior leadership team must be.' Her tone was reverential as she spoke of her leader, who now was making his way over to a girl sitting at a table by herself looking solitary, a look of defiant anger on her pretty face.

Sorrel.

Petra put a warning hand on my arm. 'Leave her, Robyn. Mason's going to chat with her. The last thing she needs is her big sister fussing over her. That really would have her heading for the hills. Pizza and chips?'

And I would have found myself calmer, more able to meet the challenge, had I not followed Petra back to the staffroom for the last ten minutes of the lunch hour and overheard a conversation.

'Woah, he is *fit*,' one of the younger members of staff was saying as four of them stood gathered around a table, perusing the front page of *The Daily Herald*. 'What's he called?'

'Carrington,' another said, reverentially. 'Fabian Mansfield Carrington. Blimey, look at those eyes. He looks like Jamie Dornan...'

'Who?'

'You know! That gorgeous actor in *Fifty Shades*. Hell, I wouldn't kick *him* out of bed.'

'You should be so lucky,' another scoffed. 'But yes, I know what you mean. He's all dark and smouldering...'

'You're *joking*.' A petite Asian girl in the white coat of a science teacher was indignant. 'How could you fancy him? He's defending that misogynistic murderer Rupert Henderson-Smith. How could you want to be anywhere near, let alone in bed with, someone who's making a shedload of money trying to get that bastard off? Blood money. What about the poor families who've lost their daughters? For heaven's sake, what's the matter with all of you?'

19

Thursday morning, 5.30 a.m. Fabian was there with me, his dark eyes full of love, and I lay, my own shut tight, desperate for the images that played behind them to crystallise into the actuality of his being beside me. Then, in his apartment, I'd wake from sleep knowing he was smiling down at me, watching me in the already light hours of another summer's day in the capital. He'd reach for me, pulling me out of sleep and towards him, and make love to me in such a way that, still half asleep, I wasn't quite sure where I ended and he began. I was a part of him, and I never wanted to be without him ever again.

I tried desperately to hang onto the dream but, like a fading memory that refuses to focus and eventually disintegrates, he was gone. I opened my eyes to being alone, back in Beddingfield, with the nausea-inducing knowledge of my first day in a new job I didn't want. I turned over, my knee aching and heavy, unwilling to get out of bed and into the first-day-in-a-new-job outfit I'd carefully set out neatly for myself, before allowing myself the luxurious, but dangerous, game of 'What if?'

There'd never been any side to Fabian; never been any time

when I'd thought he might have been flattering me simply to get me into bed, to make me fall in love with him. As far as I knew he'd always been honest with me (apart from pretending, that first night in Graphite, he didn't know who I was) and had so much integrity, which, knowing I'd deliberately not told him about my grandfather murdering my grandma and her lover, I'd not been able to match.

His bloody integrity, I reminded myself crossly, had vanished down the pan when he'd taken on the defence of a misogynistic and sadistic murderer. This thought had me more than awake and, by the time the shrill call of my alarm shattered the tiny box room – as well as my lovely memories of Fabian – I was well and truly brought rudely back down to earth with the reality of my new but unlooked-for life.

With a deep sigh of resignation, I headed for the bathroom before waking Sorrel. She took more than a couple of shakes and threats to have her up out of her pit, but she did eventually acquiesce. And, once up, came down sporting not too much make-up as well as eating the porridge I put in front of her.

'You look lovely,' I said, meaning it. 'How did it go yesterday? You said very little on the way home.'

'You didn't ask,' she said.

'I didn't want to treat you like a five-year-old on your first day at school.'

'The history was good,' she conceded grudgingly. 'The rest was shit.'

'OK.'

'And I don't get the maths. Never have. It's a waste of effing time.'

'Well, unfortunately, you'll need it. Have to say, it wasn't my strong point either, Sorrel. Jess is pretty good at maths. Much, much better than me.'

'She's always far too busy to help. And she might have been good at it at school, but it didn't get her anywhere, did it? Ended up with that pillock Dean persuading her not to go to uni, pregnant at nineteen and working in the frozen-food factory as well as at that awful care home.'

'To be fair, Sorrel, it's not that bad. I mean, as care homes go. Not that I've been in many,' I conceded. 'I've said I'll go out to Ilkley Moor on Saturday with Jess and some woman who wants to scatter her parents' ashes over there.'

'Have you? Why?' Sorrel pulled a face of utter contempt.

'You could come with us.' I tried to jolly her along. 'You know, make a family outing of it? Lunch, maybe in Ilkley? I'll treat us all.'

The look on Sorrel's face was so incredulous I nearly laughed. Nearly. Glancing at the kitchen clock, I knew we had to get off, and any further attempts at jollity went right out of my head.

Just an hour or so until kick off.

* * *

I'd tried to suss out the drama studio the previous afternoon but, finding it locked, I'd abandoned the quest, Mason promising he'd get the caretakers to have it unlocked and ready for me in the morning.

So now here I was, in a freezing-cold room in the bowels of the Victorian building. The walls and ceiling of the cellar – for that was what it was – had been painted entirely black but with a tiered and stepped area where the kids would gather at the start of a lesson and which would be used as a stage for performing. An attempt had been made to brighten the place with posters of Oscar-winning actors as well as some large stars painted onto the walls in luminous yellow paint. The effect was spoiled by every known swear word – as well as some new to me – felt-tipped onto each phosphorescent star. The posters themselves were graffitied with moustaches, beards and cigarettes, as well as one particular national treasure, in the role of Lady Macbeth, being treated to an erect penis directed towards her open mouth as she spouted, presumably, immortal lines of the Bard. Those would be coming down straight away, and I immediately set to, tearing at the tattered posters that were only adding to the sense of despondency in what was supposed to be an area of dramatic creativity.

'Ah, sorry, Robyn, I was on my way to do just that.' Mason Donoghue had appeared at my side without my realising.

'I'm amazed you've allowed it,' I said irritably, cross that he'd not got round to removing the posters himself. 'And the graffiti – there's stuff here I've never heard of, let alone considered physically possible.'

'At least the majority's spelled correctly.' Mason attempted humour but, when he saw my face, backtracked. 'I set one of the caretakers to the task during the six-week break, but he left once a vacancy came up at the Frozen factory. Said he'd rather be freezing peas than his "bloody backside off in t'bloody cellar..."' Mason did his best, but failed, to speak the words in a Yorkshire accent and not for the first time I wondered where in the UK he'd originated.

'And yet you expect me to teach down here? Kids to be educated down here?'

'You're a professional, Robyn,' Mason soothed. 'I have every faith you can sort it. No one's been down here since the end of last winter when the boiler broke. We're up and running again now – the heat's been on all morning, not that we can afford it – and I'll help you get these posters down. The kids will be raring to go – they've not had a drama lesson for... well, for a long time.'

'Now I know why you avoided bringing me down to the

"drama department"—' I put air quotes round the words '—when you showed me round the other day. What do the parents think? And your governing body should be sacked.'

'The majority of St Mede's parents have enough problems simply getting through their day without being concerned about a drama room that needs a bit of TLC.'

'A bit of TLC?'

'And there's a vacancy for a teacher rep on the governing body, if you want to put yourself forward?'

Before I could give Mason the short-shrift answer his question deserved, Petra stuck her head around the door.

'Ah, sorry, Robyn,' she apologised in turn. 'I had every intention of staying behind yesterday afternoon to take down those posters and tidy the place up a bit. And then, you know...' she trailed off when she saw my face '...stuff happens. Listen, you're down to cover Year 7 until break.' She turned to Mason. 'Sonya Harrington's just rung in, she's not well *again*.' She turned back to me. 'I'll cover instead and leave you to sort things down here. That OK with you?'

I was about to retort that, no, it was not OK. I could be visiting Mum instead, having some physio on my knee, going back to London and begging Fabian to abandon the madness of defending Rupert Henderson-Smith. But I was a professional; we needed the money; I needed to keep an eye on Sorrel, however covert a mission that turned out to be.

I could do this.

'That's fine.' I nodded towards Mason and Petra. 'That gives me some time to get this place ready.'

* * *

It was unfortunate that my very first lesson was going to be a drama session with a Year 9 group who, according to John Vaughn, Head of Maths – aka Sandy Head – were the 'worst set of wankers' at St Mede's. Ask any high school teacher and they'll generally tell you Year 9 kids are the most obnoxious. They've got through Years 7 and 8 where, as the newest and youngest kids in school, they've been kept in their place by the older pupils. By Year 10, GCSEs are imminent, with all the work that goes with them being piled on, and pressure's mounting. But Year 9 is an in-between phase when, with hormones raging, voices breaking and friendships dissolving, sex is calling, school and parents are being dissed and learning and co-operating are the last things on adolescent minds. John Vaughn had gleefully warned me that St Mede's present Year 9, despite being only two weeks into the new academic year, were particularly obstructive characters.

'Don't listen to him,' Petra had advised. 'John just doesn't know how to handle them. Think back to when *you* were thirteen, going on fourteen and I bet *you* hated the world and his wife? I know I did. And kids today have all the extra complications of social media and cyber bullying at a time when their face is full of acne, they're frightened they're going to start their period in the middle of a maths lesson, lads terrified their willy will never be big enough and, when you're not hungry for your tea, your mum is convinced you're starting with an eating disorder. Which leads you to actually *having* an eating disorder, especially when Gran suggests you've put on a bit of weight...'

I got the picture.

* * *

I found the switches for the overhead lights – four out of the ten weren't working, and neither were the footlights at the base of the tiered steps. The studio was beginning to warm up and, with as much preparation done as possible, I changed into black tights, little black skirt and ballet shoes – I didn't trust what was on the floor to go barefoot – in the drama teacher's tiny room before making my way back down to the studio.

I stretched, I loosened up, I moved and, using an old chair as a barre, went through a variety of routines trying to lose myself in simply becoming at one with my body. My knee hurt like hell, but it wasn't as bad as I'd first thought and I closed my eyes, arms raised as I swayed to the music playing in my head...

'Fuckin' hell, where does Old Hopalong think she is?'

I came back to the present, opening my eyes and turning to see a gaggle of sniggering kids, their noses pressed to the glass window of the door, elbowing each other out of the way to get a better view of this daft bint. I walked over to the door, opened it and was nearly flattened as kids and huge bags threatened to have me arse over tit.

Start as you mean to go on, Robyn, I warned myself, pulse racing.

'OK, this is a drama studio.'

'It's an effing cold cellar, miss.'

'And you will all go out, line up and come back in – without your bags – and sit down on the steps and await my instructions.'

No one moved.

'Now,' I said calmly.

No one moved.

'Now,' I yelled, all the anger and frustration of the past few days pouring out of me like venom.

'No need to shout, miss.' A small under-developed white whippety kid, obviously a ringleader, turned to the others. 'Right, she wants us on the steps.' He proceeded to jump into the lap of a well-built black girl, pulling another whippety kid onto his own knee, and the others soon got the message, piling onto each other until there were four Leaning Towers of Pisa, each pillar in competition to see which could attain the greatest height without falling over.

Which each tower eventually did, spewing its giggling or expletive-bawling teenaged contents onto the dusty steps, and the floor below.

'That were right good, miss, shall we do it again?'

'Fuck off, you've broken me bloody neck.'

Oh, the shame of having to bring in the behaviour support staff in the very first five minutes of my first lesson. No one could hear me down here; no one could come down and rescue me. What was that immortal tagline from *Alien*? 'In space no one can hear you scream...'

I felt my pulse race and wanted to get out of there but, looking on the positive side – if I could manage to salvage *any* iota of positivity – no one, apart from the twenty little sods in my care, knew what an utter dog's dinner I was making of trying to teach drama. Taking a deep breath, I tried once more.

'OK, you lot, the joke's over.' I managed to make myself heard over the chattering and giggling.

But it obviously wasn't. Little Whippety Ringleader was off, racing round the room like a whirling dervish, his bag spinning over his head in the manner of a helicopter blade.

'Oh, for God's sake,' one of the girls eventually said in disgust. 'He's like an effing five-year-old. Grow up, you pillock.'

'He's on something... again,' her mate said, retrieving a copy of *Grazia* from her bag, and the pair of them settled down to peruse the contents together.

Fight or flight?

I fled.

Up the three wooden steps to the teacher's tiny room, grabbed my phone and immediately rang Jess's mobile.

'Jess, I can't do it. I can't *do* it. They're mad. These kids are *feral...*'

'Yes, you can,' she replied calmly. 'You *can* do it. Think back to all your training. And if that doesn't work, go and get the heavies in. Go on, Robyn. Go. You can do it.'

I ended the call, wiping away the tears of anger, frustration and utter sadness that this was where I'd ended up. But instead of making my way back to the tiered steps to face the horde once more, I dithered, uncertain what to do next.

'Hey up, miss? You all right?'

A tall, well-muscled and exceptionally handsome kid stood at the bottom of the three wooden steps and I looked up at him, unable to speak.

'You Sorrel's big sister? I heard you were down here.'

I nodded.

'Right, give me five minutes. Wait there.'

Joel Sinclair, I found out later, was the Cock of St Mede's. You didn't mess with Joel and live. Watching, as I gave Joel the requested five minutes, I saw the class of thirteen-year-olds brought to heel. It was like watching an intelligent but ruthless collie dog rounding up recalcitrant sheep. His back to me, he directed a low, calm voice towards the group so I couldn't catch what he was saying, but his intention was obvious. He finished by turning to me, pointing a neat navy-blazered arm in my direction, his fabulous corn-rowed hairdo moving only slightly as he did so.

'Ms Allen, here, is a top dancer. A West End professional who has been on *Strictly...*'

Sorry?

'...who has taken the lead part in *Matilda...*'

Hang on!

'...and you lot are so fucking lucky to have her here to teach you...'

Hmm, that bit's all right.

'Why's she here, then? In this dump? If she's so famous?' Whippety Snicket sneered and the rest of the group turned for clarification in my direction.

I stepped forwards. 'As you can see, I injured my knee as I executed a *tour jeté*...'

'She's *killed* someone?' I heard a thrilled whisper.

'Killed someone?'

'She just said she'd executed somebody called Atour Jettay!'

'I was on stage in London less than a week ago,' I went on. (If I couldn't get this lot on board by my teaching methods, I'd have to try pulling the alleged fame card.) 'Unfortunately, as you see, I have a knee injury. No professional dancer, like a professional footballer, can carry on with an injury. As a result, I'm having to take a break, and Mr Donoghue asked if I would come and teach you what goes on in London's West End. In Covent Garden. On New York's Broadway.'

'*I'm* going to be a dancer, miss.'

'I'm going to be a film star, miss. Going to be famous, make loads of money and get off with Taylor Swift...' the kid paused and then went on '...and buy me mam a house instead of the council flat we have to live in.'

'Yah.' Whippety Snicket sneered. 'Dancing? Who wants to fucking dance but sissies and girls? I'm going to be a footballer. Take over from Messi at Barcelona.'

'He's not at Barcelona any more, you thicko.'

'Hang on, hang on.' Joel Sinclair put up a hand and addressed Whippety. 'How do you think Messi learned to move across the pitch so gracefully? He had dance lessons...'

Hang on, kid: do not tell this lot I taught Messi all he knows.

'Did he?' There was silence as the kids in front of me digested this unexpected nugget of information. 'Nah, he didn't...'

'So, you think only girls and sissies dance?' Joel raised an eyebrow and then, bending, slowly removed his black brogues and socks before steadying himself, taking several steps and leaping away towards the back of the room, performing a series of totally professional *jetés*.

Well, that shut them up, as nothing else had done!

20

With a quarter of an hour of the fifty-minute lesson already gone, I gave the kids instructions and, under Joel's watchful eye, the group gathered in front of me. I took them through a series of drama warm-ups with the intention of at least wearing some of them out physically, if not mentally.

For Year 9, the drama lesson should have focus on melodrama, comedy and exaggeration. My lesson plan had been to focus on these elements but I knew, jumping straight into this work, I was on a hiding to nothing and, instead, did the sort of stuff I'd used previously with much younger children.

Some of these kids were so unfit: mums or dads driving them to school; their breakfast, if any, a Mars bar and a bottle of pop consumed in the car while plugged into iPhones and iPads. Most of the St Mede's playing fields had been sold off decades ago, and persuading the pupils into the regulation games kit and onto what bit of grass was left was, according to Petra, a constant battle.

So in the time I had left, I introduced name games and team-building games and kept the fitness required to a minimum. I think we were all surprised when the bell for the end of the session sounded and we'd made some progress. This was not going to be easy, but at least the kids thought I was somebody famous and I'd managed to survive a lesson with the worst class in the school.

My knee was beginning to give me gyp, but I gathered my things and made my way to the staffroom for coffee.

'Have you survived?' Petra asked, eyebrow raised as I fell into a chair and she passed me a mug of coffee and a Twix.

'Just about.' I decided to be honest. 'I wouldn't have, if I'd not had some help from one of the older kids.'

'Oh?'

'Joel Sinclair?'

'Ah.'

'What do you mean: *Ah*?' I raised my own eyebrow in her direction. 'He soon gave that Year 9 lot short shrift.'

'Well, he would.'

'Would he?'

'He's an exceptionally bright boy...'

'And has the potential to be a superb dancer, from the little I saw.'

'Hmm.' Petra's eyes narrowed.

'Hmm, what? What?'

'He's a gang member.'

'Gang member?' I laughed. 'Aren't all kids in gangs? I know I used to be. What were we called...? The Beddingfield Barbies? Yes, that was it.'

'Presumably when you were at junior school?' Petra asked. 'And you had secret codes and knitted badges and were best friends forever, deliberately leaving out the kids who nobody liked and who were always chosen last for rounders?'

'Something like that.' I laughed again. 'I suppose we were a bit mean to the ones who didn't pass muster.'

'Yes, well, this is a bit more serious. Joel's already been up in front of the youth court for possession with intent to supply. His dad's in prison for the same sort of stuff and *his* mates, seemingly, are big into OC. Our worry is that they're now grooming Joel.'

'OC?'

'Organised crime. Where've you *been*, Robyn?' Petra frowned. 'I went over all this with you yesterday in Safeguarding.'

'Well, I didn't think it would actually be happening here, in Beddingfield. Little Micklethwaite,' I corrected myself. 'I assumed it was just precautionary stuff.'

'As I say, where've you been? We have to be police and social workers as well as teachers and constantly on our guard in all schools, but particularly ones like St Mede's.'

'Ones like St Mede's?' I stared at Petra. 'And I've encouraged Sorrel to come here? With all her problems?'

'Far better than the pupil referral unit in town, which, from what I hear, is a hotbed of trouble.'

* * *

All too soon, break was over and I joined the streams of kids making their way to their next lesson. I was down for a double lesson of English with Year 7 and, while the curriculum I was being expected to teach appeared dull, I'd done my homework and was well prepared.

Compared to the Year 9 drama class, these new-to-St-Mede's-kids were pliable, still finding, not only their feet, but their way around the school.

'You're late,' I barked at the bespectacled lad who was only just making his way into the classroom, determined I wasn't standing for any nonsense from the get-go.

'Sorry, miss, I got lost... and... and...' He broke down in tears.

'And...' he sniffed, holding up a brand-new white trainer, which he'd just retrieved from his sports bag '...she's shit in me shoe again.'

'I *beg* your pardon?' I stared at the kid, thinking if the English lesson had been focusing on alliteration, we'd have been off to a flying start.

'Uggh!'

'Gross, miss!'

'Oh, pooh...!'

A chorus of distaste and revulsion spread round the room like wildfire. (Similes, then?)

'Who did this?' I asked, glaring at the rest of these eleven-year-olds. 'And all of you, stop that noise right now.' Amazingly, they did, their eyes moving from me to the poor kid – Alfie, according to the curling name sticker on his blazer – snivelling in front of me.

Was he going to be a grass? The class held its collective breath.

'Write down who did it?' I suggested. 'But first, go and put that trainer outside and we'll deal with it later. And the rest of you, you have just five minutes to write down as many authors as you can think of.'

'Come on, Alfie.' Once he'd returned to the classroom, sans stinky trainer, I placed paper and pencil in front of him.

'Little Shove Horn?' I whispered, staring down at Alfie as he pushed the paper back towards me.

Alfie nodded, wiping his eyes.

'It's his baby sister, miss,' the class chorused. 'Siobhan. Little Siobhan. She's really cute.'

Wanting to giggle, as well as thanking God I didn't have to hunt out and bollock the perpetrator, I turned once more to the class. 'OK, we have fronted adverbials on the menu today.'

'Is that what's for dinner, miss? I'm right hungry, me.' A tall child who looked as if he really was in need of a good meal shouted out from the back.

'Well, for a start, let's not have any calling out. Jack, is it?' I scrutinised his name written in childish lower case on his sticky label, which, after almost two weeks of wear, was looking pretty tatty. I turned to the class. 'You're at high school now, and you'll have had St Mede's behaviour policy explained to you? Yes? No?'

Several heads nodded at me in response, but it was clear some of the kids didn't know what I was talking about.

'C1,' I reminded Jack and the rest of the class, 'is a verbal warning issued if you shout out or *waste the opportunity to learn* as well as *damage others' opportunities*.' I'd learned this little homily off by heart the previous evening and could already spout it verbatim.

Blank faces all round.

'Miss—' a hand was raised '—d'you mean we'll be in the doodah if we muck about?'

I wanted to laugh. At least he'd had the sense not to say *in the shit*. 'Absolutely, young man,' I said with a straight face. 'So, let's get on. Sit up, you can't listen and learn slouched over your desks. So, no, we don't *eat* fronted adverbials, however hungry we might be. We use them in our writing.'

'I hate writing, miss,' Jack shouted out, but at least had accompanied this with a raised hand.

Ignoring him, I went on, 'You will have all been taught what a fronted adverbial is at your primary school. You'll have needed to know them for your SPAG SATS exam, but let's have a reminder. Anyone remember?' I looked round hopefully but was met with a sea of blank stares, eyes dropping onto wooden desks as my own attempted to meet each one in turn.

'No? OK, let's break the phrase down. Fronted? Frontal?'

'Full frontal, miss? That's rude, my mum says.' The tiny little girl on the front row sporting a perfect pair of blonde plaits looked most put out.

'Just means *in the front*.' I smiled. 'Now, we all know what an adverb is, don't we?'

We obviously didn't.

'OK, a verb?'

'A doing word?' A red-haired lad raised his hand.

'Exactly. OK, I want a doing word from every one of you.'

'Eat.'

'Munch.'

'Chew.'

'Doesn't *have* to be about eating,' I remonstrated.

'Breakfast.'

'No, that's not really...'

'Dinner.'

'Hungry...'

'No!'

'Pizza...'

'Whoah, whoah.' I put my own hands up to stop them. 'You can't *pizza* something...'

'I have pizza every night for my tea.'

A hand shot up. 'Miss, there's a bug on my desk.' The girl stood, scraping back her chair in dramatic horror. 'I've got arachnophobia,' she explained proudly.

'I've got eczema,' another said, holding up an arm with a rolled-back shirtsleeve and scratching dutifully at the red rash on his wrist.

'OK, OK, what's the bug *doing*?' I asked, in an attempt to get back to the lesson in hand.

'Crawling, miss,' the kid in front bellowed.

'And how's it crawling?' I asked.

'Quickly, miss.'

'That's an adverb. Great, let's have more.'

'Silently.'

'Crazily.'

'Sexily,' a boy named Stefan called out, crossing his eyes in what I assumed he thought the throes of passion required.

Hoots of mirth all round.

'So, bugs.' Thinking on my feet, I decided to abandon bloody boring fronted adverbials, clapping out a rhythm as I spoke:

> *'Bed bugs, red bugs, crawling on your head bugs.*
> *Rat bugs, bat bugs, riding round in hat bugs.*
> *Blue bugs, glue bugs, those that give you flu bugs.'*

I turned to the whiteboard, writing as the kids gave me ideas:

> *'Pink bugs, sink bugs, swimming in your ink bugs*
> *Stew bugs, poo bugs...'*

'Really?'

> *'Flush 'em down the loo bugs.'*

We were on a roll and I was enjoying myself as much as they were. With five minutes of the lesson to go, the kids stood, clapping out the rhythm, clicking fingers, patting knees and moving to the beat while acting out the words.

I looked up at the open classroom door where Mason Donoghue, accompanied by two other adults, stood smiling, totally engrossed in the lesson. Mason put two thumbs up before moving away.

'That were great, miss,' Jack said. 'Are you tekking us for English all the time?'

I had, it seemed, survived the first morning in my new job.

* * *

By the end of the school day, I felt I'd never been away from teaching. You're not a probationary teacher, I constantly reminded myself, and, gaining confidence with each class, I went for it, keeping order as much as I could. In a Year 11 GCSE English class studying Mary Shelley's *Frankenstein*, I finally felt I'd found my feet. I decided we'd spend the last half-hour of the lesson changing one of the pertinent chapter's narrative into script, letting the main characters act out the story.

I'd been surprised to see Joel Sinclair sitting at the back of the room – I hadn't expected the alleged gang member to have any interest in studying the nineteenth-century English novel – but, giving no indication we'd met earlier in the day in very different circumstances, he joined in fully with the discussion, contributing sensible answers and taking the part of Captain Robert Walton with aplomb.

As the class made their way out, I called Joel back, wanting both to thank him for his intervention with the awful Year 9 drama group, and to find out where he'd learned to dance, but, with a wave of his hand, he was out of the classroom without a backward glance.

* * *

Thank God for Jess and her love of cooking: the thought of getting back to Mum's place and having to start preparing something for Sorrel and myself to eat had been filling me with almost as much dread as taking Year 9 again. But Jess had come up trumps, messaging me to say she was more than happy to cook, and for

Sorrel and me to go round there every evening she wasn't working. We'd have a kitty, share the shopping and, in return, maybe I could do some babysitting of Lola?

Sorrel hadn't hung around for a lift home and wasn't answering her phone. I did the day's marking, not wanting to take it home with me, and was just about to leave the classroom when Mason appeared in the doorway.

'Knackered?' he asked, grinning.

'Something like that.' I managed a weary smile.

'I knew you'd be OK.'

'You knew nothing of the sort.' I sniffed. 'You didn't see my drama session with the notorious Year 9 class this morning.' I glared up at him. 'And I see you've put me down for every single Year 9 drama class next week?'

'You're the expert.' He smiled winningly. 'You're the drama professional. And,' he went on, 'I did see what you were up to this morning. I came down to see if you were OK in the drama studio. You were totally engrossed, as were the kids. You'd got them moving, talking, doing what you wanted.'

'I'd had some help.'

'Oh?'

'Joel Sinclair?'

'Really?' Mason frowned.

'That was exactly Petra's reaction when I told her.'

'Let's just say he's not always as accommodating.'

'He's been nothing but accommodating with me today.'

'Good, that's good. Is there anything I can support you with? Anything you want to ask?' I glanced up at Mason Donoghue, thinking, not for the first time, what a lovely face he had. If my head hadn't been stuffed to the gills with Fabian, I knew I'd have fancied this man. 'Look,' he now said, 'I don't suppose you could get your dad in?'

'In?' I pulled a face. 'In where?'

Mason indicated with his hands. 'Here. Into school.'

'My dad?' I stared. 'Jayden, you mean?'

'Of course, I mean Jayden. Jayden Allen? It would be great if he could come and give us a talk about the history of black music. Of the roots of reggae.'

'Great for whom?' I smiled. 'The kids? Or for you?'

'For the kids, of course.' He had the grace to look slightly abashed. 'I think it would be brilliant for our students to learn how reggae music emerged in the sixties, from Jamaican ska and rocksteady, how it was influenced by social, political and cultural factors, including the Rastafarian movement.'

'You seem to know quite a bit about it already.' I smiled. 'Just do an assembly and play some Bob Marley. Getting hold of my dad, never mind pinning him down to anything, is virtually impossible.'

* * *

So it was something of a surprise to see Jayden's car pulled up on Mum's drive. He was sitting in the kitchen, drinking tea and eating toast and Marmite.

'Where's Sorrel?'

'What are *you* doing here?'

'I've been worried about you all.'

'Must be the first time you have,' I said tartly, moving over to the kettle and then ditching that idea and reaching for the bottle of wine in the fridge instead. 'Jesus, I needed that.' I allowed the first mouthful of the cold, crisp liquid to do its job, following it with another before putting down my glass and turning back to my dad. 'I reckon I could turn to drink,' I said. 'Seems all I have left in the world to rely on.'

'You're teaching, then?' Jayden asked, acknowledging the text I'd sent earlier, while ignoring my self-pitying moaning. 'You went with that head teacher's offer?'

'I didn't really have a great deal of choice.'

'So, where is she now?'

'Sorrel? Your guess is as good as mine. She's behaved herself the past couple of days. Frightened of being kicked out and put in the PRU, I guess. She's not daft, you know, Jayden. The history teacher, particularly, was full of praise for her. I need you to sit down with her... Are you staying? Because if you are, you're in the single bed in the box room... and try to get to the bottom of where she keeps going to. There was a bloke in a BMW – well, I assume it was a bloke – giving her a lift home the other night—'

'She's *fifteen*, Robyn,' Jayden snapped. 'What's a fifteen-year-old doing out at night with a man in a BMW? Why didn't you stop her?'

'Me? Why don't *you* stop her? Why aren't *you* here for her? And don't start coming the heavy father at this late stage in the day.' When Jayden didn't say anything, but simply glared in my direction, I went on, 'Is it any wonder Sorrel's going off the rails with *you* for a father? *And* Mum believes she's failed as a mother because Sorrel is running wild.'

'I'm sorry.'

'Too late to be sorry, Jayden.'

'I've tried to support you girls, tried my best to work and send Lisa money...'

'It was love and affection she wanted, not your money. You should have left her alone, Jayden; given Mum the chance to meet someone else. Heaven knows she's gorgeous enough to have the pick of any man around.'

'I'm not proud of my behaviour, Robyn. I didn't want to...

didn't want to lose you three girls. You're my daughters, my family...'

'Oh, spare me the sentimentality,' I snapped. 'You know Mum had a dire childhood with those parents of hers.'

'As did I, *without* parents,' Jayden put in mulishly.

'More reason for you to make an effort with your own family, then.' I glared at him. 'With Mum. And with *us*, Jayden.'

I held up the bottle of Sauvignon Blanc in Jess's direction as she came through the kitchen door. 'Come on, we need to work out how we're going to sort Sorrel out. Mum can't come out of hospital to find her in more trouble – that would probably finish her off.'

21

'What are *you* doing back here again so soon?' Jess pulled a face in Jayden's direction. 'Saw your car parked up.' She nodded towards the bottle and, ignoring Jayden, addressed me. 'How'd it go? You know, after you rang me this morning? Was it OK?' She glanced around the kitchen. 'Sorrel not back?'

I poured wine for Jess and Jayden – no point in pretending he wasn't there. 'Yes, I survived, with the help of one of the older kids.'

'One of the older kids? Really?' Jess pulled another of her faces, sipping at her wine.

'And I don't know where Sorrel is.'

'Why didn't you bring her back with you?' Jess was indignant. 'Isn't that one of the reasons you took the job? You know, to keep an eye on her and bring her home after school? Food's ready in half an hour. You staying?' she added, turning to our father.

'I can't be her minder.' I closed my eyes briefly. 'By the time I'd done my marking, cleared up and had a debrief with Mason, she'd gone.'

'Where?' Jayden and Jess spoke as one.

'I *don't know*!' I sat down, heavily. 'She's almost sixteen. She has a right to meet up with her friends after school.'

'What friends?' Jess tutted. 'Sorrel's never been a girly girl – you know, off with her "*bestie*".' Jess air quoted the word, obviously irritated with the world and his wife. 'God, I hate that word: Bloody *bestie*, for heaven's sake. I really don't know who her mates are any more. She's not brought anyone round since she was fourteen. Mum and I were always asking her if she wanted a friend over for a sleepover but she never did. There was a big bust-up and falling-out with her gang of girls when they got to the end of Year 9 – Mum had to go into Beddingfield High to try to sort out what was going on. I don't think we ever got to the bottom of it, and then Sorrel seemed to close in on herself. The happy little girl she'd been – you know, always doing cartwheels on the lawn or dancing and putting on shows for us – disappeared overnight. We just put it down to hormones and adolescence and' – she glared in Jayden's direction – 'not having a supportive father who was here for her.'

'He's never been here, Jess,' I protested, 'so you can't really blame Jayden for Sorrel suddenly going off the rails.'

'Oh, I think I can.'

'More likely her seeing Mum go downhill: worried she'd be left alone if Mum had to go back into hospital?'

'*I've* always been here for her, Robyn,' Jess protested hotly. 'I've had to take on the role of both father and mother for Sorrel. You know, when Mum couldn't cope or was back in hospital, she came round to me... and I was more than happy to have her with us.'

'What about Dean? Was *he* happy that you were parenting Sorrel as well as doing everything else you do?'

'Dean's a pillock,' Jess snapped tersely. 'Always has been and always will be. And I'm glad to be finally shot of him. The barmaid's welcome to him. But I'm keeping him in my life for

Lola's sake – I don't want *her* going off the rails once she goes to high school next September.'

'OK, I totally get that,' I soothed. 'And you've done a fantastic job with Sorrel – been a second mother to her and provided her with a secure home when Mum wasn't always up to it. But at the end of the day, once she hit those awful teenage years, you really can't blame yourself for what she's been getting up to.'

'I tried to do everything.' Jess dashed away an angry tear. 'It's not been easy – *you* were off having a ball and *he*' – she jabbed an angry finger in Jayden's direction – 'was off jamming and gigging and doing whatever else it is that he does...'

'Earning a living, Jess,' Jayden protested. 'I can't bring any money in by singing in Beddingfield village hall.'

'Come on, Jess,' I soothed. 'You know Jayden's always on the road, or recording in London.'

'Enjoying himself while doing it though. Not really like hard work, is it?'

'Actually, it's bloody hard work, Jess. I get fed up with it at times.'

'Sorry, Jayden, if you're looking for sympathy, you'll find it in the dictionary between shit and syphilis.' She glared once more at Jayden. Blimey, she obviously really needed to vent all her frustration and anger at where life had taken her. 'And *I've* had to pick up all the pieces,' she spat angrily, reaching for her wine glass and draining the contents. She turned, now looking daggers at the pair of us.

'I know, I know, Jess, and I'm sorry I wasn't here more to help,' I said. 'I should have been.' I went to give her a hug but, after a brief response, she pushed me away with the usual self-deprecatory tutting.

'Yes, well, I don't blame you.' Jess sniffed, trying to smile. 'And, if I'm coming over as being bitter and jealous, I'm sorry. I don't mean to – you know, don't want to rain on your parade, as it were. You had your dream of the West End; no point in hanging round this backwater. Funnily enough, our waitress in Pizza Express in town, a couple of weeks ago, was an out-of-work actor. Lovely girl, bags of personality, but I wanted to tell her, especially as she now has a four-year-old at home, that her dreams of hitting it big in the West End, or even in Leeds or Manchester, were just about over.'

'Oh, never burst someone's bubble, Jess. And I *am* sorry,' I went on, meaning it. 'It's not been easy for you. But you wouldn't be without Lola, would you?'

'That's a jolly silly question, Robyn. Of course, I wouldn't be without her, but, had I not got pregnant at nineteen – and convinced myself I was in love with Dean – I'd have been off, studying food sciences. I was always really good at chemistry – did it at A level, if you remember – and was fascinated by the actual science behind creating food dishes. God, what I'd give to have a meal at Heston Blumenthal's place.'

'Heston Blumenthal? Goodness, really? And there was me about to—' I broke off. Why tell Jess that Fabian had been somewhat cavalier about booking a table there and, worse, I'd not been overly interested or particularly excited at the prospect.

'About to what?' Jess stared.

'About to offer you egg and chips over at Mum's for tea one night,' I lied.

'You know, I've read everything about Blumenthal,' Jess went on, obviously cheering up as she spoke of her chef hero. 'Got all his books and tried out all his recipes. When I get fed up, when I can't see anything beyond the day-to-day reality of my life, I get out his recipe books, try another one; adapt them, even.' Jess gave a little self-conscious laugh and, when Jayden and I didn't scoff, she continued. 'Did you know he's been described as a *culinary alchemist*? His recipes are created by identifying molecular similarities between different ingredients and bringing them together. His white chocolate with caviar is to die for. I once saved up my housekeeping for weeks to buy some caviar.' She laughed again, Jess's indomitable spirit chasing away her bad temper, as it always did.

'But you're such a brilliant cook, Jess.' Jayden, who up until then had said very little – I think he'd always been slightly frightened of Jess – patted her arm soothingly. 'How about looking into starting your own business again? You know, outside catering? You were planning to do that at one point. I'll try to help you financially as much as I can.'

'Yes, I was talking about that, before Covid hit and scuppered everything.' Jess shook her head. 'Jayden, I don't have the energy, let alone the money, to see to Mum, Lola and Sorrel as well as the shifts at the care home, to even *think* about starting up a new business. Anyway, folks round here can't afford the luxury of outside catering any more. Have you seen the price of an avocado and truffle oil these days? As well as the cost of petrol to get to these rich people's houses out in the sticks?'

'There's always someone with money who wants their dinner cooking,' I enthused. 'Promise me, once we've sorted Mum and Sorrel, you'll look into it again? I'll help you, too.'

'You?' Jess actually laughed, bending down to kiss my cheek. 'You daft thing. With that knee? And what do *you* know about gourmet food? You've never even watched *MasterChef*, have you? And, I bet, in your fridge in London, there was nothing more than a heel of mouldy Cheddar and a jar of Nutella...'

'There was a jar of Hellmann's,' I started indignantly. 'Put a dollop of mayo onto anything and you've a fabulous meal. It was a *new* big jar as well. Tanya, at the flat, will have got well stuck into that by now,' I added crossly.

'Anyway, you've never been interested in food. Probably why you're so skinny and why I look like I do.' Jess patted her generous behind contemplatively. 'You and Sorrel got Mum's genes. Who the hell *I* inherited this big backside from is anyone's guess.'

'Actually, I did start becoming more interested in food watching Fabian when he cooked. He was a superb cook.'

'What? The Posh Bucks Buccaneering Barrister' – Jess started to laugh, falling over the alliterative consonants – 'could cook? I thought he'd have had his meals shipped in from Harrods on a daily basis? Or from some little chichi deli in Knightsbridge?'

'No,' I said, indignant on Fabian's behalf. 'Jess, you're as prejudiced about people as Fabian liked to suggest *I* was.'

But Jess, glancing at the kitchen clock, wasn't listening. 'Right, come on, food'll be spoilt if we don't eat. We can't wait any longer hoping Sorrel will be back. Lola's laying the table.'

* * *

'You've laid the table beautifully, Lola.' I smiled, admiring the artistic way my niece had arranged cutlery, dishes and even a bunch of late-blooming pink roses from Jess's tiny garden on the crisp starched tablecloth. 'Blimey, who starches tablecloths these days?' I grinned, enjoying the feel of the stiff cotton fabric between my fingers.

'I do' – Jess sniffed – 'and make no apologies for it. How you serve and present food is almost as important as the food itself. What's the point of cooking with wonderful ingredients if the first thing you see is a plastic plate on a polyester tablecloth?'

'Smells good anyway.' I grinned. 'Jesus, I tell you, after a day like today, I need a reward like this.' I felt my face fall as I remembered. 'I'm already dreading facing the hordes again tomorrow.'

'Well, at least it's Friday. One more day and then you can stay in bed and rest and read and do whatever you do to relax.'

'Dance,' I said glumly. 'I usually dance to relax.'

'Oh, yum,' I countered greedily as Jess placed dishes of food in front of us. She was trying to be casual, trying not to care too much that she'd obviously spent the last couple of hours concocting something to impress us, but really desperate for our approval.

'I thought you were off your food.' Jess smiled. 'So in love, you can't eat?'

'Oh, for two minutes there I wasn't thinking about him, Jess. Now you've reminded me.' I put down my knife and fork, my throat constricting with longing for Fabian and the reality of knowing I'd lost him.

'Was he gorgeous, Aunty Robyn?' ten-year-old Lola asked through a mouth full of the most divine linguine, her eyes wide with anticipation and interest. 'How do you *know* when you're in love? Does your heart beat faster?' She wiped at her mouth with the white paper napkin she'd spent ages – and very artistically – trying to origami into a swan. 'I don't think I'll bother falling in love,' she added once she'd swallowed and reloaded her fork. 'You have to do that thing in bed with them, don't you? And then they bugger off with the barmaid.'

'Oy, language,' Jess and I both remonstrated as one, while Jayden started to laugh.

'Or do something that makes you hurt your knee and run away.' Lola glanced hopefully in my direction, obviously wanting to know what had been so bad I'd come back home.

'Lola, elbows off the table, don't talk with your mouth full.' I loved the way Jess had brought Lola up to have such beautiful manners. No different, really, from how Lisa had insisted we two girls behave at the table when we were kids. She might have brought us up single-handedly, but our mum had always insisted on manners and good behaviour.

'Did he get someone else pregnant?' Lola was now asking.

'Did who get someone pregnant?' Jayden, Jess and I all turned in Lola's direction; she'd now gone slightly pink.

'The boyfriend you were so in love with, Aunty Robyn? Amie Thompson, in my class, said she bet that's what happened.'

'Enough, Lola.' Jess shot a look in her daughter's direction.

'Or was he cheating on you?'

'No, Lola,' I managed to get out. 'Fabian and I held very different views on very important issues. Sometimes you just have to be true to yourself.'

'Even if you're mad about him?'

'*Especially* if you're mad about him. And if his family have been unpleasant to you,' Jess now put in.

'Is this boyfriend of yours really helping that awful man, who's done horrible things to ladies, to not go to prison? He's on *his side*?' Lola pulled a face of dramatic horror.

'It's a bit more complicated than that,' I started to say, wanting to defend Fabian when he wasn't here to defend himself.

'Little girls like you shouldn't know about horrible men like... like *him*,' Jess put in.

'Rupert Henderson-Smith?' Lola was scornful. 'You can say his name, Mum; he's on the news and in the paper. I read all about him in last Saturday's *Guardian*.'

'*The Guardian*? Expensive!' I raised an eye in Jess's direction.

'Only paper worth reading,' she parried. 'Love the culture magazine and the recipes. I forgo something at Aldi for my Saturday treat. And *you*,' she went on, turning to Lola, 'shouldn't be reading about what that perverted dreadful man did.' Jess was slightly flustered. 'OK. More of this, anyone?'

'Anyway, it's all right, Aunty Robyn.' Lola grinned across at me. 'Mum says Mr Donoghue really fancies you and you'll probably end up with him and forget all about the sexy barrister.'

'Lola, *enough*.' Jess was totally red-faced. 'I told you that in confidence. I thought you were old enough and grown up enough for a bit of adult conversation without telling Aunty Robyn what we'd been discussing.'

'Discussing?' I breathed. 'That's gossiping.'

'But spot on, Robyn.' Jayden grinned. 'It was obvious from the get-go.'

'No, it wasn't,' I snapped. 'It's you he's after, Jayden; he wants you to go into school to talk to the kids about the history of West Indian music.'

'I'm up for that,' Jayden said. 'You arrange it and I'll peruse my diary.'

'What?' I shook my head in despair.

'So,' Jayden went on, removing plates to the kitchen sink before sitting down once again. 'That meal, Jess, confirms what I keep saying about you and cooking. You need to turn professional.'

'I'm not a footballer.' Jess pulled a face but I knew she was pleased at the praise.

Jayden looked at his watch. 'It's going up to eight. Where's Sorrel?'

'Jayden, Mum had this most evenings and didn't get anywhere.' Jess was cross again.

'I'm going out looking for her.' He went to stand. 'She's not been home since school finished.'

'Oh? And where will you start?' I asked.

'Well,' he conceded, sitting down again and reaching for his roll-ups, 'as soon as she gets in, I'm having words.'

'Not in here, Jayden,' Jess instructed, eyeing the cigarettes.

'Lola, go and make sure your reading's done, then start getting ready for bed.'

'But I want to stay here and listen...'

'Go. Now.'

'OK,' I said, turning to Jayden once Lola was out of earshot. 'You know, Jayden, we never really knew how you met Mum?'

Jayden settled himself back on the kitchen chair. 'I met your mum when she was just sixteen. Sorrel's age, just about.'

'Gosh, that *is* young. How old were you?' Jess was disapproving.

'Almost twenty.'

'Too old for her,' I said, pulling a face. 'Would you like to think of Sorrel being with some boy – some bloke – four years older?'

'It was different then. Well, it seemed to be. Every gig I managed to get in the pubs and clubs around here, in Bradford, across in Huddersfield, your mum turned up.'

'Really? By herself? Going into pubs and clubs by herself? At sixteen?'

Jayden nodded. 'Sometimes with a girlfriend, but usually by herself.'

'What were her parents thinking of? Letting her do that?'

'She hated them.' Jayden looked longingly at his roll-ups but they remained where they were. 'As you know, she was adopted at birth.'

'Yes, we know.' Jess was impatient, looking at her watch, eyeing the pile of washing up waiting in the sink.

'Her adopted father was a head teacher.'

'Really? We never knew *that*. I mean, we always had some idea that he was a teacher, but not actually running a school. Not actually a headteacher. Fancy that!'

'At one of the most prestigious public schools in the area. He was incredibly strict with your mum; she was their only child, was actually a pupil at the school...'

'Mum went to *public school*?' I stared. 'She didn't! When we've talked about where she went to school, she's always said the local comp where she grew up near Sheffield. Blimey, no wonder she's so articulate... I can't believe she kept that to herself. Why did she lie about it? Why have *you* never told us, Jayden?'

'She just didn't want to be reminded of who her parents were, never wanted you girls to have anything to do with them. Really unpleasant bloke he was, by all accounts, and Lisa's mum wasn't much better. Once she ran away from them when she was seventeen, she never went back. You might not think it, but your mum is a survivor and Sorrel, well, Sorrel, out of the three of you, is the most like her.'

'Mum is a survivor?' Both Jess and I spoke as one. 'Despite,' I went on, 'you not being there for her?'

'She's a survivor,' Jayden reiterated irritably. 'Look how she brought you two up. I hold my hands up to not being the best dad on the planet.'

Jess gave a cynical squawk of agreement. 'You're not kidding.'

'But your mum gave everything she'd got to bringing you two up.' Jayden reached for his roll-up tin once more. 'We just need to sort Sorrel out now, before Lisa's out of hospital.'

22

Although we were into mid-September and the nights were drawing in, the days here in the very pretty village of Beddingfield were still warm with a wonderfully mellow feel to them. I'd promised to join Jess and the Hattersleys on the ash-spreading trip to Ilkley but, two days later, I wanted to do nothing but sit in the garden and think of Fabian. Also, I was still in shock over Jayden's revelations about Mum's adopted family and longed to get over to the hospital and simply be with her. Traipsing out to Ilkley on some fool's errand ash-scattering of some old folks I didn't even know was not high on my agenda of how to spend Saturday.

Maybe, if my knee allowed, I could also have a little wander down into the village itself? Call in for coffee at the little cafe across from the village green; pick up a couple of things from the store next to the Victorian primary school where all three of us girls had spent our formative years.

But Jess was having none of it.

While she dropped Lola off at Dean's flat, ten minutes' drive away, I walked outside into the garden with my mug of coffee, testing my knee for any sign of improvement, but having to accept there was little, if any. I breathed in the fresh, if somewhat pungent, country air – Philip Rogers, the farmer across the lane, had obviously been out muck-spreading – the pale amber sunlight giving little credence to the coming cold months. The back lawn, always kept meticulously mown and neatly edged by Mum, was bejewelled with early morning dew, but now in need of some TLC. I sighed. Gardening wasn't my thing but I could see I'd have to get the lawn mower out at some stage.

Once she'd returned from taking Lola, and following Kath Hattersley's directions, Jess drove us in Mum's car to the neat bungalow on the edge of the Tythehill estate at the far end of the village. Kath and Rick had arranged to pick us up but, at the last minute, had rung to say Rick couldn't get the car started. Was there any chance Jess could pick them up instead?

'Flipping heck, I can do without this,' Jess said crossly. 'Bad enough being driven there, but at least I could have closed my eyes and nodded off in the back seat. Now I'm going to have to concentrate.'

'Make sure they cough up for the petrol,' I said. 'You're not a charity, Jess.'

'I know, I know, but I'm never any good at asking for money.' She breathed deeply. 'And once we're back, I'm going to have to cover the late shift at Hudson House. Lola's staying the night at Dean's for the first time.'

'You OK with that?' I asked dubiously. 'Will the barmaid be there?'

'I have to move on.' Jess sighed. 'And if Lola is to have any relationship with her father, then I have to let him have access. Also means I can do the late shift at work. Lola used to stay in the box room with Mum once Dean had hopped it and I was on lates or overnights. Mum loved having her there. Anyway, let's think of Ilkley as a treat, as a day out. I've never been to Ilkley Moor. It's supposed to be beautiful and it's a gorgeous day. We could pretend we've arranged to meet some friends and have some time to ourselves – a lovely lunch? – before we drive them back.' Jess's eyes lit up. 'Jayden's come up trumps' – she patted her jeans' back pocket – 'and, sorry, I'm not too proud to accept his cash. I've already done my research – the Ginger Plum Coffee Shop in Addingham sounds bliss.'

* * *

'I'll put Mum and Dad by your feet in the front with you, love, if that's OK?' Kath Hattersley raised her eyes in my direction as Jess opened Mum's car door to the waiting trio: we had an extra passenger, by the look of it. 'You see, Mum always suffered from claustrophobia and she'd hate being locked in the boot. Rick, this is Jess. You know, from Hudson House? Mum's care home? And her sister. Robyn, isn't it? Robyn's *famous*.' She lowered her voice, eliciting the word in hushed reverence. 'A famous dancer in *Covent Garden*.'

'Oh, gosh, not really...' I began, but Kath had moved on, chattering about both her long-departed dad and more recently departed mum.

Rick, I suspected, wasn't overly interested *where* we'd hailed from or that I might be somebody he should possibly have heard of. 'Hello, loves.' The ruddy-faced and heavily tattooed man climbed slowly and painfully into the back seat ('bad back – am an absolute martyr to it') leaving Kath to haul two urns – one terracotta and one plastic – into what little space there was beneath my feet. A tiny woman ('Mum's big sister, Aunty Bea') followed Rick over the front passenger seat of the car silently settling herself in like a wraith, accompanied by a large plaid flask, bulging Tupperware container and some sort of beige travel rug. 'Do you know where you're going or d'you want some help navigating?' Rick asked Jess.

'Waze.' Jess tapped at the navigation app on the dashboard. 'Never go wrong with this.'

'Oh, I wouldn't trust them buggers. You'll end up in a quarry, or down the bottom of a one-way street and not be able to turn round. Look, I'll point you in the right direction, love.'

And he did. Every left and right turn, on every road – major and minor; every T-junction, every motorway turn-off, cautioning Jess each time she went even slightly over the speed limit that 'the rozzers' would be after her. But then, once on the motorway, telling her to put her foot down and 'go for it, girl'.

Jess, I could tell, had never been so relieved to see our destination in front of us, pulling up in the car park as soon as she saw the sign for the Cow and Calf.

'A quick one, is it, then?' Rick rubbed his hands together and I realised we were in a pub car park. 'Send 'em on their way, like? What you having?'

'I'm so bloody stressed,' Jess whispered in my ear, 'I could down the contents of a bottle of gin, smoke a particularly large joint and, given the opportunity, wouldn't turn down a nice selection of Class A drugs.'

I started to giggle, but Jess merely turned back to Rick, smiling beatifically while tapping the steering wheel to indicate she was driving.

'Oh, one won't hurt, love.' Rick alighted the car with a good deal more alacrity than at the start of the journey, bounding off in the direction of the pub door. Thirty seconds later he was back. 'Not got any money on me, Kath; come on, get your purse out.'

'I've not brought my bag,' Kath said in some dismay. 'Both my hands were full of Mum and Dad when I left the house. And I'm *spitting feathers* an' all.'

Rick, Kath and Aunty Bea all turned hopefully in our direction.

Sticking a rictus of a smile on her face, Jess peeled off a twenty-pound note from the stash given to her by Jayden and Rick bounded off once more, returning with a pint and a whiskey chaser for himself, a port and lemon for Kath, a schooner of sherry for Aunty Bea and a Coke each for myself and Jess. No change from the twenty, then.

'I put a little something in that, Jess. You need to keep your strength up, love, after that drive.'

Jess sipped cautiously at the fizzy drink, obviously not happy there was some alcohol hidden in its overly sweet, murky depths. 'I won't be over the limit with one shot,' she reassured both me and herself before, shivering slightly in the damp atmosphere and sneaky cold wind that had suddenly appeared, she gave a warning nod towards big black clouds moving in from the west. 'Looks like rain,' Jess said pointedly. 'Maybe we'd better get on?' We all turned our heads to the left, looking across the road and moorland at the Cow and Calf, the large rocks that could be seen in the distance.

The other three didn't appear ready to go anywhere.

Ashamed that, as a Yorkshire girl, I'd never visited this iconic spot, I'd spent the previous evening, when I should have been getting stuck into a pile of marking, googling its history. 'You know' – I turned to the others – 'according to local legend, the Calf was split from the Cow when a huge giant called Rombald was fleeing an enemy.'

'Right?' Rick appeared more interested in his pint, which he downed quickly before reaching for the whiskey chaser.

'And then,' I went on, warming to the theme, 'he stamped on the rock as he leapt across the valley. You can imagine a great big giant racing across the moor, can't you?'

Kath frowned. 'I think you need a good imagination, Robyn, love, to picture that. Mind you, you're an arty type. So, who was his enemy, then?' She drained her glass of port and lemon and looked expectantly at Aunty Bea, who silently ignored her niece and continued to sip at her sherry.

'Well' – I smiled – 'apparently he was running away from his angry wife.'

'Come back drunk from the pub, had he? What a lad.' Rick gave a whoop of laughter.

'Anyway,' I went on, thinking this would be a great story to embellish and maybe get the kids at school to act out, 'she dropped the stones held in her skirt to form the local rock formation called The Skirtful of Stones.'

'Right.'

Maybe it wasn't such an interesting story after all. I felt a spot of rain and took a surreptitious look at my watch.

'So.' Jess obviously had the same idea. 'Do you think we'd better get on?'

'How about another before we start on the ashes?' Rick looked at Aunty Bea. 'Your round, Bea, is it?'

'I don't mind if I do.' Aunty Bea spoke for the first time since setting off, draining her sherry and offering the empty glass to Rick. No funds appeared forthcoming though, so Jess moved to the front of the car, took out both casks and, handing one each to both Rick and Kath, said, 'Come on, let's lay your mum and dad to rest.'

The five of us crossed the road and headed in the direction of the two huge rocks formed years ago of the local millstone grit. It wasn't an easy walk, Aunty Bea at ninety needing both her stick and

Jess's arm to move slowly forwards, while Rick took up a constant complaint at his every step across the tussocky grass that there'd be hell to pay with his bad back the following day. Kath carried her dad, while Jess, with the hand not assisting Aunty Bea, clutched at the green plastic cask she'd taken from a complaining Rick.

'Where do you think, then, Kath?' Jess stopped to take a breath, wiping the sheen of sweat from her brow, placing a finger down her shirt collar and giving it a shake to allow the drizzly rain down her neck. 'I think your Aunty Bea's had enough now,' she added.

'Should have brought the flask of tea with us,' Bea said somewhat accusingly at Jess. 'You forgot to take it from the car.'

'Yes, come on, Kath, let's get on with it.' Rick was becoming impatient.

Mavis, in big handfuls, was duly sent to the four corners of Ilkley Moor, Kath wiping at her eyes in between each throw. I sent up a silent prayer of thanks that the wind had dropped, while looking round for Rick, who appeared to have vanished through the miserable grey sheet of drizzly rain.

He reappeared from behind the Cow, rearranging his genitals in his trousers and zipping his flies. 'Call of nature,' he called cheerfully. 'Have we done yet, Kath?'

'Dad now.' Kath sniffed. She reached into her dad's urn with her hand but then looked in horror at the rest of us waiting expectantly – if slightly impatiently – for the first throw.

'What's up, Kath? Has he done a bunk?' Rick pulled a frightened face. 'Has he escaped?'

'I can't get him out. I can't get my dad out.'

'Give him here.' Rick took the urn, peering in. 'Well, he's in there, love.'

'Yes, but set solid.'

'Phewff.' Rick made a sympathetic little noise while banging the contents of the urn with his hand. 'What do you think, Jess? You must have come across this before, you know, dealing with all them old codgers up at the home?'

'Can't say I have, Rick. And, to be honest,' Jess went on, catching my eye and trying not to laugh as she peered into the urn and began prodding gently at the solid mass, 'I'm not sure banging Kath's dad on his head is the right way to go about this.' There'd obviously been more than a single shot of alcohol in the Cokes we'd downed because I suddenly had the most awful need to giggle.

Jess did just that, laughing until she had to cross her legs and hand the urn to me.

'You could break the urn around him,' Rick suggested, peering over my shoulder.

'Wouldn't that just leave an urn-shaped lump,' I asked. 'You know, to dispose of?' I tried my very best to look caring, reverential, but found I kept catching Jess's eye. She was in danger, I knew, of peeing her pants and that made me giggle more.

'Give him here.' Aunty Bea suddenly shuffled forward with her walking stick. 'Put him down.'

'Where, Aunty Bea?'

'Here, in front of me.' Kath did as her aunt instructed and then, hanging onto Jess's arm with one hand, Bea lifted her walking stick and started jabbing at the contents of the urn with a most amazing vigour for a nonagenarian.

'Bea, that's my dad,' Kath objected, trying to pull her aunt away from the urn.

'Been wanting to do that for years,' Aunty Bea said as Fred Crowther began to finally crumble. 'Should have hit him round the head years ago when he left me for our Mavis. He asked *me* to marry him an' all.' Bea gazed round defiantly. 'Up on't'moors. You know, near Baildon?'

'You used to go out with my dad?' Kath stared. 'I never knew that.'

'No, neither did our Mavis.' Bea started to laugh, her bony shoulders shaking, her birdlike, arthritic fingers still clutching the walking stick now covered in clumps of white and grey. 'It were all a right long time ago.' Bea patted her niece on the arm. 'Luckily for Fred Crowther I didn't catch on at the same time as our Mavis. That would have been a right to do. Bad enough at our house when Mavis had to tell my mum and dad what she'd been up to. Can you imagine if the pair of us had ended up in the family way? I'd met my Ted just as Fred had to leave for his two years' national service and, by the time our Mavis realised she was expecting you, Kath, I didn't care a jot. Just thanked God it was her and not me.' Aunty Bea grinned, her dentures white against her age-spotted skin. 'Right, let's put him with our Mavis, Kath, and then go and get the flask and sandwiches. I'm fair parched.'

* * *

'God, I didn't think they were going to agree to us leaving them for a couple of hours,' I breathed. 'I thought we'd be stuck with them for ever. *And* we'd have had to pay for their lunch.'

'No way,' Jess said. 'I'm not spending any more of Jayden's money on those three. It's stopped raining, they've got a picnic and a flask and they can have a little snooze for an hour or so before we pick them up.'

'You OK to drive?' I asked.

'Yep. I actually left most of my Coke: never liked alcohol in sweet drinks. Never liked alcohol per se really.' She started laughing again. 'It was seeing Aunty Bea bashing Fred round the head that made me laugh so much. OK,' she said, jumping into the car, 'Addingham and the Ginger Plum Coffee Shop.' She put her foot on the gas and set off at speed. 'I'm starving.'

'Stop, stop,' I shouted a few minutes later. 'Mum's brakes aren't wonderful,' I added as Jess pumped manfully on the brake pedal and we skidded to a halt on the busy A65. 'We're going the wrong way. We have to go through Ilkley and then on to Addingham. This is the way home.'

'Right, right, OK.'

I closed my eyes as Jess executed a dangerous U-turn in the middle of the road.

'What?' she asked, grinning. 'I'm starving.'

'Stop, stop!' I shouted once more as we drove through Ilkley town centre.

'What? What now?'

'Stop!'

'I'm stopped! And on double yellow lines. What?'

'Look!'

'What? Where am I looking?'

I pointed to a huge banner strung out from one side of the road to the other. 'Look. Fortuitous or what?'

We both sat and stared, reading the words in bold black capitals:

YORKSHIRE CHRISTMAS TOPCHEF COMPETITION
Final: Saturday, 16 DECEMBER
HARROGATE CONFERENCE CENTRE
TELEVISED FOR FOCUS NORTH TV
Entries being taken now
DETAILS ON FOCUS NORTH'S WEBSITE

'That's it,' I said excitedly. 'A northern *MasterChef*. This is your chance, Jess.'

'Get out.' Jess laughed. 'No way.' She laughed again. 'Don't be ridiculous. Come on, lunch. My stomach thinks my throat's cut.'

Jess pulled out into the traffic, throwing a V sign at a bloke in a flashy red sports car who peeped his horn loudly as she almost took off his rear bumper. 'Food, I need food!' She grinned. 'Food, glorious food!'

23

September morphed into October, and the only thing keeping me going was the thought of half-term and a week's respite. Respite from the daily grind of planning and executing lessons and the seemingly constant aggro that accompanied the majority of lessons I taught. The Year 9 kids were still the bane of my life, the thorn in my side, my bête-noire (I'd been teaching lessons on imagery) but, also by half-term, I had hope that Mum would be back home with us.

OK, I lie: there were three other things that were keeping me from burying my head under my pillow and, like Sorrel occasionally, refusing to get out of bed. The first was, unbeknown to Jess – and she'd have gone ballistic if she'd had any inkling – I'd entered her for the Yorkshire Christmas TopChef competition: 'to discover the county's best talent through a series of extraordinary cooking challenges, watched over by the north's most prestigious food judges'. While both Sorrel and Mum had said I was mad – *barking* was the word Sorrel had actually thrown at me – and that Jess, when she found out, would be even madder, Jayden had encouraged me to do it. Like a couple of underground resistance plotters, we'd got started on the forms before, in his usual inimitable way, he was off back down to London once more, neatly dodging any flak destined to descend on our heads once my sister found out what we'd done. 'You just cancel if she refuses to have anything to do with it,' Jayden had said airily, reversing off the drive at speed, promising he'd call in at the hospital before hitting the road back to his other life, the one he loved best, once more.

The second good thing was that my knee, after much handling and manipulation by the area's top physio – paid for by Jayden – was beginning to heal. 'You won't be doing anything with that knee, let alone treading the boards, for a good six months at least,' Maria, the physio, had warned, 'but do as you're told, don't try anything daft, do your exercises and you might eventually be able to go back to dancing.'

And the third little glimmer of light in the whole of this ridiculous pantomime darkness I'd found myself catapulted into? Well, unbelievably, Mason Donoghue.

After Lola had let out of the bag that she and Jess had been discussing me in terms of *Robyn and Mason*, I found myself unable to be in his presence without thinking of him as a... well, as a *man* rather than as a head teacher – as my boss, for heaven's sake. Instead of reading through the latest handout on 'Funding and Budgets', or 'How Best to Disarm a Child with a Bladed Article' with the other teachers in an early morning staff meeting, I'd find myself studying Mason, blushing slightly if he looked my way.

What did it say about me that I was lugging my broken heart around in its permanently shattered state, and yet I could sit back and view Mason Donoghue – actually enjoy the view – quite objectively as one very handsome, very hot, red-blooded male? I wasn't the only one: a surreptitious glance around the room revealed the younger, single – as well as those older attached – teachers hanging onto his every word, stumbling over their own if he directed a question their way, pink-faced with pleasure if he praised, as he so often did.

This man had, what was the word? Charisma. Yes, Mason Donoghue was charismatic with a capital C.

Mind you, he didn't think twice about bawling out any member of staff he felt wasn't treating the kids fairly, wasn't teaching how he wanted them to teach; ordering loitering drug-pushers to move on and then reporting them to the police; or breaking up fights between our kids and warring gangs from other schools who had, as one kid told me as he rushed excitedly out of the school gates, scores to settle.

So, my mind wandering from the government directives in front of me, I'd find myself appraising Mason Donoghue, comparing him – sometimes and sometimes not so favourably with Fabian. Both tall and well built. Mason had the upper hand when it came to sheer muscle power. A little subtle eye movement in the direction of our boss's pecs beneath the blue striped shirt was de rigueur as he abandoned his navy suit jacket before either bollocking or praising us.

As far as I knew, from information gleaned from Petra Waters, who was always happy to wax lyrical about the main man, Mason was originally from the south but had migrated to the north for university, settling here after marrying his wife.

'His wife?' I'd asked, trying not to appear too interested or display my little flicker of disappointment.

'Doesn't talk about her much.' Petra had nodded sagely. 'Not even sure they're still together,' she'd confided. 'He's a bit of an enigma – doesn't reveal anything of his personal circumstances.' She'd paused. 'Even to me, as his deputy, and you know, that's what deputies are for – to be there for a bit of offloading when things get tough.' Petra had pulled a face. 'He doesn't wear a wedding ring,' she'd added, knowingly.

'Doesn't mean anything, these days,' I'd replied. 'How many couples do actually marry these days? *And* wear rings to advertise the fact?'

'Well, *I* certainly do,' Petra had said, holding up her left hand as proof. 'Mind you, doesn't stop me looking.' She'd given a dirty laugh. 'Blimey, most disconcerting having a head teacher who looks like Mason does. You know, when you've only ever been used to the dandruffed shoulders, comb-overs and men who've stopped caring about changing the lives of kids and are counting down to a full pension and the excitement of a tour of the Isle of Man in their new camper van.'

I'd laughed at Petra's picture of a species of head teacher that probably went out with the ark but it gave me food for thought. Although I'd determined, on my next visit to Mum, I'd try to get her to open up about the headmaster and his wife who'd adopted her, and from whom she'd run away when she wasn't much older than Sorrel, Mum was equally determined that her past was just that. She had, it appeared, no intention of opening up to us about her life as a child with these adoptive parents.

The weeks slipped by and, before I knew it, October, with its promise of mellow fruitfulness, was halfway through and I felt I'd never been anything else but a high-school teacher. That my former life with Fabian, and as a performer in the West End, was nothing more than a dream, blown into the ether every morning when my alarm went off at 6 a.m. and I was brought back into the reality of my life. What with school, with visiting Mum in hospital and trying to keep Sorrel on the straight and narrow, as well as doing the laundry and making some sort of food for us to eat, I was absolutely knackered.

* * *

I was slumped over my desk at 5 p.m., a couple of days before the start of the half-term break, trying to get my breath back from a particularly horrendous session with the most notorious of the four Year 9 classes. Catching sight of myself in the fly-blown mirror adjacent to the whiteboard (why the hell there was a mirror in a classroom I wasn't sure, but can only assume it was there so the previous incumbent could have eyes in the back of her head while writing on the board) I put my head down on the desk, closed my eyes and let out a loud groan of utter tiredness and frustration. My hair, tied up with a rubber band, was in dire need of a good cut; any make-up I'd attempted at seven that morning had caked and smudged as I'd sweated my way through various dance and drama sessions with either totally over- or under-enthusiastic – dependent on age and disposition – pupils, and a familiar low-down ache heralded the start of my period.

'Great stuff,' I muttered into my sleeve. 'Bloody great stuff...'

'You OK?' Mason Donoghue stood at the classroom door, arms folded, looking concerned. Or was it amused? 'You'll frighten the cleaners.'

'I'm fine,' I said. 'Absolutely fine, as you can see.' I raised both a hand and a pair of bleary, mascara-smudged eyes in his direction, hoping he'd go away. 'Two days to get through and then it's me, a bottle of SB and my bed for a week.'

'Oh, that's a shame.'

'What is?' I peered across at him suspiciously.

'So, there's a production of *Grease* being put on in Midhope over half-term. Petra and I have arranged to see it with the idea of our own kids putting on a performance of it at Christmas.'

'Well, good luck with that!' I laughed hollowly, stopping him in his tracks before he went any further. 'A performance of *Grease*?

With this unruly lot?' (As I say, I was feeling particularly shattered and belligerent, otherwise wouldn't have had the temerity to offend Mason's sensibilities re his pupils.) 'And in...' I counted off the weeks on my fingers '...just eight weeks or so?' I laughed again, genuinely amused. 'As I say, good luck with that.'

'And,' Mason went on, undeterred, 'as we'd like you to choreograph, direct and produce our production, I've bought another ticket.'

'Sorry, I'm washing my hair that day.' I pulled at the rubber band but my hair, being so dirty, didn't fall as a sexy waterfall around my shoulders but, instead, stood out at all angles so that I resembled one of those exotic, desirous-of-mating male birds from David Attenborough's *Planet Earth*.

'Which day?'

'Sorry?' I raked a hand through my hair, meeting nothing but tangles, and in the end tied it back up again.

'Which day are you washing your hair?'

'The day you're off to the theatre. *And* all the days you think I'm prepared to be putting in producing some ridiculous Christmas concert. Any production like this should have started its rehearsals at the very beginning of term. Oh, and you have to have permission from the owners, whoever they are; copyright and all that. You can't just glibly say you're going to perform *Grease* without getting permission.'

'You see? You know all about this kind of thing.'

When I just shook my head but said nothing, Mason went on, 'Oh, well, if you won't help, I suppose I'll just have to do it all myself as usual.'

'As usual? You've done it before, then?'

'No, not really,' he admitted. 'But I'm prepared to have a go. OK, Christmas is probably a bit ambitious.'

'More than a bit.'

'So, Easter, then? That would give you more time?'

'No, I'm sorry, it wouldn't. Because I'm not doing it. If you remember, Mr Donoghue, I'm here on a supply basis and I'm very much hoping that by Easter I'll be back looking for work in London.'

'Oh, well, that's a shame. Especially as I have three tickets for next week. Why don't you come with Petra and me anyway?'

'No strings attached?'

'What sort of strings?' Mason held my eye for longer than was necessary and I had to look away. Hell, he was sexy.

'None of your trying to persuade me that there's any chance of turning our kids into something from *Glee*.'

'*Glee*?' Mason frowned.

'Oh, you've no idea, have you? Look, a lot of these kids wouldn't listen to a word anyone was trying to tell them; they'd not turn up for rehearsals and more than likely go AWOL on the opening night when something better came up.'

'Still not got a very good impression of the children in my school, then?'

'In a word – no.'

'OK, just come with us – it'll be a night out. Shame to waste a ticket.'

'I'll think about it,' I offered ungraciously. 'If I can recover from what your kids are putting me through on a daily basis.'

'Robyn, have faith in yourself. I saw you the other day showing great empathy with the class you were teaching; you understand some of the kids have issues and respond accordingly. And they're beginning to not only respect you, but really like you too. I've stood and watched you teach a couple of times.'

'I really wish you wouldn't.' I frowned, embarrassed at the

thought I'd been prancing about, giving it all I'd got, while not realising Mason was observing.

'And you're good. You know your stuff, you're enthusiastic.'

'That enthusiasm is pure adrenaline,' I scoffed. 'If I can act a part in front of them, take on a role, then at least it stops them butting in and trying to take over the lesson. If I'm talking and attempting to jump about' – I held up my sore knee to remind him I still wasn't capable of much gallivanting about – 'then at least I have some control over what's going on.'

Mason laughed at that. 'OK, ticket's here.' He left it on the table at the back of the classroom. 'Meet Petra and me outside Midhope Theatre at 7 p.m. next Wednesday. If you don't show, well, I get it. Even though it'll be a waste of a ticket.'

* * *

'I suppose this is your handiwork?' Jess flapped the A4 piece of paper in my face before screwing up the offending article and lobbing it neatly into the wastepaper bin. 'Don't be so ridiculous, Robyn. There's absolutely no way I'm putting myself forward for Yorkshire Christmas TopChef. Bloody silly name, anyway, just aping *MasterChef*.'

'You don't have to put yourself forward, Jess, because I've done it for you.'

'Well, you can jolly well get it undone, then. You know,' she added, glaring at me as she whisked egg white for some pudding she was experimenting with, 'you were saying how Mason was trying to manipulate you into producing a show for him, and how you most certainly weren't going to be manhandled into doing it? Well, I feel the same about this.'

'It's not the same at all.' I tutted. 'Come on, what do you have to lose?' I moved to the bin, retrieving and smoothing the letter before reading its content: 'You just need skill, enthusiasm, drive, a love of food and a desire to change your life,' I said, enunciating each requisite clearly so she got the message. 'You've got *all* of those things but especially the bit about wanting to change your life.'

'What's up?' Lola, coming into the kitchen and seeing Jess's face, as well as the way she was angrily bashing the egg whites in their bowl, stopped and stared. 'Mum, you've always told me that if you whisk meringues too much the stiff peaks will go back to liquid.'

'Lola, Jayden and I have entered your mum for a cooking competition—' I started.

'Oh, I might have known *he'd* have something to do with this,' Jess snapped, folding melted chocolate into the meringues.

'I don't know why you're so mean about my grandfather.' Lola pouted. 'I really like him. And *of course*, you've got to enter. Will you be on the telly?' she asked excitedly.

'No, because I'm not doing it.' Jess sniffed crossly. 'I'm not having anyone looking at my big behind on TV.'

'It's only local TV,' I said. 'And they film you from the front – no one would ever see your bum. It's a very nice bum anyway. You really have to get over this hang-up with your bum, Jess.'

'Will you stop saying *bum*?' Jess frowned, starting to laugh. 'Even if I had a *little* bum like... like... Kylie Minogue, I still wouldn't go in for this daft competition.'

'Of course you have to,' Lola said calmly, her manner belying her ten years. 'Come on, Aunty Robyn, let's both fill in these new forms with the further details they're asking for, then she'll *have* to do it.'

'Is it just for northerners, then?' Jess asked, peering over our shoulders as Lola and I started filling in the new form. 'Do you have to come from Yorkshire?'

'I would imagine so.' I nodded, smiling as I saw Jess begin to relent. 'Anyway, you probably won't get chosen. There'll be loads of people all wanting their five minutes of fame with their Yorkshire puds on *Focus North* and they're just choosing ten from the application forms for just one heat. And then three will go forward to a grand final. Don't get your hopes up too high!'

24

At the end of that first half-term at St Mede's it felt as though I'd never known any other life than the one that had me up at six every morning banging on Sorrel's bedroom door, chivvying her out of her pit and into the shower. There was always a huge sense of relief that she was there, burrowed under her duvet like some little woodland creature, and had actually come home.

It had been cold and miserable all week, the rain coming down in vertical stair rods, the kids cooped up and unable to let off steam in the yard or the one bit of remaining water-soaked and muddy grass over on the playing field. Days like this were dreaded by teaching staff throughout the land, but particularly those in inner-city schools and in areas of abandoned industry, where whole communities had been left to rot, and where the ensuing unemployment and social deprivation, after the closure of factories, pits and textile mills, were rife. The last day of this particularly wet week of the first half of the term, then, was more hellish than usual, resulting in disorganised chaos in my drama sessions, as well as the exclusion of a child.

The torrential rain being the very best autumn could muster, the drama studio had sprung several leaks, with the caretaker, Ken – an ex-army jobsworth perennially sporting an immaculately pressed brown overall – insisting (health and safety, love) he arrange several small orange cones around the resulting puddles. This was a gift made in heaven for Whippety Snicket, who proceeded, not only to stamp in the puddles like the five-year-old he still appeared to be, but to kick the cones around the room, shouting 'goal' every time he scored a hit on one of the girls' backsides. My furious intervention had resulted in him turning on me, kicking the cone at my gammy knee while shouting at me to, 'Fuck off and get back where you came from.'

With no Joel Sinclair to protect me (I'd actually begun to consider paying the sixteen-year-old protection money) I had no alternative but to call in the senior leadership team to remove the boy from the studio. The other kids in the class were left restless and sullen at one of their own being escorted off the school premises.

Mason had formally excluded Whippety from school for a week for racial harassment (although as it was half-term the following week, there appeared little point) and, too upset to talk and debrief with either Mason or Petra, all I wanted was to cry on Jess's shoulder. Sorrel was nowhere to be seen, not appearing at my classroom door for a lift home as she sometimes did when the weather was inclement. But that wasn't unusual and, to be honest, I was relieved I wasn't having to face yet another truculent teen. How many prospective parents, longing for their own little bundle of joy, would, if they could only have a snapshot of said child fifteen years hence, abandon all plans for the pastel-painted nursery and convert the room into a study or recording studio, a gym or Airbnb? As well as blowing the quarter of a million pounds this child would eventually cost them on a round-the-world trip?

I went straight over to Jess's, but her cottage appeared as dark and unwelcoming as Mum's. I assumed she was either on a late shift or had gone to the hospital with Lola to visit Mum, who was hopefully being discharged during the half-term break. Unwilling to face the cold house with last night's unwashed dishes in the sink without alcoholic sustenance to see me through, I went back out to the car and headed for the village Co-op. I bought a bottle of cheap red and a box of Mr Kipling mince pies (hell, Christmas already?) and, once home, downed the lot in an orgy of self-pity.

I lay on the sofa, red throw over me, while a sardonic Roger eyed me with a mixture of pity and contempt. Until, unable to stand the cheap wine and burp-inducing festive tarts' fumes I was breathing over him, he offered one final disdainful stare at me before heading for his basket by the unlit wood burner.

'Don't you abandon me as well, you supercilious rabbit,' I sobbed in Roger's direction before reaching for the TV control, which, I remembered too late, needed new batteries. Heaving myself off the sofa to manually change channels, I searched for a nice escapist thriller or at least a wildlife documentary, but instead found a rerun of *Fatal Attraction*. Watching the bunny being boiled, I chortled drunkenly over at Roger, turning his basket towards the TV in revenge for his abandoning me, but then felt so mean, I got up, changed channels and gathered him up into my arms, apologising profusely for my behaviour.

And there on the TV was Fabian. *Fabian Mansfield Carrington*. *My* Fabian. *My* heart. *My* racing pulse. Jesus. Was I having a heart attack? The news channel – some obscure Japanese or Taiwanese programme with subtitles – was reporting on the UK's Rupert Henderson-Smith's alleged murders and the cameras were outside Fabian's apartment. Actually outside his apartment! I clutched at Roger, staring at the screen, reading the subtitles and trying to work out what was going on and why there was a crowd of mainly women with banners on Fabian's doorstep as he hurriedly disappeared inside. I needed to rewind, see Fabian again, but Mum's TV control was no longer capable of such sophisticated action. Instead, I watched in fascination as first Julius Carrington, followed by Judge Gillian, walked grimly through the banner-waving women before disappearing together through the West London apartment's main entrance.

I couldn't quite work out – not helped by my alcoholic state and a struggling, disgruntled lop-eared rabbit – whether the TV news programme was live or, as probably was the case, a few hours or even several days old. I did the only thing that I could: brushed off mince-pie crumbs and rabbit hair and, with as much acting ability as I could muster in order to counter my inebriation, immediately rang Fabian's number.

Which came back as number not known.

Fabian was no longer on that number. He'd erased me from his life. I was blocked. Persona non grata.

To my utter shame, I took myself off to bed, the front door unlocked, the TV still on, and crashed out, still in my school clothes, teeth uncleaned, not caring that my little sister, Sorrel, wasn't back home.

* * *

'So, absolutely no reason, then, to not have a date with Mason,' Jess opined the following Wednesday as the pair of us, under Jess's direction, did our best to give Mum's cottage a thorough bottoming in readiness for her coming home at the weekend.

'It's not a date,' I snapped, breathing heavily as I found fresh linen for both Mum's bed and the single in the box room, which I knew I'd be demoted to once she was home. 'Jeez, my fitness has gone,' I puffed as we turned mattresses, re-made beds, hoovered and dusted.

'Not a date?' Jess grinned as she pummelled pillows into submission. 'You're off to the theatre with one of the most attractive men I've ever come across.'

'You've not met Fabian...' I started.

'Oh, Fabian Schmabian,' she scoffed. 'I've seen him. On TV... Well, to be honest, just the back of him... Yes, on TV, Robyn. I wasn't going to tell you...'

'You didn't need to tell me.' I sniffed sadly. 'I've seen him too.'

'Oh?'

'Yes. And I tried to ring him. He's at the centre of a hate campaign, by the looks of it.'

'Not surprised,' Jess said tartly. 'You can't be on the side of that misogynist Rupert Henderson-Smith, trying to get him off so he can be back out there to do awful things to more women, without consequences.'

'Everyone has a right to a fair hearing, Fabian said...' I began, wanting to put his point of view.

'Don't you try to defend him, Robyn,' Jess snapped. 'Anyone who defends a serial killer, to get him off to menace women again, deserves the same contempt as the murderer himself. His hands are tainted with those women's blood.'

'Hardly,' I tried again, but Jess was having none of it.

'In my opinion, take it for what it's worth,' she went on, squirting Pledge along every wooden surface within range, 'Mason Donoghue knocks spots off your Bucks Barrister. And,' she added, 'Mason is more your tribe.'

'My *tribe*? What the hell is that supposed to mean?'

'You know exactly what I'm saying,' Jess said, giving me one of her looks. 'So don't pretend you don't. You go to the theatre with that gorgeous head teacher. Because, I tell you now, if you don't,

I'm definitely going to make a play for him, invite him here for a meal next time he's visiting his grandmother at the home.'

'How come his granny's up here?' I asked. 'When Mason's from the south?'

'That's just the sort of lovely caring man he is,' Jess said, obviously determined to sing Mason's praises. 'I had a chat with him only a couple of weeks ago: his father's working abroad, and his mother wasn't prepared to take on the responsibility for her mother-in-law once she'd had a fall. So Mason brought her up here to Hudson House where he can visit her. I tell you, Robyn, he is one very lovely man.'

'He's married.'

'No, he's not.'

'He is.'

'Was.'

'He still is. Petra said.'

'Petra?'

'The deputy head at school. She's now told me she thinks he's separated.'

'Well, there you go, then. Don't look a separated horse in the mouth.'

'Sorry?'

'You will be if you don't go to the theatre with Mason.' Jess turned. 'Right, come on. Sorrel's room. Get the bin bags.'

* * *

Despite telling both Jess and myself that I most certainly *wasn't* off to the theatre with Mason and Petra, it was Sorrel who had me changing my mind about going.

'You *can't*,' she said in horror. 'Please don't tell me you're going out with the head teacher? On a date? No way!'

This was a red rag to a bull: 'I most certainly am,' I said, enjoying winding her up. She'd been particularly elusive and obnoxious this half-term holiday, staying in bed until midday, refusing to go and see Mum in hospital and sloping off, leaving the kitchen as if a bomb had hit it and not returning until the early hours of the morning. I'd tried gently reasoning with her but with little response, so reverted to wielding the metaphorical big stick with a warning that if she continued to stay out late again, I'd have social services, the police and whoever else I could think of out to find out what she was up to.

'Oh, yes? The AA?' she'd quipped through a mouthful of toast and jam. 'The RSPCA? The Lifeboat Service? Ooh, probably not, seeing as how we're around sixty miles from the nearest coastline at Blackpool.'

Well, at least her geography was on track: I'd had a fifteen-year-old in a geography GCSE class I was covering tell me: 'Germany's an island, miss, just off the south coast of France.'

I'd tried ignoring her, hoping that eventually she'd get through this phase relatively unscathed. Then I'd changed tack, pleading with her to tell me what the problem was and telling her that I could help her with whatever was worrying her. Before Jess had come over that morning to help clean Mum's house, I'd actually done something I'd sworn I'd never do, and gone through her room, her bags and drawers looking for alcohol, for drugs, for weed, the contraceptive pill, for condoms, for rolls of banknotes: anything that might give me a clue what she was up to.

'Been there, done that.' Jess shrugged, later that afternoon when, sitting in her kitchen, I confessed to searching Sorrel's room. 'You don't think I've not done that myself? And,' she added, 'I'd have read her diary if she'd had one. *And* gone through her laptop, if I knew her password.'

'She *is* almost sixteen,' I countered, slightly taken aback by what Jess was saying. 'Old enough to be legally married, live apart from a parent, legally entitled to be sexually active...'

'She's a child, Robyn,' Jess said, patting my arm and reaching for the kettle. 'A vulnerable and unhappy child. Probably the same as quite a few of the kids you teach, who you appear to think are idle, bolshy, under-achieving layabouts.'

'That about sums some of them up.' I nodded, stung at what I saw as criticism of both my parenting and my teaching skills. 'Not all of them, by any means. And I'm sorry if that's the impression I've given you of my pupils. To be honest, I'm beginning to under-stand and empathise with them—'

'You've lived too long in the south, Robyn,' Jess interrupted almost kindly. 'With rather more privileged—'

'While you, Jessica,' I interrupted in turn, 'are on your way to becoming somewhat provincial and prejudiced. You need some-thing to look forward to, to jolt you out of the rut you've got your-self into, now you're thirty, for heaven's sake. A Yorkshire cooking competition would do the trick nicely, I believe.'

Leaving Jess to tutt crossly, I headed back next door, going straight upstairs to the bathroom and running the full hot bath Jess said we couldn't afford. I added a liberal dose of some of Mum's bubble bath and climbed in, soaking for a long time while contemplating my injured knee. According to Maria, my physio, I'd not damaged the actual meniscus and, as such, it would even-tually recover completely.

There was light at the end of the tunnel. I might yet find myself back dancing in the West End. My favourite fantasy scenario was that Fabian would be in the audience of *Mamma Mia!*, unaware not only that I'd returned to London, but that I was wowing audiences with my interpretation of Sophie, the free-spir-ited daughter of the protagonist, a part I'd long coveted. He was with Fish Face, of course, who'd persuaded Fabian to accompany her with the best possible box tickets. She would be leafing through the programme before turning to Fabian with a derisory chuckle, pointing out my photograph. 'Darling, isn't this the waitress you once had a bit of a thing for? The one Julius warned your parents was only after one thing...' At which juncture, Fabian would snatch the programme from her, focusing on the action on stage before jumping up, startling those in the cheap seats below by yelling that he would always love me... always...

'Can you hurry up in there?' Sorrel was banging on the bathroom door, bringing me back to the reality of my cooling bath in a rather damp cottage in Beddingfield. 'I'm off out in ten minutes.'

'So am I,' I retorted, refusing to pander to her. 'Wait your turn.'

'You're not actually going out with Mr Donoghue and Ms Waters, are you?' This was progress – Sorrel actually taking an interest in what I was up to.

'Might be,' I shouted through the closed door.

'Bloody hell, what *are* you turning into?' She sniggered. 'I'll never live this down if it gets out.'

'So you have made friends at St Mede's?' I called hopefully. 'You know, with whom you apparently *need to live this down*?' I knew that didn't make a great deal of sense, but it soon became apparent it really didn't matter. In the time it took to quickly dry myself and rub in what was left of my precious Clarins body lotion, Sorrel was gone, the fading tail-lights of the Uber winking conspiratorially down the lane.

25

'Oh, you came? Good.' There was genuine pleasure on both Petra and Mason's faces as I walked towards the pair waiting outside the town's main theatre. 'I hope you've a pen and paper with you?' Mason added.

'Pen and paper?'

'To make notes for St Mede's production next term.' Mason grinned, taking my arm and leading the pair of us towards the main entrance.

'In your dreams,' I said, eyebrow raised. 'I'm here for a free night out to one of my favourite musicals.'

'We'll see.' Mason laughed, showing us to our seats.

'You OK?' I asked Petra, who I noticed didn't seem her usual self.

'Think so.' She smiled. 'Hope so.'

'What's that supposed to mean?' The three of us sat down, Petra in the middle and, for that, I was grateful. I wanted to take in every bit of the production without worrying that my arm might be making contact with Mason's, that his leg might brush against mine.

'Pregnant,' Petra whispered.

'Sorry?' I stared.

'I'm pregnant.'

'Oh, wow! Gosh. And are you happy to be pregnant?' I realised as soon as I said it that this was a totally personal question and hurriedly added, 'I mean, you appear to be such a career girl, loving your job.'

Petra laughed. 'I do love my job and I'll have to go back to it once the baby is born. But I'm so excited, I can't tell you. Mind you, I thought the sickness would have finished now I'm twelve weeks and can tell people.'

I glanced across her towards Mason, who was studying the theatre programme intently. 'Mason won't know what to do without you.'

She laughed. 'His face did fall when I told him, but there you go. We have to produce the next generation or there'll be no one to teach.' She laughed again. 'You know, Robyn, I realise you think you're no good at this teaching lark, but both Mason and I have watched you. You're a natural.'

'A natural?' I scoffed. 'I hate it.'

'No, you've just had to handle exceptionally difficult kids at the beginning of your career. If you move to an easier school, where kids aren't bringing baggage from home with them, where they've been given breakfast before they set off, where the whole family's not living in one room in a B & B...'

'Shhh,' Mason warned, smiling across at us while conspicuously brushing at his sleeve. 'Leave the chalk dust where it belongs, you two. We're here to enjoy the performance.'

'And make notes.' Petra grinned, nudging me. 'We're here for a purpose, don't forget.'

I didn't need to make notes: the whole performance was stamped on my memory from the very beginning of what turned out to be a quite spectacular production from joint local amateur companies. Both leads – Sandy and Danny – were, according to the programme, professional performers who had worked in big productions in Birmingham and Leeds.

I was so envious. I jumped, I *pliéd*, shimmied, leapt and danced with them all on stage, but particularly Sandy, a nineteen-year-old who, I could tell, had a whole performing life in front of her. With a thud of my heart, I had the sudden realisation that at twenty-eight, with a knackered knee and my early dance career chances scuppered by bloody Covid, I was maybe on a one-way track to the elephants' graveyard of spent musical theatre performers. There must be loads of us, desperately trying to claw our way back out of the mire that both age and injury had had a hand in toppling us into. But with gorgeous young things like this Sandy ready to tread on our heads and push us back down, what producer would even look at us?

'You OK?' Petra whispered, putting a hand on my arm. I realised I was crying.

'Sorry, just a bit hormonal,' I whispered back, trying to smile.

'Me too,' she said. 'Need the loo. Sorry.'

I couldn't believe the effect this production of *Grease* was having on me. I'd assumed it was going to be a local amateurish performance, with proud parents enthusiastically cheering on their little darlings when they missed a cue or fluffed their lines. But this was slick, professional, fabulously executed. Blimey, if a small area of West Yorkshire was able to produce and showcase such incredible talent, there must be a whole pool of young performers dreaming of heading to the West End and beyond.

I felt sick at the thought.

'I feel really sick,' Petra said, sliding back into her seat on my right. I realised she'd been gone for a good fifteen minutes.

'You OK?'

'I've actually been throwing up as well as peeing. Bloody hell...'

'Shhh.' An elderly red-faced man behind us leaned forward and prodded Petra's shoulder as she stood once more, white-faced.

'Excuse me,' I hissed at him. 'My friend isn't well.'

'Just pregnant...' she started.

'Can you sit down? I can't see.'

'A mint?' Grandad's other half offered sympathetically, scrabbling in her bag and rustling paper. I was immediately taken back to the Central Criminal Court when I'd first spotted and fallen in love with Fabian, when Minty Breath had chummily offered me a Polo mint. Oh, Fabian, where are you now?

Petra sat, but the elderly man behind sighed audibly as she stood again. 'Sorry, you two...' she said turning to Mason and me, a hand to her mouth. 'Look, I'm spoiling this for you both. I'm going.'

'I'll come with you.' I made to stand.

'I'm fine,' Petra whispered through her hands. 'If I don't go, I'm going to throw up here.'

* * *

I was now not only totally immersed in my own misery with the realisation that I was more than likely a has-been, but the offering of a mint to Petra had just brought back all my longing for Fabian. I was seriously thinking of following Petra out of the theatre and home, until Mason moved next to me, fished out a clean folded hanky from his jacket pocket and handed it in silence to me.

I hadn't realised just how much I was crying and, embarrassed, I wiped at my eyes before handing it back to Mason.

He shook his head, indicating I should keep it, but took my

hand briefly in his own before releasing it and concentrating on the production once more.

This was ridiculous. It was about time I got my big girl's pants on and started to accept my lot in life.

'Do you think we could get it together?' Mason whispered, a hand on my arm, his face turned towards me as his eyes met mine, holding them almost in challenge.

'Get it together?' I stared back before, embarrassed, I turned away. Please don't say my boss was propositioning me. 'Get *what* together?'

'A production of *Grease*? At St Mede's?' He smiled, obviously amused at my reaction. 'What did you think I meant, Robyn?'

'Oh, right, of course.' I was so glad the lights were down, and he couldn't see my flushed face. 'Actually, I don't see why not,' I added, relieved there appeared to be no hidden agenda in his request.

Relief or disappointment?

We stayed put during the interval making polite conversation about school, how he was going to miss Petra once she was on maternity leave. He asked about Sorrel, how she was behaving at home, because he felt she'd settled at St Mede's a lot better than he'd anticipated. While she was only six weeks in, he admitted he'd not been certain she would stay the course, would possibly still end up at the PRU. Or, as was more likely, her education would just peter out and no one would really be bothered to get her back on track for her GCSEs and beyond. 'And, to be fair' – he grinned – 'I didn't expect *you* to be still here by the time half-term arrived.'

'Not much option really,' I said, slightly put out he'd thought me flaky enough to get out when I couldn't cope. Mind you, I had taken on the job kicking and screaming.

'You've not had it easy, have you?' Mason smiled. 'An often

absent, famous father? A single mother with a condition that meant her being taken into hospital at the drop of a hat?'

'How on earth do you know all this?' I looked at him in some indignation.

'How do you think?'

'Sorrel?'

'Sorrel? No, she's only just deigning to say good morning to me. She's certainly not at the stage of opening up to me or Petra, although Petra, I know, has tried several times.'

'Ah, Jess? Of course, I forget that you and she meet up at Hudson House.'

'And,' Mason went on, briefly touching my hand once more, 'how you two had to be taken into care when your mum was poorly again?'

I nodded, not wanting to remember. They hadn't been good times: on one occasion Jess and I had been split up – her sent to one set of foster parents, while I was taken, shouting for Mum and particularly for Jess, with whom I'd always shared a bedroom, to another set. I'd been so homesick, so desperate to be with my mum and my sister. Luckily Jayden had returned from some gigs in the Caribbean to rescue and care for us the best he could. During our teens, Mum's illness appeared to go into remission, but then she was pregnant with Sorrel and went downhill again when a bout of post-natal depression took hold. I think because Jayden seemed to me, at the age of four, to have rescued me from the foster family I'd not liked, of all three of us girls I was the one to have developed more of a relationship with him. Jess and Sorrel were always in agreement that he was a waste of space and Mum was better off without him.

And like Jayden I had performing in my blood. Now Mason and this wonderful production of *Grease* had gone some way to persuading me that I could after all be up for producing a show at St Mede's. No way could we be up and running for Christmas, but maybe, just maybe, we could be ready for Easter. Did that mean, then, despite all my protestations, I was still going to be in Beddingfield and at St Mede's until Easter? I spent the remaining second half of the production with ideas buzzing in my brain, simultaneously trying to work out how I could take such a mammoth task on board and what direction I would take.

By the time the production had come to its conclusion and Mason and I, along with the rest of the audience, jumped to our feet to join the standing ovation, I was feeling something akin to excitement. Anticipation at any rate.

'Can I give you a lift home?' Mason asked as we descended the theatre steps before facing the chilly evening outside.

'Got my car,' I said. 'Well, Mum's car.' I held up the keys as proof. 'Actually,' I said, and, to this day, I don't know why, added, 'I'm really thirsty. Do you fancy a drink?'

Mason hesitated and I thought, oh, hell, what on earth was I thinking? A supply teacher asking her head teacher out for a drink?

'OK.' He smiled. 'I could murder a pint.'

We walked in embarrassed silence, across the road from the theatre and into the warmth of The Albert, a traditional pub adjacent to the town's library.

'I'll get them,' I said purposefully. 'I invited you. And you bought the tickets.'

'I earn more than you.' He grinned. 'What do you fancy? Look, there's a couple of seats over in the corner. Go and bag them before someone else does.'

Seeing as it was after ten and there were very few other drinkers in the pub, that seemed unlikely, but I did as I was told. I took off my jacket and sat, watching as Mason got into an easy conversation with the landlord before coming over with our drinks.

I was genuinely thirsty and, so it seemed, was Mason. We drank gratefully, putting our drinks down on the table at the same time.

Now what?

'So...' Mason began.

'Have you...?'

We both started talking as one and had to stop, smiling inanely at each other.

'OK,' I said, leaning over the table and meeting his eye, 'I reckon we could try it.'

'Really?' His eyes widened in pleasure, and I thought once again what a really gorgeous-looking man he was. Easy to be with, confident in his own abilities, determined against the odds to make a success out of his school.

'Really. Although' – I grimaced – 'I must be mad even contemplating it.'

'You know, taking on the direction and production of something like this would really enhance your status with the kids at school. They all want to be stars...'

'Or footballers.' I smiled.

'Or footballers,' he agreed. 'The thing is, it won't just be for those who can act, dance and sing. I want this to be a whole school and community production, with all staff, as well as mums and dads, helping with stage management, making costumes.'

'I can't see many of these kids' mums with a sewing machine,' I started. 'And how many of their dads are actually around?'

'Don't stereotype,' Mason warned. 'Don't let your prejudices make you think our kids' parents won't be around for them.'

'I'll believe it when I see it,' I said with a raised eyebrow. And then, because I was nosy, or because I was beginning to feel some sort of warm glow in the presence of this man, I asked, 'So, kids? Do *you* have any?'

'Five hundred and sixty at the last count.' He grinned.

'You know what I mean.' I tutted. 'Although that's probably more than enough.'

'Actually, it isn't,' Mason said.

'Oh?'

'If our numbers decline much further, the school will close. With the new head in place at Beddingfield High, we're seeing a quite serious drift away from us. The authority would love to get our site, bulldoze it to the ground and sell it off for housing.'

'Right.' I was still at the point of thinking razing St Mede's to the ground wouldn't be a bad thing.

'And, to answer your question, no, I don't have children of my own.'

'You'd make a great dad.' I tittered nervously. Where had that one come from? One minute I'm asking my boss out for a drink and the next I'm giving him the idea I'd like him to father my children. Well, almost.

'I think so,' he said seriously.

'Think so what?' I was spending too much time gazing into his amazing chocolate-brown eyes – oh, hell, what a cliché – and couldn't quite remember what I'd asked him.

'I think I'd be a great father. Trouble is my wife doesn't agree. Actually, that came out wrong. I don't know whether she thinks I'd make a good father or not: it's a long time since we discussed it.'

'Right,' I said once more, not quite knowing what to say, feeling a little flare of disappointment he was actually married.

'My wife and I are separated,' Mason said, holding my eye for slightly longer than was necessary.

'Oh, I'm sorry.' Liar, liar, pants on fire. Petra had been right, then. I felt a little flare of hope replace the previous flare of disappointment.

'So.' Mason appeared to want to change the subject. 'What are you up to the rest of the week?'

'A ton of planning for next term, I guess.'

'You're getting there.'

'I suppose I am. I really *think* I am and then a *series of unfortunate events* happens, like Friday when Whippety Snicket tells me to eff off.'

'Whippety Snicket?' Mason started to laugh. 'How descriptive! But don't take it personally, Robyn. Blane Higson's told all of us where to go at some point in his career at St Mede's.'

'Even you?'

'Even me.' He grinned. 'If you knew his background, you might understand why he reacts as he does. You know, dad upped and left when Blane was tiny and I'm not sure where his elder brothers are now. Mum's a heroin addict and more than likely on the game to pay for her next fix. He has ADHD—'

'Haven't they all?'

'Quite a few have,' Mason said seriously. 'Don't believe *The Daily Herald*, which would like us to believe it's all a made-up syndrome, designed to bleed more benefits from the state.'

Feeling I'd been put in my place, I changed the subject. 'Lola and I are determined to get Jess onto TopChef.'

'Oh? What's that?'

'Cooking competition along the lines of *MasterChef*. But only for those living in Yorkshire.'

'I hear she's a great cook.'

'She's better than great. She really is superb. You'll have to come and eat with us one evening.' Bloody hell, now what was I doing, inviting the man home for dinner?

'Thank you. I'd really like that.' Mason looked at his watch. 'Better be going.'

Why? Did he have someone at home waiting for him?

We pulled on jackets and scarves, picked up our phones and bags and went to leave. At the pub exit, Mason smiled. 'I go this way – are you OK getting back to the car park?'

But I wasn't listening.

I'd just seen Sorrel disappearing into one of the newly refurbished apartments across from the town's main square.

With a man I'd hoped I'd never again come across in my lifetime. A man so repulsive he'd set your teeth on edge, make your skin crawl. A man old enough to be my father and who, as far as I knew, had left for Thailand over fifteen years ago.

26

When I was eight, Mum, at first amused and encouraging, and then rapidly fed up of me constantly under her feet as I danced around the tiny sitting room and attempted *jetés* off the sofa, took me along to the one and only dance class in the village. The teacher, Miss Julia Grenville, had been at it for years and, Mum said, always reminded her of someone called Thelma Mayne who was, apparently, the disabled ballet teacher of some character called Lorna Drake in *Bunty* comic that Mum had devoured as a child. None of these fictional characters meant anything to me at the time, but it always amused Mum to see Julia Grenville shaking her walking stick in despair at some poor kid in a white tutu whose predilection for Mars bars and fish and chip suppers kept her grounded when Julia insisted she soar.

Little girls, desperate to be the next Darcey Bussell, were introduced to the rudiments of ballet, tap and musical theatre, and every Saturday morning, after we'd walked Jess down to the local hockey club where she was already showing promise both in defence and in goal, Mum would walk with me to Miss Grenville's

Academy of Dance. This was the absolute highlight of my week, where I soon became Miss Grenville's protégée.

I stayed with Miss Grenville for almost four years because, quite frankly, there was little alternative. One Christmas, Mum, having saved up her family allowance for weeks, had taken Jess and me on the train to a production of *The Nutcracker* at the West Yorkshire Playhouse in Leeds. We'd gone for pizza first in Pizza Hut, piling our bowls with the complimentary salad, loving the stringy, cheesy pizzas, and then queuing in the rain for what seemed ages before being shown to our seats. It was the first time I'd ever been to the theatre, to a proper professional ballet production, and I was hooked. Mesmerised. At the age of twelve, I knew I was going to make ballet my life. This was at the same time that Miss Grenville had taken Mum aside and told her I had promise and that I should be looking further afield if I was to progress. Had we thought about the Northern Ballet Theatre company in Leeds?

I was too young, Mum insisted, to be going to Leeds on the train by myself, even though Jayden, on one of his visits back home, had done his usual trick of peeling off enough twenties to pay for a few months' tuition and travel, as well as the required outfits.

Of course, the money soon ran out, buses ran late and trains didn't run at all, especially when it snowed or there were leaves on the line. After just two months, and with Mum back in hospital for a couple of weeks and Jayden once again forced home to look after Jess and me, that little foray soon came to an end.

Then, fortuitously, Julia Grenville, herself on the point of retirement and moving back to the Midlands from where she'd originally hailed, phoned Mum to tell her that Peter Collinson had returned to his home town of Midhope and his dance and musical theatre academy was up and running and flourishing.

Hopefuls were travelling from as far away as Manchester and Leeds, she said, and this was a big opportunity for me.

Who was Peter Collinson? Mum had asked. Julia had apparently tutted crossly at Mum's ignorance about the man who'd danced with Moving States, for heaven's sake, one of the most innovative dance companies in the UK, up there with Matthew Bourne's New Adventures dance company. He had disappeared from the limelight for several years, working in South Africa, where she'd read he'd orchestrated a career move from ballet to more contemporary dance. She didn't know the full story, she'd explained to Mum, but the main thing was that he was back, and this was my big opportunity to go further.

Mum, who still hadn't passed her driving test, accompanied me on the bus the very next Saturday morning, walking us from the bus station to Imperial Chambers in the town's Victoria Gardens where the new and impressive studios were waiting. Mum had a long chat with a couple of minions, enrolled me into both a Saturday morning and a Wednesday evening session, handed over some of Jayden's ubiquitous twenties and then took herself off for a coffee, leaving me to it.

The classes were great, taken by several young, talented, and, through my twelve-year-old stargazer's eyes, incredibly trendy teachers. I know now they were more than likely frustrated performers themselves, paying the bills by teaching until their big break came. If it ever did. No spent and aging former ballet dancers with walking sticks in *these* studios, then.

I didn't know who Peter Collinson actually was. For several weeks he was simply the huge blown-up photograph of a young man executing an amazing leap in a production of *Desdemona* that had apparently won every accolade going in the late seventies. This had been hung for all to see in the tiny reception area, above a blue velvet sofa and adjacent to the door leading to the one lavatory. And then, one Wednesday evening, I looked up from the session at the barre taken by Danny, to see a middle-aged man, arms folded, watching at the door. He was probably there to check that Danny was teaching to his exacting standards (aren't all dance teachers sticklers?) because Danny himself was obviously nervous, beads of sweat appearing on his forehead and darkening the armpits of his white top.

I still didn't realise who he was because this man, scowling at the door, was middle-aged so I assumed he was one of the students' fathers.

'No, no, no!' the man shouted, leaving the doorpost and walking determinedly to the front of the class and facing the barre. '*This* is a *rond de jambe*! *This* is a *battement degages*,' and, pushing poor, mortified Danny to one side, he took over the lesson himself. He was good, I'll give him that, but as an ex professional ballet dancer with one of the UK's top dance companies he should be. I think he taught me more that lesson than I'd ever learned in the four years with Miss Grenville, never letting up, pushing the ten of us in the session until I was almost weeping with frustration and fatigue.

Poor Danny *was* weeping at the meting out of such wrath on his head by Peter Collinson, and it took him quite a while to regain the confidence needed to take up the class once more after Peter had sailed out.

I adored these sessions, particularly when Peter Collinson deigned to take a whole class himself. I was learning so much, would practise and practise at the studio and in the gym at school now that I was at Beddingfield High, determined to be the best.

One Wednesday evening, I'd changed into my usual leotard, tights and ballet pumps and was making my way along the corridor to the smallest of the studios. I was taking a contemporary dance class with Greg, who had, it was rumoured, once taken the role of Mr Mistoffelees in *Cats* on Broadway. I loved his sessions and was beginning to think I might actually prefer contemporary dance to the classical ballet I'd always revered. Greg, though, had auditioned for and been given a part in some new West End show and, without a by your leave, had upped sticks, leaving Peter in the lurch.

Peter was already waiting to take the session and was soon putting the twelve of us through another of his gruelling training classes. On my way out, he waylaid me, placing a hand under my chin, moving my face from side to side as he scrutinised every angle of my features.

'You'll do well,' he finally said, a hand now on my shoulder. 'We'll make a star out of you.'

My twelve-year-old self glowed with pleasure and embarrassment as, scarlet-faced, I ran off to change and meet Jess who, at fourteen had been sent, complaining, down on the bus to meet me and bring me home.

Most sessions from then on involved Peter either singling me out for a chat, for a little extra tuition on a particular step or – and difficult for a young starry-eyed adolescent to understand – him totally ignoring me. Every time he blanked me – ghosted me, I suppose you'd call it these days – I knew I must be rubbish; I would never make the big time. But on the occasions he smiled down at me, took me through a short routine after class and laid a fatherly hand on my shoulder, around my waist, I knew I must be special. I was going to be famous. Peter had said so.

When, after he'd given me a fifteen-minute solo instruction on how to execute my very first *jeté* and, desperate to please, I'd passed with flying colours, Peter had smiled. Then he'd put his arms around me, held me in front of him, his front pressing into my back with what appeared to be something hard and strange. I was twelve and a half, tall for my age, very thin and only just beginning to develop breasts, for which I was sometimes taunted by the other kids at school. The boys weren't averse to calling me ironing board, but I was also dissed by some of the girls who were already filling bras with 36C chests to be proud of. I had no brothers or male cousins, and a more-absent-than-not father, so understood little about the male species. I was a total innocent, ripe for the plucking by the paedophile sex pest that Peter Collinson turned out to be.

A week or so after this strange hugging incident, Mum was once again rushed into hospital, and Jayden, who was touring Australia and New Zealand, was uncontactable. At fifteen, Jess was allowed to stay with her best mate's parents, sharing Isabelle's bedroom and sleeping on a put-up bed. However much I pleaded to be allowed to go there too, there was simply no room for me and, once again, I was placed in the temporary care of the local authority. Jean and Brian, the elderly couple I went to stay with, were absolutely lovely and more than happy to drive me to my dance classes twice a week. But Peter must have got wind of what was happening because he told Jean, when she dropped me off, that he was happy to give me a lift back to their house, save her a trip coming back out in the rain.

On the drive back to Jean and Brian's place, Peter stopped the car down a quiet country lane and proceeded to tell me that if I wanted to make dance my future, he'd help me get there. I was special, he said, and he'd chosen me to work with *because* I was so special. I had all the makings of as big a name as Ruthie Henshall or even Elaine Paige. I'd never even heard of Elaine Paige, but Ruthie Henshall was my hero after Jayden had found me DVDs of her as Roxie Hart in London's revival of *Chicago*, as well as making her debut of Velma Kelly in the Broadway production of the same show.

'You'll have to practise until you're ready to drop,' Peter told me, stroking my arm in the dark. 'And you'll have to exercise, stretching your body to the limit.' At that juncture, he'd moved his hand to my bare leg, lifting, pulling and stretching as he explained the leg exercises I must commit to every day. Even though I was uneasy, unsure why he should be touching my leg, I nodded in agreement, wanting to get back to Jean and Brian's but unwilling to offend this man when he was being so positive about making me into a star.

'I think I'd better get back now, Mr Collinson,' I said, shifting my leg from his grasp and inching myself away from him as best I could. 'Jean'll be worried, and I don't want her ringing the police.'

'The police?' Peter laughed at that, but the word was obviously enough to break the spell and he turned away irritably, put the car into gear and drove to my foster parents' house.

I might have been only twelve, but I wasn't daft. I knew Peter Collinson was acting in a way he shouldn't. That if I'd told Mum or Jayden or even Jess – particularly Jess – any one of them would have had me out of that academy and reporting his behaviour to the police. But I didn't want that: I wanted to dance; I wanted to be in musical theatre. I wanted Peter's help. When the following Saturday came round and Jean said she'd pick me up after class and take me into the town centre to buy the new school tie to replace the one I'd lost the previous week in Midhope, I felt a sense of relief. Peter wouldn't be driving me home in the dark, and nothing could happen in daylight with others around.

How wrong can a kid be? When the class taken by Cherie came to its conclusion ten minutes early and she rushed off saying she had a train to catch to London, I gathered my things and went to wait in Reception for Jean to pick me up. As, one by one, the rest of the kids made their way out, I wandered to the window to watch for Jean. She was late and I was last man standing.

Peter appeared at my side, telling me he had some forms I

needed to sign to audition for an upcoming production of *Oliver!* in Leeds.

'I can sign them here,' I remember saying, not wanting to follow him into his office. 'Or I can take them back to Jean and Brian's with me to sign.'

'They need to go off today.' He smiled. 'They've sent them over as a special favour to me, when I told them how good you were.'

'Jean'll be here to pick me up in a minute,' I demurred.

'It'll only *take* a minute.' He smiled persuasively. 'Come on, what's the matter? I thought you and I were mates? That I was going to help you become a star? Can't do that if we don't sign the forms.'

Reluctantly I followed Peter into his office, and he was right, it did take only a minute. Thirty seconds for me to sign the forms and thirty seconds for him to grasp my hand and shove it, with a guttural sigh of pleasure, down his trousers and onto his semi-hard flesh while, with the other hand, his fingers moved quickly under my ballet skirt towards my knickers.

I never went back to Peter Collinson's Academy of Dance and Musical Theatre.

I spent the rest of that weekend, much to Jean and Brian's consternation, crying but unable to tell them what I was actually crying about. They assumed it was because I was missing Mum and Jess, and fed me ice cream and let me watch an old VHS video of *Bambi* that had apparently been their son's favourite when he was ill or upset.

Brian drove over to fetch Jess the following day to join us for a Sunday tea of tinned salmon, tomatoes and cucumber, followed by tinned peaches and condensed milk and a huge chocolate cake Jean had spent the morning making for us. They were truly a lovely couple. I still go and visit Jean in her care home, though she doesn't remember who I am.

Mum came out of hospital a few days later and Jess and I went home.

I never told a soul about what Peter Collinson did to me until, one evening during lockdown when I was back at home sitting in the garden with Jess, and both of us had too much to drink, I confided in her. Surprisingly, she was fairly philosophical – I thought she'd have threatened to cut off Collinson's balls with a rusty razor – though she did say that if anyone did the same to Lola, she *would* be after him with a rusty razor. She was proud that I appeared psychologically undamaged by the experience: I hadn't allowed myself to become a victim and hadn't been put off musical theatre – or men.

She was almost right. Mum and Jayden couldn't understand why I refused to go back to Collinson's academy, eventually assuming I was exercising my adolescent right to be bloody-minded. A new young PE teacher at Beddingfield High started an after-school dance session and bit by bit I returned to my first love of dancing, but it was all contemporary stuff rather than classical ballet. Jayden paid for me to have singing lessons – with a woman – and when the Midhope Amateur Dramatics were looking for their Liesl in a production of *The Sound of Music* I went for it and never looked back, taking part in all their major productions until I went off to uni in Manchester.

I might have thought I'd weathered the Peter Collinson incident unscathed and without recourse to counselling, but as I stood gazing across at the apartment Sorrel had just followed the bastard into, my blood was boiling, my pulse racing and I wanted nothing more than to kill him.

'Robyn?' Mason asked. 'What on earth's the matter?'

27

'Robyn, what is it?' Mason had to put out an arm in order to physically stop me dashing across the road and into the path of a speeding car.

'It's Sorrel!'

'*What's* Sorrel?' With his hand still on my arm, Mason kept me back on the pavement while glancing round in some bewilderment. 'There's no one here.'

'I've just seen her go into an apartment across the road.'

'Are you sure? You don't think, because you're worried about her at the moment, you've manifested her. Thought it was her?'

'It was *Sorrel*.'

'Well, maybe she has friends in this part of town?'

'Friends? Friends? She's fifteen! You know as well as I do, Mason, that kids from St Mede's don't have friends in places like this. In one of the trendiest parts of town? All new apartments with Waitrose and Ottolenghi on tap?' I could hardly get my words out. I took a deep breath, trying to calm down, trying to explain. 'Mason, my fifteen-year-old sister went into that apartment across the road…' I looked at my watch '…over five minutes ago with a man old enough to be her father... her grandfather, for heaven's sake.'

'Are you sure?'

'Mason,' I hissed through gritted teeth, 'I'm going across.'

'Hang on, hang on, just think this thing through,' Mason insisted, grabbing hold of my hand. 'You can't just bang on a stranger's door because you think you've seen someone that looks like your sister going in there.'

'I know it was Sorrel,' I said angrily. 'I know the man she was with.'

Five more precious minutes passed as Mason tried to persuade me to knock on the apartment door calmly, rather than with all guns blazing. But, finally breaking free from Mason's grasp, I dashed across the road, Mason following closely behind, and was about to bang on the door I'd seen Sorrel entering, when he physically stopped me once more.

'There's an entryphone,' he hissed. 'You'll have to say who you are. If Sorrel hears your voice and knows you're there and after her, there's no way she'll come down.'

'Ring the bell and say you're the police,' I urged Mason.

'The police?' Mason looked at me. 'Isn't it against the law to impersonate a police officer?'

'I'm sure you've done much worse at some point in your life,' I snapped. 'Just *ring the bell*.' I pushed Mason towards it, not caring that he was my boss and that I was getting him involved in our family problems.

Mason gave the bell a long hard ring and, after a few moments, the entryphone crackled into life.

'Pizza?' a disembodied male voice asked.

'Yep,' Mason immediately replied. 'Come and get it while it's hot.'

'*Come and get it while it's hot?*' I whispered, pulling a face in his direction.

'Well, better than "I'm arresting you for—"'

'Shhhhh!' I hissed.

The apartment door opened and the man I'd not seen for sixteen years or so stood there, frowning, seemingly unable to take in the one woman and one man on his doorstep who obviously weren't pizza delivery boys from Deliveroo.

'Hello, Peter.'

'Sorry, do I know you...?'

Ignoring him, I pushed my way past him, racing up the stairs, shouting Sorrel's name as I went, Mason and then Peter following in my wake.

'Excuse *me*,' Peter snapped, overtaking Mason at the top of the stairs and grabbing at my arm. 'Who the fuck d'you think you are, breaking into my home like this...?' He trailed off as the entry-phone sounded once more and he appeared unable to make any decision about what to do next so instead stood dithering.

'That'll be your pizza you were obviously expecting,' Mason said, calmly. 'I'll go and get it for you. I assume you've paid for it?' He headed back down the stairs, accepted the pizza and started his ascent once more. And then I ran, flinging back doors on each room in turn, looking for Sorrel. The apartment was large, beautifully and artistically decorated and lit, myriad framed photographs of Peter dancing hanging on every wall. I went through a sitting room, a kitchen and utility and, with pounding heart, terrified of what I was going to find, a large bedroom with an enormous king-sized, black satin-covered bed.

Sorrel was in none of these – I even looked in the wardrobe and under the bed – and I turned to the one remaining room, opened the door and went in.

I couldn't quite work out what I was seeing to begin with: the woman sitting upright at a dressing-table mirror wasn't Sorrel. In her place was a heavily made-up female with a blonde chignon dressed in a plunging white dress emphasising a quite remarkable pushed-up bosom sporting strands of diamonds. Her lips were painted in the brightest of red but as the woman glared at my reflection, I saw that her face appeared strangely lopsided, one dark brown eye completely made up and including a ridiculously feathery false eyelash, while the other was completely natural.

"'I am my own woman,'" the woman in the mirror said solemnly.

'Sorry?' I stared. 'Sorrel?'

"'My biggest fear in life is to be forgotten,'" she went on, holding my eye and then, pulling off the blonde chignon to reveal her own beautiful dark wavy hair, added, 'Oh, for fuck's sake, Robyn, what are *you* doing here?'

"'Suffer little children and come unto me,'" I snapped furiously, grabbing at her arm. 'Yes, Sorrel, *I* know my Eva Peron quotes as well as you appear to do. Now, get that dress off, get your jeans on and get out of here with me. This minute.'

'No way,' Sorrel snapped. 'The man out there is *Peter Collinson*, for heaven's sake, and he's going to help me get into the West End. He's famous.'

'Sorrel.' I sighed wearily. 'The man out there... I know who he is. You're fifteen, without any training...'

'You know him? Well, you know how famous he is, then? You're just jealous because your dance career is over,' Sorrel sneered. 'And without any training? Robyn, I've been going to dancing class since I was eight. You know that. Just like you did.'

'But you've not been going anywhere for over a year, have you?'

'They'd taught me all I know; I was fed up with them all,' she said sulkily.

'You have to have the basics, Sorrel.'

'I know the basics,' she almost shouted. 'I've been doing the basics for seven years. I needed to move on, to bigger and better things, but Mum couldn't afford for me to go anywhere else. Jayden said he'd look into it, but he never did.'

'Stop trying to run before you can walk.'

'I want to go to the Susan Yates Theatre School in London. Jayden said he'd look into it for me. But of course, again, he never did.'

'Oh, Sorrel, you know what Jayden's like.'

'I do *now*. Mum tried to help but then she got poorly again.'

'Sorrel, the competition for a place at Susan Yates' is huge. Emily Benton was there...'

'Who?'

'Sweet Girls – a group from the nineties,' I said vaguely. 'Ava Wheathouse, and... and...' I couldn't think of any other past pupils.

'Duo Lister,' Sorrel put in helpfully.

'So, you just gave up?' I asked. 'Stopped going to your dance class?'

'The girls at Beddingfield High said I was a full-of-it-all; a know-all. Especially when I said I was going to the Susan Yates Theatre School in London.'

'What, you were being bullied?'

'Bullied? Me? I wouldn't let any of those bitches bully me.'

'So you decided to bunk off school?'

'Wouldn't *you*, if they were putting stuff up on Snapchat about you and constantly sending awful stuff to your phone?'

'Why didn't you tell Mum? Jayden? Jess?'

Sorrel rubbed at the one made-up eye, smudging the heavy

eyeshadow. 'And make Mum even more ill? Have her back in hospital? Jayden? He's never around and when he is, he's always telling me to chill, it will all get better if I just hang on in there. He hates anything to do with school and education, you know that. And Jess? Oh yes, Jess would have been right in there, wouldn't she, lying in wait for the mean girls? It would have been even worse for me if she'd intervened.' Sorrel rubbed at her eye again. 'It just got worse and worse, so I stopped going to school—'

Sorrel broke off as the doorbell went again.

'Stay there,' I ordered Sorrel. Had Mason called the police? I could hear him and Peter Collinson talking in the kitchen, Peter no doubt trying to convince Mason he only had Sorrel's interests at heart.

'Sorrel is very talented,' I heard Peter gush through the open kitchen door. 'Someone needed to help her, Mason; to understand her full potential. I am her teacher, nothing more, so I don't know what her sister's implying. Because, I tell you now, her bloody irresponsible parents and dysfunctional family don't appear to be helping her...'

The doorbell sounded again, but still no one seemed to be opening the door. I made my way downstairs and, as the bell went for a third time, opened it.

'Oh?' I frowned in surprise. 'What are *you* doing here?'

The boy, obviously startled, threw a nervous look in my direction before attempting to turn and make off, but I grabbed hold of his jacket while shouting for Mason to come and help.

'Joel?' Mason said, running down the stairs towards the pair of us. 'What's going on?' He took hold of Joel Sinclair's other arm and together we pulled him inside and closed the outer door, Mason leaning heavily with his sturdy weight against it, blocking any potential flight. 'Come on, Joel, you can tell us. What are you up to here? And *don't* tell me you're here to dance as well.'

'Well, actually, I am.'

'Sorry?'

'Peter's been giving me lessons—'

'Oh,' I interrupted, beginning to understand a little, 'so the fabulous *jeté* you did out of the drama studio that first morning...'

'Yep.' Joel gave me a hard stare, daring me to come back at him.

'There you go, then.' Mason smiled at both of us. 'It appears to be all above board. Peter's a ballet teacher and is helping these two kids to achieve their dreams. Good on him. Come on, Robyn.' Mason looked at his watch. 'Get Sorrel and go home.'

'I *know* Peter Collinson,' I snapped. 'I know what he is...'

'And what is he?' Mason held up his hands. 'What, Robyn?'

'He's a paedophile, a sex pest: preys on young girls. Maybe young boys too?' I stared hard at Joel who, with hands shoved into his hoody pocket, was looking angry. 'When I was twelve he was my dance teacher. He groomed and sexually assaulted me...'

'What you suggesting, miss?' Joel glared in my direction. 'He's never touched me. Ugh, I wouldn't let some bloke touch *me*.'

'So, what *does* he get from you, then, Joel, if it's not sex?'

Joel went on glaring at me but, as I continued to hold his eye, he eventually dropped his own. And then the penny dropped. What had Mason said about this kid not always being as accommodating as he had been when he'd jumped in as my minder that very first morning at St Mede's?

'Where d'you meet him, Joel?' I asked softly. 'Where did you first meet Peter?' I still had to find out where Sorrel had come across him, but assumed it was at one of her previous ballet-class sessions. Had he persuaded her she was too good for that class and needed to have private sessions with him? 'At a dance class?'

'Never been to any dance class, miss.' Joel shook his head in my direction. 'Mum couldn't afford it and Dad said I were a pansy even asking to go.'

'So, here, then?' I asked gently.

'Here?' Mason frowned. 'Oh, right! You were delivering, Joel? And I assume not something to eat?'

Joel shrugged and glared at the pair of us. 'Look, I need to get the dosh off him or... you know.'

'Joel, we can help you, support you,' Mason said, glancing up as Sorrel appeared at the top of the stairs, make-up removed, jeans and hoody back on instead of the ridiculous Eva Peron dress Collinson must have laid out for her.

'No, you can't,' Joel said grimly and in some exasperation. 'Of course you effing well can't.'

''Lo, Joel.' Sorrel made her way down towards him and I saw a look of recognition pass between the pair of them.

'What happens if you don't get the money for the dust from him, Joel?' Mason was now asking, this boss of mine obviously au fait with the street lingo for cocaine.

'What d'*you* think?' Joel scowled.

'You'd better go and get it, then.' Mason nodded and I immediately tried to intervene.

'You can't let him—'

'I *can*, Robyn.' Mason sighed. 'Joel's got the drugs on him. Whoever he's working for won't let him off what's owing them.' He turned to Sorrel. 'Just go home with Robyn, Sorrel. Listen to what your sisters are telling you. They know about these things.'

'Hang on, before you do that, Joel.' I dashed upstairs to the kitchen where a white-faced Peter Collinson was pouring himself a glass of wine with a trembling hand.

'This, Peter, is from my twelve-year-old self,' I said calmly, aiming a kick at his balls. With no rusty razor to hand, a kick was as good a substitute as any.

'What the fuck...?' he began, bent double with pain. 'I'll have the police on you for assault.'

'No, you won't,' I snapped right in his face, pulling at his hair and forcing him to look into my eyes. 'It's Robyn, Peter. Robyn Allen. All grown up, and a West End dancer to boot. You go to the police, but you'll find I've already been there before you. I suggest you move on again before the police come knocking on your door...'

Collinson's eyes narrowed, a flicker of some sort of recognition there, but I knew he didn't really remember me. I was probably just one of many kids he'd groomed.

Back downstairs, I was expecting Sorrel to stick her heels in, to refuse to come back with me, but to my surprise she followed me. But not before glaring at Mason and then, to my surprise, leaning into Joel to kiss him.

* * *

'How did you meet him?' I asked, once we were in the car and heading back to Beddingfield.

'At school.'

'At *school*?' I turned to Sorrel in absolute fury: the pervert had been hanging round school, taking his pick from the girls there?

'Yeah, school. Duh. He does go to school.'

I stared. 'Oh, Joel?'

'Who d'you think I meant?'

'Collinson.'

'Why would Peter Collinson be at Beddingfield High?' She gave me the look only a fifteen-year-old could give.

'Joel Sinclair was at Beddingfield High?'

'Yes. Course. That awful head, Ms Liversedge, kicked him out almost as soon as she arrived last Easter. Main reason I said I'd go to St Mede's was because I knew Joel had ended up there.'

'Right. So, is he your boyfriend? Are you going out with him?'

'Going out with him? Oh, for heaven's sake, Robyn. You sound like Mum. Joel's my mate.'

'OK, OK.' I pondered this for a while. 'I like him,' I said.

'So do I.'

'But he's involved in county lines?'

'Yep.'

'He's bright,' I went on, knowing how hard he worked in my English lessons. 'Very good at English Lit. And he has the potential to be a very good dancer.'

'Peter's been teaching him.'

'In that flat?' I frowned. 'Not a huge amount of room to *jeté*.'

'Garage,' Sorrel said. 'He's turned his garage into a studio. With a barre and everything.'

'Where does he put the BMW?'

'How do *you* know he's got a BMW?'

'I assume that's Collinson's car that you sometimes come home in?'

'He gives me a lift home sometimes after a session. Or pays for an Uber.'

'A session?' We were stopped at red lights and I turned fully towards her.

Sorrel sighed. 'He likes me to dress up.'

'I bet he does,' I said in anger. 'Annie? Matilda?'

Sorrel nodded. 'Young Cosette from *Les Mis*. Once Oliver...'

'*Oliver?*' Flaming hell, the man really did have fantasies including young boys as well as girls.

'Did you not realise what he was up to, Sorrel?'

'Yes, suppose.' She sighed. 'But he's arranged an audition for me at the Susan Yates Theatre School; he knows her really well.

And honestly, Robyn, he is *such* a brilliant teacher. He's taught me so much.'

I had to concede that I remembered how much he taught me, the steps, exercises and routines he put me through over and over again, always wanting perfection, insistent on getting the very best out of me.

'Sorrel,' I said as we pulled into Mum's drive. 'He's sick. He's a paedophile, preying on kids who are desperate to become famous. He told me I was going to be in *Oliver!* in Leeds when I was twelve. Had me signing the papers. Before grabbing my hands and forcing them down his pants. I was a kid, Sorrel. I was in foster care because there was no one to look after me when Mum had to go back into hospital.' I found I was crying, great fat tears falling down my cheeks. 'He assaulted me and I never told anyone; I refused to go back to his academy. No one could understand why.'

Sorrel scrabbled in her hoody, passing over a tissue. 'Sorry, it's a bit used. You were twelve?' She sat in silence, contemplating. 'The bastard.'

'But, Sorrel' – I sniffed – 'he's been grooming you too. You must have realised?'

'Yeah, course, but he never got anywhere. He tried to kiss me a couple of times, stroke my leg, put his hands all over me, especially when I was dressed as Annie. Pervert's obviously got a thing about kids with red hair and freckles. I just kicked him off, told him to fuck off. You know, Robyn, when you've had to deal with the girls at school – when a whole gang of them are lying in wait in the toilets and after school, when they're sending messages to my phone that I was an absolute rubbish dancer, telling me to die, to kill myself – then one slimy perverted old man like Peter Collinson is a doddle.'

'Sorrel, we have to go to the police or we're condoning what he does. And he'll keep on doing it.'

'Yes, I know, I know. S'pose so. OK.' She turned to me once again. 'But we can't mention Joel and what *he's* doing.'

'OK.'

'And, I s'pose there'll be no going to the Susan Yates Theatre School now?'

'Sorry, Sorrel.' I moved to hug her and, for the first time in months, she allowed me to do just that.

And I really was sorry.

28

It had been one hell of an interesting week's break from school.

'You know, Jess,' I said on the Sunday morning before the start of the new half-term, 'I've been googling, and I don't see why Sorrel can't apply to the Susan Yates Theatre School herself.'

'Are you sure?' Jess, buttering toast, looked up. 'Don't you have to go through a dance school? And is she any good? She's not had an actual lesson for the last year or so.'

'Apart from with Peter Collinson... Look, I've no idea if she's any good or not. I feel a bit guilty that I've never been to watch her in any of the concerts she used to be in. She's been classically trained like I was, but, like me, much prefers the contemporary stuff: musical theatre and the like.'

'But the cost, Robyn? Don't go getting her hopes up, will you? We just can't afford it.'

'There's bursaries available apparently, and she wouldn't have to wait until next September – they take new kids on at Christmas and Easter. The big problem, as far as I can see, is that they only take academically sound kids: you have to be up to scratch with schoolwork as well as absolutely brilliant at dancing, singing and acting.'

'Well, forget that, then, Robyn. Sorrel's been bunking off school for the last six months. She must be way behind with her GCSE work.' Jess drained her coffee cup. 'And do they take these older kids, who're already in Year11? I thought they'd only be interested in much younger ones they can train up. Right, are you off to fetch Mum while I make us a lovely roast as a welcome-home dinner? We're going to eat about fiveish if that's OK?'

'I thought *you* might want to go?' I said, straight-faced.

'Me? Why? I'm the cook round here. *Your* job is to chauffeur.'

'One last look at a certain consultant?'

'Don't know what you're talking about.' Jess turned away, slightly flushed.

'I *knew* it.' I smiled in delight. 'You've not stopped talking about Dr Spencer ever since I got home from London.'

'He's *Mr* Spencer. Give him his correct title, Robyn. He's lovely though, isn't he?' Jess grinned, reaching for a pack of butter. 'I have real fantasies about him, you know.'

'Involving his stethoscope on your chest?'

''Fraid so.'

We both chortled conspiratorially.

'Shall I invite him back to eat with us?' I asked, determined to do just that.

'Don't you dare,' she warned. 'No.'

'Are you daring me?'

'No, just don't.'

'I'm going to.'

'You do that and I'll ring Mason and ask him as well.'

'You don't have his number.'

''Course I do. For if I need to get in touch with him about his granny.' Jess indicated her phone with a floury hand, pushed her tongue out at me and began to chop the butter before thrusting her hands into the bowl once more.

'Lovely. Do it.'

'What?'

'Invite Mason. And I'll invite Matt Spencer.'

'Oh, God, really?' Sorrel, on the scrounge for peanut butter, had come round from Mum's cottage. 'Please, *not* the head teacher.'

'Robyn fancies him,' Jess whooped.

'I do not.' I found myself flushing.

'Just listen to the pair of you,' Sorrel said, shaking her head. 'You're like a couple of adolescents. Grow up, would you, and act your age?'

That really set Jess and me laughing, relief that Sorrel appeared, almost overnight, to have had a bit of a reality check. I think she knew the situation she'd got herself into and, seeing this, Jess suddenly turned from her mixing bowl and demanded, 'Sorrel, why in God's name did you *keep on* going to his apartment? You're not daft, you must have known he had ulterior motives – apart from to make you "a star"?' She air-quoted the words irritably.

'He said if I didn't keep on coming, I'd *never* be any good,' Sorrel replied. She hesitated and then went on, 'But I was worried about Joel too.'

'Joel?' I asked, frowning. 'Joel Sinclair's big enough and daft enough to take care of himself.'

'He's not actually. He's a very sensitive person under all that Mr Big bravado.'

I wanted to smile at that: Sorrel being aware of how another kid was actually feeling under all the hard exterior he had to portray to keep at the top of his game was heart-warming. 'And?' I now asked gently.

'And what?'

'Why were you worried?'

'Peter said I had to do as he instructed or he'd tell school and the police about Joel being a drug dealer and a gang member. He's already on a referral order from court.'

'Well, that's utter rubbish for a start.' Jess tutted. 'Peter Collinson would be in just the same shit as Joel. More so actually. Joel's selling, probably been groomed and at the hands of whoever's gang he's got himself involved in. He's a minor, he's vulnerable, the courts would take a view—'

'Yes, and the gang would take *another view*,' Sorrel snapped. 'You live in a cosy world, Jess, where the police and authorities will protect you from your dad's druggy mates...'

'OK, OK!' Jess put up her hands. 'You obviously know more about it all than Robyn and me. But, as far as I can see, that slimy Peter Pervert was *buying* drugs, *using* drugs and having kids in his apartment for ulterior motives. When are you going to the police about him, Robyn?'

I glanced across at Sorrel. We'd already discussed this, and she'd been quite adamant she didn't want me to even though earlier she'd agreed we should. I'd argued that he needed stopping, he'd just move on to groom and hurt other children, some, as I'd been, too young, scared and without the understanding of what was really happening to do anything about it. I determined I was going to discuss what to do with Mason. 'It's in hand,' I said and then, changing the subject, asked, 'And do you like Joel, Sorrel?'

'He's my mate,' she replied.

'Mr Donoghue will be able to help him...' I started.

Sorrel pulled a face as she spooned peanut butter straight from the jar into her mouth. 'Really?' Her voice and face held nothing but cynicism. 'He's a head teacher! Ms Liversedge at

Beddingfield High did nothing to help me when I was being bullied. Anyway, he's old.'

'Oy, use a knife and spread it on some bread.' I passed a loaf of Jess's home-made sourdough in her direction. 'Old? What's that got to do with it? Anyway, he's only mid-thirties,' I protested. 'I asked him – wanted to know how he'd made head teacher at his age. And he told me how old he was then.'

'Put the head teacher down, Robyn.' Sorrel grinned through a mouthful of bread. 'Stand away from the head teacher.'

That made me laugh.

'D'you *really* fancy him?' Sorrel went on. 'Half the teachers at St Mede's do. Even the men: I see how they look at him in assembly. Like he's a god or something.'

'Since when have you ever made it to assembly?' Jess asked.

'I have, haven't I, Robyn?' Sorrel was indignant. 'I've only bunked off a couple. I like his assemblies.' She swallowed and made to cut another slice of bread and then stopped. 'D'you think Mum'll be OK?' she suddenly blurted out. 'It makes me really nervous, watching her, just waiting to see if she's about to have another attack. I feel panicky. I don't know what to do if she has one and has a fit or passes out.'

'Have a chat with Mr Spencer about it, Sorrel. Come with me now to pick her up.'

'OK.'

'Really?' Jess and I both turned in her direction.

'Stop looking at me,' she ordered, 'like I'm some strange specimen.'

'There's no way Matt Spencer will come to eat with us,' Jess said, almost sadly. 'He's probably got a wife and four kids at home.'

'All the more reason to come here then.' Sorrel smiled. 'Get away from the kids.' Goodness, I'd forgotten what an utterly bonny girl she was when she smiled. Of the three of us, Sorrel was the most like Mum to look at: slim, petite and very, *very* pretty.

'He's single,' I said. 'I asked him.'

'You didn't!' Both Jess and Sorrel looked aghast.

'Well, not in so many words,' I said seriously. 'I didn't say: "Are you single? Are you up for a bit with my sister?"'

'Up for a bit? God, Robyn.' Jess closed her eyes.

'I *didn't* say that.' I grinned. 'It just came up in conversation that he moved up to Yorkshire from Nottingham three months ago and he doesn't really know anyone here. OK, I'm going to ask both Mason and Matt Spencer. If they come, great, if not it'll just be the four of us Allen girls – five now with Lola. As it's always been.'

* * *

'Wow,' Matt Spencer said as he wiped his mouth on his napkin – an origami swan attempted by Lola with much muttering and concentrated hanging-out of tongue – smiling across at Jess, who went visibly pink. 'I've had months of hospital canteen food since moving up to Yorkshire from Nottingham. I can't tell you how wonderful this is, in comparison.'

'Mum's going to be on *MasterChef*,' Lola boasted.

'Really?' We all turned in Jess's direction.

'Oh, Jess, you didn't say!' Mum's eyes were wide with delight. 'At last. I've been telling you for years you should be up there with them on TV. You're just as good. And you've always yelled at the screen telling them not to cook mussels like that... or, or... not to handle filo pastry like that bloke from – where was he from, Jess? Dewsbury? And when there was that skills task and none of them knew how to prepare and cook sea urchins... do you remember? You knew...'

'I'm not going on *MasterChef*,' Jess said firmly, utterly embarrassed as four pairs of eyes turned once more from Mum back to her.

'Aw, Jess.'

'I am not going on *MasterChef*,' Jess repeated, glaring at Lola, who just laughed. She sighed. 'But I do have an interview and audition for the Yorkshire Christmas TopChef.'

We all cheered and Mum leaned over to take hold of Jess's hand.

'Which is just a little, local competition for those living in Yorkshire,' Jess went on. 'It's *nothing*.'

'It certainly isn't nothing,' I argued, remembering the big banners across the street in Ilkley, while reaching for my iPad and googling. 'Look, hundreds of people go in for it and don't get past the application-form stage.'

'They just wanted to fill their diversity requirements,' Jess snapped. 'Mixed-race, female, single mother, care worker.'

'Oh, you cynic, Jess.' Matt laughed. 'Believe in yourself.' From the way this lovely, shy consultant was looking across at Jess, not taking his eyes off her, I could see he'd been believing in Jess for a long time. 'You are an absolutely superb cook. What can we do to help you get there? To win?'

While Jess, Mum, Lola and Matt cleared the dishes and spread the TopChef information on the table to go through all the steps and instructions for Jess's first audition, Mason and I moved to the kitchen, stacking plates and cutlery in the dishwasher, scrubbing the plethora of pans Jess had used to create the amazing meal we'd just eaten.

'She really *is* good, you know,' Mason said. 'She'll do OK.'

'Depends on the competition.'

'Only regional.' He smiled. 'Only from Yorkshire.'

'Big county, Yorkshire.' I laughed. 'Hang on, where's Sorrel sloping off to...?' I made my way to the front door. 'Where're you going, Sorrel?'

'Stop panicking,' she said, looking slightly flustered. 'I'm just going to make sure Mum's bed is all ready for her; she's already gone back next door with Lola to help her.'

'Oh?' I looked at her suspiciously. 'It is ready. Jess and I made sure of that a couple of days ago. What have you got behind your back? What are you up to? You're not going out, are you? It's school tomorrow.' I realised, with sudden insight, my heart hadn't plummeted at the horror of going back to school after the week's break. My lessons were all planned and there were some new dance classes I was going to be taking. My knee, I also realised, wasn't hurting as much, didn't need half the painkillers I'd been on seven weeks or so earlier.

'What are you hiding? What have you got there?'

'Nothing!' She tutted crossly.

I turned her around. *'GCSE Maths?'*

'It was Jess's, so probably out of date now.' She was embarrassed. 'I heard you and Jess talking. I might be able to apply for Susan Yates' myself. Without Peter Collinson's recommendation. I need to look at this maths.'

'Jess will help you. I'm hopeless at maths.'

'I know,' she said, heading for the door. 'That's why I never asked you.'

'So, what do you think?' Mason asked as he folded tea towels and hung the dishcloth over the taps. Obviously house-trained.

'About Jess? And her cooking?'

'No, I meant about Sorrel.' Mason raised an eyebrow.

'I don't know. It would be far too simplistic to think we'd

rescued her from what was making her unhappy, and that everything is going to be wonderful from now on. She may have appeared fairly pliable today, but she's no angel.'

'She's fifteen, Robyn. I've never yet come across an angelic fifteen-year-old.' Mason laughed, holding up the kettle. 'Can I make coffee?'

'Sorry, of course, yes.' I found mugs and the cafetière while Mason moved to the sink.

'What I *was also* asking was what you thought about putting on a performance of *Grease*.'

'I think you're absolutely mad.' Any enthusiasm I might have garnered after the theatre visit last week was now beginning to wane when I thought of the hard work involved.

'Very probably, but: "there is a pleasure sure, in being mad, which none but madmen know…"'

'Samuel Johnson?'

'John Dryden.'

'Right.'

'So?'

'You'd never pull it off, Mason, not with the kids we have to work with at St Mede's.'

'You can't see Sorrel as Sandy?'

'Sorrel?' I stared.

'And you tell me Joel Sinclair can dance. Would he be up for Danny?'

'Mason, I've no idea if Joel can dance. Or sing? Or act? Don't forget, this isn't just about dancing; you have to be able to stand up there and speak, remember lines, hold a tune. Yes, sure he can do fabulous *jetés* out of a room to impress Year 9, but that could be mere gymnastics. Mind you, if Peter Collinson was taking him in hand…' I trailed off.

'Not just for the cocaine the bastard's addicted to, then?'

'From what I remember of Peter Collinson, he was so arrogant he wouldn't lower himself to teach anyone who didn't have a great deal of talent...' I trailed off once more, flushing slightly. 'Sorry, that makes me sound like a total bighead, doesn't it?'

'You've answered your own question, Robyn.' Mason grinned. 'I reckon we've got our Sandy and Danny.'

'Actually, I can just see Chardonnay Booth's Year 9 gang as the Pink Ladies. They're already halfway there.' I laughed at the very thought. 'And the T-Birds? And all the students at Rydell High...' My eyes widened with excitement at the thought of how I'd somehow get these kids to take part.

'There you go, then. Is that a modicum of enthusiasm?' Mason came to join me at the ancient battered Aga where I was standing for warmth and, as he passed me a mug of coffee, I saw him hesitate. I looked across at him, taking in his height and incredibly toned arms underneath the cream cashmere sweater, before moving my eyes up to his face. Yep, this was one very handsome man, and I knew there was some connection between us other than the bloody Year 9s and this mad idea to put on a full-scale production of *Grease* by Easter.

'Robyn?' He put out a hand to my arm, and I felt a traitorous stirring of lust. OK, OK, I might be utterly heartbroken over Fabian, but, at the end of the day, I was a woman and here was this man – my boss – an exceptionally bloody gorgeous man about to make a pass... A pass? Oh, for heaven's sake, Robyn...

'Could we...? D'you think...?'

This was the first time I'd seen Mason anything but totally sure of himself. In front of his staff, his kids in assembly, he was supremely confident. And yet, here, in Jess's kitchen, I was seeing another side to him.

'Could we...?' Mason moved closer, but not in a creepy way. In a warm, friendly, loving way and I realised just how much I'd missed having a pair of strong male arms around me.

'The thing is, Mason—'

'I know, I know.'

'You know?'

'Jess gave me the low-down on why you're back. I know it wasn't just your knee...'

'No.'

'And, as your boss, your *superior*...'

'My *superior*?'

'Superior in a professional capacity.' Mason started to laugh and that was enough to counter any hesitation and embarrassment we were both obviously feeling.

'And as I'm your boss, anything other than a professional relationship between the two of us really shouldn't be happening.'

'Is something happening?' I continued to hold his eye.

'I don't know what's happening, Robyn.' Mason rubbed a hand across his forehead. 'But from the minute you walked into the school with Sorrel and your dad—'

'I thought it was Jayden you were after.' I grinned, relaxing and finding myself moving tantalisingly closer to the enticing warmth of his sweater, but not yet touching.

'Him as well, of course.' Mason laughed. 'So... Robyn...' Mason moved a hand to my arm.

'I'm not, you know...?'

'Me neither...'

'Your wife?' I asked. 'Does it still... you know...?'

'A little less every day.' Mason smiled.

'What happened?'

'We're very, *very* different people: different politics, different backgrounds, different ideas on just about everything.'

'Sounds like me and Fabian.'

'The guy who's defending the serial killer?'

'Jess told you?'

'Yep.'

'She'd no right.'

'I asked, Robyn. I wanted to know. Goodness, that must have been *so* hard for you, being with someone prepared to be on the side of that bastard Henderson-Smith.'

'Different politics, different backgrounds, different ideas, different *tribe*,' I said sadly. 'We learn and we move on.'

'We have to.' Mason put out a warm hand and stroked my face.

Could I do this? Was I ready to kiss another man?

I obviously was. I leaned into Mason and he bent his head, kissing me hesitantly at first and then, as I reacted, pressing me gently back against the warm stove so that all my senses were warm and on fire... and this was fine... more than fine... and although it wasn't Fabian, this was a man who was exceptionally hot, exceptionally kind and *of my tribe*. I found myself kissing him back.

'Bloody quadratic equations,' Sorrel muttered as she returned from Mum's, coming back through the kitchen door. 'Jess...? Oh, gross,' she added, hiding her face from where we stood before hurrying into the sitting room. 'Oh, not *you* as well, Jess? What the hell's the matter with the pair of you?' Sorrel backed out of the sitting room, laughter following in her wake, Mason and I joining in as she turned to us in the kitchen. 'I'm off back to Mum and Lola where it's safe. And, it's *school,* you do realise, tomorrow?' She sniffed. 'Time you were all in bed... Oh, no, I didn't mean that.' She started laughing and, once she'd started, couldn't stop.

29

'You OK now?' I popped my head round Petra's office door the next morning at school.

'OK?' Petra appeared slightly surprised. 'Oh, after throwing up at the theatre? Yes, I'm fine. By the time Joe picked me up I was starving and desperate for cheese on toast with mint sauce.'

'Yuck! Is that a pregnancy thing?'

'What, cheese on toast?'

'No! The addition of mint sauce.'

Petra looked across her desk at me. 'No, I always have mint sauce on cheese on toast. Don't you?'

'Er, no, not always! Right, it seems our lord and master has finally managed to get his own way with me—'

'Oh?' Petra interrupted, narrowing her eyes slightly. 'In what way? You do know, Robyn, that while—'

'About the idea of putting on *Grease*,' I hurriedly interjected.

'Oh? Lovely! Right! That's fabulous, then.' The apparent relief that I wasn't actually getting more than friendly with our boss had rendered Petra utterly effusive about any forthcoming production the school might attempt to put on. I reckon if I'd told her we were presenting a nude production of *Hair* or *The Full Monty* she'd have been just as relieved there was nothing going on between Mason and me. And, if I *had* told her, I'd have had the total lecture about how it wasn't the *professionally done thing* to have a liaison with another member of staff, but particularly between *the head teacher and the supply teacher*. But, Petra, I'd have had to add, while I'd not been rendered a *total* quivering mess, not in the same way I'd melted into ecstasy with Fabian Mansfield Carrington, there was certainly a connection between our head teacher and myself.

'Well, anything I can do to help.' She now smiled, still looking at me a little strangely as these thoughts went through my head. 'Although, to be honest, I can't hold a note or act my way out of a paper bag.'

'We're a long way off that, yet.' I laughed as the bell went for the start of the school day. First day back and I was already covering registration for one member of staff who was, apparently, notorious for taking sick days off at the start and end of each half-term. 'First got to obtain permission to perform it and then find the cheapest way to get scripts. It's actually not as difficult as it sounds – I did a module when I was at uni in Manchester on producing and directing musical theatre... oh, hang on... sorry...'

Seeing Joel Sinclair walk past Petra's open door, I followed him down the corridor.

'Joel?'

'Miss?'

'You OK?'

'Why wouldn't I be, miss?' Joel held my eye.

'Look, Joel, you do know what type of man Peter Collinson is?'

'I know exactly what he is,' he snapped. 'He's a coke-head with a predilection for young girls.'

Predilection? I stared. Joel Sinclair certainly knew his English language.

'But I tell you this now, miss, he was also one of the best dancers the UK's ever produced. I've seen loads of his clips on YouTube. And he's an effing good teacher as well.'

'I do know that.' I sighed. 'He taught you those *jetés*, you said?'

Joel nodded. 'It's good Sorrel's out of there.'

'Do you really think she is?'

'Yeah, def. Been texting her ever since Thursday. She doesn't need *him*.' His tone was scornful. 'She can make it without him.'

'And you can't?'

He shrugged. 'Sorrel's got you to help her... look, miss, I'm late for registration. Don't want another bollocking from Mr Mallinson.'

'OK, OK.' I put up my hands. 'But thank you for helping to keep her safe, Joel.'

He laughed somewhat hollowly at that. 'She's more than capable of looking after herself.' He made to move away but, as he did so, I called him back.

'I can help you, Joel.'

'Help me?' He turned, a look of utter cynicism on his handsome young face. 'No, you can't. And anyway, I don't need any help.'

'Meet me in the drama studio after school.'

'Sorry?' His face turned wary.

'I want to see if you can dance.'

'Dunno if I can or not.'

'Well, let me be the judge of that. Sorrel will be there.' I crossed my fingers behind my back.

'I've got to get off, miss, after school. Can't hang around.' He turned once more.

'Four o'clock, Joel. Be there.' I headed for the class I'd been asked to register, but not before texting Sorrel to meet me and Joel in the studio after school.

I wasn't convinced either of them would turn up.

* * *

'OK,' I breathed, delighted to see not only Sorrel but Joel as well waiting in the drama studio for me at the end of the day. 'Hang on, I need a hit of something after double drama with 9AT.' I reached for my can of Coke, draining the contents in one long thirsty gulp. 'Right, I need to know if you two can dance.'

'You must know that Sorrel can,' Joel snapped irritably. 'You're her sister.'

'Yes, I may be, Joel, but she's not shared with me what she's been up to for a while. I've been away, working in London; as far as I know she could be on a hiding to nothing.'

'Oh, thanks very much!' Sorrel shook her head. 'Great confidence boost there from my big sister.'

'Right, you know where the changing rooms are. Get yourself into whatever you wear when you dance.'

Sorrel gave me one of her looks but took her bag and headed off to get changed. Joel stayed where he was.

'Joel?'

'I've nothing with me.'

'OK, you're about the same height as me.' I threw him a pair of joggers and a white T-shirt. 'Bare feet are fine. Come on.' I smiled, patting his arm as, scowling, he also headed off. 'Relax, enjoy yourself. What d'you like to dance to?'

'Kygo remixes.'

My heart missed a beat, but I kept smiling.

'You won't have ever heard of his stuff, miss. Techno house.'

Want a bet? I was immediately back in London at the end of the summer, Fabian and I dancing, utterly losing ourselves to Kygo's music in a one-off concert at Gunnersbury Park. Knowing how much I absolutely adored the man's music, Fabian had managed somehow to get tickets.

It had been one of the best evenings of my life.

I reached for my phone and scrolled to Spotify. 'Any particular track?' I asked. 'Please not Selena Gomez singing "It Ain't Me".'

'Selena Gomez,' Joel said, obviously embarrassed. '"It Ain't Me". You won't know it – Kygo's remix.'

Five minutes later the pair were in front of me.

'Now what?' Sorrel asked, hands on hips.

'Selena Gomez?' I asked. 'Joel says he knows it. You as well?'

'Yeah, we've worked together on this at Collinson's place.'

'Look, pretend I'm not here.' I smiled as they both stood there, not looking at each other. 'Warm up, do your own thing. I've some tidying up to do.'

'Oh, for God's sake,' Sorrel muttered as I turned my back on them and started the music, but I sensed her bending, stretching, starting to move and then, as the first evocatively soul-stirring notes of the utterly wonderful track sounded in the room, knew that Joel, too, was simply unable not to.

Oh, that haunting music; the words. I was back at Gunnersbury Park, dancing with Fabian, lost in him and Kygo's music, loving every single minute, wanting it never to end.

With an effort, I wrenched myself from memories of Fabian singing along, holding me, loving me.

I turned to find Joel and Sorrel moving, at first utterly self-conscious, horribly embarrassed, Joel missing a step, swearing at himself, and then beginning to lose himself in the music, becoming oblivious now to me, to the dingy, badly lit drama studio, to anything but being in the moment.

I stood and stared because I couldn't do anything else, my hand to my mouth, as they danced a routine they obviously both loved and had practised under Collinson's direction.

'Bloody hell.' Mason had joined me by the door; utterly capti-
vated, I'd not realised he was there. 'How've you got them to come
down here and do this? Wow, they're good.'

'Dance is a part of them both,' I whispered. 'It's just what they
have to do.'

'Well, there's your Sandy and Danny.' He grinned, placing a
hand on my arm before, obviously remembering we were no
longer in Jess's kitchen by the Aga, removing it.

As the track came to its conclusion, Joel's embarrassment
returned, but doubly so at Mason's presence. But there was
another look: a mixture of pleading, hope and also pride as they
both joined us.

'Oh my *God*,' I exclaimed. 'You are both *so* exceptionally
talented; no wonder Collinson wanted to work with you. Sorrel,
I'm so sorry, I just didn't realise how good you've become, how
you've progressed...'

'Well, no, you wouldn't,' she said, feisty as ever. 'You were
never around.'

'Well, I am now. I can teach you both... I can...' I broke off as
two kids, probably in their late teens, appeared at the studio
door.

'Hey, Joel, bro, move it. We've been waiting for you outside.
Get the fucking fairy outfit off and get back out here with us
where you belong.'

Joel hesitated, but only for a couple of seconds, and when
Mason, frowning, moved across to the door and the newcomers,
Joel picked up his things and headed towards them.

'I don't know how you've gained entry into school, gentlemen,
but you need to leave. Right now.' Next to Mason's height and
stature, these two youths appeared slight, weedy, but they stood
their ground, ignoring Mason until Joel was with them.

'Joel, you don't need to go,' Mason was saying. 'If you're not happy to leave with these...' Mason hesitated '...*friends* of yours, then stay.'

'It's fine, Mr Donoghue.' Joel smiled, but his face was pale. 'They're mates of mine. No problem. Thanks, miss...' He looked directly at me. 'See you, Sorrel.' He turned and left, a lonely figure in the wake of the other two.

'He's still got your joggers and T-Shirt, Robyn,' Sorrel said, almost apologetically. 'I'll get them back for you tomorrow.'

'Not a problem.'

'Jess's waiting for me,' Sorrel went on, checking her phone. 'She's picking me up because she didn't know what time you'd be finished.'

'Oh? You're going to do some maths?' I laughed at that, trying to lighten the atmosphere the two older boys' presence had made dark.

'Yes, *actually*.' Sorrel glared at me. 'And off for what's left over from yesterday. Better than what you call your shepherd's pie.' She sniffed. 'Don't think it's ever seen a shepherd.' She turned to Mason. 'She can't cook you know, sir.'

'Sorrel, you were amazing.' Mason smiled. 'You'll go far.'

'Just back to Jess's with Mum this evening.' She grinned and then became serious. 'Look, can't you do something? You know, for Joel?'

Mason patted Sorrel's shoulder. 'Doing what I can at the moment, Sorrel. Not your problem. You go home and have the rest of that fabulous cheesecake.'

'It *is* my problem,' Sorrel insisted. 'Joel's my mate. He always tried to make sure he was around when I was at Collinson's place.'

'As I say, I'll do what I can,' Mason reiterated.

When Sorrel had left, I turned to Mason. 'What *can* you do?'

'Already liaising with the local authority, their gang team and the police.'

'They have a *gang team*?' I stared. 'Those two who appeared just now won't like that. They'll think Joel's grassing them up. Is that fair on Joel? You need to be careful.'

'That's why I'm saying nothing further to you, Robyn. I don't want you or Sorrel in any way involved. And I suggest you also do nothing at the moment about going to the police.'

'Jeez, this is scary.' I sighed. 'Got some marking to do.' I turned to leave.

'I've an M&S lasagne for two in my fridge at home. Needs eating before it's out of date. We could think further about *Grease*?'

I laughed at that. 'Well, I've never before been wooed with going-off pasta.'

'Always a first time. So?'

'Thank you.' I smiled at him. 'Yes, why not?'

'I've an hour's work or so to do before I leave. I'll text you when I'm leaving with my address.'

'Petra won't be impressed,' I said, pulling a scary face.

'Petra won't know,' he replied. 'And, if she finds out, we're simply having an extraordinary general meeting of the St Mede's spring production.'

And with that, he loosened his tie, removed his suit jacket and set off in the direction of his office.

* * *

Mason lived in a rented cottage, not dissimilar to Mum and Jess's cottages, but on the other side of Beddingfield in the lea of what we kids had always called Bluebell Wood, where we'd spent many a day having picnics.

'I love this part of the village.' I smiled as I followed him through the front door. 'How long have you been here?'

'Ever since I separated from my wife. She's remained in the house we bought together in the swankier part of town.'

'Right.'

'So, just over two years, ever since I accepted the headship at St Mede's.'

'Where were you before?'

'I was deputy at a private boys' grammar school at the other side of Midhope.'

'Really?' I stared at Mason's back as he bent down to light the log fire in the sitting room. 'I'm amazed the governors gave you the job at St Mede's, then. Going from a posh school to a sink school without the experience needed for that new challenge.'

Mason turned and stood. 'No one else wanted it.' He grinned. 'There was just me and one other up for it and, after his tyres were let down during the first rounds of interviews, he withdrew. I'm probably there by default. But,' he added, 'I was just so fed up with statistics and trying to get kids into Oxbridge and bolshy, arrogant parents with a lot of money who assumed that was the gateway to life. I was bored; I needed a professional challenge.'

'And now?'

'Now, I'm probably feeling somewhat disillusioned. I thought I could make a difference, but I'm not convinced anyone can. There's always the spectre lurking in the shadows that St Mede's really *is* a sink school, and sinking further into the mire with every term that passes. Right, glass of wine?'

'On a school night?'

'Particularly on a school night.' He grinned. 'But just the one.'

'You've no photos around the place,' I observed, looking round before following him into the large dining kitchen.

'All left behind at the house,' he said. 'Except for this one.' He pointed to the photo of an elderly woman on the sideboard.

'Your gran? Up at Hudson House?'

Mason nodded. 'She's my father's mother, but my father's opted to spend the last few years of his career in the States – he's a surgeon – and my mum's got a new husband and family and not overly interested in Denise, my granny. So, it seemed the best solution all round to move her up near me. Dad keeps in touch with her best way he can.'

'And your wife?'

'What about her?'

'You're still on speaking terms?'

'Just about.' He smiled and then, obviously not wanting to talk about her, changed the subject. 'OK, food's in the oven.' He clinked his glass of wine with mine. 'I declare the first meeting of the newly formed St Mede's spring production 2024 well and truly open.'

We spent the next couple of hours with notebooks and pens, outlining our ideas as I took Mason through the steps we'd have to take.

'I'm not convinced we're going to be able to do all this by Easter,' I said. 'Why don't you aim for the summer term, you know, an end-of-year thing?'

'With Year 11 already left by May to revise for the GCSEs? And half the kids being taken off for the bargain weeks in Benidorm and Turkey that their parents can't afford during the school holidays?'

'So, you've six months,' I said with raised eyebrows, while simultaneously counting on my fingers.

'Need to crack on, then.'

'Like a pit pony.' I smiled, thinking how much I'd like Mason to kiss me again.

'Look, Robyn.' Mason put down his pen and half-drunk cup of coffee. 'Last night...'

Oh, hell, was this the brush-off coming? Just when I didn't

think I could cope with any more rejection?

'...was really wonderful...'

'But?'

'But?' Mason reached for my hand. '*And*, actually.'

'And?'

'And I'd quite like to do it all over again.' He grinned across at me and, not for the first time, I was getting the sense that Mason Donoghue didn't really give a fig for protocol, for the rules of the game, about his having a relationship with the lowly supply teacher.

This wasn't going to be easy. I'd been so hurt by Fabian, I didn't know if I could ever really feel anything more than this passing frisson of lust. It had only been, what? Two months? Maybe this wasn't such a good idea? Maybe it really was too soon to get back on my bike, as it were. And riding pillion with my boss into the bargain? *Riding?* Oh, hell! And Petra wouldn't be happy. Mind you, Jess would. And Mum: Mum had really taken to him when he was round yesterday.

'Sorry,' I said, in an attempt to push away these conflicting thoughts that were buzzing round my head like an out-of-control mosquito. 'Could you repeat that?'

'Which bit?'

'Something about wanting to do it all again?'

'Last night was really wonderful, and I'd quite like to do it all over again? That bit?'

'On a school night?' I asked primly.

'Especially on a school night,' he replied, leaning in.

PART III

30

The autumn term rolled on. More than rolled on, really: in fact, it galloped on.

By the time I'd been teaching at St Mede's for three months, I was gaining in confidence and actually beginning to enjoy my days at the chalkface. Year 9 still had the ability to wind me up, and that little sod, Whippety Snicket, took great pleasure in goading me into losing my temper whenever he could. But now I was able to see him for the unhappy, unloved, immature adolescent he unfortunately was and, instead of being confrontational with him, I either ignored him or rang for the senior leadership team to remove him from my lessons.

And I now had a secret weapon with these kids.

Two, actually.

With my knee much improved I'd started both lunchtime and after-school dance sessions, which could only be attended when accompanied by good reports from class teachers. *Anything* less than a clean sheet for behaviour – and that included C1: shouting out in class – and they'd forfeit that week's chance to join in.

'Yah, you're all big sissies,' I heard various kids mock those who were up for it. 'Who wants to be a fucking ballet dancer?'

'Oh, grow up,' one tiny Year 7 lad had the temerity to come back at a much bigger, extremely truculent Year 8 girl. 'It's hip hop.'

Well, some of it was. I'd started with easy dance routines, stepping, pivoting and shimmying to tracks such as Taylor Swift's 'Shake It Off', and when the kids were able to cope with those, we were soon into working to the tracks of Swedish House Mafia, Illenium and Teddy Swims.

* * *

After a couple of weeks, when I found some of the young mums watching at the door, tapping their feet and dancing in the corridor, I invited them in as well and soon I had a class just for parents: all mums – there didn't appear to be any dads interested. Maybe there just weren't any dads around full stop?

And, of course, the other secret weapon was the production of *Grease*. I'd been absolutely astonished when, after Mason had announced in assembly that St Mede's was thinking of attempting this, and that anyone interested in taking part should meet with him, Mr Mallinson, in charge of English, and me that very lunchtime, we were absolutely inundated with kids. To be honest, it was jolly cold outside that day – an icy wind blowing across the playground from the Pennines – and it was a good opportunity to remain inside, but there was a genuine frisson of excitement in the ranks as Mason explained just what was entailed in their signing up.

There were some rumblings of disapproval from one quarter of the staffroom, particularly from those with responsibility for the summer GCSEs, but, on the whole, positive vibes were soon winging around the school and the four of us, Mason, Petra, Dave Mallinson and myself, immediately got down to auditioning for parts.

By early December, parts had been allocated and rehearsals started. Sorrel was the obvious choice for Sandy, despite some backchat and downright badass comments from a couple of coteries of Year 9 and Year10 girls – as well as their mums – who complained of favouritism and actually bandied around the words *bias* and *nepotism* (with which I was most impressed).

Joel would have nothing to do with the part of Danny Zuko or, indeed, the production itself, despite Sorrel, Mason and myself constantly haranguing him to change his mind.

'Leave him,' Sorrel advised. 'He's got enough on his plate at the moment.' And, eventually, after much auditioning (some truly terrible, some rather surprisingly promising and some that had Mason, Petra and me in absolute hysterics) the part was given to a Year 10 lad – Seb Kingsley – who might not have been anywhere near Joel in the dance stakes, but could sing and act and was confident with his lines.

* * *

I'd called an after-school rehearsal for both the Pink Ladies and the T-Birds.

Mason had gone off to some meeting of head teachers and Petra had spent the afternoon at the hospital having a scan, so it was just Dave Mallinson and myself left to organise the kids. They were enthusiastic but over-excited, and after a couple of hours putting them through their paces I was shattered. It was going up to 6 p.m. by the time Dave and I were satisfied we'd done enough, and all I wanted was to get off home and a soak in a hot bath.

Sorrel had missed the rehearsal, Jess picking her up to take her to the dentist for a filling. I went to retrieve marking I'd not got round to earlier and then, desperate for a pee, made a quick visit to the nearby girls' toilet block rather than the staff facilities a good five minutes' walk at the other end of the building. Humming along to 'Look at me, I'm Sandra Dee', I did what I'd come for and went to the basins to wash my hands. I was running a hand through my hair, belting out at the top of my voice the actual, more controversial, lyrics – about being lousy with virginity instead of the words appropriately doctored by Dave for our young performers – when a scuffling noise behind me stopped me in my tracks.

One of the cleaners had reported seeing a rat on the playground earlier in the week and I froze, poised to leg it out of there. The shuffling noise came again, but this time accompanied by sniffing. Sniffing rats?

'Hello?' I called, assuming it to be one of the girls from rehearsal and now utterly embarrassed I'd been overheard really going for it with the original words to the song. 'Hello? You need to get off home before Caretaker Ken locks you in.'

Silence.

Then more sniffs.

I walked the length of the toilet block, bending to peer underneath cubicle doors. 'You'll be here until the morning,' I warned once again. 'You need to get off home.'

The end cubicle was closed and, when I put my hand to it, I found it was locked. I bent down once more but could see no telltale shoes or trainers.

'Who's in there?'

Silence.

I walked into the adjacent cubicle, stood on the toilet seat and, hoisting myself up, peered over into the locked one.

'What on earth are you doing?' I'd called the kid Whippety

Snicket for so long that, for a second, I couldn't remember his real handle. How awful of me. Blane, that was it. Blane Higson. 'What are you *doing*, Blane?' I repeated. 'This is the girls' toilet.' He was sitting on the closed toilet seat, his knees scrunched up to his scrawny chest, his head in his hands, and sniffing. 'Have you found yourself locked in?' I asked with a laugh. 'Come for some tissue for your nose and got yourself locked in? Come on, open the door and go home.'

'I've lost the bloody key,' he muttered, and I realised he was crying.

'You don't need a key to get out, you daft thing,' I encouraged. 'Just turn the lock on the door.'

'No. I'm staying here.'

'Why?'

'Just am.'

'All night?'

Silence.

'All night?' I asked once again. 'It'll get cold. It's December. Heating'll go off.'

Silence.

'Hang on, I'm coming over. Shift out of the way, Blane.'

Putting all the weight on my hands, I hoisted myself over, feeling for the toilet cistern with my feet before dropping down beside the boy.

'Blimey, haven't done that for a while.' I smiled, turning in the narrow space and unlocking the door.

'Don't,' he snapped, kicking out towards the door before hugging his foot to himself once more.

'Why not?' The atmosphere in that cubicle was fetid as well as slightly claustrophobic and I needed to get out. I realised Blane, as well as the lavatory, was somewhat odorous. His scrawny neck, peeking out from the frayed and dirty collar of his greying school shirt, was filthy.

'Can't go home.'

'Why not?'

'Told you, I've lost the bloody key.'

'And your mum'll be cross? Convinced a burglar might find it and let themself in?'

'Me mam's not there.'

'Oh?'

'She's gone off somewhere.'

'Where?'

'Dunno.'

I remembered Mason telling me Whippety's dad had left years ago and his mum had a heroin addiction.

'You've brothers, haven't you? Big brothers? Won't they be at home?'

'Dunno where they are. They've scarpered; couldn't stand living with me mam any longer.'

'OK. Well, at least let's get out of this toilet. You hungry?'

'I had me school dinner,' he muttered.

'What are you having for your tea?'

Blane shrugged but uncurled his legs from beneath him and stood.

'I've some chocolate in my classroom. D'you fancy some?'

'If you want.' He shrugged again, but looked hopeful as he followed me out of the toilet block.

'Oy, what you two still doing here?' Jobsworth Ken was doing his final rounds. I looked at my watch and realised it was going up to 7 p.m.

'Just going, Ken. We've been in rehearsal.'

'Him as well?' Ken nodded in Whippety's direction. 'Can't see *him* as the next Fred Astaire.' He gave a sneery chuckle. 'Come on, the pair of you, out, my wife'll have my tea on the table.'

'Ten minutes, Ken, and then we'll be off.'

* * *

'Right,' I said, once Blane had devoured not only the chocolate but my left-over cheese and pickle sandwich from lunchtime. 'I'll give you a lift home.'

'I told you, I've no key to get in.'

'Neighbours who might have one? Granny you can go to?'

Blane shook his head.

I needed Mason or Petra to tell me what to do but when I rang, both their numbers went straight to voicemail. I left messages and then tried Dave Mallinson but, again, no response.

'Where d'you think the key might be?' I asked hopefully, not sure what else to do.

'I'm locking up. Now,' Ken ordered, coming back into the classroom with his coat, hat and scarf on before retreating once more.

'OK, OK, we're coming,' I called after him. I turned back to Blane. 'When did you lose this key?'

'Dunno.'

'Have you ever actually had one?'

'Yeah, course.' He didn't look at me.

'Blane, where did you stay last night?'

He shrugged.

'Here? In school?' I felt my heart plummet. The poor, poor kid. 'Right, OK, you come home with me now and I'll ring Mr Donoghue again. He'll know what to do.'

'Don't you bring in no social lot,' Blane warned, heading for the door. 'I'm not going into no care again.'

'Come on,' I said gently, taking hold of his arm. 'Come home with me and then we'll work something out.'

* * *

'What the hell's *he* doing here?' Sorrel looked up from the kitchen table where she was struggling with not only a post-dentist numb mouth, but pages of algebraic equations. Mum, at the ironing board, was equally surprised.

'Long story,' I said. 'Blane here's lost his key and can't get in at home.' I threw both Sorrel and Mum a warning glance. 'So, he's going to stay for tea and then, if I can get hold of him, Mr Donoghue will take him home.'

'There's a casserole in the oven,' Mum said. 'Might be a bit dried up now, but there should be enough for both of you.'

Throughout this, Blane had stood, head down, scowling, refusing to speak or meet anyone's eye.

'You hungry, Blane?' Mum asked gently. 'You look it.' She moved towards him and then drew back slightly as the smell of unwashed teen assailed her nostrils. She raised an eye in my direction and then we all turned as Jess came through the back door.

'I've come to help with your maths, Sorrel...' she started, but stopped once she saw Blane. 'Hello, who's this?'

And then, in typical Jess style, once she'd been brought up to speed on the situation, she took over. 'You look all in, Blane. How about Ms Allen here gets on the phone to Mr Donoghue again? Then, once you've had your tea you can come round to my house – I just live next door – and you can have a lovely warm shower and we can find you some clean clothes?'

'I'm not going into no home again,' Blane warned.

'Well, we can't throw you out on the street, can we?' Jess

smiled. She nodded her head slightly in my direction and I followed her out into the sitting room.

'You can't just bring a child home like this,' she warned. 'Not convinced it's ethical.'

'What else could I have done? I couldn't leave him to spend another night by himself in school.'

'I'll ring the right people.'

'Who are?'

'Robyn, don't forget I'm a registered foster parent.'

'Oh, I had forgotten that. You've not fostered a child for years, have you?'

'Yes, I have.' Jess spoke calmly. 'The spare bed's always made up in case of emergencies. Not so many now when I'm virtually full time at the care home but, yes, my number is still on lists.'

'So, what are you saying?'

'I'm saying, you feed him and I'll make a phone call. I'll take the poor kid next door after he's eaten and keep him overnight if necessary. You keep ringing Mason and then he and the authorities will have to sort it tomorrow.'

Which was what we did. Blane and I sat at the table and ate while both Mum and Sorrel tried to act as though it were an everyday occurrence that one of my pupils – a neglected, unhappy kid from a broken family – had joined us.

Jess made just the one phone call to whoever, determined that Blane should have at least one night's stopover with her before the real interrogations started the following day.

* * *

'I didn't know what else to do,' I told Mason the next morning. 'You didn't answer your phone. Didn't get back to me.'

'The heads' meeting went on and on,' Mason said. 'And then I crashed out. Been a busy term. Sorry. You did well. Thank you.'

It turned out that Blane's mum had been working the daytime streets as usual and had overdosed and ended up in hospital, totally out of it. No one appeared aware, or even to care, that a thirteen-year-old child had come home to an empty house and a locked door. The upshot of all this was firstly that Blane did have to spend several weeks at one of the local places for looked after children until his mum was back home, supported by social services. But secondly, he and I had established a much better relationship and I'd often look up from my desk at the end of the day to find he'd sidled in wanting to talk. Or just for company. And a bit of affection.

* * *

One bitterly cold Friday morning, I was in the studio trying to heat up the place in readiness for a Year 7 session and, shivering, realised the best way to warm myself up was to actually move. I'd been growing in confidence about my knee, extending my movements when teaching my dance classes, and now I decided to see just how much my knee would take. I was stiff, awkward to begin with, but I built up slowly, repeating the exercises and routines I knew my knee could take and then extending myself, pushing myself, going through the less complicated set moves I knew by heart from *Dance On*.

'Hey, you're getting there; you're nearly back to what you were.' Sorrel had appeared in the studio without my noticing.

'Not really.' I sighed. 'I'm terribly stiff; really lacking the confidence to jump. Terrified I'm going to fall again. What are you doing here?' I turned to her. 'Bell's gone.'

'I have to go home.'

'Aren't you well?' She looked fine. Buzzing actually. 'Need some Tampax?'

'No! Jess has just texted me.'

'You shouldn't have your phone on you.'

'Jess just texted me.' She tutted, ignoring the rebuke. 'Don't go all teacherish on me. She's probably texted you as well.'

'Oh, not Mum?' I wiped the sweat from my face with a towel. 'She's not had another turn, has she?'

'No!' Sorrel tutted again. 'Why d'you have to be so negative? She says the post's just come.'

'And?'

'She says there's two letters. One for her, and Mum's been round to say there's one for me.'

'*And?*'

'She daren't open them. One's from Yorkshire Christmas TopChef—'

'Oh, blimey—'

'And mine's from the Susan Yates Theatre School.'

'Oh, Sorrel.'

'So, can we just bunk off and go home? Come on, drive me, will you? Because Jess says she won't open hers – and she won't open mine, though I've texted her to open mine and text me back – until we're all there. And she's off to work in an hour. Come *on*!'

'Registration, Sorrel?' Mason popped his head round the studio door. 'You're late.'

'I need to go home.'

'You *don't*,' I butted in. 'Exercise a little patience.'

'So, how about I tell you *Focus North* is going to come to a rehearsal next week?' Mason's face was alight with anticipation. 'They've a feature which looks at the creative arts in local schools. Lucy Bennet's boyfriend works on the programme, apparently. She had a word with him last night and he's just messaged her;

they're coming to a rehearsal next Wednesday. It'll only be five minutes at the most, but it'll give the kids a buzz.'

'Oh, that's great.' I felt really pleased, but with misgivings. 'They do know we've only just started?'

'Absolutely. Have you never seen the programme? It tries to feature different activities at different stages of production. If we're lucky, they'll come back later on to see how we're progressing.' He turned away from Sorrel and, with a lowered voice, said, 'Sorry, Robyn, can't make this evening, after all.' He'd asked me over to his place for the drink and takeaway that had become a bit of a Friday evening routine. 'Got a really important meeting over in Leeds.' He turned again in Sorrel's direction. 'Right, Sorrel, registration,' he barked before hurrying out as his phone started.

Sorrel glared at me, but set off in the direction of the door.

'We'll sort it all tonight,' I called after her. 'If it's good news, we'll go out for pizza. Yes?'

'And if it's bad?' She turned at the door, a look of comic melancholic dejection on her pretty face.

'I'll treat you to somewhere posh.' I smiled, trying to work out what was left in my bank account that month.

* * *

'Come *on*.' Sorrel was at my classroom door as the bell went, waiting with her coat on and irritably elbowing the younger Year 7 kids and their voluminous bags as they barged into her in their bid for freedom.

'Oy, don't rush. Walk!' I shouted at their departing backs. And then, grabbing my jacket, added, 'I'm coming, I'm coming.' Luckily, Friday was the one afternoon I didn't have a staff meeting, rehearsal or one of my extra-curricular dance classes. 'OK.' I jingled my keys in Sorrel's direction as we attempted our own quick getaway through a throng of pop-drinking, chocolate-bar-eating and phone-scrolling kids.

'You OK?' I asked once we were belted up and negotiating our way through the dissipating crowd of pupils.

'Duh! No!' Sorrel snapped. 'Of course not. What if they turn me down for an audition? *Of course*, they'll turn me down for an audition,' she added crossly.

I patted Sorrel's hand in sympathy, but slowing to a standstill at the main gate where kids and parents had gathered was just too much for her and, pressing down the window button, she shouted, 'Get out the fecking way, can't you?'

'Sorrel,' I spluttered. 'There are parents there.'

'I'm sure they've heard a lot worse.' She grinned. 'Sorry.'

Mum, Jess and Lola were all waiting in Jess's kitchen, hovering impatiently over a devil's food cake brimming with chocolate and cream.

'I made it to stuff our faces if it's not good news,' Jess said apologetically while Mum poured tea.

'What if one's good news and one isn't?' Lola asked, holding the two letters reverentially to her chest.

'Oh, for God's sake,' I said. 'You're all drama queens. Get the damned things opened.' I took the envelopes from Lola and handed them to their rightful recipients. 'Just do it.'

Jess and Sorrel did as they were told and, without another word, opened the letters.

'Yes!' Sorrel immediately shouted, thumping the air and jumping up and down. 'Yes, yes, absolutely yes! Got an audition after Christmas.' She hugged Mum so hard the pair almost fell over.

'Jess?'

We all turned in her direction where she stood, stock-still, grim-faced, her demeanour one of utter disappointment.

'No?' I asked gently. 'Aw, Jess. Look, you can try for the *big one* next. Actual *MasterChef*…'

Sorrel grabbed the letter angrily from Jess's hand and then started to hoot. 'You big fraud, Jessica Butterworth,' she yelled, turning back to Lola, Mum and me. 'She's got it too: she's one of the ten picked to show what they can cook in the first round of just two rounds in Harrogate. Blimey, Jess, filming starts the beginning of the week after next!'

* * *

Mum had immediately messaged Jayden touring in South America to tell him the good news and he'd (amazingly) immediately got back saying he'd transfer the necessary readies to Mum's account and for her to book somewhere fabulous for the five of us to celebrate.

'You don't think we're being a bit premature?' Jess worried. 'I mean, we're only both at the first stages.'

'Yes, and let's face it, being realistic, you might not get to the finishing line.' I patted Jess's arm. 'So, best to take up Jayden's offer of a fabulous meal and make the most of celebrating this first step of the way while you can.'

Three hours later, showered, coiffured, dressed in our best and made up (including Lola, who was immediately ordered back upstairs to take off the badly applied startlingly pink lipstick and blue eyeshadow) we were in an Uber and heading for Cream, an up-and-coming and ridiculously expensive restaurant in the town centre.

'Do we just get cream?' Lola wanted to know as we were

shown to our seats. 'You know, like at the chippy, we just get chips?'

'Yes,' Sorrel deadpanned. 'You just have to choose from single, double, clotted, whipping or sour.'

I glanced over at her. What a difference three months had made to my little sister's whole life. She was still feisty, probably always would be, and, let's face it, that wasn't a bad thing if she was to make it and *survive* in the West End. I couldn't see Sorrel getting as upset as I had been with the mean girls who'd turned on me backstage at The Mercury. Sorrel, this evening, was animated, glowing, her hair, released from its usual scrunched-up ponytail, a cloud of dark smoke around her ravishing little pixie face.

'Ugh, sour cream? Why's it gone off?' Lola pulled a face. 'I'll have clotted cream, I think. Can I have Coke, Granny?'

'She's having you on, sweetie.' Mum smiled. 'Yes, one Coke if your mum says that's OK.' Mum, too, was so much better than when I'd rushed up – as much as one *can* rush up with an ACL injury – three months earlier, terrified that this particular downward spiral into her condition might be her last. Thanks to Matt Spencer and his team at Midhope General, she'd pulled through again and was trialling new drugs, which appeared to be working. Slight, pretty, her beautiful facial bone structure a heads-up to her Asian heritage, she looked more like my and Jess's older sister than our mum.

Jess, herself always a worrier, appeared, despite the nerve-racking Yorkshire Christmas TopChef rounds ahead of her, much more relaxed and happier now that Dean Butterworth was out of her life and Matt Spencer very much in it. I watched as she perused every bit of the menu, frowning at a dish she obviously didn't think would work, but nodding sagely to herself at an idea I knew she'd be emulating in her own kitchen the following day.

She'd lost quite a bit of weight recently – whether through worry or, as was probably the case, through falling in love with Matt – and, with Jayden's Caribbean heritage, rather than Mum's South Asian genes, her stunning dark eyes and full mouth reflected her own striking good looks.

Mum looked up from her perusal of the menu. 'Right, I know what I'm having,' she said, turning to me. 'So, Robyn, how's it going with the magnificent Mason?'

'Magnificent?' I laughed at that. 'Yeah, he is quite nice.'

'Nice?' Mum looked askance. 'Nice? Robyn, he's absolutely lovely. Quite stunning. Reminds me a bit of your dad in his younger days.'

'Does he?' I thought about it. 'Actually, you're right. Don't they say you always end up marrying your father?'

'Oh, gross.' Sorrel sniffed, overhearing our conversation, and Lola started giggling. 'Please don't say you're serious about him, Robyn? Mind you, you are getting on a bit now. Pushing thirty is so-o-o-o ancient. Maybe settling back down here, up in Yorkshire...'

'Is that grammatically correct?' I interrupted, embarrassed as all eyes turned on me.

'Good job I'm going to Beddingfield High rather than St Mede's next year,' Lola said sagely, saving me from answering Sorrel. 'I certainly don't want to be sitting in assembly singing "Fight the Good Fight" knowing the headmaster's just got out of bed with my aunty.'

'Oy,' Mum, Jess and I chorused as one.

'No, not the best situation.' Sorrel grinned. 'I'm with you on this, Lola. Mind you, that bitch of a headmistress – Ms Liversedge – is an utter witch. You'll have to watch your step there. In fact, you'd probably be better going to St Mede's in September. I'm sure Robyn will be back in London by then, so you don't have to worry about conjuring up pictures of the pair of them together.'

'Oy, you as well, Sorrel,' I said. 'Enough already.'

'Yes, but, Robyn, you are getting a bit serious with Mason.' Mum was refusing to let it go. 'He's fabulous: good-looking, bright – dad's a surgeon – he must be OK – and he's *here*.'

'What's that supposed to mean? He's *here*?'

'Well, unlike the Bastard Bucks Barrister...' Jess started.

'Oh, come on,' I snapped, hating any criticism of Fabian still that wasn't coming from me. 'I'm sure you three can be even more alliterative if you try.'

'Perfidious Patronising Pillock?' Sorrel suggested.

'Lousy, Loathsome Lawyer?' Lola giggled.

'Enough,' Mum warned, seeing my face. 'I'm sure he was very nice...'

'No, he wasn't,' Jess came back at Mum. 'He knew how Robyn felt about his defending a serial misogynistic murderer; he messaged that there was no future in their relationship; blocked her from his phone and, even *without* all that, Robyn couldn't have put up with his racist family.'

'Only his brother and mother,' I started, wanting to defend Fabian, knowing how much he'd loved me. Though not enough, obviously. 'His dad was quite nice; his sister, Jemima, fabulous. Right,' I went on, suddenly close to tears, 'we're supposed to be celebrating, not pulling my ex to bits.'

'We're just trying to balance Mason against your barrister,' Mum said calmly. 'Mason has a lot in the credit column whereas, from what you've told us, and what we've seen of him on TV, Fabian – is it? – is clearly in the red, if not totally morally bankrupt.'

'You know, Mason Donoghue's no *angel*,' I snapped, as we

didn't appear to be moving on. 'He'll do anything to get what he wants. Look how he blackmailed me into going to work for him.'

'There you go – he *is* a bit like your dad,' Mum said gently.

'Oh?' I glared at her. 'That's why you like Mason, isn't it, because he reminds you of Jayden? And look how *he's* led you a merry dance all these years.' I shook the menu meaningfully. 'Before I lose my appetite altogether, can we just order?'

The food was utterly fabulous and the wine went down well. I started with North Sea crab with *ajo blanco* and seared grapes; Mum and Sorrel had scallops with white asparagus and a smoked egg yolk, Jess went for prawn bisque croquetas with a charcoal mayo and Lola, although unfazed by Jess's concoctions at home, went for a less exotic-sounding chorizo Scotch egg.

'Hey, look! No, *don't look, don't look,*' Sorrel spluttered as we all did just the opposite. 'Isn't that the horrible Ms Liversedge herself?' she asked as we all turned in the direction of the ladies' loo where Sorrel indicated she'd just seen Beddingfield High's headmistress go in.

'Definitely her,' I said once the woman exited and Jess nodded in agreement while Lola, who knew the infamous woman only by hearsay, lurched out of her seat to get a good look at her future head teacher.

'Lola, stop gawping,' Jess and I hissed.

'*You* all are.' She pouted. 'Kyle Meadows in my class says she's really sexy and he can't wait to move up to the high school.'

'She does look a lot more glamorous than I remember.' Jess nodded, turning back to the table. 'D'you see her tight leather skirt and high heels?'

'All the lads in Year 10 used to fancy her.' Sorrel said in agreement. 'I never got it.'

'You're not a red-blooded male.' Mum laughed. 'She's certainly got something, I agree, but I found her so intimidating when she was always calling me in because of you, Sorrel, I never really dared look at her face. I think I was constantly eye to eye with that cleavage of hers that was always out on display.'

'I'm going to see who she's with.' I grinned, the surfeit of wine making me frivolous.

I stood and walked over to the loo and then past it, peering into the dimly lit area beyond. This was obviously set up for more private dining – each white-clothed table set for just two diners – compared to where we were seated in the marginally cheaper seats out at the front.

Oh. I stopped, for a second, unable to take in just what I was seeing.

Ms Liversedge – I didn't know her first name but, from then on, would always give her the handle Ms *Loversedge* – was leaning into, and being fed forkfuls of food by, the exceptionally handsome man opposite.

By, in Mum's opinion, the Magnificent Mason.

31

'I'm sorry.'

'What are you sorry for, Mr Donoghue?' Monday morning and I was back in the drama studio, even more Arctic now that Jobsworth had turned off all the heating over the weekend, despite the icy conditions and thus the real threat of burst frozen pipes. I turned to Mason, who was hanging back at the entrance looking sheepish.

'I should have told you,' Mason said, obviously embarrassed but coming into the studio and walking over to me. 'Hell, it's cold in here.'

'Told me what? That you were having a bit of a thing with a rival head teacher? At the same time as with me? At least you're hedging your bets, going for a bit of variety: a head teacher and a lowly supply teacher.'

Mason hesitated. 'Bit more than having a bit of a thing with Angel...' he began.

'Angel?' I started to laugh. 'Not even Angela?' I laughed again. '*Angel* Liversedge?'

'Angel Donoghue actually.'

'What?' I stared at the man in front of me. 'Ms Liversedge is your *wife*?'

Mason nodded. 'I'm sorry, I should have come clean about it with you. With all the staff really. And, the thing is…'

'You're no longer estranged?'

'That obvious?'

'Mason, your fork was just about down her – rather magnificent, I'll admit – cleavage at the restaurant. How obvious does it have to get?'

'You're upset?'

'Upset?' I didn't need any time to reflect on the question as I'd been trying to work out just how I felt all weekend. 'Erm, disappointed, I suppose.'

'Ooff, not good.' Mason offered up a conciliatory smile. 'I used to hate it when my father said my behaviour disappointed him.'

'And did it?'

'Often. Particularly, you know, my going into teaching rather than following him into medicine.'

'So why on earth does no one on the staff know you were – you are – married to… to *Angel*?'

'The governors know, I think Petra suspects, but, really, it's nothing to do with anyone. My private business.'

'Right. Well, you certainly have kept it private.' I didn't know what else to say.

'You will stay, won't you, Robyn?'

'Stay? What, with you? Carry on with the relationship we were *sort of* having?'

'No, obviously that's not going to continue.'

'Obviously!' I wanted to laugh out loud at that. The arrogance of the man! That this conceited bloke might consider I wanted to continue any relationship with him while he was back with his wife was laughable.

'St Mede's needs you...' he now started.

'Oh, give me a break, Mason. This school does *not* need me. What it needs is a kick up the pants. Or a demolition order.'

'I'm still trying to do the first,' Mason said. 'And I really think we're getting somewhere. This production, you know...' he trailed off, but I wasn't prepared to make it easy for him '...we can still work on it together?'

'Absolutely! Why wouldn't we? Just because you're shagging your ex-wife, sorry, *estranged*-wife, I see no reason to take it out on the kids.'

Mason visibly winced at the crude language but said, 'Thank you.'

'You're welcome. Now, if you don't mind, the only way I'm going to get warm is to move.'

'You're right, you're right. Sorry, Robyn...' Mason trailed off and then, taking my hand, he said, 'Look, we had a good time together, didn't we? You and me? There for each other when the one we *really* wanted wasn't around?'

'Sorry?' I stared. 'Is that supposed to make me feel better? That I was a... a *comfort blanket* when your favourite duvet had fallen off your bed?'

'What?' Mason's mouth twitched and I wanted to laugh myself at the ridiculous analogy I'd come up with. 'Look, Robyn, I really fancied you...' He moved towards me and put out a hand. 'Still do, of course.' He stroked my arm and I looked down at it pointedly before giving him the same look I offered up to recalcitrant Year 7s who'd crossed a boundary. Mason hurriedly dropped his hand. 'What I mean is, I know, deep down, you're still in love with this London barrister bloke.'

'No, I'm *not*,' I snapped crossly. 'I most certainly am *not*.'

'And if he came knocking at your door...'

'Like the *Angel* Loversedge came a-knocking at yours?' Every time I uttered her ridiculous handle, I found myself about to snort with glee. 'Lo, she appeared before you, saying: "Verily, Mason, you are the chosen one..."' I started to giggle. 'Blimey, good job she never went off and married Peter Gabriel.'

Ignoring me, Mason went on, 'A chance meeting at AA.'

'You're both alcoholics? Well, you kept that quiet.'

'Alcoholics?' It was Mason's turn to stare. 'Where've you got that from? A chance meeting at AAH: Amalgamated Association of Head Teachers. Look, Robyn, all I'm saying is, if you had a second chance with this barrister bloke – mind you, I can understand you refusing to have *anything* to do with a bastard who's on the side of another bastard who tortures, rapes and murders women—'

'Enough!' I put up both hands in Mason's direction, furious with him for reminding me of the awful decision Fabian had made to defend Rupert Henderson-Smith.

'All I'm saying—' Mason refused to let it go '—is that if he appeared here, this morning, you'd listen to him.'

'I most certainly would *not*,' I snapped. '*I've* moved on. *I've* had the strength of character to know when a relationship is irretrievably broken. One can *never* go back,' I added loftily. 'I would *never* go back to him. Now, if you don't mind, I need to get on.'

'Yes, fine. Don't forget *Focus North* is here on Wednesday,' he reminded me. 'I'll arrange cover for all your lessons so that you can be down here all morning. I'll try and get Kenneth to have the heating running constantly before tomorrow.'

'Good luck with that one.'

'He'll want to interview you, you know?'

'Who? Jobsworth Ken?'

'No! The bloke in charge of the *Focus North* feature. You'll really go for it, won't you? Really sell yourself? Tell them you're a West End star.'

'But I'm not,' I said irritably.

'You *were*. All impressive stuff. Telly features like this will help boost our numbers. I'd like St Mede's to be designated a performing arts school.'

'In your dreams, Mason.' I almost laughed in his face. 'But don't worry, I'll really sell the school because the kids, more than anyone, deserve that if nothing else.'

So, was I upset? Had I been telling Mason the truth when I'd said the only emotion I was feeling was disappointment? Certainly, I was feeling something akin to regret, but I think it probably boiled down to a sense of embarrassment that I'd allowed myself to be seduced and that I'd then been usurped by a bountifully bosomed angel. Angel, my backside! I couldn't help grinning to myself as I conjured up the best way to relate her name to Jess and Sorrel.

Once Mason had left the studio (I didn't think for one moment his apparent self-reproach on being caught with his ex-wife would last even down the corridor and back to his office) I started to stretch and limber up. Things were looking promising, my knee allowing me to consider moves I'd not dared to just a week earlier. I blasted out Walk the Moon's 'Shut Up and Dance' on the crappy sound system – this studio definitely needed a new one – and, slowly at first, I started swaying, bending, rolling, and before I knew it, I was dancing again. Really dancing. Sod bloody Mason Donoghue. I grinned to myself as I step-touched and shimmied, turned and leapt and then, before thinking better of it, started a full, no-holding-back, extravagant routine to the music.

Mason, I considered as I soared, could never have been the love of my life, had no way touched my soul as Fabian had. Maybe, I thought as I covered every inch of floor, we only ever have the chance of one great love in this life of ours. That after knowing, and then losing, a perfect love, one is forever chasing an unobtainable high.

Dance would be my high, I vowed and as, sweating and slightly trembly, I slowed and came to a standstill, and a chorus of applause came from the door where my first class of the day was waiting and watching, I knew I was going to be heading back to London: to the life I'd left behind, to dance professionally once more.

'You're looking very... very...' I couldn't quite work out *what* Jobsworth Ken was actually looking when, two days later, the drama studio had become a hive of activity around the cameraman and sound recordist deciding the best positions for their equipment and apparatus. Ken was being officiously but smarmily protective of both the visitors and the drama studio, one minute brown-nosing in the manner of Uriah Heep with the *Focus North* presenter before turning to glare and bark at the kids who'd gone AWOL from registration in the hope of catching themselves on telly and who were now springing, in the manner of Masai warriors, at the windows into the studio from both outside in the yard and inside along the corridors.

A toupee! Of course! Jobsworth Ken had donned a gingery-coloured hairpiece to hide his balding pate and, wanting to laugh, I turned to Petra to share the revelation.

But Petra, beginning to lose her rag with the kids, was, with dire threats, attempting to send them back to their classes so appeared to be in no mood for a laugh. Mason, in his best navy three-piece suit, burgundy tie and polished brogues was ingratiating himself with the *Focus North* team, explaining how the school was hoping to become a designated performing arts school under the direction of St Mede's professional West End musical theatre performer: i.e. me.

Oh, but he was a smooth talker, determined that people should fall in line with his ideas before, I was now beginning to realise, he became bored with that particular whim and moved on, flitting erratically to something else that caught his eye and his restless energy.

Mason Donoghue the butterfly.

I stood and watched, quite objectively, rather enjoying the performance Mason was putting on for the benefit of the *Focus North* team, until he turned and called me over, introducing me to Leanna Pottinger, the programme's director and presenter, as 'our resident expert in musical theatre, direct from a stint in the West End'.

I spent the morning under direction from Leanna, a tiny vivacious woman I liked enormously and who appeared to want to make me central to the five-minute clip that would go out that evening. The kids were brilliant, waiting their turn, showcasing their moves and explaining how their lives had been transformed with the arrival of a proper London performer at the school, and how they were turning away from hanging round the Co-op car park every evening, now that they had true meaning to their lives.

They'd obviously been well tutored by Mason about what to say and, after a particularly sycophantic outpouring from one Year 9 kid, I turned to glare in Mason's direction where he stood with the group of Pink Ladies who were about to perform for the camera, throwing up my hands in despair and mouthing 'Over the top!' at him.

Despite having had only five weeks learning the score and the moves, I was hugely proud of their efforts, giving the thumbs-up as they trooped off from being filmed, high-fiving each other in their excitement.

'We've been practising in Mia's dad's hen hut,' Isla Boothroyd whispered as they came back towards me, their faces glowing, their bodies still excitedly and compulsively moving.

'Didn't the hens mind?' I laughed.

'No, they loved it!' Isla said seriously. 'Thought we were really good.' She wiped the sheen of sweat from her brow. 'Miss,' she went on, 'I'm going to do this when I leave school. I'm so-o-o-o-o glad you came to teach here.'

'Me too,' Fatima Khan added, turning to hug me. 'You're great, miss. Best teacher here. You won't go off back to London, will you?'

'Thank you, girls,' I said, genuinely touched. 'And good for you, Isla,' I went on. 'You stick to your dreams, and you'll get there.'

'Well, your Sorrel's doing all right, isn't she?'

We all turned to the centre of the drama studio where Sorrel was limbering up, dressed in the skintight black trousers and top Olivia Newton-John, playing Sandy, wore for the iconic dance with John Travolta. Adjusting the blonde curly wig – God knew where she'd found it – she sashayed over to the camera, pouted, said, 'Tell me about it, stud,' before taking off her jacket and flinging it towards the edge of the room. She made love to the camera, grinding out her cigarette prop with her red high heel and dancing so professionally, so fantastically, we all just stood and stared.

My little sister was going to go far.

I felt the tears start, knew I'd never been as good as Sorrel, knew that if the clip was shown on *Focus North* that evening, she'd be able to download it and show it at her interview and audition at the Susan Yates Theatre School the following month.

'You were fabulous,' I whispered as she came towards me, pulling off the wig as she did so.

'Was I OK?' she breathed, her eyes shining while the Pink Ladies crowded round her, congratulating and patting her like Premier League footballers after one of their team has scored a winning goal. 'Oh, hell,' she snapped as Blane, having previously derided any coming performance of *Grease* as 'fucking bollocks', had obviously snuck out of his class, donned the blonde curly wig and was now attempting a ludicrous Egyptian sand dance in front of the camera. 'Get him off.'

Without hesitation, the pair of us descended, laughing, on the skinny lad and, taking an arm each, removed Whippety from the studio, praying the cameraman had stopped filming before he'd taken centre stage.

32

With the excitement of *Focus North* coming into school and the subsequent airing of the film on the local BBC news programme that Wednesday evening at 6.30 p.m. – and which was actually extended to almost ten minutes rather than the anticipated five – the kids at St Mede's were fractious and un-cooperative. They'd had their five minutes of fame and, with the exception of Year II, who were facing GCSE mock exams in the new year, with just two weeks to go to the Christmas break the younger kids had obviously had enough and were voting with their feet and downing tools early.

Back at home, we alternated watching the *Focus North* clip over and over again – Sorrel highly critical of her performance, Mum just one proud mum that both her daughters were being shown in such a good light – with being force-fed Christmas concoctions that Jess thought she might make on the Friday while being filmed for the Yorkshire Christmas TopChef competition. All she'd been told was that round one involved the ten competitors coming up with and cooking a two-course Christmas meal of their choice using ingredients that were to be set out in front of them, before three of them would be chosen to go through to the final round.

'Isn't it cheating, practising like this?' Sorrel asked, downing heavenly lemon and maple roasted carrots.

'Not at all. They admit to it on *MasterChef*,' I said, pulling a warning face at Sorrel as Jess, behind us at the stove, looked worried.

'It's not cheating, is it?' she asked, wiping her hands on her pinny before handing over tiny, deliciously crisp Hasselback potatoes swimming in chive and cranberry butter, and delicate slices of a turkey wellington made with the flakiest pastry, delicious duxelles and tender meat.

'Course not, darling,' Mum added her own reassurance. 'But buying this little lot must have set you back a fortune?'

'Two months' child benefit,' Jess admitted somewhat guiltily. 'Oh, and Dean arrived with the goose.' She offered a plate of sliced goose crackling with orange and rosemary and, with forks at the ready, we all dived in.

'Dean? Dean did?'

'Probably off the back of a lorry somewhere.' Jess sniffed before lowering her voice as Lola left the kitchen to watch TV. 'He knows he's going to be by himself at Christmas now that the barmaid appears to have gone back to her husband.'

'Oh, Jess, you're not taking him back?' I pleaded through a mouthful of delicious stuffing.

'No, no, of course not. Lola wants her dad back here, of course, but...'

'Dean's well and truly cooked his goose.' Sorrel grinned.

'And Matt Spencer's got his feet well and truly under her table,' I added, joining in the banter.

'*And* under her duvet.' Sorrel cackled.

'Oy, d'you mind?' Jess threw Sorrel a look as Lola strolled back in looking for pudding.

'You do like Matt though, don't you?' Mum asked, desperate to hear the correct answer. 'I liked him from the minute I met him. He really helped me get better this time, you know.'

'She's in love with him.' Lola grinned. 'Mum's fallen in love.'

'Matt's coming with me to Harrogate – to the conference centre where the competition is taking place.'

'Oh, good for him. You'll need to set off early to avoid the Friday-morning traffic. I'll come over as soon as you're ready to go,' I added, 'and make sure Lola's up and ready for school.'

'I'm not sure I can do this,' Jess now said, absent-mindedly offering the plate of potatoes again instead of the rounds of fig and sweetened roast chestnut crumble tart topped with Bailey's ice cream. 'I'm absolutely terrified.'

'You can do it. We'll be cheering you on from here,' I said, going to give her a hug. 'We'll be there with you in spirit.'

* * *

By Friday we were all as nervous as Jess, who'd started hyperventilating whenever she attempted to prepare anything more exotic than toast and Marmite for Lola's breakfast. When, in the middle of the night, she sat bolt upright, said she couldn't remember how to scramble eggs or how long it took to actually boil an egg, Matt simply took her in hand, calmed her down and soothed her back to sleep.

I went next door at 6 a.m. to see to Lola. Jess was showered, dressed and looking as if she was on the way to her own personal execution.

'Off you go,' I said, pushing her gently towards Matt's car. 'Just do your best and enjoy yourself. Let us know what's happening.'

I spent the day anxiously looking at my phone, tearing strips off the kids who were getting right up my nose and giving out detentions like sweets for the least iniquitous offending.

'Blimey, what's up with *her*?' I heard a couple of Year 11 kids discussing me as they made their way to lunch. 'I'd got to really like her recently – best teacher in this dump – but she's been just as bad as the rest of them today.'

As soon as the final bell for the day – and the week – sounded, I waited for Sorrel and together we drove home in silence, leaving Little Micklethwaite and its school behind for the weekend. We motored slowly through Beddingfield, the main high street decked out in opulent but elegant seasonal white and silver, the huge Christmas tree stylishly decorated by the parish council. No garish multicoloured lights in *my* village, I thought before smiling inwardly. I finally appeared to be happy and content to be back home in Yorkshire with my family, proud to live in this beautiful part of the country once more.

'I've been feeling so anxious all day,' Sorrel finally admitted. 'If my stomach is in knots just thinking of Jess not being able to remember how to make a béchamel sauce or her ice cream not setting, how the hell am I going to feel when it's *my* turn to head off down to London and Susan Yates's next month? You will come with me, won't you?' she pleaded. 'Oh, and just so you know, all the Pink Ladies have gone off you. Isla Boothroyd says you're a bossy bitch and Mia's dad's hens appreciate them and know more about dance and musical theatre than *you* will *ever* know.'

That made me laugh, and by the time we got back home we were both hiccupping with giggles and ready to face the news of how Jess had got on, whatever the outcome.

Matt's car was in the drive and Sorrel and I raced straight round, flinging back the kitchen door in our eagerness to see how it had gone.

Mum, Matt and Jess were sitting at the kitchen table, drinking tea, looking serious and certainly not as if there was any good news in the offing.

'Oh...' I hesitated, scanning Jess's face. 'Not good news? How'd it go?'

'Absolutely terrifying,' Jess finally said, glancing across at Matt, who took her hand. 'I can't tell you how frightening it was.'

'She was brilliant,' Matt said.

'You don't know that.' Jess tutted, slightly crossly. 'You weren't allowed in. They wouldn't let anyone in with us. It was just the ten of us, the three judges and the camera crew.'

'And? And?'

'Yes, yes, I'm through. Three of us were chosen to go to the final.'

'Well, flipping heck, Jess, show a bit of enthusiasm, will you?' I went over to hug her but she felt stiff, unyielding. I stood back, looking down at her. 'What? What's happened?'

'So, there were ten of us there, all at our own worktables just like on *MasterChef*.'

'And?'

'And we all had our white Yorkshire Christmas TopChef aprons on.'

'Yes? And?'

'With our names on the apron. Beautifully embroidered in red and green so they'd look Christmassy...'

'And? The embroidery wasn't up to standard? They spelled your name wrong?'

'And it just never occurred to me, even when I eventually saw his name. The thing was, Robyn, I was so nervous, so desperate to get on with the actual cooking, that I didn't really look at the other competitors.'

'Name? Whose name, for heaven's sake?' I asked irritably.

Jess glanced across at Matt, who nodded slightly in my direction. 'Look, Robyn, I think... possibly... maybe... you *said* he could cook...'

'*He?* Well, it can't be Mason because he's as terrible a cook as me; it can't be Jayden because he's still touring and it can't be Fabian because he's not from Yorkshire...' I trailed off. 'Fabian?' I stared. 'Fabian Carrington? Fabian was there?'

'Well, it said Fabian on his pinny,' Jess said, slightly huffily. 'I mean, how many good-looking... all right, sorry, Matt... absolutely *gorgeous*-looking blokes called Fabian are there who can cook? Anyway, this Fabian bloke, me and another girl called Bea are through.'

'Fabian's not from Yorkshire, Jess,' I interrupted crossly. 'Just because there's some bloke there called *Fabian* doesn't mean he's suddenly *my* Fabian. For heaven's *sake*, Jess!' I felt my pulse, which had revved uncomfortably at his name and the possibility of his being just thirty miles or so away, now race out of control as I lost my rag with Jess. 'And, if you remember, he's *not* my Fabian,' I corrected myself. 'Look,' I went on, trying to speak calmly, 'even if he lied and said he lived in Yorkshire, he's far too involved in preparations for the Henderson-Smith trial to be having time off from London. *And* to have entered himself into a provincial cookery competition. *And* he was nowhere near as good a cook as you, Jess.'

'Not *that* provincial, Robyn.' Matt was straight in there, defending the status of Yorkshire Christmas TopChef as well as his new love. '*Focus North* were there.'

'They get around,' I said irritably. 'Look, Jess, just concentrate on the fact that you're through to the final round next week. That's fantastic. Well done. Let's open a bottle to celebrate.'

'Absolutely,' Matt said, going to the fridge, where he'd placed a bottle of fizz earlier. 'You're through to the final, Jess. It may be just a "provincial competition"...' here he glared in my direction '...but you got there. You and the other two, whoever they are.'

'So, what happens now?' Sorrel asked.

'Mum and the other two have to cook again next week.' Lola, who'd just joined us in the kitchen, was totally overexcited. 'Mum's in the final three. And it's on a Saturday, so can I come with you?'

'Who was he with?' I asked Jess idly.

'Who was who with?'

'This Fabian bloke?'

'Why? Why does it matter?' Jess said spikily, still upset that I'd had a go at her.

'Just interested.'

'Well, he came out of there really excited.' Matt laughed. 'And this absolutely ravishing blonde ran over to him and nearly knocked him over as she hugged him and showered him with kisses.'

'Yes, absolutely ravishing,' Jess agreed. 'Although a bit over the top, to be honest.'

'Hey, I kissed you.' Matt smiled. 'And she was nowhere near as gorgeous as you, Jessica.'

'Keep on,' Jess encouraged. 'This is just what I want to hear.'

She leaned in, kissing Matt until both Lola and Sorrel chorused, 'Yuck,' and I was on the point of suggesting pouring a bucket of water over the canoodling pair.

* * *

While I was utterly thrilled that Jess was not only in the throes of a wonderful new relationship with the lovely Matt Spencer but also showing the world – well, OK, Yorkshire – what a great cook she was, and Sorrel was spending every available moment in St

Mede's drama studio going through her audition moves, I was envious of both of them. I had to continually berate myself for feeling this way.

Mason had given me permission – and the key – to use the drama studio out of school hours, much to the chagrin of Jobsworth Ken, who refused to put the heat on while we were there and constantly stood at the door tutting while looking at his watch and asking how much longer before he could lock up and put the alarm back on. What he thought was going to be nicked from the place was anyone's guess. Determined that Sorrel should win one of the coveted scholarship places at the Susan Yates Theatre School at the end of January, I was a hard taskmaster and on more than one occasion she flounced out and began walking home. But, on the whole, she worked her socks off before going round to Jess's for help with her maths, while Jess simultaneously experimented with new recipes for the upcoming Yorkshire Christmas TopChef final.

The following Monday morning I was standing in for the PSHE teacher who'd gone home with – allegedly – excruciating period pain. I'd never got on with Sonya Harrington, whom I considered both unfriendly and arrogant, and, convinced her period pain was really a chance to get over to Meadowhall for Christmas shopping while it was relatively quiet, I wasn't in the best mood for teaching her Year 8 class the planned lesson of 'Learning to learn and the acquisition of thinking tools'.

What the hell did that mean anyway? I'd quickly scanned Sonya's lesson plan, but it was written in such a user-*un*friendly way and made little sense (to anyone, including, I suspected, Sonya herself) that I gave up on it and, instead, started a discussion on 'Disability', which, looking at the PSHE long-term planning, I'd spotted was on the following term's curriculum. Tough,

Sonya, I thought scathingly, when the kids, in January, all chorus, 'We've already done this, miss.'

I'd started the lesson, and had reminded the kids that not all disabilities, particularly mental, are visible, when Sol Baxter, gazing out of the window, suddenly shouted, 'Caretaker Ken is fighting with some nutter down there who's off *his* rocker, miss. Look, look!'

Twenty-four kids left their seats and rushed as one, stampeding across the floor to the classroom's second-floor window, opening it as wide as Health and Safety allowed, to get a good look. Knowing it was pointless telling them to get back into their seats, I walked over to see what all the commotion was about – maybe I could use whatever was going on as a teaching aid.

Jobsworth Ken was losing his rag with some bloke – a drunk? A vagrant? – who'd seemingly wandered onto the school playing field and was now trying to make his way onto the paved area down below, Ken equally determined he should not. Ken had hold of the man by his arm, attempting some sort of military hold he'd obviously learned from his days in the 2nd Battalion, Yorkshire Regiment, but the intruder was having none of it. With a couple of choice swear words that drifted up through the classroom's open window, the man wrenched himself from Jobsworth's grasp, smoothed himself down and stood looking up at the windows where myriad cheering kids were now applauding his bid for freedom.

At which point Mason Donoghue himself appeared on the scene accompanied by Sally, one of the school secretaries. As the bell rang out loudly for the start of lunch break, Mason looked up and, seeing me standing at the open window, shook his head slightly before shouting: 'Ms Allen, would you join us in my office, please?'

33

Racing out of the classroom, heart pounding and without dismissing the class first, I took the steps two at a time down to Reception and Mason's office, scattering kids and staff as I went.

'Oy, wotchitmiss, that's me best Gucci,' floated crossly in my wake as my shoulder separated an oversized bag full of books and papers from its owner.

'He's in *there*, Robyn.' Sally nodded in some excitement towards Mason's open office door. 'Is he really the bloke who's defending the Soho Slasher?' she added excitedly. 'I saw him on TV. He's—'

'Thanks, Sally.' I cut her off and walked into the office, closing the door firmly behind me.

'What the hell are you *doing*?' I asked, leaning against the door, my arms folded against my racing heart in a futile attempt to calm it down.

'He wouldn't let me see you.' Fabian spoke calmly but his face was pale.

'Who wouldn't?'

'This head teacher of yours.'

'What do you mean?' I stared at Fabian and then across at Mason, who was looking slightly sheepish, but came out fighting.

'He was here last Thursday,' Mason said indignantly. 'Hanging around like some pathetic stalker, trying to see you.' Mason sat back in his chair, somewhat portentously, looking down his nose at Fabian in the same way he addressed recalcitrant pupils. 'Said he'd seen you on *Focus North*. I assumed he was just a random viewer at first, then I realised who he was, once he gave his name. I don't know how he could have seen you on *Focus North* when it's our local TV programme and he's living in London. Defending that bastard Henderson-Smith. Unbelievable.' Mason was at his most righteous, lecturing the pair of us in the same tone he used at meetings when castigating the staff for the week's misdemeanours that had come to his notice.

'What? And you never told me?'

'I think, Ms Allen, if you recall, you assured me there was no way you'd ever want to see this man again. I had only your interests... your mental health and well-being... at heart.'

'My mental health? Oh, for heaven's sake.' I gave Mason my best withering glare. He was jealous! Despite all the conflicting emotions whizzing through my head, I could see clearly that he didn't want me going off with anyone else.

I turned to Fabian. 'So, what are you doing here? How can I help you?'

'Robyn' –he took my arm – 'can we get out of here?'

'She's back teaching in' – Mason glanced at his watch – 'forty minutes.'

'Robyn?'

Oh, but he was sublime. He'd lost weight, I saw, his dark hair even longer than before and his face pale, but he was still consummately glorious and just looking at him was enough to have my pulse racing like the winner of the 3.30 at Aintree.

'I lost all my frees last week, Mr Donoghue,' I said, turning to Mason. 'I'm sure you won't object to my taking the afternoon off to take care of my... my *mental health*? I'm sure you won't mind covering the two Year 9 classes on my timetable?'

* * *

Fabian's silver 911 was parked in the far corner of the staff car park, sticking out like a sore thumb amongst the teachers' Corsas, Minis and VWs and gathering a crowd of Year 7 petrolheads who were gazing upon it reverentially. We walked in silence towards it, the eleven-year-olds parting like the Red Sea at our approach.

'Nice car, miss,' Cameron Halliday called.

'Nothing to do with me,' I said, pulling a face but getting in nevertheless.

'Where to?' Fabian asked, leaning across as I fumbled with the seat belt, my fingers seemingly unable to undertake the simple task my brain was instructing them to do.

'You appear to be taking *me* somewhere,' I snapped.

'I don't know the area, Robyn,' Fabian said without a smile. 'Just point me in the direction of a park or a pub or... or somewhere we can sit and talk.'

'There's the one pub in Beddingfield,' I said. 'Mind you, you'll have to be on your guard: the barmaid there ran off with Jess's husband last time he was in there.'

'Jess?'

'My sister.'

'Of course.'

Of course?

Fabian drove too quickly down the narrow winding lanes that led from Little Micklethwaite across to the rather more upmarket village of Beddingfield, following my instructions but saying nothing else. We pulled up outside The Green Dragon, which was already decked out in its seasonal festive best.

'Pretty pub,' Fabian said as he got out and looked round.

'Pretty village too,' I said. 'Yorkshire isn't all mill chimneys and *eeh bah gum*, you know.'

'I don't think I ever thought it was.'

'Not a patch on Marlow, of course.'

'You'll have to show me round some time and let me make that judgement.' He sighed but didn't smile. 'I need a beer. What'll you have?'

'Wine gives me a headache at lunchtime, but I'll have one anyway,' I said, moving to the back of the pub where most of the tables were free. I sat and watched as Fabian smiled and chatted to the girl behind the bar – not Jill who'd been at school with Jess and who had run off with Dean – loving the way his dark hair curled onto the collar of his denim shirt beneath the navy sweater. I'd never stopped loving this man. I might have tried, tried hard to move on by having a fling with Mason, but sitting here, unable to take my gaze off Fabian's back, feasting my eyes on his backside in the faded jeans, I knew it had been to no avail. And if he was just here to bring back the cardigan I'd left in his flat, before zooming off back down the M1, at least I could refill my senses with enough of him to sustain me through his absence over the coming months.

'Are you here to return my cardigan?' I asked as he sat opposite, taking a long drink from his glass of Budweiser.

'Your cardigan? What cardigan?' Fabian pulled a face.

Right, not my cardigan, then.

'Fabian, why are you here?'

'I wanted to see you. To explain.'

I sipped at my wine, wanting to cry as I remembered that final message he'd texted telling me not to get in touch ever again.

'You just couldn't hack the fact that I was just doing my job, could you?' Fabian said crossly after a long silence. 'The job I'd spent years being trained to do.' He shook his head. 'Running back home when you found out about the Henderson-Smith case. When I needed you most.'

'There wasn't much running involved with my damaged knee.' I glared at Fabian. 'And, you never actually told me you were defending him.'

'I knew what your reaction would be.'

'You never told me!' I insisted. 'I had to find out from that brother of yours.'

'My half-brother.'

'Does it make a difference?'

'And *you* never told me about your grandfather.' Fabian was equally angry.

'Do you blame me?'

'Yes, I do blame you.'

'Your Marlow set would have *loved* knowing that little nugget of information.'

'We've all got something in our families we're not proud of.'

'I bet *you* haven't.'

'How about my great-great-great-grandfather building his fortune on the back of the slave trade?'

'You've just made that up!' I said indignantly.

'No, I haven't. The last thing I was going to do was come out and confess that to you! And then you blocked my number...' Fabian shook his head, furious now. 'Did what we have mean *nothing*? Nothing, Robyn?'

'You blocked me,' I countered. '*And* I hurt my knee badly. *Very* badly,' I added mulishly.

'I know that, Robyn. I went round to the theatre to see you once I'd calmed down after you'd blocked *me*. The guy in charge there – Carl, is it? – said you were injured and wouldn't be dancing again for a long time. That you'd returned to Yorkshire.'

'And you didn't think to come up to Yorkshire, knowing not only that I'd damaged my ACL, but that my mum had been taken into hospital again?'

'Your mum? And again?' Fabian glared at me. 'What do you mean, again? That theatre guy didn't say anything about your mum. *You* never once talked about any illness your mum had, Robyn. I didn't know. Why didn't you tell me?'

Because Mum had always been embarrassed about her seizures. And, to my shame, always afraid that her condition was hereditary and that, one day, I too might be affected, I'd always kept poor Mum's ailment at a distance.

'You blocked my number, Robyn,' Fabian went on. 'What was I supposed to think? I didn't have your address up here in Yorkshire; you'd never once suggested a weekend up here to meet your mum and your sisters. I was never even allowed to meet your father, although he was often in London.'

'You wouldn't have liked him. You're both very... very different. From different worlds.'

'I'd have loved anything, anyone connected with you, but no, you were ashamed of your family.'

'I was not,' I snapped indignantly, but acknowledging a slight sense of guilt that was gnawing at me like a bad toothache. 'Don't you come all self-righteous with me about not getting in touch...' I put down my glass of wine on the table, scrabbling about in my bag for my phone. 'There,' I said in triumph, once I'd scrolled through and found that awful final message from Fabian. 'Don't you make me out to be the baddie when I messaged you almost immediately I was back here in Yorkshire, and you reply with a message like this.'

I think everything that needed to be said has been said, Robyn. I also think it best for both our sakes that we formally terminate our relationship and have no further contact with each other.

Fabian

Fabian stared down at the screen, shaking his head in apparent bewilderment. 'Look, it's probably all water under the bridge now, Robyn, but you need to know, I never sent this. I promise.'

All water under the bridge? What did he mean by that? I felt my heart plummet.

'So, who did, then?' I asked, trying to ignore the despair I was feeling at what he'd just come out with. 'The phone fairy? And don't tell me you left your phone somewhere and someone else wrote that. You were more attached to your damned phone than to me. You never let it out of your sight: I'd wake and find you scrolling in the middle of the night.'

'Exactly that.' Fabian sighed, closing his eyes and obviously thinking. 'I was called out in court one morning by an extremely irritable – and irritated – judge, fed up of me constantly picking up my phone, hoping for a message from you. He said if I brought it into his court just once more, he'd ban me—'

'Oh, come on, that only happens on *Judge Judy*.'

'When I remonstrated and said, "With all due respect, Your Honour," he actually shouted back: "When someone begins a sentence with 'with all due respect', Mr Carrington, you can expect to be *disrespected*. Now, take that infernal device out of my court and leave it there, or I'll have you for contempt…"'

If I hadn't been feeling so confused, I'd probably have laughed at that. Instead, I said, 'You're having me on. He didn't!'

'He did. I had to leave it in my chambers.'

'Whereupon someone else picked it up? And this someone else replied to my message? Is that what you're saying?' I raised an eyebrow at Fabian while scrutinising his face for the truth.

'Robyn, when you rushed off, I was desperate to see you, not desperate to tell you I didn't want to see you ever again – so, yes, that's the only explanation I can come up with.'

'Fish Face?' I asked.

'Who? Oh, Araminta?' Fabian frowned, shaking his head. 'While she's absolutely delighted that I'm "no longer seeing your waitress, darling", she's never been to my chambers.'

'So, someone else, then? I wonder who that could be.'

'He wouldn't!'

'Of course he would,' I snapped. 'Julius would have done *anything* not to have me with you...' I trailed off as Fabian looked at his watch, terrified he was going to get up and leave. 'Fabian,' I eventually managed to ask once more, 'why are you here?'

'I've been living in Yorkshire for the last two months.'

'What?' I stared. 'Up here in Yorkshire?' I shook my head, unable to take in what he was saying. 'But why? How can you live up here, but work in London?'

'I no longer work in London, Robyn.'

'Yes, you do. I saw you on TV. Some Japanese... or... or some programme I was watching.'

'Japanese? Why in God's name were you watching Japanese TV? And you saw me on it?' Fabian pulled a face.

'But what about your work? What about the Soho Slasher?'

'I couldn't take it any more...' Fabian's voice cracked and eventually he stopped speaking, struggling to carry on. He looked away, trying to control his voice and his emotions. 'I just couldn't take Julius and my mother constantly trying to do my job for me; a job I finally admitted to myself I no longer wanted to do. Hadn't wanted to do for a long time, if I'm being honest. It's taken a lot of counselling to make me understand where I was in myself. Anyway, it all came to a head when I just couldn't take knowing the terrible – *really* terrible – things Henderson-Smith had allegedly done to these poor women. I was tainted by it; didn't want to be a part of it. And then the stuff on social media started: there were people – sometimes crowds – outside the apartment. I had eggs and dog shit thrown at me. And the daft thing was, *I agreed* with their sentiments, *agreed* with why they had it in for me for defending the bastard.'

'Oh, Fabian.' I took his hand, then just as quickly released it, holding my breath. 'You're with a blonde now?'

'A blonde?' Fabian frowned. 'What blonde? What d'you mean I'm with a blonde?' He looked round as though any number of blondes were about to descend and claim him for their own.

'You do know who you're going through to the next round of Yorkshire Christmas TopChef with?'

Fabian's eyes widened and he stared for a good few seconds. Eventually, he gave a little smile. 'You *know about that*?'

'I do now.'

'Jess? She *is* your sister, then?'

'You realised?'

'She looks very much like you. She's a cook. She's in Yorkshire. She kept looking at me as if she might know me, once she'd seen my name on my apron.'

'I told her it couldn't possibly be you. That you were not eligible to enter. Got quite cross with her, actually, when she kept going on about you. And then, when Matt said you were set upon by some ravishing blonde—'

'Matt?'

'Jess's new man. *Dr* Matt Spencer,' I added proudly. 'My mum's brilliant consultant. When Matt said you were with a blonde...'

'What? What did you think?' Fabian kept his eyes on mine but I couldn't quite work out what he was thinking either.

'All right, I just didn't want to know any more. I sort of shut off. If there was even a tiny percentage chance that it *was* actually you who'd suddenly descended on Yorkshire... and with some blonde in tow...' I trailed off '...I didn't want to know...'

'Well, yes, OK, I *am* living with a blonde, as you call her. I've known her a long time, she's always been there for me and she loves me. When she moved to Harrogate, I decided to move up here with her. The thing is, she's been trying to get me to come and find you. Knowing how I used to feel about you, she wanted me to come over to Beddingfield and see you. To explain what was going on... you know, with her and me...'

How he *used* to feel about me?

'So you wouldn't get the wrong idea...' Fabian raised an eyebrow and drained his glass.

'Right.' I upended my own glass, not knowing quite what else to do, feeling sick with longing for him. 'I need to go,' I said, standing, but then turned back to Fabian. 'But why? Why all that fuss down on the playing field?'

'Seemed to be the only way to get in touch with you after that pillock of a head teacher wouldn't let me see you. I just needed you to know.'

'Know what?'

'That I'm happy. Really happy. That you were right all along.'

'About what?'

'About my taking on the Henderson-Smith case. I shouldn't have.'

'And what are you doing with yourself? How are you earning a living?'

'I'm not really.' Fabian smiled. 'I'm cooking a lot, helping out with foodbanks in Harrogate.'

'Foodbanks?' I stared.

'And volunteering legal advice for those who need it, but can't afford it.'

'While living with The Blonde?'

'*Living off* The Blonde at the moment, to be honest... God, you're pig-headed, Robyn. And bloody dense as well.' Fabian folded his arms and leaned back on the chair until the front legs left the floor and the chair rested against the wall. If he'd been one of the kids in my class, I'd have had him for doing that.

'Excuse me?' I snapped instead.

'I'm staying with Jemima. In Harrogate.'

'Your sister?' I shot Fabian a look of disbelief. 'But Jemima is as dark-haired as you.'

'Not any more she's not.' Fabian actually laughed, bringing his chair back onto all four legs and reaching for my hand. 'She made the big decision to not only go blonde but move north, taking a job in Leeds to be nearer to the man she's fallen in love with – he's a consultant oncologist at St James's Hospital. She continues to fly off at a moment's notice all over Europe – while I house-sit – but just flies from Leeds Bradford airport, which, she says, is actually much easier than driving out to Heathrow or Gatwick when she was in central London.'

'Right.'

'Right, so that's sorted, then.' Fabian took my hand.

'And no other blondes I should know about?'

'Apart from Boris.'

'Boris?'

'Jemima and I appear to have inherited him, the rest of the family being too busy to really care for him properly. Mum's come out of retirement again, taking on another high-profile case.'

'Not the Soho Slasher?' I felt my eyes widen at the very idea.

'No! Henderson-Smith has a whole new defence team

working for him. It's been kept out of the news up until now – I guess the barrister who's taken him on has been advised to keep a low profile after the media onslaught and protest that came my way.'

'But what are you going to do? Up here, I mean. In the sticks. Away from your family.'

'Walk Boris, read a lot, cook a lot, get to know Yorkshire, hope that some gorgeous brunette I know will come and visit. Maybe even stay with me at the weekends? And...' he paused, slightly embarrassed '...and I'm already looking into this... looking for premises.'

'Premises?'

'My own restaurant... Early days yet, of course... Hell of a long way to go.' Fabian bent his head, kissing my mouth, tentatively at first, as though asking permission, and then, with my knees actually trembling – and I could do nothing *but* acquiesce – he drew back, starting to laugh. 'Do they do ice cream here?' he asked.

'I don't need ice cream,' I murmured, reaching for him once more, not caring that we were apparently putting the two old dears at the next table off their chicken in a basket.

'Robyn.' Fabian finally sighed. 'I've *never* changed my mind about you. I knew from the moment I glanced up at you in that courtroom that I had to get to know you. And when I did, despite your constantly jumping out of my car and running away, despite your pride, your bloody awful prejudices and stereotyping, I *never* wanted to let you go.'

I felt tears well and had to brush them away. 'You know, Fabian,' I finally managed to get out, 'while the last thing I wanted was to lose my career and I never *ever* wanted to lose you, this has all been a bit of a journey for me. And,' I went on, standing and holding out my hand, suddenly excited at the prospect, 'I want you to meet my family. Right now. I want you to meet Jess, meet her properly this time... mind you, you are competitors... but that doesn't matter, does it...? And Mum and Sorrel. Sorrel is *so* lovely. And she's absolutely going places. I'm so proud of her.'

'And Roger?' Fabian started to laugh. 'I've been wanting to meet Roger Rabbit since, well, forever.'

He stood then, taking me in his arms and kissing me until I thought he'd never stop.

'They'll all love you,' I murmured, once we came up for air. 'Just like I do!'

ACKNOWLEDGEMENTS

A Class Act is my fourteenth novel, but my first with Boldwood. It's always very exciting to be writing for a new publisher, but particularly exciting to be back working once more with my original editor, Sarah Ritherdon, who took me on several years ago and helped make *A Village Affair* the great success that it was. Thank you, Sarah.

I have to say a big thank you to Kate Winch for sharing her stories as a drama teacher, but particularly for sharing the experience of her first day as a new teacher at a local high school. Robyn's account of her first day in the drama studio (cellar) at St Mede's is virtually word for word how Kate described her own scary experience of facing a recalcitrant set of thirteen-year-olds who weren't prepared to listen and take part, until ordered to by one of the older, looked up to, pupils who came to her aid.

Thanks, as always, to my lovely agent, Anne Williams at KHLA Literary Agency, for her unstinting help, advice, friendship and loyalty.

To all the wonderful readers and reviewers who read my books and write such lovely things about them, a huge, heartfelt thank you.

I've dedicated this book to my fabulous women friends who have been there for me while writing this book, but I would like to acknowledge them here as well. My much-loved only sister, Valerie, was diagnosed with terminal pancreatic cancer while I was in the middle of writing *A Class Act*, and passed away earlier this year. My wonderful, supportive friends – as well as my husband, Nigel, and kids Ben and Georgia – have been with me every step of the way through this difficult time. To all of you – thank you.

ABOUT THE AUTHOR

Julie Houston is the author of thirteen bestselling novels set in and around two fictional West Yorkshire villages.

Sign up to Julie Houston's mailing list for news, competitions and updates on future books.

Follow Julie on social media here:

facebook.com/JulieHoustonauthor

x.com/@JulieHouston2

instagram.com/juliehoustonauthor

bookbub.com/authors/julie-houston

LOVE NOTES

LOVE IN EVERY CHAPTER

WHERE ALL YOUR ROMANCE
DREAMS COME TRUE!

THE HOME OF BESTSELLING
ROMANCE AND WOMEN'S
FICTION

 WARNING:
MAY CONTAIN SPICE

SIGN UP TO OUR
NEWSLETTER

https://bit.ly/Lovenotesnews

Boldwood

Boldwood Books is an award-winning fiction publishing company seeking out the best stories from around the world.

Find out more at www.boldwoodbooks.com

Join our reader community for brilliant books, competitions and offers!

Follow us
@BoldwoodBooks
@TheBoldBookClub

Sign up to our weekly
deals newsletter

https://bit.ly/BoldwoodBNewsletter

Printed in Great Britain
by Amazon